THE UNSUITABLE
MISS PELHAM

THE UNSUITABLE
MISS PELHAM

A NOVEL

by

JUNE DRUMMOND

LONDON
VICTOR GOLLANCZ LTD
1990

First published in Great Britain 1990
by Victor Gollancz Ltd
14 Henrietta Street, London WC2E 8QJ

British Library Cataloguing in Publication Data
Drummond, June
 The unsuitable Miss Pelham.
 I. Title
 832 [F]

ISBN 0-575-04878-6

Typeset at The Spartan Press Ltd,
Lymington, Hants
and printed in Great Britain by
St Edmundsbury Press Ltd, Bury St Edmunds, Suffolk

I

AT THREE O'CLOCK on the last day of March, 1821, a carriage bearing the Linslade coat of arms turned through the gates of the estate Foxfare, near Shipton-under-Wychwood in Oxfordshire. It swept past the gatehouse without a check, and moved at a brisk pace along an avenue edged on either side by a double row of oak trees. These did something to blunt the teeth of an icy north wind, a respite welcomed by the coachman Cheadle, the groom Belper, and the four splendid bay horses that drew the equipage.

They had yet a quarter of a mile to travel before they reached their destination, a mansion in the Palladian style that stood on a gentle rise of ground, against a lowering sky.

The building was of imposing aspect. Its three wings enclosed a courtyard set with baroque fountains, at present stilled. Lights shone in the central block, and smoke curled from several of its chimneys, but the east and west wings appeared dark and lifeless. Clearly the Fromes were entertaining no house guests.

The well-tended woodland which bounded the estate gave way first to a home park where fallow deer grazed, then to a shrubbery with neatly-gravelled walks, and finally to a succession of grassed terraces, clipped and mown to perfection.

The passenger reclining at his ease in a corner of the carriage paid no heed to these marks of good husbandry. A casual observer might have taken him for a man of fashion to whom country pursuits were a matter of indifference; yet there was nothing foppish about the powerful muscles of shoulder and thigh; and the aquiline features held a decisiveness that gave the lie to the indolent pose.

His gaze was fixed on the road ahead, and when he caught the flutter of a white kerchief among the oaks, he raised his hand to rap on the carriage roof.

The vehicle slowed and stopped. The passenger leaned across to open the offside door, and a girl in a black cloak darted from the shelter of the trees, sprang up into the carriage, and collapsed breathless on the seat next to him.

"Alex," she said in a tone of profound relief. "Thank God you are here! No one else can save us now!"

Alexander Frome reached up and signalled for the carriage to resume its course. Though fifteen years lay between him and his sister — he was thirty-two and Emily had just turned seventeen — they were much alike in countenance and character. They had inherited their dark hair and eyes, their quick intelligence and lively sense of humour from their late father, Julian Frome, whom folk had accounted a handsome man; but it had to be admitted that at the moment Emily did not look her best, her hair being wind-blown and her nose quite red with cold.

Her brother picked up a fur rug and cast it over her knees. "Wrap up, Em," he said. "How long have you been lurking in the grove?"

"It seems forever," she answered, "though I suppose it is only three days since I wrote you. I was in a torment in case my letter should have gone astray."

"I had it this morning, at the Tarletons." He gave her a sidelong smile. "Naturally, as soon as I had read it, I ordered the horses put to, and came here *ventre à terre*. A matter of life and death, I believe you said?"

Emily gave him a darkling look. "It's all very well for you to poke fun, Alex, but I swear that between them they'll kill poor Nicholas, unless you stop them."

"Nick?" The dark man turned his head sharply. "Nick is in Greece, digging up temples."

"No, that's just it. He's home. He's been at Foxfare these past ten days, and he's in very poor case, whatever Dr Rumbole may say."

"Ten days? Why the devil wasn't I told? George knew my direction, he had only to send word."

"Mama forbade it. She said she would not permit anything to disrupt your well-earned holiday."

"Oh, gammon! As if that were of more importance than Nick's health."

"So I told Mama, but she wouldn't listen. She said I was

pert, and forward, and knew nothing of such things; and with Rumbole insisting that Nick's indisposition is the merest trifle . . . "

"Rumbole? Squat, reddish fellow with hairy nostrils?"

"The same, and Mama's oracle in all things medical." Emily drew the rug more snugly about her. "Though, to be plain with you, it's my conviction Mama did not wish you to leave the Tarletons. She lives in hopes that you and Amelia will make a match of it."

"Heaven forbid!"

Emily closed her eyes and put on a saintly expression. "Amelia", she said, "is all that a gentleman could desire in a prospective wife. Not only can she paint on china, but her performance at the pianoforte is extremely creditable. Her manners are such as must please, her lineage impeccable, and her marriage-portion handsome. She is in every way suitable." She opened her eyes. "I heard Mama tell George that she feared you are interested only in unsuitable females."

Alex sighed. "They are so much more amusing."

"Mama cannot conceive of a single reason for your taking Amelia in dislike."

"She's bigger than I am," said Alex. He bent a thoughtful eye on his sister. "No bamming, Em, Mama may be busy matchmaking, but what reason can George have for keeping me from home?"

"I think," she said slowly, "he doesn't wish you to know of his latest economy drive."

"Ah! And what has he cut this time?"

"Everything," said Emily simply. "The guest wings are under Holland covers. Half the hunters have been sold. Mrs Hackaway has been ordered to serve no desserts and to use less butter in the sauces. The worst is that George has stopped the draining of the north acres, and closed down the experimental farm."

"But, Heaven save us, those are precisely the measures that will increase our yield. I thought I had drummed that lesson into his skull, by now! But let it pass. Tell me about Nick. What ails him?"

"Some sort of fever," Emily answered. "It lessens by day, but

7

at night he has dreadful onsets of shivering, and perspiring. He never complains — you know that's not his way — but he's so thin, Alex, so weak, it terrifies me."

"What's Rumbole's diagnosis?"

"A passing inflammation of the blood, that will be cured by fasting and laudanum. Oh, how I detest that man! I asked him whether Nick might have contracted malaria, for I remembered how many of the Duke's army returned from Spain with just this sort of malady. Rumbole informed me, in the most rude and snubbing way, that malaria is caused by miasmas that rise from swampy ground, and that as Nick has been in the driest part of Greece he cannot possibly be suffering from the disease."

"Why did you not say outright that Nick was home, and ill? Why all the secrecy?"

Emily met his eyes. "I was afraid George would stop the letter."

"Do you tell me he reads your mail?"

"Indeed he does, and a very vulgar trick I think it, for a man to be spying on his own flesh and blood. However, that doesn't signify. I knew if I said it was a matter of life and death you'd not fail me. I asked James the footman to carry the letter to the post. I dursn't entrust it to Bungay, he'd have run straight to George. Bungay," concluded Emily bitterly, "is a fawning lickspittle!"

"Not a doubt of it. Where's Mama at present?"

"Gone with George and Augusta to Witney, to consult with Mr Spalding. I doubt they'll be home much before seven."

"Good. I'll have time to talk to Nick alone."

The carriage now left the avenue, and swung on to a drive that led directly to the stable yard. Belper jumped down to lower the carriage steps, Cheadle and a brace of stable lads set about unloading the baggage and unharnessing the horses. The two passengers slipped quietly into the house by a side door.

As they entered, there came a scuffling noise on the back stairway, and a small woolly terrier shot down to meet them, circled them twice, and finally cast himself on his back at Emily's feet, tongue lolling and tail thumping.

8

Alex bent to scratch the animal's ear. "And who is this?" he asked.

"His name's Pebble," Emily answered. "He was the runt of the litter. George said he should be put down, but Amos wouldn't hear of it. He said, 'The little tyke's as game as a pebble. You take and raise 'im Miss, and you won't be sorry.' I had to hand-feed him for weeks, but he's strong as a lion, now, and a champion ratter, as well as being the best of company."

"He looks to me to be a shameless toadeater," said the dark man with a smile. "Em, you'd best go and tidy yourself before Mama sees you."

Emily disappeared up the stairs with the terrier at her heels. Her brother lingered in the hallway long enough to divest himself of his curly-brimmed hat, tan leather gloves, and many-caped greatcoat. As he tossed these articles on to the hall-stand, he caught sight of his reflection in the looking-glass; a face of cold annoyance, brows knit and lips compressed.

Why was it invariably the case, he wondered, that within minutes of returning home, he found his temper to be in shreds?

It was not Foxfare itself. That would always stand high in his affections. He remembered it as it had been in his father's time: the focus of a bustling county round, a place not scorned by the pink of the London ton, a Mecca for sportsmen and scholars alike. Now, thanks to George's cheeseparing ways, the Frome reputation for hospitality was forgotten, and the very prosperity of Foxfare was being sapped by a spate of pinchbeck economies.

It did not help to reflect that one had none to blame but oneself. The tasks imposed by King and Castlereagh left no time for the family, or Foxfare. One spent months in Vienna, or Paris, or Rome, argued with hairsplitting diplomats, picked over the details of trade agreements, attended endless dreary receptions, and came home every so often to squabble with George. It was all an intolerable bore.

Perhaps Mama was right. It was time to find some dull but suitable girl, and marry. Remembering Emily's description of Amelia Tarleton, Alex grinned. He hadn't come to that, yet.

He reminded himself that it wouldn't do to let Nicholas see

him in such a depressed frame of mind, and he walked quickly up the stairs and along the gallery that would bring him to the bedroom quarters.

His progress did not go unnoticed. The butler, Bungay, about to cross the entrance lobby with a Dresden candelabrum he had been washing, glanced up in time to see the tall figure stride along the gallery.

Bungay was startled and perturbed. For a moment he considered making his presence known, but he quickly stifled the impulse. If Alexander Frome, sixth Baron Frome and Fourth Earl of Linslade, chose to enter his ancestral home unannounced, and to sneak up the back stairs like a menial, then it was not for Bungay to kick up a dust. As that national hero, Horatio Nelson, had demonstrated, there were times when it was expedient to put the telescope, metaphorically speaking, to one's blind eye.

Nicholas Frome's bedroom was on the north side of the house. Normally its three tall windows, which overlooked the park and rose-garden, provided ample light and ventilation, but at present they were tightly shut and the curtains half-drawn. The room was both gloomy and cold. No fire burned in the grate, and the air had a stale, sweetish smell, as if someone had been burning incense.

As the Earl came through the door, a housemaid who had been engaged in placing a carafe of barley-water on the bedside table, turned in surprise, and dropped a flustered curtsey. The Earl signed to her to withdraw, closed the door after her, and advanced to stand beside the big fourposter bed.

Nicholas Frome was asleep. Dressed in breeches and shirt, he lay spreadeagled on his back. His breathing was light and rapid, and it was easy to see that, though Emily might have exaggerated the gravity of his illness, he was very far from well. His fair hair was darkened with sweat. The skin about his mouth was blistered and cracked. He had lost a great deal of weight. In sleep he looked far younger than his nineteen years, as vulnerable as a child.

The Earl leaned down and took his brother's fingers in a light clasp. "Nicholas? Nick, old fellow, wake up!"

The young man stirred, muttered, and opened his eyes. For a moment he stared blankly, then his face lit in a wide smile.

"Alex, by all that's wonderful! How come you to be here?"

"Em wrote to tell me you weren't in too plump currant. I only wish Mama had sent for me sooner."

Nick turned his head restlessly, as if he did not wish to speak on that topic.

"When did this start?" enquired Alex.

"Oh, in Greece. Several of the men on the dig came down with it. Perhaps the water supply was to blame. I shall be well in a trice, never fear . . . despite old Rumbole's best efforts."

As he spoke Nick struggled to raise himself higher on the bed. The Earl put an arm behind his shoulders and lifted him bodily, easing him back against the pillows. As he did so, he noticed a linen bandage wrapped round Nick's right arm, and said sharply, "Has that quack been bleeding you?"

Nick gave a shaky laugh. "Yes, he's a regular bloodsucker, comes of fine old vampire stock I shouldn't wonder. The devil of it is, I was better yesterday . . . on my feet and spent the day downstairs. If Rumbole would but leave me to mend, instead of cupping me, and dosing me with his foul potions . . . "

Alex did not reply. His gaze had fallen on the bedside table, on which reposed a number of black bottles of lethal aspect, and a bowl of greyish, turgid liquid.

"What in God's name is that?" he demanded.

"Gruel," answered Nick. "Em usually contrives to pitch it out of the window. Smuggles in the occasional plate of victuals, too, when the kitchen patrol's off guard. Good little soul, Em. Pluck to the backbone."

The Earl perceived that he had to deal with a reign of terror. Walking to the bellrope that hung beside the chimneypiece, he tugged it sharply. This produced, in double quick time, the little chambermaid and a young footman.

Alex addressed the latter.

"What is your name?"

"James, my lord."

"The same that took Miss Frome's letter to the post?"

James, looking apprehensive, admitted this to be the case.

"Then," said his lordship, "you're the man I want. Go to the kitchen and tell Mrs Hackaway, with my compliments, to send a collation for two here to this room. Strong broth, bread and butter, cheese, a piece of pie if that's available. Also a dish of fruit. I suppose there is fruit in the succession houses?"

Staring straight ahead of him, James agreed that there was, but added that Mr Bungay did say as how Mr George was wishful to send the lot up to Lunnon, to the market.

"Bungay must have mistaken the matter," said the Earl. "Bring grapes, James, and some peaches." He glanced at Nick. "I feel sure Rumbole prohibits wine?"

"Absolutely."

"A bottle of hock," his lordship instructed James, "and two glasses, if you please."

The footman sped away, and the Earl turned to the little chambermaid. Her face, pink and shining, struck a chord in his memory, and he said pleasantly, "You are Lizzie, are you not?"

"Yes, my lord."

"Then Lizzie, be so good as to light the fire and open the two end windows at the top only. When that's done, take the mess of pottage in that bowl and feed it to the pigs . . . if they will accept it."

While Lizzie set about these tasks, his lordship fetched a chair and set it down at the bedside.

"Now," he said easily, "tell me about Greece."

Nick's face brightened. "Oh, it's the most splendid place. Mountains and sea, beautiful beyond description, and the light as clear as crystal. You can't imagine how enjoyable it was . . . and what a privilege to be able to work with Lord Brayshaw. He knows all there is to know about the ancients. He believes that the old legends contain the germ of fact, and will lead us to all manner of discoveries . . . the site of Theseus's palace . . . Troy . . . the lost cities of the Bible. There's so much to be learned, Alex, so much to be accomplished!"

It was plain that Nick's visit to Greece had launched him on a lifelong career, and in speaking of it he forgot his present ills; but later, when the food was brought, he fell into a brooding silence, and at length said abruptly, "Alex, I have to get away from Foxfare."

"Of course, just as soon as you feel up to the mark."

"No, I must leave at once! It's not only a question of my health. It's the family. Mama, George, Augusta, even Emily, each one of 'em professes to know how I should conduct my life, and they brangle over me as if . . . as if I were a dog's bone. I can't make 'em understand I don't wish to be cosseted, I don't wish anyone to make decisions for me, I wish to be my own man. So will you please arrange for me to go back to Oxford, or to London, without delay?"

"We'll see what can be contrived." Alex rose to his feet and saw anxiety flash into his brother's eyes.

"Where are you going?" The young man raised himself on one elbow and seemed about to clamber off the bed.

"Don't fret. I'm only going to see Turner in his office. We'll talk again later, I promise."

"How long will you stay at Foxfare?"

"For as long as you need me." Alex dropped a reassuring hand on Nick's shoulder. "Now try to rest."

Nick stared at him for a moment, then apparently satisfied, fell back against his pillows and closed his eyes.

II

As MAY BE supposed, the house was by now buzzing with the news of Lord Linslade's arrival. In the kitchen Mrs Hackaway had unhesitatingly scrapped the frugal menu prescribed that morning by her mistress, and was assembling a dinner more in keeping with the return of the prodigal.

Fires had been kindled in every room in which the Earl might conceivably set foot. In the red dining-room, extra leaves had been added to the long table, and the best crystal and silverware brought out.

When his lordship reached the master-bedroom, which was always reserved for his use, he found his portmanteau had been unpacked, his best evening coat of dark blue superfine freshly pressed, and a change of linen laid ready for him. Since his lordship had committed the folly of travelling without his own valet, Bungay had taken these duties upon himself, and was now carefully wrapping towels round a canister of hot water on the wash-stand.

Bungay had had time to reflect. He saw clearly that there was to be a clash of wills, and he was resolved to declare at once for the Earl's cause. He had accordingly prepared a little speech of welcome, expressing his own and the staff's gratification at seeing their master safe home, after so many months of absence.

He was not permitted to deliver this encomium, the Earl announcing as he entered the room that he intended riding over at once to see his farm agent, and requesting Bungay to send a message to that effect to the stables.

Bungay, retiring wounded to the servants' hall, told his subordinates that they'd best mind their ps and qs, as his lordship was in a downright crusty mood, and like to make any error on their part a hanging matter.

A little after seven o'clock, an elegant carriage drew up under the portico of Foxfare, and set down the Honourable George Frome, his mother Elvira, Countess of Linslade, and his wife Augusta.

All three were tired, chilled, and longing for their dinners. It did nothing to lift their spirits when Bungay greeted them with the tidings that Lord Linslade had returned unexpectedly from his travels, spent an hour with Mr Nicholas, gone out to see Mr Turner, and now awaited them in the grey drawing-room.

"Dashed inconsiderate of Alex," burst out George, as soon as Bungay was out of earshot. "What's he mean by it, I'd like to know? Dropping on us without a word of warning, going off to see Turner without first consulting me? I won't tolerate it, d'ye hear? I shall tell him so to his face."

Augusta, who had a genius for saying the wrong thing, reminded her husband that Foxfare was, after all, Alex's house.

This won her an impatient frown from Lady Linslade. "To say so, my dear Gussie, is to state the obvious. We will naturally afford Alexander the respect that is due to the head of the family. Pray, George, go and say all that is proper, and tell him I shall be down just as soon as I've had time to see how Nicholas does, and to change my gown. Gussie, if you please, your arm on the stairs. All this junketing to Witney has quite worn me out."

The ladies retreated, and George made his way across the hall and through an ante-chamber to the grey drawing-room. This was quite the most beautiful room in the house, its dove-grey panelling ornamented by delicate carving picked out in white and gold, its ceiling set with exquisite medallions by Angelica Kauffmann. Lady Linslade had long ago ruled that this salon was to be used only on formal occasions, but it was plain that her oldest son did not feel himself bound by any such ukase.

He stood now, his left elbow resting on the chimneypiece, and in his right hand a glass of what George felt sure was the best Amontillado sherry. He appeared to be listening with considerable amusement to Emily, who was perched on a tapestried stool, close to the fire.

Unnoticed in the doorway, George studied his brother. Coat by Weston, he thought. Boots from Hoby. Ruby pin stuck in the folds of the cravat. It was infuriating that Alex should spend a fortune on his clothes, and then wear them as if he were unconscious of the effect they had on others.

Young Emily had tricked herself out in her best gown, and set a cherry-coloured ribbon in her curls, all in honour of Alex's homecoming. Alex was her favourite . . . was everyone's favourite, if the truth be told.

As a child Alex had been his papa's constant companion (whenever, that is, that indefatigable traveller was to be found in England). It had given him an unfair advantage over his siblings, helped him to excel in all he did as sportsman, student, man of fashion and man of affairs. "Julian Frome's oldest," declared the *beau monde*, "does him credit."

Nobody said that of George. Nobody sent George on sensitive diplomatic missions to the capitals of Europe. Nobody sought George's advice on the purchase of a painting, or a horse. Nobody tried to copy the way George tied his cravat.

The early death of the third Earl had given Alex the title at the age of nineteen; and as if looks, talent, wealth, and an earldom were not enough, Alex possessed the Frome charm, an ease and frankness of manner that made him everywhere liked. Emily had it too. So did Nicholas. People made excuses for Nick's frail constitution. He might not be robust, they said, not quite up to a day in the field or with the guns, but he was uncommon stout of heart. George, alas, was only stout of waistline.

Even George's older sister Arabella, who had come within an ace of disgracing the family, and whose name was never mentioned in George's hearing, enjoyed an undeservedly cosy niche in polite society. The fact that she was quite bird-witted seemed not to count with the ton, who insisted that her eye for fashion, and her skill as a hostess, were second to none.

Life, thought George moodily, was very unfair.

At this juncture the Earl, happening to glance up, noticed the gloomy figure in the doorway, and at once turned and held out his hand.

"George, my dear fellow, how are you?"

George crossed the room and shook hands. "Well enough, I thank you. A pleasure to see you at Foxfare. Unexpected," he could not resist adding.

Alex smiled. "Yes, it was shabby of me to arrive without warning, but when I heard that Nick was ill, I felt I must come at once."

George brushed that aside with a wave of the hand. "Bungay tells me you've been to see Turner."

"Yes." The Earl gave George a pensive look. "I wished to ask him why he has seen fit to close down the experimental farm."

"He did so on my orders."

"Ah! I expect you had your reasons."

George saw heavy ground ahead. He began to enumerate, in a blustering tone, the difficulties he had had to face: how his best labourers had deserted him and gone north, lured to the cotton manufactories of Liverpool and Manchester; how the weather, taxes, blight, maw-worm and malign fate, had conspired against him, to the extent that it was now necessary to prune expenditure to the bone.

Alex listened without comment. In due course the estate would have to be steered, for the nth time, towards more enlightened farming methods, but for the moment he had no wish to cross swords with George. His chief concern must be to bring Nick back to health. If that problem could be amicably settled, so might the rest.

A short while later, Lady Linslade and Augusta entered the drawing-room. Her ladyship had exchanged her day-gown for one of dark blue silk, and a Kashmiri shawl was draped over her shoulders and secured at the bosom by a pearl brooch. Her fair hair was covered by a cap of fine gauze trimmed with lace and fastened under the chin by black ribands.

She was a slender woman in her late forties who retained much of the fragile prettiness of her youth. Her disposition was not sanguine and, although she was sincerely devoted to her children, she found their energy and strong opinions exhausting. Unpleasantness of any sort quite overset her nerves, and at the first hint of dissension she was wont to retire to the chaise-longue in her boudoir, where she would remain, vinaigrette in hand, until the storm blew over.

Augusta still wore the gown of tartan challis she had put on that morning. Her excessive weight made her physically lazy and disinclined to obey the dictates of fashion. She affected drab colours and an outmoded style of dress. Her looks were undistinguished. Though her complexion was good, her nose seemed too small for the plumpness of her cheeks, and her eyes, large, brown, and set wide apart, gave her a rather bovine expression.

Lady Linslade advanced to embrace Alex, and began to shower him with questions about his most recent journey. He cut her short.

"Later, Mama. First tell me about Nick."

His mother smiled brightly. "Why, to be sure, he's fast asleep, and his fever seems much reduced. I'm sure that seeing you here has done him a power of good."

"Why didn't you send for me earlier?"

"My love, I didn't wish to incommode you, particularly as dear Dr Rumbole is so pleased with the way Nick goes on. Rumbole has been a tower of strength in our time of need. He is truly an excellent man. You'll recall that he attended on Ralph Gillingham and old Mr Humphries and Viscount Amesbury."

"All of whom," said Alex bluntly, "are dead."

As Lady Linslade began to protest, Alex found an unlooked-for ally in Augusta, who said loudly, "Quite right, all knocked into doornails by Rumbole! Starved to death, I shouldn't wonder. Couldn't keep a sparrow alive on the diet he advocates. I'll lay odds the reason Nick is feeling more the thing is that he has a square meal in his belly."

Lady Linslade shot George an anxious glance. "I do agree! A good bowl of broth does wonders for the convalescent patient."

"Not broth," insisted Augusta. "Lizzie told me it was fresh-baked bread, mutton pie, and a piece of Stilton cheese. Half a bottle of hock, too. And," she concluded with a wistful sigh, "peaches and grapes from the hothouse."

"Peaches?" cried George in a shrill tone. "My peaches, that I've been bringing to peak for the market? Do you stand there and tell me Nick has eaten one of my peaches?"

"Two, in point of fact," said Alex.

"But I told Slade they were on no account to be touched."

"I took the liberty of countermanding your order. I must say, George, you're to be congratulated. I've never tasted better fruit, not even in France."

"It was indeed a liberty," said George, scarlet in the face. "You have overset my plans and Dr Rumbole's, as well. He gave express orders that Nicholas must not eat meat or cheese. Such viands inflame the blood. Rumbole will be seriously displeased when he hears what you have done."

There was a moment's tense silence. Then, "Rumbole's displeasure," said the Earl gently, "is of no importance, since he won't be visiting this house again."

"Not visiting? What d'ye mean? Do you propose to leave that poor boy unattended? There's no other doctor this side of Charlbury. Or do you mean to call in one of your fancy London practitioners?"

"If necessary, yes."

"And you, I take it, will foot the bill? A pretty penny it will cost you, to fetch a doctor from London."

"Luckily I'm well able to stand the racket."

"Ah, yes, you are always very ready to spend, are you not? Spending is all you ever do — spending, and jauntering about to the ends of the earth, wasting the blunt I earn by the sweat of my brow!"

"I think you have that wrong." There was a new edge to Alex's voice. "While I appreciate that you work hard at

18

Foxfare, our chief revenue does not come from our lands. Indeed, if that were the case, with corn prices at rock bottom, we should soon be in Queer Street. What keeps us plump in the pocket, George, is the very handsome income from our properties in London, and the sound investments our father made in gilt-edged stock."

"At the rate you spend, that will soon be gone."

"On the contrary, if we continue to follow papa's rule, which was to invest in the development and enterprise of this country, we shall remain extremely well-to-do."

"I suppose that in the term enterprise, you include planting seed that has never before been tried, and interfering with the established laws of nature?"

"Exactly so, which is why I've instructed Turner to re-open the experimental farm, and to keep it open until I decide otherwise."

"You decide? Well, if by that you mean that you intend to come home and run the estate, let me say that I for one am heartily glad of it. You've made it plain that you consider my humble attempts to be quite beneath contempt, so I won't mince matters, either. I've had enough of your absenteeism, and your autocratic demands, and your crackpot innovations. You're so full of your own damned consequence that you think you have only to nod, and the world will grovel at your feet! I tell you, I'll not do so. From now on you may manage Foxfare any way you please. I am done with the place, and all its works."

Lady Linslade, looking distraught, hurried across the room and placed a hand on George's arm. "Pray, my love, don't speak in haste. We are all of us conscious of the sterling efforts you have made on our behalf. I know that Linslade, like the rest of us, feels himself to be very much in your debt."

"No, he don't," said George pettishly. "He thinks I'm a clodpole, the veriest bumpkin, unfit to make the smallest decision. He don't trust my judgement in anything, and nor do you, Mama, or you wouldn't have sent for him to come home."

"I? I did no such thing, and I must say, George, that it's the outside of enough that you should speak so harshly to one who has been at all times your loyal and loving champion."

Dabbing at her eyes with a lace kerchief, Lady Linslade moved with tottering steps to the nearest sofa and sank down upon it, the picture of lacerated feelings. Emily rose from her place by the fire and approached George.

"Mama didn't send for Alex," she said. "I did."

"You?" George clutched at his shirt-front as if he expected to surprise a nest of vipers there. "You deliberately flouted my orders? Well, Miss, don't imagine I will let such duplicity go unpunished. There'll be no London season for you, this year. If you've not yet learned the meaning of obedience, then you are certainly not fit to be launched in polite society."

The injustice of these words, and the rough tone in which they were couched, reduced Lady Linslade to a fresh burst of tears, and Emily to speechless rage. Once again, Augusta took it upon herself to intervene.

"Not for you to decide, George. You ain't Emily's guardian. Alexander is."

Alex, seeing George to be on the verge of apoplexy, stepped forward.

"For God's sake, let's have no more brangling. George, it's true that I see no reason to alter Mama's plan to bring Em out this year. It's also true that I owe you an apology. You've carried the load for me all these years. I'm deeply grateful to you, for your care of Foxfare, and your devotion to the family interests."

George was not mollified by this speech. Shouting that Alex, Foxfare, and the entire Frome clan might go to the devil for all he cared, he brushed past his brother and would have stormed out of the room, had not Bungay appeared to announce that dinner was served.

It was not a convivial meal. Mrs Hackaway had, in her own phrase, wellnigh bust her stays to set something creditable on the table, and had prepared a roast baron of beef, a brace of glazed chickens, a trussed goose, and a steak and kidney pie of gargantuan size, all supported by numerous side-dishes, vegetables, and sauces. This course was followed by a great many creams, jellies and custards, as well as a large bowl of George's forbidden fruit. Bungay, not to be outdone, had fetched from the cellars the finest claret and burgundy, and a flagon of champagne for the ladies.

The extravagance of this repast caused George to sink into a fit of the sullens, and he refused to utter a syllable to anyone. Augusta, who had been on short rations for weeks, made no other contribution to the conversation than the word "truffles", spoken in tones of deep satisfaction. It was left to Alex to entertain his mother and sister, which he did by giving a lively account of Paris society, and the extremes of fashion affected by Louis XVIII and his mushroom court.

The party broke up as soon as the dessert dishes had been removed. George picked up a bottle of port and retired with it to the library. The ladies withdrew to the red salon. The Earl made his way upstairs to Nicholas's room.

Nick had put on a dressing-gown, and was seated in a wing-chair by the fire, poring over a sheaf of papers. He laid these aside as Alex entered, and said anxiously, "I heard George bellowing, down there. Fur and feathers flying, was it?"

"I'm afraid so." Alex sat down, smiling ruefully. "I never did learn the trick of handling him."

"I doubt if there is one. Dashed short fuse, has George. Explodes at a touch."

"I told him to give Rumbole his marching orders."

"Did you, by Jove? I won't say I'm sorry."

"Unfortunately, I can't trust George to abide by my wishes. He'll very likely reinstate Rumbole as soon as my back's turned. It's best you leave Foxfare for a time. The question is, where do we send you?"

"To London," Nick said eagerly. "I've thought it all out. Frome House will be opened soon enough, and my wants aren't great. Braddock can look after me until the full staff arrives. I shall rest, and study, and work on my notes. Did I tell you I plan to write a book? Nothing spectacular, just a journal of my time in Greece. So if you will ask Turner to hire a post-chaise for me, I shall set off tomorrow, and reach Town quite comfortably in a day or so."

"That won't serve, Nick. For one thing, you're in no state to handle all the changes of team. For another, I shan't be in London for another week at least, and I've no intention of leaving you to Braddock's tender mercies." He saw the disappointment in Nicholas's eyes, and went on reassuringly,

"But here's a scheme you may like. I've been promising for an age to visit Grandmama . . . was on the point of setting out for Evesham when I had Em's letter. Why don't you come with me? Grandmama will be in alt over having you to stay, and you can bear her company when she removes to London in April."

This idea found instant favour with Nick. It was agreed that, unless he suffered a setback overnight, they would leave for Evesham the next day.

Alex went at once to convey this news to his mother. It was not to be imagined that Lady Linslade would easily accept a plan that entailed snatching her ewe lamb from his sickbed and transporting him in inclement weather to what she unequivocally described as the wastes of Herefordshire.

Not all Alex's assurances, that they would travel by easy stages, that Grandmama Alice lived in a style far more luxurious than that obtaining at Foxfare, and that the excellent Dr Henry Gifford would be called to examine Nick the instant they reached Oakengates, sufficed to calm her ladyship's fears. She very soon worked herself into such a lachrymose state that it took the combined efforts of Emily and Augusta to help her to her bed, from which, she declared, she did not expect to rise again.

George's reaction was more blunt. He said that as tomorrow was All Fools' Day, he supposed Alex might commit any folly he pleased, and added that if the venture proved to be the death of Nick, then he for one would accept no part of the blame.

It remained only for the Earl to instruct Cheadle and Belper to be ready to quit Foxfare at short notice. That done, he retired to bed, and slept the sleep of the man who has burned his boats.

He woke betimes next morning, and went to the window of his bedchamber to study the weather. What he saw was far from heartening. The sky to the north hung low and yellowish, and the air had the oppressive stillness that warns of snow.

Going to Nick's room, he found that young man already dressed, and instructing his valet Braddock what to pack in his valise. Alex's suggestion that they postpone their journey was dismissed out of hand.

"If it snows," Nick said, "we'll be trapped here for days. There are plenty of good posting-houses on the route north. If push comes to shove, we can put up at one of 'em."

Braddock now enquired if he was to be allowed to accompany his master. The Earl shook his head. "No. It will be more comfortable with only two of us in the carriage, and taking the baggage chaise would slow us down. I've sent Finch to Oakengates already. He's quite well able to look after the pair of us."

Braddock indicated by the stiffness of his bow how little he thought of this arrangement; and he later remarked to Bungay that in the Old Earl's time, no gentleman would have dreamed of travelling without his own courier, valet, and postillions, and it all went to show that there'd been a sad falling-off in the manners and morals of the world.

The departure from Foxfare took place immediately after breakfast. Of the family, only Emily came to bid the travellers Godspeed. She had made up a parcel of nostrums for Nicholas, with copious directions for their use, and had caused hot bricks, rugs and pillows to be placed in the carriage.

Alex knew that she was bound to face a good deal of unkind criticism from her relations, and he said, as he bent to kiss her cheek, "This won't be for long, Em. We'll meet in London very soon, I promise. In the mean time . . . "

"I know." She smiled at him. "I'm to stay in the ring, keep my guard up, and roll with the punches."

He laughed. "Where did you learn such vulgar cant?"

"From you, of course." She gave him a hug. "Take care, Alex. Don't let Cheadle spring the bays."

"They shall never exceed a trot," he said. "Don't fret about us, Em. It's barely thirty miles to Evesham, as the crow flies. Nothing very terrible can befall us in that short distance."

Fate, thus tempted, lost no time in proving his lordship wrong.

III

THE ROUTE LORD Linslade had chosen to take lay through Shipton-under-Wychwood, and thence up the river valley to Moreton-in-Marsh, Chipping Camden and Evesham.

It was not as popular a road as the main pike to Stratford-upon-Avon, but it was a good deal shorter. Going by Stratford would mean delays, perhaps the need to change horses, or even to spend a night at an inn. Moreover, Alex was familiar with every twist and turn of the river route, knew the ostlers in the various hostelries, and could count on them to give him accurate advice on the state of the track ahead.

For the first two hours, all went swimmingly. Nicholas was in high spirits, and strenuously denied feeling any symptoms of fever. The bays stepped out sweetly, and the miles sped by.

As they moved north, however, the weather grew rapidly worse, black clouds crowding low over the valley, and a cold wind keeping up a ceaseless, ominous keening.

At the White Hart in Moreton, when they stopped briefly for refreshments, they received bad news. Josiah Chubb, the landlord of the inn, warned the Earl that it would be unwise to take the Chipping Camden road.

"My lad Simeon came from thataway not an hour since, m'lord, an' 'e do say as there's snow lyin' thick on the tops, an' closin' down fast. You'd not want to risk those prime uns o' yourn on black ice, now would 'ee? Do better to bide here for the night, an' try for Stratford tomorrow."

Alex shook his head. "If I can't reach Evesham today I must return to Foxfare. My brother's in poor health. He must be within reach of a doctor should the need arise."

Mr Chubb rasped a hand over his chin. "You might go by Swallowford," he said pensively. "It's a roughish road, mind, but sheltered, an' if you can go no further, you'll find good lodgin's at the Merry Man. Stablin' for the 'osses, decent victuals an' 'omebrewed for yoursel'n. As to Mr Nicholas, if 'e was to be took bad, there's Dr Chase lives in Swallowford. They do say as Sir Sholto Curle pays 'andsome to 'ave 'im close at 'and, and Sir Sholto's not the man to waste 'is ready on a quack."

Told of the situation, Nick said at once that they should try the Swallowford route.

"We can't go back, Alex. Just imagine the rumpus, George saying 'I told you so', Mama indulging in another set of conniptions, and the whole performance to be repeated next

24

time we set out. Flesh and blood won't stand it. I say let's cut line and run."

Alex hesitated. He already regretted having embarked on this expedition. Nick's pallor alarmed him; but so did the expression in Nick's eyes, the look of a rabbit that has seen a stoat. Foxfare wasn't the place for him. Their mother, and George, had the terrible tenacity of the weak. George used ill-temper to get his way, and Mama used tears. Only their victims understood how powerful such weapons could be. To take Nick back to them, and to Rumbole's ministrations, would be cruel, even dangerous. Sighing a little, Alex agreed to make for Swallowford.

Mr Chubb came out of the inn to set them on their way, gave them precise instructions how to reach Swallowford, and cautioned Cheadle that some of the road signs were hard to find. "Just 'ee keep to the left o' the river," he adjured as the carriage started forward, "and 'ee can't go wrong."

His confidence proved to be misplaced. Though Cheadle obediently kept to the left of the water, there was often a choice of roads and no way of telling which was the right one. At the end of fifteen miles they found themselves on a cart-track that grew steadily rougher and at last petered out altogether.

There was nothing to do but go back. There followed what seemed an eternity of snail's-pace travel along narrow, twisting lanes. It was after three in the afternoon when they came upon a signpost pointing the way to Swallowford.

The sight made Alex sweat with relief. For the past hour he had been cursing himself for a fool. The light was failing, snow seemed imminent, and Nicholas was in extremely poor case, unable to suppress the violent bouts of shivering that racked his body, and admitting, when taxed, that his head ached like the very devil.

"Only a mile or so more," Alex assured him. "We'll have you warm and comfortable in no time."

Ten minutes later the carriage checked at the head of a gentle rise from which the road wound down between steep, wooded banks to a broad and pleasant valley. To the right of the road was a stream, which flowed to join a much larger body of water on the floor of the valley, and at this meeting-point was a good-sized village. Alex was able to discern a church with a tall steeple, a green with a duck-pond, a forge, an inn and a number of cottages built of the mellow local stone and deep-thatched. There were, besides, a few larger houses, set back from the road, which he judged to be the homes of wealthy farmers or the local gentry. Swallowford, if it did not promise the luxuries of life, at least seemed to offer some of its comforts.

He was about to tell Cheadle to drive on, when the peace was shattered by the sound of a shot, not the heavy thump of a sporting-gun, but the lighter crack of a pistol. It appeared to come from the woods above and to the right of the carriage.

The next moment, with a great noise of threshing and trampling, two horsemen burst from the cover of the trees and plunged down towards the road. The first, mounted on a rangy grey, wore a shabby frieze coat, thigh boots and a beaver hat. The second was dressed all in black: tight black trousers, black boots embroidered in silver, a black cloak that swirled on the wind like the wings of a bird, a wide black hat secured under the chin by a heavy silver chain.

The first horseman forced his mount down the last of the slope and across the stream. Wheeling in the saddle, he levelled a pistol at his pursuer and fired, then spurred on past the carriage, heading away from Swallowford.

The second rider continued to race along the bank, apparently in the hope of cutting off the other's escape. He too brandished a pistol, and as he came closer he loosed off a shot. His aim was poor. The ball shattered the window on the Earl's right, and whistled past his ear to bury itself in the leather squab.

The man on the grey was out of sight. Thwarted, the pursuer uttered a cry of rage and turned his horse downhill. The slope was steep and treacherous. The beast pecked, missed its footing and rolled down into the stream. The rider, unable to jump clear, crashed headfirst into the water and lay motionless.

Shouting to Belper to catch the horse, the Earl ran to lift the fallen rider from the stream and lay him on the grassy verge. He felt for the pulse at the throat and found it to be beating, though faintly. Blood was pouring from a gash in the man's scalp, and from his nose. Alex drew off his own scarf and wound it round the man's head, trying to staunch the flow of blood. He caught the glint of metal at the edge of the stream and leaned over to pick up a long-barrelled pistol which he slipped into the pocket of his greatcoat.

Nicholas thrust his head out of the carriage window. His teeth were chattering with cold.

"Alex? Is the f-fellow alive?"

"Breathing, barely. We must get him to shelter. I imagine the village is our best bet. We can lift him on his cloak. Belper, lend a hand here."

But Belper was staring fixedly at the bank.

"There's another on 'em, my lord, up yonder."

The Earl turned his head. Some ten yards away, on a promontory of rock, stood a truly splendid horse, pale honey-coloured, his mane and tail streaming in the wind. Bridle, stirrup-leathers and saddle were heavily ornamented with silver in the Spanish style. Astride him sat a rider in the now-familiar black, but his raiment was of a far richer quality than his companion's. His cloak was lined with scarlet silk and secured at the throat by a jewelled clasp. Silver braid adorned the brim of his hat. His breeches, cut full in the Cossack mode, were tucked into half-boots of soft red leather. His gauntleted left hand held the reins, and in his right was the twin of the pistol the Earl had retrieved.

"Footpads?" muttered Nicholas, and Alex answered softly, "I think not." He raised his voice. "Sir, your friend is badly hurt. Be so good as to come and tell me what you wish done with him."

The rider remained stock still for a moment, then turned his mount and brought it in a slithering rush down the bank and across the stream. Reaching the road, he dismounted and without a word handed the reins to Belper. Kneeling beside the injured man, he pulled off his gauntlet and began to check for broken bones, gently feeling the victim's limbs and rib-cage. His hands, Alex noticed, were those of a gentleman, narrow and well-kept. The injured man, beginning to regain consciousness, groaned and rolled his head from side to side.

"At least his neck's not broken," Alex said.

The other glanced up. The shadow of his hat hid the upper

half of his face. He appeared to be young, little more than a boy, with delicate features, a pale skin, and reddish hair tied back in a queue. His voice when he spoke was light and husky.

"We'll take him to Ringwood."

"Surely, a doctor . . . " began the Earl, but the youth cut him short.

"The doctor will come to us." The voice was English, without accent, and coolly sure of itself. "Sir, if you will be kind enough to permit us to use your carriage? It's no distance. The house is behind these woods."

As Alex hesitated, thinking of Nicholas, Nick himself settled the issue. "Do it, Alex. C-common decency."

The young man threw Nick a brief glance, then turned back to his lordship.

"Perhaps your groom will help me lift Ramon?"

"He'll help me to do so. Hold the horses."

The young man obeyed without a word, swinging himself into the saddle of his own mount, and taking the reins of the other horse from Belper. The Earl and Belper lifted Ramon on to his spread cloak and laid him on the floor of the carriage. Nick stretched out along the seat, Alex climbed up to the driver's box beside Cheadle, and Belper swung himself to the perch at the rear. The young horseman called over his shoulder: "Follow me. The gates are two hundred yards down, on the right."

The carriage rolled forward. The light was now almost gone, and the first flurry of snow obscured their view of the valley.

Lord Linslade was later to remember his arrival at Ringwood as having the quality of a dream.

Their guide led them through an ancient stone archway and along a drive overarched by dense and sombre foliage. From this they emerged into a large level area, on the far side of which stood a manor-house built of brick, its many gables roofed with slate, its windows fitted with diamond panes that glowed with rosy light. The building was sheltered from the elements by the shoulder of the hill. No wind stirred the air here, and the snow fell silently over all.

28

On the sweep of gravel in front of the house, there were signs of frantic activity. Lackeys ran to and fro, brandishing torches. A group of farm hands was engaged in doling out lanterns and billhooks. A game-keeper stood to one side, his gun in the crook of his arm, a spaniel at his heels. Two wolf-hounds paced restlessly back and forth, shaking their massive heads. On the broad steps of the house, a woman in a grey mantle was in what seemed to be heated discussion with an elderly man whose black clothes and chain of office marked him as the steward of the establishment.

As the cortège approached, this old man broke off the argument and hurried to greet the horseman, raising both arms in obvious relief. The youth leaned down to speak to him, then dismounted and beckoned to two servants who were waiting with a trestle-board, indicating that they should bring it over to the carriage. The men hurried to do his bidding and in a matter of moments had lifted the still-unconscious Ramon from the coach and borne him within doors.

The Earl climbed down from the box and helped Nicholas to alight. The young man approached with outstretched hand.

"My name is Pelham," he said. "This house is Ringwood. It belongs to my grandfather, Sir Sholto Curle."

Alex shook hands, bowing slightly. "Linslade, of Foxfare. My brother, Nicholas Frome."

"We are much in your debt, sir."

"Pray don't consider it."

"We shall of course make good the damage to your carriage."

"There's no need. It will be repaired by my own people when I return to London."

"At least let us offer you a glass of wine? Grandfather will wish to thank you for all you have done."

Alex cast a glance at the thickening snow. "Forgive me, but I believe we should make for Swallowford without delay. I beg you will present my compliments, and regrets, to Sir Sholto."

The young man tilted his head enquiringly. "You have friends in Swallowford, sir?"

The Earl frowned slightly. "No, Mr Pelham, we are strangers to these parts. We intend to lodge at the Merry Man. I'm told it's adequate."

The youth appeared not to notice the coldness of this reply. His attention had switched to Nicholas, who was leaning against the carriage door, very white of face.

"You are ill, sir!"

"M-merest chill," said Nick, summoning up a death's-head grin. "B-better directly. Assure you."

For answer, the young man applied the palm of his hand to Nick's forehead.

"You have a high fever," he said, turning an accusing stare on Alex. "Mr Frome should not be abroad in such weather!"

Since this conviction had been plaguing his lordship for the past five hours, he naturally resented being reminded of it. He said repressively, "You may leave my brother's welfare in my hands, Mr Pelham. I shall call a doctor to him just as soon as we reach the inn."

The youth shrugged. "You'd be better advised to remain here. There's only one doctor in Swallowford, and he resides in this house. At present he's busy with Ramon, but Mr Frome may see him shortly, and in far greater comfort than can be found at the Merry Man. You're welcome to such hospitality as Ringwood can offer."

Alex opened his mouth to frame a refusal, and closed it again. In the past half hour he had been embroiled in a vulgar shooting affray on the public highway. He had narrowly escaped a bullet in the brain. His carriage had been severely damaged. All of these events the insufferable Mr Pelham treated as if they were run-of-the-mill, offering neither explanation nor apology for his part in them.

Linslade of Foxfare was accustomed to be treated with a great deal more deference. People, particularly very young people in bizarre apparel, did not issue reproofs — or invitations — in this imperious manner. He was tempted to give the young bantam a sharp set-down; but there rose to his mind the memory of George's recent strictures. Arrogant, George had called him. Overfull of his own consequence. These were not epithets that Alex wished to deserve.

Moreover, he was recalling what Chubb had told him, back at the White Hart. If it were true that Sholto Curle retained the services of this doctor to his own exclusive use, then it would be pointless to let Nick wait his turn in the village.

He bowed stiffly, and said, "You are very kind . . . and if it is not too great an imposition . . .?"

"None at all." The young man was already raising a hand. A groom with a lantern ran forward, signalling to Cheadle to bring the carriage round to the stableyard. At a nod from his master, Cheadle complied, and the carriage rolled away.

Looking about him, Alex saw that the terrace had emptied while they talked. Torches flared in the brackets flanking the steps, and at the head of these the tall double-doors stood open, light streaming through them.

Mr Pelham was already leading Nicholas towards the house. With a feeling that he might live to regret it, the Earl followed.

IV

THE ENTRANCE HALL of Ringwood was immense, panelled from flagged floor to lofty ceiling in oak, and lit by three massive chandeliers of Waterford glass suspended on gilded chains. Two fireplaces accommodated burning logs of formidable girth. Above each chimneypiece was an array of antique pikes. The wall between was hung with a double row of portraits in heavy frames.

A minstrels' gallery lay at the west end of the hall, and at the east was a broad stairway, the balustrade carved with heraldic beasts.

As the Earl entered, a footman hurried forward to relieve him of his coat and hat. Shrugging out of his greatcoat, he remembered the pistol in the pocket, and retrieved it. A discreet cough sounded at his side. The elderly steward was watching him with a faintly quizzical smile.

"May I say, my lord," murmured the old man, "that it is a great pleasure to be able once again to welcome a member of your family?" At the Earl's enquiring look, the smile widened. "I recognized the arms on your carriage, Lord Linslade. We were used to see them on occasion, when your father was alive. He was on terms of friendship with Sir Sholto. They fenced together. A notable swordsman, your father, though not, I venture to say, quite up to Sir Sholto's mark."

"I look forward to making Sir Sholto's acquaintance."

"Thank you, my lord. Now that my poor master is unable to leave Ringwood, he regards such fortuitous visits as yours as manna from Heaven. Dinner is at six-thirty, my lord. It is the custom of the family to assemble in the drawing-room at six."

The old man bowed, and withdrew. The Earl, turning to look for his host, suffered his second shock of the day.

Mr Pelham, divested of his broadbrimmed hat and heavy cloak, proved to be not Mr Pelham at all, but a young woman of striking appearance. She was above average height, her figure slender but pleasantly rounded. Her face was oval, the nose straight and delicately formed, the lips full, the eyes of a dark, fiery blue. Her hair, tied at the nape of the neck by a black riband, was the colour of old brandy. Her expression was amused, and a little defiant.

"I am Lucilla Pelham, Lord Linslade. Welcome to Ringwood."

Alex recovered his wits. "Your servant, Miss Pelham. You must forgive my gaucherie. I mistook you for the grandson of the house."

"I expect it was the breeches," she said. "Females don't in general wear them."

"True," agreed the Earl politely, "though I believe Caroline Lamb was apt to appear at costume balls dressed as a page."

The blue eyes flashed. "Ah, but Lady Caro was weak in the attic, was she not, besides being very bad ton? I assure you that I only put on man's garb when necessity demands."

"As, for example, when you are chasing armed bandits across the countryside?"

"Exactly so."

"And is that a common occurrence, Miss Pelham?"

She met his gaze coolly. "More common than I like, sir." She held out her hand. "Shall I take that?"

With a start, Alex remembered the pistol. He held it out to her and she took it casually, at once turning to Nicholas, who was standing by with a dazed look on his face.

32

"You will wish to go straight to your bed, Mr Frome. I shall send Dr Chase to you as soon as may be." She signed to the footman who waited near the bottom of the stairway. "Robert will show you to your rooms, and act as your personal servant while you're at Ringwood. Pray ask him for anything you may need."

She bestowed a brisk nod on his lordship, a friendly smile on Nicholas, and strolled away towards the rear of the house, leaving her guests to follow their guide upstairs.

The antiquated style of the great hall had led Alex to expect Gothic discomfort in the domestic regions of the manor, but he found this not to be the case.

The bedroom allotted to him could only be described as magnificent. The walls were hung with cream-coloured Spitalfields silk. The curtains and bed-hangings were of darker gold brocade. A fine Aubusson carpet covered the floor, the furniture was Louis Seize, and a charming Watteau was displayed above the chimneypiece.

He walked through a dressing-room, to Nick's bedchamber. Here the predominant colours were white and China blue, and the furnishings by the hand of Mr Chippendale.

Sir Sholto was evidently a man of taste as well as means.

Dr Chase, a cheerful figure with cherubic features and a head of tight grey curls, arrived a few minutes later. The man Ramon, he told them, was suffering from a nasty laceration of the scalp and a severe concussion, but had not incurred any internal injuries. "The rogue is as tough as my boot," he said. "He'll do, provided there's no infection of the wound. And now, Mr Frome, let's take a look at you."

He examined Nicholas thoroughly, and questioned him closely about his sojourn in Greece. "There's the cause of your trouble," he said at last. "Drinking foul water from a village well. We'll set you to rights, soon enough. The first thing to do is keep you in bed for twenty-four hours."

"That's impossible," Nick protested. "What will my hosts think of me if I take to my bed the instant I arrive?"

"Sir Sholto will think you a sensible man who follows the advice of his doctor," responded Dr Chase with a smile.

"He'll wish me at Jericho!"

"No, he won't. Not only are you the son of an old acquaintance, but you have lately been to Greece. Mad about Greece, and Greek literature, is Sir Sholto. He'll be wanting to show you his library as soon as you're up and about. He's a lonely man, Mr Frome, a very lonely man. His heart is not strong, and he suffers acutely from rheumatism. It's a sad affliction for a man who was a regular out-and-outer, rode to hounds four days a week, and could handle the ribbons in style. Now he seldom stirs from this property, and must rely upon chance visitors to bring him news of the world."

As he spoke, the doctor drew a writing-tablet from his pocket and began to scribble on it.

"Here is the regimen I wish you to follow, young man. Rest, sleep, and a plain but nourishing diet. Tonight perhaps you may like some broth, and buttered eggs? I shall mention it to Miss Pelham. As to the fever and headache, I shall leave you a paregoric draught. It's something quite new. The principal element is the bark of the cinchona tree. Miss Pelham brought back a supply with her when she returned to England from the Americas. Devilish bitter to the taste, but swallow it down, sir, swallow it down, it will do you no end of good. Now you are to let Robert help you to bed. I shall look in tomorrow, to see how you go along. Good night, Mr Frome. Sleep well."

As the little doctor moved towards the door, he said in a low voice, "Lord Linslade? A word with you, if you please."

Outside in the corridor, Dr Chase regarded Alex with some severity. "Your brother, my lord, is severely debilitated. I don't like to criticize other members of my profession, but I must tell you frankly, Mr Frome has been bled beyond what is wise. He's very weak."

"My view entirely," agreed Alex. "In fact, I removed him from home because I disliked the treatment doled out by Dr Rumbole. Too much leeching and not enough food."

"Yes, well, those are the old-fashioned methods. Now we will see what rest and sustenance can achieve." Dr Chase paused, then went on. "There is something else I wish to raise with you, my lord. The recent encounter on the highway . . . I beg you won't make mention of it to Sir Sholto."

34

"Surely he must know of it already?"

"No, sir. Soan — that is the Steward — has told him only that there was an accident, that Ramon was injured and that you very kindly conveyed him to this place. He knows nothing of the shooting. It would distress him to know that Lucilla — and your good selves, of course — have been exposed to such danger."

"Forgive me, doctor, but if the neighbourhood is being overrun by bandits surely the proper course is to hand the matter over to the Justice of the Peace?"

"Sir Sholto prefers to deal with it himself."

"Can he do so?" said the Earl bluntly. "It seems to me that it's Miss Pelham who runs the risks."

Dr Chase reddened. "I know. I know how it must look, to an outsider. I've done my best to reason with Lucilla — to persuade her that these breakneck tactics won't do. But she's as hot at hand and stubborn as her grandsire! I daresay it's the result of her upbringing, which was far from orthodox. Her papa, you see, was Sidney Pelham, the explorer. You may perhaps have heard of him?"

"I have indeed, and read his book on the Incas of Peru."

"He made many journeys, my lord, to many outlandish places. His wife Elizabeth — Sir Sholto's daughter — could not stand the hardships of his expeditions. She died when Lucilla was no more than seven years old. Mr Pelham would not surrender the child to be raised in England, but took her on his travels. They lived in wild and dangerous territories. Lucilla had perforce to learn to be intrepid, and to rely upon her own resources. Her father was her only guide and mentor. He taught her to read and write, but she had no other education until she was brought to England at the age of twelve. I take credit for that. I was able to convince Sidney Pelham that if he continued in his obstinacy he would lose the daughter as he had lost the wife.

"Lucilla attended a Dame School in Cheltenham for four years, and spent her holidays with Sir Sholto. At sixteen she returned to her father and me in New Orleans. It was from there that Mr Pelham launched his last venture, to Brazil. There he perished of fever. Lucilla returned home. That was six months ago."

"I see. And does the man Ramon hail from Brazil?"

35

"No, he's a Mexican, and an idle, untruthful rogue. Nothing to commend him but his skill with horses and his loyalty to Lucilla." Dr Chase sighed. "This is an unusual household, my lord. There are circumstances which I'm not at liberty to discuss. All I can do is urge you to spare a frail old gentleman unnecessary anxiety."

Alex shrugged. "Whatever you wish, Doctor."

Dr Chase thanked him, and bustled away. Alex returned to his brother's room. He found Nicholas comfortably established in bed, and the footman Robert busy gathering up boots and discarded clothing. Alex dismissed the man, saying he'd send for him when it was time to dress for dinner.

When they were alone, he smiled at Nick. "Well? What do you make of our hosts?"

"A dashed rum set of characters," said Nick. "First they try to kill us, then they bring us here and treat us *en grand seigneur*. Makes me feel we're being fattened for the slaughter!"

"In that case, you're in no immediate danger."

"I thought Miss Pelham a dashed pretty gal."

"Oh, a gem of the first water," said Alex carelessly, "but lacks polish, I think. Hardly conformable for a female to be careering about in breeches, brandishing a horse-pistol."

"Since when have you liked 'em conformable?" demanded Nick. "What about that opera-singer you had in keeping last year? Gave her a coach lined with blue velvet! Four white prancers with ostrich-feathers on their heads! If that's conformity, you may bite me."

"I admit to the carriage," said the Earl, "but those knock-kneed screws and their trappings were Marie's idea. They put an end to our friendship. I don't intend to become a figure of pantomime . . . or to be part of such melodrama as we've just witnessed."

"The truth is, you're miffed because Miss Pelham took you in aversion."

The Earl grinned. "She did, didn't she? Which is further proof that she lacks proper judgement." He stood up. "I'm going to look at the bays. Try not to fall into any more scrapes while I'm gone."

He made his way out to the stables, which proved to be

36

splendid enough to have impressed even Belper, who confided that he'd counted twenty-six hunters in the loose-boxes, as well as carriage and work-horses, all of them prime blood and bone. Belper, once satisfied that the bays had taken no harm from their rough journey, was enjoying the luxury of his surroundings; but Cheadle was less sanguine.

"Havey-cavey lot, hereabouts," he said darkly. "Bunch o' cut-throats. Murder us in our beds as soon as look at us."

Alex turned to Belper. "Jack, did you manage to catch a glimpse of that ruffian on the grey?"

"I did, my lord," Belper said, "an' a proper wicked customer I thought 'im. Nose as flat as the palm of yer 'and. Been in a few mills, I reckon. Wouldn't like to run into 'im of a dark night."

"Was he a foreigner, do you think?"

"Not 'im, me lord. Cussed me in the King's English as 'e went by. I took 'im fer Lunnon scum. Gallows-meat, as sure as I stand 'ere."

Alex was inclined to agree with Belper, but it puzzled him to know what brought such Town riff-raff to a backwater like Swallowford . . . and why Sir Sholto was reluctant to call in the Law to deal with the fellow. Aloud, he said:

"It seems likely we'll be forced to stay here a day or two. Luckily my brother is comfortable, and Dr Chase seems competent to care for him. Jack, if the road permits, you will ride to Evesham tomorrow to tell my grandmother we're safe. The rest of us . . . " he cast a warning look at Cheadle . . . "must bide our time in patience, and keep still tongues in our heads."

V

LORD LINSLADE, ARRIVING in the drawing-room promptly at six o'clock, found himself forestalled. Six faces turned towards him as he made his entrance, their expressions ranging from mild amiability to lively curiosity.

Lucilla Pelham came forward to meet him. She wore a gown of French-blue silk which, to his lordship's practised eye, bore the stamp of a London *modiste*. Cut low over the bosom, it had sleeves very full at the shoulder and tight at the wrist. A deep band of ruching adorned the hem of the skirt. Miss Pelham's hair was arranged in a high knot on the crown of her head, with a fall of curls over each ear. Her only jewel was a locket set with seed pearls and sapphires. The Earl could scarcely credit that a short time earlier he had mistaken her for a boy.

He saw that, though her face was demure, mockery sparkled in her eyes. The minx was enjoying his discomfiture. He smiled down at her, raising his hand in the fencer's acknowledgement of a hit, and a small chuckle escaped her.

"Good evening, my lord. I trust your brother is comfortable?"

"Most comfortable, thank you, ma'am. I left him on the verge of falling asleep."

"The best thing for him. My Grandfather sends you his apologies. He has been detained and will join us as soon as he's able. In the meantime, may I present my cousins, Miss Tamar Curle and Mr Adrian Curle? Their companion, Mrs Marion Gray? Our neighbour, Mr Giles Ayliffe? Dr Chase you have already met."

Lord Linslade dutifully bowed, smiled and shook hands with the company. They were, he thought, a somewhat odd assortment.

Miss Tamar Curle he judged to be fresh from the schoolroom, the promise of beauty still veiled by the plumpness of youth. Her hair was the pale gold of a pussy-willow catkin, her features regular, and her complexion rosy with health. She was clad in a gown of embroidered jonquil muslin, and a velvet spencer-jacket of a slightly darker hue. The fleeting glance she directed at his lordship was shy, but not awkwardly so. In a year or so Miss Curle might be counted upon to break a few hearts.

Her brother Adrian was perhaps two years older than she, fair like his sister, and a little on the plump side. He wore his hair in the Byronic style, and thick spectacles exaggerated the size of his eyes so that Alex was put in mind of the story of the dog with eyes as big as windmills. Mr Curle's manner was abstracted and, once he had made his bow, he lapsed into a reverie that seemed to render him deaf to what went on about him.

Mr Giles Ayliffe, on the other hand, was very much on the *qui vive*. He was a tall young man, well set up, with a narrow, eager face and tow-coloured hair. He fixed the Earl with a stare of such intensity that his lordship wondered if he might be a little touched in the attic; but in time he saw that Mr Ayliffe favoured every person and object in the room with the same intense gaze. Only when it touched Miss Curle did it soften. It did not take much to guess that Mr Ayliffe was nutty upon the girl, and that she returned the sentiment in full. First love, thought his lordship, and moved with a smile to address Mrs Gray.

He was startled to find her watching him with cold animosity. She masked the look at once, lowering her lids and forcing a smile to her lips. He made some commonplace remark and she answered civilly but without meeting his eye, her head averted.

She must have been handsome, he thought, before the years sharpened the line of nose and jaw. She had the fine skin that lines early, and her black hair was streaked with white at the temples. Her eyes were her best feature, very large and luminous, the eyes of a tragedy queen. Her frame was thin to the point of emaciation, and her style of dress sombre, though by no means shabby. He put her down as some dependent of Sir Sholto, called in perhaps to take temporary charge of his grandchildren; in which case, where were their parents?

As if she sensed and resented his question, Mrs Gray slipped an arm round Miss Curle's waist and, with a murmured excuse, drew her away to where Lucilla Pelham stood talking to Dr Chase. The Earl found himself alone with Mr Ayliffe.

"Uncommon good of you, sir," the young man offered, "to come to Lucilla's aid this afternoon. Most men would have driven by without lifting a finger, in which case it'd have been all over with Ramon." He fixed Alex with his unnerving stare. "Poachers, was it? Been a lot of 'em about, this year."

Having no wish to be drawn into a discussion of the fracas, Alex merely said, "My dear sir, no thanks are due to me. We're in Sir Sholto's debt for taking us in."

"He likes company," said Mr Ayliffe simply. "Converse all day and all night if you let him. I spend what time I can with him, and don't count it wasted."

Amused, the Earl said, "Is Greek literature your interest, Mr Ayliffe?"

The young man gave a crack of laughter. "Lord, no, I'm no hand at the Classics! No, we discuss my work." He paused, then said somewhat defensively. "I'm an inventor, and Sir Sholto is my patron."

Lord Linslade regarded his companion with a fascinated eye. "Indeed? What do you . . . er . . . invent?"

"Anything," said Mr Ayliffe largely. "I've perfected a broad harrow, and an automatic loom, and a threshing-machine which Mr Cobb believes has merit, but I design smaller items as well. I've made a study of Mr Joseph Bramah's work, and I fancy that the Ayliffe Indoor Water Closet is a distinct improvement on his design. Bathrooms are the coming thing, you know. Soon no man or woman of distinction will be without one. I've achieved piped water, hot and cold, to the bathroom I've built for my mama. She's in alt about it, though m'father says it's decadent and will mark the end of British supremacy over lesser nations. But that's all old history. My present interest is steam."

"Steam?"

"Steam. Steam propulsion, or traction. The steam engine will revolutionize the world, you may depend upon it. I've not yet convinced Sir Sholto I'm right, but I shall. In matters scientific he's sharp as they come."

As he spoke, Mr Ayliffe cast a wistful glance in the direction of Tamar Curle, which made Alex think that on other subjects Sir Sholto might have shown himself to be less persuadable. Mr Ayliffe's next words strengthened this impression.

"Tell me, my lord," he said, "is it your opinion that marriages should be arranged by the parties concerned, or by their families?"

The Earl thought of his Mama. "By the parties concerned, without doubt," he said.

"Exactly my view," said Mr Ayliffe. "Mind, I'll concede that a man of your rank and standing has important considerations to weigh when he comes to choose a wife. But for ordinary folk, where there is no compulsion of title or social ambition to be met — where perhaps the female is orphaned and has no parent to please in her choice of a partner — in such a case, should not her feelings outweigh all else?" Mr Ayliffe abandoned the indirect mode of speech, and said warmly, "I mean, sir, if Tamar and I wish to marry, why should obstacles be set in our way? I may not be of the nobility, but there've been Ayliffes at the Hall as long as there've been Curles at Ringwood. I'm no Croesus, but I have Expectations. I intend to make my mark in the world. I know that with *her* to inspire me, I can achieve anything. Sir Sholto has no objection to me as a man, he's told me so. It's only the damned tontine that is queering the pitch."

Mr Ayliffe checked suddenly, his face reddening. "I beg pardon," he said, "I've no right to speak so. Pray forget what I said."

This was the second time within hours that his lordship had been invited to forget the evidence of his eyes and ears. He began to think that Nick was right to categorize this as a rum household; but his years of diplomacy stood him in good stead. He preserved a blank face and turned the subject, asking Mr Ayliffe if there was any road by which a man on horseback could reach Evesham, as he was anxious to send word to his grandmother of their enforced delay.

The young man nodded. "Yes, there's a bridle-path along the river. Provided it doesn't snow too heavily tonight, a rider should get through quite easily, though I'm afraid the carriage-roads will be impassable for a time. After the thaw, it will take a full day of sun and wind to harden them. If you wish, I'll come over tomorrow and show your man the way he should take."

Alex accepted this offer gratefully. A moment later there was a trundling sound in the passageway and his host appeared, riding in a wheeled chair propelled by a liveried footman.

In the course of his travels, Lord Linslade had met many powerful men, but none with a more imposing presence than old Sir Sholto Curle.

The frame hunched in the wheelchair must once have been massive but was now much shrunken, the shoulders arched and the hands knotted by rheumatism. The face too was scamed by pain. Yet the blue eyes looked out, brilliant and amused, and the voice was brisk and resonant.

"You will forgive me, Linslade," said the old man, "if I neither rise, nor offer you my hand. My infirmity precludes the signs of welcome, but we are heartily glad to see you at Ringwood." The bright eyes were scanning Alex from head to foot. "You're your father's son, by the look of you. He was a man to reckon with, in the saddle or out of it. Tell me, is your grandmother still alive?"

"Very much alive, sir. My brother and I are on our way to visit her."

"Alice Frome," Sir Sholto said, smiling. "The Incomparable, we used to call her, but it was your grandfather won her." He turned his head a little. "Lucilla, why do we sit here gossiping when his lordship has been on the road all day, and must be well-nigh famished? Ring the bell, girl! And you, Prentiss, open the doors. No, don't bother about me — Mr Ayliffe will steer my plaguey infant's cart. He has the trick of it. Why is it that no one seems capable of building an invalid-chair with wheels that run true? Linslade, you will take Lucilla in, if you please. The rest of you may follow as you choose. We don't stand on ceremony here. A dull thing, ceremony, the resort of those who have nothing else to commend them."

The footman hurried to throw wide the doors that led from the drawing-room to the dining-room. Giles Ayliffe pushed Sir Sholto's chair through them, and the rest of the company flocked after in as good order as they could contrive.

The dinner, though excellent, was not protracted. Alex, no lover of port wine, was glad when Sir Sholto limited the passing of the decanters to a mere half hour before leading the gentlemen back to the drawing-room.

Miss Pelham was not to be seen, having gone, her grandfather said, to give the staff their orders for the next day. Dr Chase sat down beside Mrs Gray, who was engaged in sorting a parcel of silk embroidery-threads, and the youngest members of the party embarked on an argument about an expedition they planned to make to Oxford.

Sir Sholto, having established himself in a position close to the fire, beckoned to Alex to take the chair next to him, saying cheerfully, "That's the ticket! Now we may have a comfortable chat."

42

He proved to be an expert in the art of conversation, as anxious to listen as to talk. He cross-examined the Earl closely on his latest visit to Vienna, showing by his questions that he was as much abreast of events on the continent as many a London pundit.

His views were surprisingly radical. He had stringent criticism to offer on the present administration's handling of the Anglo-Irish difficulties and on the case for Catholic emancipation. He roundly condemned the use of child-labour in the new manufactories, saying that laws must be passed to forbid such unchristian exploitation. He had not a good word to say for the soon-to-be-crowned monarch, George IV. "Spendthrift, erratic and wingeing," he said, "and not to be trusted, least of all by his friends." At times he appeared to be testing his guest's views, as for example when he asked what would be his lordship's reaction to an extension of the franchise to include the labouring class.

"I'd have no objection," said Alex, "provided none of 'em has his eyes on my job."

Sir Sholto chuckled. "And so say I, Linslade, but I fancy we'll have to concede a portion of what we own, or Madame Guillotine will be called upon to make the necessary cuts."

"You think there could be revolution in England?"

"Why not? The seeds of it are everywhere in Europe. I hope we'll avert it by following the path of reform, but I can tell you this much. Whoever rules, Whig, Tory, or Radical, I'll do my best to hang on to my lands. There've been Curles at Ringwood since Plantagenet times. We've clung here like barnacles through war, pestilence and famine, and I trust we'll do so for a few hundred years, yet." He sighed. "It was the wish of my heart to hand the place over to my son Charles, but he was killed at Waterloo. Now it must pass to Johnny-Head-In-Air, yonder." He scowled in the direction of Adrian Curle. "The boy's not such a looby as he looks. Takes his fences in good style, and is as fine a shot as any man twice his age, but won't settle to anything. Spends his time chasing whatever is new-fangled. Last month he was off to Stratford to see a man who claimed he could fly. Fellow tied wings to his shoulders and jumped off the Corn Exchange. Broke both legs, which put paid to Adrian's ambitions in that direction. This month it's poetry.. The mooncalf plans to write another *Don Juan*. He'll go up to Oxford in the autumn, but I'm sending him to London for the Season in the hopes that he'll acquire a little town bronze, if not a modicum of common sense.

"Lucilla and Tamar go, too, to make their come-out. Tamar's maternal grandmamma, who's also Lucilla's god-mother, has been kind enough to say she'll launch 'em. Not that either of 'em has need of that Marriage Mart. They'll find husbands easily enough. Indeed, Tamar is already as good as promised. Her husband-to-be is the son of an old friend, and will be here in a day or so to arrange about marriage-portions. The wedding won't be until the end of the year. I want Tamar to try her wings a little — grow ac-customed to society before she settles down to married life. As for Lucilla, she's never lacked for admirers, and will do very well for herself as long as she doesn't try to set the world by the ears."

"And you, sir," enquired Alex. "Will you come to Town?"

The old man sighed. "It's my duty to come for that Fat Fool's coronation, I suppose, but I shall delay the journey as long as I can. Winter travel plays the devil with my joints and, besides, I don't like to leave Ringwood before the new crops are established. I shall have Dr Chase to bear me company, and friends will come in to help me pass the time. I'll survive. We Curles are survivors. I've outlived ninety-and-seven better men, I can hold the line a little longer."

Before Alex could reflect on the meaning of this last utterance, the door of the room opened to admit Lucilla Pelham followed by a footman bearing the tea-tray. The talk became general, and at ten o'clock the members of the company went their separate ways to bed.

The servant Robert was waiting outside the door of the Earl's bedchamber, but Alex, having allowed the man to help him off with his coat and boots, said he would have no further need of him, and sent him away.

Before undressing, Alex walked through to Nicholas's room and found him sleeping soundly, with none of the distressful signs of high fever. Dr Chase's physic, it seemed, was more effective than Dr Rumbole's.

Rumbole and Foxfare seemed a long way away. Strange, mused his lordship, how easily one shed the habits of a lifetime. Yesterday he would have baulked at the thought of accepting hospitality from strangers. Tonight it seemed quite natural, even salutary, to do so. He felt curiously at home at Ringwood. He liked his host, whom he took to be a man of incisive mind and strong character. Miss Pelham and the good doctor might choose to think they were shielding Sir Sholto from harsh reality; Alex thought that very little escaped that penetrating eye.

Returning to his own room, he went to the window to see if the weather had improved. It had not. Snow was still falling, though lightly. The terrace was blanketed, the shrubs heavy-laden. It was possible to see as far as the dark line of forest that marked the roadway, but beyond that stretched a white wall.

He was about to let the curtain fall when his glance fell on the figure of a woman moving quickly along the driveway below. Wrapped in a cloak, the hood drawn up, she hurried towards the archway that led to the stableyard. A lamp burned over the arch, and as she reached the pool of light she was met by a man whom Alex recognized as the gamekeeper he had seen on arrival at the house. The two stood in earnest conclave for some minutes, the man doing most of the talking, and several times raising his arm to gesture vehemently towards the east.

The discussion ended abruptly, the man ducking back towards the stables and the woman hastening towards the front door of the house.

As she climbed the steps the hood of her cloak fell back revealing the sharply anxious features of Mrs Marion Gray.

VI

NEXT MORNING ALEX was awakened by the muffled sounds of an altercation in his brother's room. Pulling on his dressing-gown he went to see what was afoot, and found Nicholas protesting loudly that he meant to get up and take his breakfast

45

downstairs like a civilized being, while Dr Chase insisted just as. firmly that he must remain in bed for another twelve hours.

"I am perfectly well," said Nick stiffly. "Linslade, be so good as to explain to Dr Chase that I'm not made of china, and don't like to be mollycoddled."

"Split the difference," suggested Alex. "Stay abed until midday."

"But Sir Sholto has sent me a message inviting me to tell him about the expedition."

"Sir Sholto," said Dr Chase, "never rises before noon. If you go down now, you will have to kick your heels for hours."

As Nicholas continued to look rebellious, Alex signed to Dr Chase to leave them alone and, when the door closed, said placatingly:

"Come, Nick, don't cut up rough. Chase is right, you know. No point in risking a relapse."

"It's the old story, isn't it," said Nick bitterly. "I'm to do as I'm bid and not argue!"

"Just so. I see myself in the rôle of gaoler. From time to time I will fetch you up water and a crust of bread, and, while you languish in solitary, I shall be downstairs doing the pretty by Miss Pelham and Miss Curle."

"Miss Curle? Who the devil is Miss Curle?"

"Sir Sholto's younger grand-daughter. A real dazzler."

"Dark or fair?"

"Oh, angelically fair, with eyes like dewy violets."

"That settles it," said Nick, throwing back the bedcovers. "I shall dress at once."

"I fear you'll be wasting your time. Miss Curle is already promised to another. I wasn't told the lucky man's name, but it is not Mr Giles Ayliffe, with whom she fancies herself to be in love."

"Why 'fancies'?"

"The chit's hardly out of the schoolroom."

"What's that to say to anything?"

"At that age, females fancy themselves to be in love with a different man every day of the week."

"Who is this Ayliffe?"

"The Squire's son, and a near neighbour. He's also an

46

inventor and has promised to show Belper a safe path to Evesham. I don't want Grandmama to fall into a panic over us."

"Grandmama never falls into a panic."

"True, but she might worry. According to Ayliffe we're likely to be snowed in for several days."

Nicholas eyed his brother narrowly. "You take it very calmly, I must say. I suppose you're planning a flirtation with Miss Pelham?"

"Nothing of the kind," retorted Alex. "If you must know, what keys me to fever pitch is the prospect of being invited to inspect Mr Ayliffe's inventions . . . particularly his new and improved version of Mr Joseph Bramah's Indoor Water Closet."

This sally having reduced Nicholas to stunned silence, Lord Linslade sauntered away to shave and dress for breakfast.

An hour later, immaculate in riding-breeches, top boots, a bottle-green frock coat and a snowy stock, Lord Linslade arrived in the breakfast-parlour. He found Miss Pelham on the point of leaving it. She was dressed for riding, in a dark blue habit, her hair twisted into a chignon and confined by a net.

She greeted him pleasantly, enquired after Nicholas, and said she regretted she could not stay to chat. "I have an appointment with the bailiff in ten minutes," she explained. "Giles Ayliffe told me last night that you plan to send a messenger to Evesham today, my lord. He must take a hack from our stables. The ground's too treacherous to risk one of your beautiful bays. If you wish to ride out yourself, I beg you will speak to our head groom, Whitton. Tell him what you'd like and he'll find you a suitable mount."

She was gone before he had time to thank her. Turning to greet his breakfast companions, he found that none of them was paying him the smallest attention. At the foot of the table sat Miss Curle, staring straight ahead of her, the tears rolling down her cheeks. Next to her Mrs Gray spoke in low and urgent tones, apparently urging the girl to eat some of the devilled kidneys on her plate. At the head of the board was Adrian Curle, nibbling toast and sipping coffee with an abstracted air.

His lordship helped himself to home-cured ham, baked eggs and a tankard of ale, and sat down next to Adrian. The young man gave him an exasperated glance.

"Can you think of a rhyme for contumely?" he asked.

His lordship thought a moment. "No," he said.

"No more can I." Adrian's tone was pettish. "A poet should never be at a loss for a rhyme. Byron was never at a loss." Closing his eyes, he quoted:

> " 'But — Oh! ye lords of ladies intellectual,
> Inform us truly, have they not henpecked you all?' "

He opened his eyes and said abruptly, "Marion, it's no use: Tamar can't abide kidneys."

This had the effect of making Miss Curle burst into loud sobs and rush headlong from the room, with Mrs Gray in pursuit. Adrian shook his head.

"Dicked in the nob, both of 'em."

His lordship, reflecting that this looked to be a family failing, addressed himself in silence to his breakfast.

"Crossed in love," supplied Adrian. "Tamar, I mean, not Marion. Wishes to marry Giles. Don't see why she shouldn't, myself, but Grandfather has set his face against it, so there's an end to the matter."

The Earl glanced up, a prey to vulgar curiosity.

"Dashed obstinate, the old man," continued Adrian. "Wouldn't let me enlist when I wanted to. Came after me and hauled me home by the ear."

"How old were you at the time?"

"Twelve, I think. The news had come that m'father was killed, you see, and I felt it my duty to avenge him. I confess I'm thankful, now, that Grandfather put his foot down. The army's no place for a poet." Adrian poured himself a second cup of coffee and added cream and sugar. "Tamar's a silly widgeon, but Marion at least should know better."

Alex murmured deprecatingly.

"Goes about it the wrong way," Adrian said. "Cries. Falls on her knees. Grandfather detests Cheltenham tragedies. Lucilla never cries, she just does what she wants, and Grandfather lets her get away with it." Tired of contemplating the plight of his

48

sister, Adrian turned to study Alex. "What do you ride at, sir? Twelve and a half stone?"

"A little more."

"Trouncer will suit you," Adrian said. "Mouth like silk, good paces, good over heavy ground. Ask Whitton for Trouncer."

"Will you come with us, Mr Curle?"

"Count on it," said Adrian succinctly. "This house will be fit only for madmen till Tamar's over her megrims."

Breakfast concluded, they repaired to the stableyard. Giles Ayliffe was already there, explaining to Belper exactly what route he must follow to reach Evesham. He had drawn a map indicating the main roads, the short cuts, various landmarks, and the footpaths most likely to be free of snow.

The party set out soon after eleven, the Earl riding Trouncer, as advised. The day was cold and still, the leaden sky giving no promise of a thaw. Adrian, no doubt lured by his Muse, soon fell behind the other riders. Giles went ahead to show the way past pitfalls hidden under the blanketing snow.

The course led steadily upward and westward through woods, and across open pasture. The arable lands were at a lower level, near the village. There was plentiful water, several good streams running down to join the river. They crossed the streams by wooden bridges, which prompted Alex to ask if they were meant for woodcutters' carts.

Giles shook his head. "No. The foundations aren't strong enough for that. They were designed only to take Sir Sholto's invalid carriage. He had that built for him in London. His wheelchair can be run up a ramp at the back. That way, he can handle the ribbons himself."

"Driving must be painful for him, surely?"

"Very, I think, but he values his independence." Giles paused, then said awkwardly, "My remarks last night went beyond what's permissible. I admire Sir Sholto greatly and I've no right to challenge his decisions. He may look as high as he pleases in choosing a husband for Tamar. He believes he's found the right man for her. It's up to me to prove him wrong."

"Can you do so?"

"Yes, just as soon as I patent my Steam Horse."

"Your what?"

Giles laughed. "Not of the equine breed. It's an engine to power a traction machine. I've worked on the design for two years, and I have it right, at last. It'll be launched long before Tamar's betrothal is announced."

"I'm afraid I don't see how . . . "

"Simple. Once my name and fortune are established, no one will be able to object to my marrying her." Giles sighed. "The difficulty is to convince her of it. The nuptial contracts are to be drawn up this week, you see. Tamar believes that once that's done she won't be able to cry off. I've told her, over and over, that ain't so. A gentleman mayn't jilt a lady, but the reverse is quite acceptable. Happens all the time."

Not wishing to challenge this sweeping statement, Alex changed the subject. "Will Sir Sholto sponsor your Steam Horse?"

"No. I couldn't ask him to furnish the dibs for something that's meant to overset his plans. Too shabby by half. I've used the money my great-aunt Phillida left me. Once the Steam Horse is in production, I'll have no difficulty in finding other patrons."

This Alex doubted. He liked Giles, and thought him both honest and resourceful; but he could not envisage a flood of investors prepared to see their money turned into steam. Rather to his own surprise he heard himself saying that he'd very much like to see Giles's brain-child.

"Would you?" Giles's face lit up. "There aren't many men in Swallowford who appreciate the science of mechanics. It'll be a pleasure to have the opinion of a man of experience like yourself."

It was agreed that his lordship would ride over to the Hall the following morning for an inspection *in situ*, and the two men, having set Belper on his way, started back towards Ringwood. There was no sign of Adrian, but as they drew closer to the manor they saw two riders moving along the edge of a spur of woodland.

"It's Lucilla and Whitton," Giles said. He stood up in his stirrups, raised his arm, waved and shouted, but neither of the two made any response. Instead they moved slowly onward, their heads bent as if they were scanning the ground about them, and were soon lost to sight among the snow-laden trees.

VII

A LIGHT NUNCHEON, served in the great hall, provided Nicholas with his first opportunity of meeting the Curle family.

His attention was at once drawn to Tamar, who was looking ravishingly pretty in a gown of pale blue challis, with a matching ribbon threaded through her curls; but before he could do more than throw her an admiring glance, he was cornered by Sir Sholto, who placed the young man at his left hand and began to ply him with questions about his experiences in Greece.

Neither Mrs Gray nor Adrian Curle put in an appearance at the table, and as Lucilla Pelham and Dr Chase were deep in a discussion of an outbreak of scarlet fever in the village it fell to Alex to entertain Tamar.

He was casting about in his mind for a topic likely to please a sixteen-year-old damsel crossed in love, when Miss Curle proved that, like the other inhabitants of Ringwood, she preferred to come straight to the point.

"Sir," she said, fixing him with a limpid blue gaze, "you were out with Giles Ayliffe this morning, were you not?"

"I was."

"Giles," said Miss Curle, "is a genius, though some people don't choose to admit it."

"I believe genius often goes unrecognized."

Miss Curle clasped her hands at her breast. "Our paths may sever, but I shall always be proud to have known him." She glanced out of the window beside her and said distractedly, "It has grown warmer. Distinctly warmer."

"You think a thaw is on the way?"

"Oh, I hope not. If I had my way it would snow forever."

"You'd find it a dead bore, in time."

"You don't understand! As long as the roads are closed Mr Cleve can't reach Ringwood."

"Mr Cleve, I take it, is your grandfather's solicitor?"

"My uncle's. Did Giles tell you?"

"He said something about nuptial contracts."

"Mine," said Tamar in a voice of doom. "That dread document will seal my fate. I'm resolved not to make any more fuss about it. I know where my duty lies. I cannot go against Grandpapa's wishes, when he has given me the only home I remember and shown me every kindness, every indulgence."

"You've lived at Ringwood since your father died?"

"Since my mama died. That was when I was no more than four years old. Papa was in the Army, and away most of the time, so Grandfather said Adrian and I must come to him, and Marion too. It was the same with Lucilla. Grandfather said that as long as she was in England, she must make Ringwood her home. Now he's giving us a Season in London, and . . . and trying to secure our futures . . . in the m-most n-noble way . . . "

Miss Curle seemed to be on the brink of tears again, and, to give her thoughts a more cheerful direction, the Earl launched into a description of the festivities to be held at the coronation of King George, saying that it would be a more splendid Season than any for years.

Tamar nodded. "I know. Marion says we will witness events that come only once in a lifetime. I'm sure it will be very elevating and that I shall meet a great many interesting people; but I shan't forget Giles."

"I have a sister making her come-out this year," Alex said. "Her name's Emily. I imagine she's much of an age with you. Perhaps you'll meet her on your dizzy round."

"I should like that above all things. I dread having to face all those strangers. We are to stay with my grandmother, who knows everybody and entertains a great deal. She wrote last week to say she has procured vouchers for Almack's April assembly. I find the thought quite terrifying. Marion says the patronesses are such high sticklers that if one makes the smallest *faux pas*, one is crossed off the list. And what if one doesn't take, Lord Linslade? Only think how dreadful it must be to be a wallflower and to sit all night among the chaperones!"

"I assure you, that won't happen." The Earl spoke with conviction knowing that pretty girls with handsome marriage portions never lacked for attention. Whoever had charge of Miss

Curle and Miss Pelham would be more exercised in fending off hardened rakes and gazetted fortune-hunters than in securing dancing-partners for them.

He turned his head to find that Miss Pelham was watching him with a quizzical smile.

"And you, ma'am," he said, "how do you feel about the gorgons of Almack's?"

"I suppose they can't be worse than the headhunters of Borneo," she said.

"Don't be so sure. Lady Sefton is kind, and Sally Jersey's a rattle, but in the presence of Mrs Drummond-Burrell, or Countess Lieven, we all behave with the utmost circumspection."

Her long lashes dipped demurely. "Butter will not melt in my mouth," she said.

Lord Linslade smiled appreciatively. He was ready to wager that, whatever might be Miss Pelham's effect on the dragons of the *beau monde*, she would be an instant success with the younger set.

She was refreshingly unlike the droves of girls herded up to Town each year by their ambitious mamas. She didn't simper or strike attitudes, or affect the tiresome lisp so fashionable at present. Her regard was direct, her smile enchanting, and she appeared to have a sense of the ridiculous that would stand her in good stead during the more vapid hours of a London Season.

It might be amusing to flirt a little with Miss Pelham, secure in the knowledge that she would not mistake dalliance for anything more serious.

He said easily, "What will be your first aim when you reach London?"

"To buy clothes," she said promptly. "I've nothing to wear."

"No female ever has anything to wear."

"Would you care to be seen in company with a dowd, sir?"

"Not at all, but you hardly fall into that category. The gown you wore last night was charming."

"It came," said Lucilla, "from the House of Clemence in Bond Street. My godmother frequently buys from Madame Clemence, and I expect your mama does, too."

The Earl perceived the nature of the problem. "I believe there are modistes who cater to younger females," he said.

"I hope so," said Miss Pelham, sighing. "The melancholy truth is that I'm too old to wear muslins and dimities."

He nodded gravely. "You're somewhat stricken in years, I agree. Nothing could be worse than to see mutton dressed as lamb."

She dimpled. "I'm rising twenty, sir, and I promise you that in muslin I look perfectly ridiculous . . . like . . . like a Neapolitan donkey in a straw hat. I wish for something more striking . . . more . . . individual. Something that speaks of Lucilla Pelham, and not of Madame Clemence."

"In a word, you wish to lead fashion, not follow it."

"It might be enjoyable to try. I've a notion that fashion is about to change. It's time for a new line, a new profile. If I can discover a modiste who understands what I mean . . . "

"You will," he assured her. "Don't overstep the mark, though. The ton likes to be startled, not shocked."

She looked at him thoughtfully. "Would it be overstepping the mark to drive my own carriage?"

"That depends entirely on how well you drive it."

"Oh, I can handle the reins," she said carelessly. "If I decide to order a carriage, which coachmaker would you advise?"

"Hooper and Sons," he answered. "They make for Tommy Onslow, and various members of the Four Horse Club. What are you contemplating? A phaeton?"

"A high-perch phaeton. Would that be thought shocking?"

"Dashing, certainly. Do you aim to be a dasher?"

"I fear I am one, like it or not. Marion says I have no sense of propriety. I suppose it comes of having spent so much of my life in places where there is no society, polite or otherwise."

"Will you bring your own horses to Town?"

"Oh, yes." A small frown creased her forehead. "I shall have to hire a groom, I suppose. Ramon won't be fit to travel for weeks."

"How is he today?"

She turned to face Alex, and he saw that the bantering expression had quite vanished from her eyes. "He's conscious," she said, "but he remembers nothing of what happened. Nothing at all."

He would have liked to question her further, but she shook her head warningly, indicating that the subject was closed. A short while later the meal came to an end, and Sir Sholto carried off Alex and Nick to the library, "to read, smoke, or sleep," he said, "whichever pleases you best."

The library, which lay at the east end of the mansion, was reached by a series of antechambers housing the artefacts collected by the late Mr Sidney Pelham. Nicholas, whose interest lay in the Ancient rather than the New World, paid little heed to the display of masks, weapons and pottery that lined the walls; but at one cabinet he came to a halt.

"Why," he said, "this is Inca work, is it not?"

"So they tell me." Sir Sholto's tone was harsh. "I find it repellent. That squat fellow, like a toad . . . enough to keep a man awake at nights."

Nick shook his head. "Such figurines are extremely rare," he said. "You're a lucky man, sir, to possess such a treasure."

"I don't. It's all Lucilla's, and she hates the sight of it. Can't blame her, when one remembers it cost the lives of both her parents. Come, let's move to happier things."

In the book-room Nicholas and his host were soon engrossed in a learned work on the possible site of the Oracle of Delphi. The Earl left them to it. Like most men of rank and wealth he'd received an excellent grounding in the classics, but he had no wish to expand it. He preferred living languages to dead, and current mysteries to those of the past.

His thoughts kept returning to Lucilla Pelham . . . to the look of anxiety on her face when he spoke of Ramon. It was not poachers that frightened her, he felt sure, but something closer to home: something connected to the man on the grey horse. Something she wished to keep from her grandfather.

He felt sure there must be a simple explanation. The facts were to hand if only he could string them together in the right sequence.

An idea struck him, and he moved along the bookshelves, scanning the titles. He found what he sought at last: a paragraph or two in an Italian text dealing with the life of that famous banker, Lorenzo Tonti.

Reading the passage gave his lordship much food for thought.

After dinner that night, Sir Sholto expressed a desire to hear some music. An impromptu concert was got up, Sir Sholto, Mrs Gray and Nicholas forming the audience, and everyone else contributing at least one item to the programme.

Lucilla and Tamar began by performing a duet, Tamar singing in a clear, sweet voice, and Lucilla accompanying her on the Spanish guitar. Dr Chase rendered a suite of sea-shanties, *basso profundo*, and the Earl and Lucilla responded with a spirited version of "The Ballad of Anthony Rowley". The star of them all, however, was undoubtedly Adrian. He played the pianoforte with a brilliance that impressed Alex, moving him to ask Dr Chase why a young man with such a talent should waste his time poetizing.

Dr Chase shrugged. "Adrian will inherit Ringwood, my lord. He'll have no time for artistic fiddle-faddle."

Watching Adrian's absorbed face and flying fingers, Alex frowned. "Does he want to manage the estate?"

"His ancestors have done so for four hundred years." Dr Chase seemed surprised at the question. "He has a duty to his grandfather, to his tenants, and to himself. Surely you, of all people, understand that?"

Alex fell silent. Like Adrian, he had been born to a great inheritance. He was destined to be master of Foxfare, to sit in the House of Lords, to be head of the house of Frome; an enviable rôle in the eyes of the world.

Yet suddenly he felt a great sympathy for Adrian Curle, and a great dislike for the whole concept of *noblesse oblige*.

Lucilla went to her room that night in a pensive mood. The chief focus of her thoughts was Lord Linslade.

She had, in the course of an adventurous existence, met a number of men who showed admiration for her. She had met even more who found her fortune irresistible. She had learned to deal even-handedly with both sorts of suitor.

She had spent the greater part of her life remote from the pleasures of the civilized world, and had wasted no time in lamenting the fact. Since balls, assemblies and fine clothes were beyond her reach, she put them out of her head. She learned to do without cosy friendships and desperate affairs of the heart, which other girls of her age seemed to find so important.

Sidney Pelham chose to interpret her acceptance as happiness. Though he did not consider himself a selfish man, his devotion to his work left him no time to think about Lucilla. He raised her to be independent and resourceful. He provided her with four years of formal education. He knew that when he died she would inherit a handsome income, and he trusted that she would, as he put it, "come safe to port somewhere."

After his death, Lucilla found herself able for the first time to do precisely as she pleased. She returned with all speed to England, determined to explore its possibilities as her papa had explored South and Central America.

Her needs she felt to be moderate. She hoped to become a member of polite society, and she expected, once she had found the right man, to marry.

It was quickly borne in on her that she was ill-equipped to achieve either aim. Her ability to speak Spanish, Portuguese, Italian and French counted for little in Swallowford. Though the local gentry praised her horsemanship, they did not consider it an advantage that she could break in a colt, or shoot the pips from a playing-card at ten paces.

In their book a female should be modest, compliant and decorous at all times. She should be content to spend her days among rustics, caring for her family, and attending to the running of her household. Visits to Town must be regarded as the exception rather than the rule, and to travel abroad was seen as a penance, not a prize.

Mrs Gray was not slow to inform Lucilla that a wife could cherish no ambitions of her own. Her wishes must be subordinated to those of her husband, and success could be achieved only through his good offices.

Even Sir Sholto, unconventional and indulgent in so many ways, warned her that she must learn to put a curb on her tongue, and express her opinions less boldly.

It all sounded, thought Lucilla, a dead bore.

Hopes that London might offer a less demanding sort of

gentleman were crushed by her godmother. Lady Charlotte Brampton wrote to stress what was expected of a young girl making her debut: "It has come to my ears, dear Lucilla, that you are a sad romp, and inclined at times to act the hoyden. Be assured that such conduct will cause people of quality to take you in disgust. Nor should you allow romantical notions to blind you to the realities of life. If you hope to secure a husband of rank and influence — as I am sure you do — you will have to keep a level head. Sentiment cannot be allowed to intrude. Once you are married, of course, you may please yourself, provided you do nothing that will cause your family embarrassment."

This Lucilla understood to mean that a lady, once married, was free to take lovers, as long as she was discreet about it.

It was hard to credit that people of fashion took such a cynical view of things, but one had to take Aunt Charlotte's word for it. She was very much of the *beau monde*, and versed in all its ways.

It was plain to Lucilla that her choice lay between a life of respectable boredom in the provinces, or of dissolute pleasure among the members of the ton.

When Lord Linslade made his appearance at Ringwood she knew at once into which category he fell. His splendid horses, his carriage, his liveried servants, his exquisite apparel and air of well-bred ease, all marked him as a pink of the modality . . . just the sort of man her godmama would hold up as a desirable parti.

Lucilla took him in instant dislike.

His manners might be graceful, but they lacked warmth. He was, in a word, toplofty. He would without doubt have preferred to ignore poor Ramon's plight, and had consented to carry him to Ringwood merely to please his younger brother. Once at the house he had been anxious to escape as quickly as possible, remaining only when he realized that Dr Chase resided at the manor. He was far too high in the instep. The fact that he had shown his disapproval of Lucilla's riding-breeches by no more than a raised eyebrow, did not make the criticism any less offensive.

He was obviously a practised flirt. The way he had surveyed her from head to toe, the glint in his eyes when he smiled, were proof that he was used to having females fall at his feet like so many ninepins. He probably kept a mistress in London, and was looking for no more than a little casual dalliance to wile away the tedious time he was forced to spend in Swallowford.

Contemptible.

As time went on, however, she began to revise her opinions. It had to be admitted that Lord Linslade was devoted to his brother and considerate of his servants. He spent long hours chatting to Sir Sholto and never once showed any sign of ennui. He did not patronize Giles Ayliffe, nor laugh at his harebrained schemes. He treated Adrian's foibles with tolerance, and Tamar's crotchets with tact.

His conversation showed him to be of superior intellect. He had a pleasant sense of humour. Tonight, for instance, he had entered into their amateur concert with every mark of enjoyment. A man who could give such a lively impersonation of a frog could not truly be described as toplofty.

Studying her reflection in the looking-glass, Lucilla was inclined to think that the word might better describe her own behaviour. She had allowed herself to be prejudiced by Godmother Brampton's strictures. She had treated Lord Linslade as a potential enemy, instead of a potential friend, and had no doubt given him a very poor opinion of her.

From now on, she resolved, things would be different.

VIII

NEXT DAY THE thaw set in with a vengeance.

Lord Linslade, surveying the grounds from the window of the breakfast-parlour, saw that the snow had melted from the terrace, and remained only along the fringe of the woods. The sound of dripping and running water was everywhere, and the air had a softness that spoke of the coming Spring.

He reflected that, in such conditions, the roads were like to become quagmires. He could hardly hope to drive to Evesham for another two days at least.

A footman arrived to inform him that Trouncer had been brought round to the front door, he collected gloves and hat, and strolled outside. He was surprised to find the groom walking not one but two horses on the driveway, and turned to see Miss Pelham coming down the steps of the house.

She gave him a radiant smile. "Good morning, sir. Shall you object if I go with you to the Hall? Mrs Ayliffe has some copies of *The Ladies' Monthly Museum* that she's promised to lend me."

Lord Linslade expressed himself delighted to have her company, and a few minutes later they set out. Lucilla was on Dandified, the palomino she'd been riding on the night of his arrival. The animal was inclined to be skittish, taking exception to everything he saw and heard, but Miss Pelham kept him firmly in hand, and said with a laugh that she preferred a firecracker to a slug, any day.

The Ayliffes' acres lay to the northwest of Ringwood, and the first part of their journey took them across the hill Alex had traversed the day before. On the far side they reached a bridle-path free of snow, and conversation became easier. Alex enquired if Miss Pelham had seen the Ayliffe Steam Horse.

"I imagine everyone from here to Oxford has seen it," she answered. "It's very large, and noisy, and dirty, and according to Giles it's the miracle of the Modern Age."

"He has an infectious enthusiasm."

"He's the salt of the earth. Aside from being our nearest neighbour, he's also our dearest friend." Lucilla caught the guarded expression on the Earl's face, and said quickly, "I know you must be wondering why he is not permitted to marry Tamar . . ."

"My dear ma'am, it's no possible business of mine."

"No, but it's not fair that Grandfather should be blamed for forbidding the match. I couldn't help overhearing what Tamar said to you at luncheon, yesterday, and I feel obliged to tell you that it is the Ayliffes who are against the marriage . . . or, rather, Mrs Ayliffe. She's one of those nervous, pinching sort of women who cannot bear to see their sons leave home. Grandfather says that a union opposed by the parents can never be happy, and that Tamar doesn't have the strength of character to deal with such a situation."

"You don't agree?"

Lucilla shrugged impatiently. "How can I judge? If I were in

60

Tamar's shoes, I'd marry Giles and tell the world to go hang, but I'm not, so my opinion can't signify."

A short while later they rode into the Ayliffes' stableyard, where they found Giles awaiting them. He greeted them eagerly, begging them to come at once into his workshop. Lucilla declined the invitation, saying she wished to talk to his mama, but Alex followed Giles into the large shed that housed his invention.

The Steam Horse stood in the centre of the floor. It was a massive metal structure mounted on wheels and with a tall funnel painted in red and white stripes. It put Alex in mind of the legendary Juggernaut of India. Giles lost no time in explaining its workings to his lordship, and insisted on giving a practical demonstration of how the steam powered the engine. The noise and smoke created was truly diabolical, and Alex was thankful when his host at last stopped the mechanism and wiped his hands clean on a piece of cotton cloth.

"Well," said Giles proudly, "what do you think?"

"Impressive," said Alex.

"The future of Britain," Giles said. "Traction. Haulage. In a word, railways."

"But is that concept so new? We've had a rail-track at Foxfare since my great-grandfather's time."

Giles looked contemptuous. "Wooden lines," he said, "and wooden carts to run on 'em, towed by horses. That, sir, is primitive stuff. We're speaking now of trains, metal trains that run on metal rails."

"Er . . . who precisely is 'we'?"

"Oh, there are any number of men already on the scene. Smeaton, for example. He holds that the flange that keeps the wheel in place must be on the wheel itself, and not on the rail. Then there's Huskisson, and Rys, and Trevithick who built a steam-train as long ago as 1804, though it didn't work too well. William Murdoch designed a locomotive machine while he was working for Boulton and Watt of Soho. They didn't wish to lose his skills, so they refused to develop his idea, a shocking lack of foresight on their part. But my Bessie, here, is better than Murdoch's machine. She has features that neither Rys nor Huskisson has thought of. One day you will see Bessie flying across country at twenty, thirty, fifty miles an hour!"

61

Lord Linslade eyed Bessie uneasily. "I suppose you will have to lay tracks to carry her?"

"Oh, yes, a whole network of 'em. Lines to carry minerals to the canals, coal to the cities, cattle to the fairs."

"Surely you may expect a great deal of opposition from landowners and the like? It must play havoc with a man's herds, to have such a monster thunder past?"

"Not at all. Only consider, my lord, the monster will take the slaughter-beasts to market, and bring back feed and seed. It will convey people, too. In a year or so, you'll be able to travel from Oxford to London in the twinkling of an eye."

Alex laughed. "I hope I won't be obliged to part with my horses; for that, you know, I should very much dislike."

"There'll always be room for horses; but try to picture what it will be like to go from one city to another, at any time of the day or night, and in every sort of weather."

"Is it lawful to operate such a machine?"

"Yes, though it requires a special Act of Parliament for each enterprise." Giles gave Bessie an affectionate slap on the flank. "We shall meet with opposition, I'm sure, but we won't be stopped. We can't be stopped. The Age of Steam has arrived."

On that point, Lord Linslade was not prepared to argue. He doubted that the Juggernaut would ever leave its shed, but he did not underestimate the force of young Ayliffe's ambition. That might indeed move mountains.

They strolled from the shed to the Hall, where they found Lucilla and Mrs Ayliffe drinking tea and discussing the relative powers of crushed strawberries, raw egg, and china clay to purify the complexion.

Mrs Ayliffe, a thin and dyspeptic-looking female, insisted that his lordship remain to drink a glass of madeira wine. She apologized several times for her husband's absence. He had gone, she said, into the village, to take stock of the damage caused by the snowstorm; a mission his wife described as arrant folly.

"He knows there is scarlet fever in the cottages," she said fretfully. "Two infants have died of it already, and others are gravely ill. Heaven knows we don't wish the infection to be carried to our homes!"

Her eyes were on Giles as she spoke, indeed they seldom left him. She spoke in a gushing way about his inventions, praising them to the skies. "Every gentleman," she asserted with a tittering laugh, "should have a hobby, to fill his time when the weather's too inclement for hunting."

Alex felt it was foolish of her to belittle her son's work, but he kept his thoughts to himself. At noon, Lucilla said it was time they returned to Ringwood, and they took their leave of the Ayliffes.

They followed a different route, this time, as Lucilla wished to see how much flooding had occurred in the lower pastures. The path took them southward along the course of one of the streams that fed the river. The water was in full spate, streaked with foam and carrying with it masses of tangled vegetation, mud and stones. In some stretches it had overflowed its banks, and the riders were forced to move with caution. In the upland woods they passed, snow still lay thick and white.

They reached the first of Sir Sholto's bridges and prepared to cross it; but Alex's mount Trouncer, who was in the lead, refused to set foot on it. Alex urged him on, but the animal reared and tossed his head, the whites of his eyes glinting.

Dismounting, Alex handed the reins to Lucilla. "Stay here," he directed, "and I'll take a look."

He walked to the edge of the stream. Its course at this point was steep and narrow, and the water plunged down-hill with a roar loud enough to drown out most other sounds; but after a moment Alex picked up what had frightened Trouncer, the slow steady groaning of weakened timbers.

There was a sapling rooted in the bank a yard above the bridge, and by kneeling in the mud and gripping its trunk he was able to lean forward over the water and examine the underpinnings of the bridge. He returned to Lucilla looking grim.

"We owe this fellow a vote of thanks," he said, as he swung himself back into the saddle. "The supports on the far bank are gone."

She stared at him, white-faced. "The floodwater," she said. "It must have washed them away."

"I think not, Miss Pelham. From what I can see, the chief shafts have been sawn almost through. The breaks are too clean to be natural. You should send men at once to barricade the bridge before anyone tries to cross."

She nodded silently. Her gaze was on the water hurtling down towards the valley, dashing against rocks and sending up spouts of spray.

Alex said quietly, "If the fall hadn't killed him, the cold and shock must have done."

Her head jerked round. She stared at him for a moment, then began to turn her horse, but Alex reached out and grasped the bridle.

"No, ma'am," he said. "This is the second time in three days that my neck has been at risk. I think I deserve an explanation."

"I have none to give you, Lord Linslade."

"Come, you can do better than that! Two nights ago, one of your servants tried to shoot a man on the public highway. Today we find evidence to suggest someone is trying to murder your grandfather . . . "

"One can't know that . . . "

"It's a fair assumption. He's the chief user of the bridge, is he not? You must have some theory to offer for this mayhem."

Her eyes blazed at him. "If I had a theory, sir, do you think I would waste time talking about it? I would take action. I have no theory, no clue, I am totally confused."

His expression softened a little. "Have there been other attempts, Miss Pelham?"

She hesitated, studying his face as if she were considering how far he could be trusted. At length she shrugged. "I think so," she said.

He released her bridle, saying, "Tell me as we go."

They set off once more towards Ringwood.

"On Christmas Day," Lucilla said, "Grandfather was sent a box of sugarplums. He thought it was from Mrs Singery, the gamekeeper's wife, who always sends a gift of preserves at Yuletide. He opened the box, but left the contents almost untouched. One of his wolfhounds discovered the sweets and ate one or two. They made him very ill. A smaller dog would have died."

"You think someone tried to poison Sir Sholto?"

Lucilla shook her head. "At the time such a thought never entered my head. I thought that the plums must have fermented, nothing more."

"Did you examine what was left of the sweets?"

"No. Grandfather bade me throw them away and warned me not to make any fuss for fear of hurting Mrs Singery's feelings. Two days later, I chanced to meet her in the village and she told me she'd be sending her gift a little late because her children had all been laid low with the measles. I never learned who sent the sweetmeats, nor did I refine upon the matter. So many people send gifts to the manor. You know the way of it."

Alex nodded. Gifts often arrived at Foxfare, from neighbours, from tenants or from further afield. It wasn't always possible to identify the giver.

"When were your suspicions first aroused?" he asked.

"In January," Lucilla answered. "Grandfather had decided to attend the funeral of a very old friend, in the village. Our coachman drove him to the church and back. As they were coming through the home woods, a tree fell and missed the carriage by inches. The woodmen searched carefully and said the tree had been undermined by heavy rains and the roots loosened. I was troubled, but I could find no trace of deliberate interference with the soil, and the idea that someone harboured such malice towards Grandfather seemed . . . grotesque. But then, in February, someone tried to shoot him."

Lucilla turned to meet the Earl's questioning gaze. "It was at the end of the month," she said, "and the first fine day we had had in ages. Grandfather asked for his wheelchair to be taken out to the kitchen garden. He likes it there because it's so warm and sheltered.

"The woods come very close to the house at that point. A shot was fired. It would have struck Grandfather had he not at that very moment leaned down to stroke the kitchen cat. He shouted for help, and the assailant made off. We heard him running through the woods, but we never caught him."

"What did your grandfather make of the attack?"

65

"He refused to admit that there was one. He said it must have been a poacher firing at a rabbit. He refused to lodge a complaint with the Justice of the Peace."

"Didn't you find that strange, Miss Pelham?"

She looked at him with troubled eyes. "At first I was too shaken to think at all. Later, I came to see that he didn't wish to believe anyone could want him dead. Arguing with him only caused him distress. I decided that I must . . . must keep watch over him, without alarming him. I warned all the outdoor servants that there were thieves in the district, and that they must tell me if they saw strangers in the village. I arranged for Singery and Ramon and the other grooms to patrol the grounds after dusk."

"What happened on the day of my arrival?"

"Ramon came to the house," she said, "to say he'd seen an intruder up on this hill. I gave directions that a search must be organized, and I went with Ramon to try and pick up the man's tracks. He was hiding in the woods. We flushed him out, and drove him down to the road. The rest you know."

"Miss Pelham," said Alex urgently, "my groom saw this fellow clearly, and described him as gallows-meat. You must go to the Justice at once, ma'am."

"And what shall I tell him? That someone is trying to murder Grandfather? He'll say what everyone knows . . . that Sholto Curle hasn't an enemy in the world."

"He has at least one . . . probably more." Alex was thinking of the conversation he'd had with Giles Ayliffe on his first night at Ringwood. He had promised Giles not to repeat what was said then, but if Sir Sholto's life was in danger, such a promise couldn't be binding.

"Tell me," he said, "is your grandfather a member of a tontine?"

She frowned slightly, "Why, yes, he is. What of it?"

"How many of its members are still alive?"

"Three."

"Three, out of how many?"

"One hundred, I believe." Lucilla sounded impatient. "I must say I fail to see what significance some old lottery . . . "

"A tontine isn't a lottery," he answered. "It's a form of life

66

annuity, invented by a hard-headed banker named Lorenzo Tonti. The principle is simple. A group of people invest a sum of money in property. The income is shared, each year, by all of them, and when a member dies the share of those still living becomes proportionately larger. Finally, one person remains to scoop the pool. If Sir Sholto is one of three survivors in a long-running tontine, his death will greatly enrich the other two."

She stared at him for a moment, then burst out laughing.

"Oh, no, that's absurd!"

"People have killed for gain before now, ma'am."

"I beg your pardon, I didn't mean to be rude; but, sir, the other survivors, as you call them, are members of our own family. One of them will be arriving here tomorrow, and you'll see for yourself he's not the desperate villain you describe."

She gathered up her reins. "I must go and warn the bailiff to make the bridge safe. I shall be very much obliged to you if you will speak to Soan as soon as you arrive at the house. Warn him, if you will, that the bridge at the millstream crossing has been weakened by floodwater, and that no one must use it."

So saying, Lucilla wheeled her mount and, with a farewell flourish of her hand, set off at a gallop across the hillside. Lord Linslade sat in frowning thought for a while before turning Trouncer towards Ringwood.

IX

HAVING DELIVERED Miss Pelham's message to her Steward, Alex went in search of his brother. Nick was in the library, seated near the window, a large tome open on his knees. Hearing the Earl's footstep he looked up eagerly.

"Alex, Sir Sholto has given me his copy of Herodotus! A truly splendid text, and with illustrations beyond anything I've ever seen. What a stroke of luck we had to chance on this house."

"Ill luck, I'm afraid," said Alex.

"What can you mean?" Nick's startled gaze shifted to the Earl's muddied coat and breeches. "Good God, man, did you take a toss? You're white as a ghost."

"No ghost." Alex set a chair for himself and sat down. "I've reason to think that someone is trying to kill our host."

"Sir Sholto? Kill? Oh, come, Alex, such things don't happen outside of a penny romance."

"I'm not romancing, I assure you." Alex proceeded to give a full account of the events at the bridge, and his subsequent discussion with Lucilla. "The earlier incidents might be ascribed to chance," he said, "but not this last. If the old man had driven across that bridge, he'd be dead as mutton by now."

Nick slowly laid his book aside. "Will you speak to him?"

"I don't know that I should. Dr Chase warned me Sir Sholto's heart is not strong. A shock could finish him."

"And Miss Pelham? Surely she must . . . "

"Miss Pelham is not persuadable. When I spoke of the tontine, she laughed at me."

"Well, stands to reason, Alex, she won't suspect her own family . . . people of rank and standing."

"I've yet to find that rank sets a man above crime."

"Yes, but consider! The attacks can only have been staged by someone on the spot, someone living in Swallowford."

"Not so. Assassins can be hired, you know. It's pretty obvious that bridge was wrecked by the ruffian we met on the highway. The question is, who paid him for his trouble?"

"What do you propose to do?"

Alex shrugged. "Sir Sholto told me his solicitor will be here shortly, to draw up the terms of Miss Curle's marriage settlement. Perhaps I'll find a chance to speak to him. In the mean time, I'd best change these clothes before the bell sounds for luncheon."

That afternoon Sir Sholto invited the Earl to play a few hands of piquet. It quickly emerged that his real wish was to talk, for he announced over the first hand that Lucilla had told him of the damage to the bridge. "Sabotage, she says. Do you agree with her, my lord?"

"I do, sir. The timbers were sawn clean through."

"I see." Sir Sholto drew a card. "No doubt the work of some mischievous yokel," he said.

68

"'Mischief' is hardly the right word, sir. I'd say rather, 'malice aforethought'. I believe you will be well advised to . . . "

"My lord," Sir Sholto held up gnarled fingers, "pray don't be anxious on my account. We live in turbulent times, times of violence and revolution. People of our sort, who own so much, are the natural target of those who have nothing."

"All the more reason why you should try to protect yourself."

"Oh, tush, I'm an old man! At my age, one doesn't fear death. I'll not have a witch hunt in Swallowford, I'll not have my dependents harried and my family exposed to vulgar gossip."

"Fine words, sir, but what of Miss Pelham? Is she to continue to risk her neck, on your behalf?"

"No. I have told Lucilla to drop these unnecessary heroics."

"She does not," said Alex carefully, "strike me as being a very biddable female."

Sir Sholto chuckled. "You're in the right of it, there. Devilish hot at hand, sometimes, and stubborn as a mule! That's why I'm sending her to London . . . which brings me to my point, Linslade. I shall take it as a great favour if you will lend her a little support when she reaches Town. She knows no one there, aside from her godmama, and she'll find the going heavy just at first. You're a man of sound reputation and you have influence with the right people. A word from you will smooth her path. I wouldn't ask it of you, save that I'm unable to get about much, myself."

"Please say no more," Alex answered. "I'll count it an honour to vouch for your grand-daughter. It's little enough return for the kindness you've shown me and my brother. Had I guessed that we'd be imposing on you for so long . . . "

"Gammon," said the old man. "Haven't I made it plain that I welcome company? Not but what I know you must be chafing to be on your way. Shouldn't be long, now. Word came through from Moreton, not an hour since. The roads to the east are drying nicely, and Jason Cleve expects to be able to reach Ringwood tomorrow. Provided the fine weather holds, the western route will be dry in another twenty-four hours, and you'll be free to press on to Evesham." Sir Sholto played his last card with a deft gesture. "Capot, my lord! That is forty points to me!"

The imminent arrival of Mr Jason Cleve now occupied the forefront of every mind. Sir Sholto was distrait, and at dinner that night made little contribution to the conversation. Tamar pleaded the headache and went early to bed. The rest of the company were not long in following her example.

Alex retired to his room but not to bed. He sat for some time by the fire, thinking over the day's events. Troubled as he was by them, he could see no way to help his host. He had presumed to offer advice and been snubbed for his pains. Perhaps Sir Sholto was right to blame the attacks on some village lout. Certainly, argument wasn't going to change his mind. The old man had as good as said he'd rather be dead than admit one of his close circle was trying to kill him. Miss Pelham must have inherited her stubborn streak from her redoubtable grandsire.

Thinking of her, the Earl smiled a little wryly. He was wondering what his mother would make of Lucilla Pelham. She was certainly not "suitable". Brash and indecorous were adjectives that sprang to mind. Yet he found himself thinking how diverting it would be to watch her effect upon the ton, how amusing it would be to show her about Town, take her to the places he especially enjoyed, squire her to one or two select parties, and introduce her to some few of his friends.

Launching the unsuitable Miss Pelham might help to alleviate the tedium of another London Season, and he in no way regretted his undertaking to Sir Sholto.

As to the rest, he would have a word in private with Mr Cleve and advise him of the situation regarding Sir Sholto. More than that, he could not do.

Next morning the Earl woke to hear the shutters of the manor rattling. A south wind was tossing the treetops in the home woods, and warm sunlight bathed the surrounding hills.

After an early breakfast he summoned Cheadle and rode with him to inspect the roads to the west. Sir Sholto had been right in his estimate. The tracks were drying, but were not yet firm enough to bear the weight of a coach.

"We shall leave tomorrow," the Earl said, and Cheadle nodded.

"Can't say I'll be sorry, m'lord."

"Have you been uncomfortable here, Cheadle?"

The coachman hesitated. "Not to say uncomfortable, m'lord. Good quarters and prime grub. But the folks ain't friendly. Watch me all the while, as if I might snitch the siller or summat. You'd think it was us that caused the rumpus, and not that Ramon."

"How is Ramon, do you know?"

"I ain't seen 'ide nor 'air of 'im, but Mrs Grover, she's the cook, says 'e'll do." Cheadle fixed his gaze on his horse's ears and said, "I did 'ear tell there's been trouble afore, m'lord . . . bad trouble . . . but what it is I dunno. Ma Grover won't speak o' that."

"Nor should we, Cheadle."

"Oh, aye, m'lord, I'll stay mum, but like I say I'll be glad to be out of it, and that's the plain truth."

They returned to Ringwood by the path along the hilltop which afforded a good view of the surrounding countryside and of the manor itself. It was as they were descending the last slope that they heard the sound of a posting-horn and saw a procession of three vehicles emerge from the woods and advance up the driveway.

Leading the cavalcade was a large travelling-coach with its accompanying postillions; next came a heavy baggage-chaise; and bringing up the rear was a sporting curricle, its dark green and cream paintwork gleaming in the sun.

As the coach reached the steps of Ringwood, the front doors swung open, and the Steward Soan bustled through them, followed first by a bevy of servants and then by Miss Pelham.

The steps of the coach were let down and Soan moved forward to assist an immensely fat gentleman to alight. He was richly, even flamboyantly dressed, his plum-coloured great-coat being heavily frogged with darker braid, and his high-crowned hat perched on a wig whose bright brown curls accorded ill with the sagging red face beneath it. His hessian boots had very deep white tops, and he leaned on an ebony cane decorated with two gold tassels.

71

Behind him appeared a tall, thin man dressed entirely in black. This sombre hue, and the angularity of his limbs, gave him something of the look of a water-spider. He clasped a briefcase to his chest, as if he feared someone might snatch it from him.

Lord Linslade turned to survey the curricle. The man now flinging the reins to his groom, and leaping down to the ground, was of middle stature and compact build. He was dressed in the height of modality, wearing a long straight overcoat cut in the Cossack style and trimmed with a heavy fur collar. His boots shone like glass. He wore no hat and his light gold hair was romantically windswept.

Ignoring his companions, he marched straight to where Lucilla Pelham waited on the steps and made her a flourishing bow. He then tugged off his right glove, caught her hand, and raised it to his lips.

Cheadle ignored this display of gallantry. His attention was on the curricle and the two magnificent horses harnessed to it.

"I know them greys," he said aloud. "Seen 'em in The Park, not two weeks ago." Glancing round, he was surprised to see a look of angry consternation on his employer's face. "Them's Mr Warsop's cattle, me lord."

"They are, Cheadle. The counter-coxcomb on the steps is Mr Francis Warsop, and the gentleman in puce is his father, Lord Everley. I take the other gentleman to be their lawyer, Jason Cleve." He remained silent for a moment, then said tersely, "We won't disturb them, I think."

When Lord Linslade entered his brother's room some ten minutes later, Nicholas took one look at him and said in a voice of concern, "What's up, Alex? More trouble?"

"Yes." Alex cast aside his riding-whip and gloves and threw himself down in a chair. "The new arrivals. You've seen them?"

"No. I heard the post-horn and came upstairs. Didn't wish to intrude. Who are they?"

"The Everleys, and their lawyer; from which I gather that Tamar Curle is about to become betrothed to Francis Warsop, and that his father Lord Everley is one of the two

surviving members of Sir Sholto's tontine. Put together, those facts do present us with a problem."

Nick stared in consternation. "Alex, you're surely not suggesting, are you, that Lord Everley's behind the attacks on Sir Sholto? Because that won't fadge, you know. Everley's very well thought of in society. Why, you may find him at White's any day of the week."

"You may indeed," agreed the Earl, "in the gambling rooms. Henry Everley has gambled away two fortunes in his time, and it's common talk that he's in devilish low water at the moment."

"Yes, but murder . . .! And if his son's to wed Miss Curle . . . he wouldn't butcher his son's future papa-in-law, would he? Why kill the goose that lays the golden egg?"

"For the tontine money, obviously."

"Well, I'm damned if I think Everley's a murderer. He was one of the Carlton House set, until Prinny became king and cast off his old cronies. Very high in the instep, the Everleys! There's a sister, Lady Charlotte Brampton. Starchy as they come. Can't see her hob-nobbin' with a set of hired cut-throats. As to Francis Warsop, he's a Melton man, and a pink of the ton besides. What Warsop wears today, the rest will be mad for tomorrow."

"Francis Warsop," said Alex flatly, "is a liar, a shabster, and a cheat. He's capable of anything. He seduced our sister Arabella when she was no more than sixteen years old, and then tried to extort money from Papa in return for his silence."

"Bella?" Nick shook his head in shocked disbelief. "No one told me of it."

"How should they? You were scarcely out of short coats when it happened. Bella was in her first Season, and privately betrothed to John Ruthven. We believed her to be happy with the match, but a week before it was due to be puffed off in *The Times*, Bella eloped with Warsop. It was two weeks before we tracked them down, in a seedy inn in Taunton."

"We?"

"Papa and I, and John Ruthven. John learned Bella's whereabouts from one of Warsop's toadies. Paid a high price for the information, too. It's my belief Warsop intended us to

find them. He imagined that by compromising Bella, he could force Papa to consent to their marriage. His pockets were to let, and Bella's marriage portion was handsome.

"Be that as it may, we posted off to Taunton. Papa was in killing mood, as you can imagine. Challenged Warsop as soon as he clapped eyes on him. Warsop refused the challenge."

"Chicken-hearted!"

"No, merely cunning. He was convinced Bella must marry him or be ruined. He thought she would welcome his offer. He was wrong on both counts. Bella had had time to see Warsop for what he was. She said she'd rather retire to a nunnery than marry him. Then dear old John stepped in and said there was to be no more talk of nunneries, as he intended to marry Bella himself."

"In spite of all?"

"Yes. His generosity at that time was wholly admirable. He spoke with such kindness to Bella . . . said he knew she'd been led astray by Warsop's smooth talk; said he loved her and wished the wedding to take place as soon as possible. In short, he called Warsop's bluff.

"Once Warsop saw how the wind lay, he changed his tune. Tried to blackmail Papa. Said he'd keep his mouth shut about the affair if he was suitably recompensed. Papa told him that if so much as a word was breathed by Warsop, or any of his acquaintance, he would run him out of England. Warsop knew it was no empty threat. Papa was a man of great influence, which he wouldn't scruple to use.

"Warsop went away empty-handed. John and Bella were married within the month. Thank God, no child was born whose paternity could be called in doubt, and the marriage, as you know, has proved to be extremely happy."

"Do you think Lord Everley knew of the affair?"

"He's never admitted to knowing. Naturally, we Fromes haven't spoken of it and, to avoid gossip, we've kept up the pretence of civility towards the Everleys."

"George hasn't. He ain't even been civil to Bella!"

"George blames Bella for the pain she caused our parents. For two weeks they never knew if she were dead or alive. I daresay that's what makes Mama over-careful of the rest of us.

It certainly hastened Papa's death. He suffered his first seizure a week after Bella's wedding, and died a year later."

Nick frowned as a new thought struck him. "You've as good as accused the Everleys to Miss Pelham, haven't you?"

"Not by name, but by implication perhaps. She laughed at me. My dilemma now is, how to broach the matter to Sir Sholto?"

"You can't broach it. We're guests in this house."

"What if I stay mum, and another attempt is made on his life? How shall I feel then?"

"We must leave at once," Nick said, then sighed. "No, we can't, can we?"

"No. Even if the roads were open, we'd still be indebted to Sir Sholto. We owe him the truth."

"Won't Warsop spill the beans when he sees you?"

"I doubt it. If he hopes to marry Tamar, he'll hardly wash his dirty linen in public." Alex got to his feet. "Stay where you are, Nick. I'll ask for luncheon to be served to us here . . . say you're unwell, or something. I don't intend to run into Francis Warsop until I've decided what's to be done about this imbroglio."

X

ALEX FELT THAT Fate had served him an ill turn in bringing him to Ringwood. He was faced with the choice of making accusations against his host's friends, or of remaining silent and putting Sir Sholto's life at risk.

Speaking out would not be easy. Francis Warsop, trumpery character as he was, might still prove a formidable opponent. He owned a sharp intelligence and a glib tongue. Moveover, he was the son of one of Sir Sholto's oldest friends. His word was likely to be believed over that of any passing stranger.

Warsop would be on his guard the instant he learned that there were Fromes at Ringwood. He might not provoke an open quarrel, but he would do all he could to protect his ambitions, notably that of marrying Tamar Curle.

That in itself raised another problem. Warsop's amorous

intrigues were a byword even in a society that was far from prudish. His tastes ran to married women with complaisant husbands, or the hard-eyed harpies of the demi-monde, and he had no compunction in living off their money. It could only be Tamar's dowry that he coveted. Once he'd run through that, he'd treat the chit with the same callous cruelty he'd shown Arabella.

Did Sir Sholto, living here in isolation, know of Warsop's reputation? If he did not, would he thank Alex for mentioning it?

Alex considered his earlier plan to speak to Mr Cleve, and dismissed it out of hand. Cleve, by the look of things, was in the Everleys' pocket. He'd do nothing to overset their plans.

The only possible source of help appeared to be Dr Chase, and Alex went in search of him.

The doctor had been in the village since early morning, attending to the latest victims of the scarlet fever. He returned to Ringwood about three in the afternoon, and the Earl, seeing the gig turn through the archway to the stables, was able to intercept him in the Great Hall and request some private conversation with him. The doctor led the way to the morning-room and listened gravely to all that Alex had to say, remarking at the end that it was a relief to him to be able to speak frankly about the situation at Ringwood.

"I make no bones to say, my lord, that I've been at my wits' end to know what to do. Here's Sir Sholto impervious to reason, won't tolerate the thought that anyone could be plotting against him; and here's Lucilla, a mere slip of a girl, trying to play the guardian angel, at Heaven knows what peril to herself."

"Sir Sholto doesn't accept that she's in danger?"

"Because he refuses to doubt his own kith and kin."

"I wasn't aware that the Curles are related to the Everleys."

"By blood, sir, and by marriage. Lord Everley's sister is Lady Charlotte Brampton. Her daughter Caroline married Charles Curle, Sir Sholto's son. Tamar is her grandchild. The marriage of her nephew Francis Warsop to Tamar would further strengthen the family ties."

"Are Henry Everley and Lady Charlotte members of the tontine?"

"Yes, they are."

"Then both of them stand to benefit by Sir Sholto's death."

Dr Chase looked distressed. "In theory, yes, but I must tell you, my lord, that I cannot believe that either of them would harm Sir Sholto. Lord Everley is a rake and a gamester, but he's known Sir Sholto for fifty years and I'm sure their friendship is sincere."

"And Francis Warsop? What's your opinion of him?"

"I know little about him." The doctor directed a keen glance at Alex. "Less, I fancy, than you do, my lord."

"I know a great deal about him, and none of it to his credit." Seeing Dr Chase pull a long face, Alex continued, "Whom do you hold responsible for the attacks?"

"I had thought some rogue with a grudge — a servant dismissed, a poacher sent to gaol — but I confess you've raised doubts in my mind . . . and put me in a damned difficult position, into the bargain."

"I know. You've no need, of course, to take my word that Warsop's a twister. Plenty of reputable people will tell you the same story."

"I don't doubt it. I've seen enough of the man to mistrust him heartily. A real here-and-thereian. The fact remains that I'm a doctor, and a paid retainer in this house. As the first I'm expected to be discreet, as the second I'm bound to abide by Sir Sholto's wishes."

"Even if it kills him?"

Dr Chase met the Earl's eye. "My lord," he said, "I can see my way clear to making a report to the Magistrate. I cannot see myself accusing an Everley of attempted murder. The result could only be my immediate dismissal from Ringwood . . . and that would leave Miss Pelham quite unprotected."

Alex nodded. "Very true. I wonder, though, if you could come at the problem another way? How if you were to tell Lord Everley about the attacks on Sir Sholto . . . mention casually that the affair is in the hands of the Law . . . ask him to inform his son and Mr Cleve? Mightn't that be enough to forestall any other incidents?"

"It might." Dr Chase began to brighten. "His lordship is in conference with Sir Sholto and Cleve at the moment. Later on I shall find a way to speak to him. I shall ask him to inform his party of what's afoot, and warn them to say nothing whatsoever to Sir Sholto. Yes, I think that will answer the case very nicely. I shall report the outcome to you as soon as I'm able."

He bustled away, and Lord Linslade retired to his room, nursing the uneasy feeling that he had rushed in where angels feared to tread.

"I now understand," said Nicholas, as he and Alex descended the stairs that evening, "how the French aristos felt in the tumbrils."

Alex smiled. "*Courage, mon brave*! Show the *canaille* that a Frome knows how to die!"

Nick sighed. "Perhaps Chase hasn't yet had time to speak to Everley."

This hope was quickly dashed, for as they reached the Great Hall they found Lord Everley awaiting them.

He looked to be in a poor state of health. His body, always fat, was swollen by dropsy, his legs much bloated, the right one swathed in bandages up to the knee-clasp of his old-fashioned black satin breeches. His face had the sheen of an over-ripe plum, and his lips were mottled grey. He wheezed a greeting as they approached.

"Linslade. Frome. Your servant. Desire a word with you before we join the rest. That demmed sawbones . . . what's his name . . .?"

"Dr Chase," said Alex.

"Chase, that's the one! Told me about these dastardly attacks on my dear friend Curle. I was never more shocked in my life. Recent turn of things, eh? Nothing of that sort when I was here last Christmas?"

"Was there not?"

"Nothing at all. Stayed here for the best part of five weeks. Ill, you know, and Sholto wouldn't let me make the journey to London. So, some madman that's got a bee in his bonnet. Some maniac, d'ye see? That's the explanation."

"If you're right, the Law will settle his account fast enough."

"I hope so, Linslade, but we shouldn't leave things to chance, umh? Must get Curle away. Persuade him to come to London."

78

"He told me he'll be in Town for the Coronation."

"Should come now. Stubborn as a mule, that's the trouble. Diggin' in his heels because he don't wish to run from the enemy."

"He says he's needed at Ringwood."

"Rubbish! Place runs itself. And of what use will he be to Ringwood if he's dead, eh? Man's a pigheaded dolt, and I shall tell him so to his face."

"That must, of course, make him see reason."

Lord Everley gave a breathy chuckle. "Oh, I'll wrap it up a little better. Turn him up sweet. Play on his family feelin'. Two gals to launch in society, need his support, that kind of thing."

"According to Sir Sholto, the arrangements for the début are best left to Lady Charlotte."

"Stupid notion. Very proper, my sister, knows all the ton, but she ain't liked. Cold sort of fish, y'know. Puts folk off. I don't like her, and I'm her brother! No, Sholto must come to Town, there's nothing else for it."

Alex had been watching Lord Everley closely as they talked, looking for any sign of hypocrisy. He could detect none. Either Everley was a master of deception, or he'd had no part in the conspiracy against Sholto Curle.

Aloud, he said, "He'd certainly be less vulnerable in London. I wish you success in bringing him there."

"Thankee, Linslade, thankee. Want you to know, I'm grateful for what you've done. Delicate situation, very. You acted just as you ought. Now we'd best join the company before they send out a search party for us. Francis ain't down yet. Fiddlin' with his neckcloth, most likely. Demmed if I'd let m'self be such a slave to fashion, but there it is. Won't change his habits at thirty-four. Have to take him as I find him, I suppose."

Entering the drawing-room they found Sir Sholto already there with Mr Jason Cleve. Lord Everley did not introduce the lawyer to the Fromes but drew him aside and began to speak to him in a low voice.

Alex thought that Cleve resented this cavalier treatment. He was a tall man, and not ill-favoured, his features finely drawn and his skin pale and matt. His thick dark hair was brushed into careful disarray and he was dressed in the height of modality. Only his tucked-in chin and too-bright eyes hinted at some hidden discontent.

Alex recalled a family of Cleves he had met, years before, in Ireland. They belonged to an obscure branch of an impoverished Irish title, and scraped a living where they could. If Cleve was one of that brood, it explained much. It must be galling to be thought enough of a gentleman to sit at the host's table, but not enough to merit the small courtesies of life.

Nicholas had become involved in an argument with Adrian Curle about the rival worth of spermacetti ointment and goose-fat in the treatment of a grazed fetlock. The Earl moved to join Sir Sholto, who told him that neither Lucilla nor Dr Chase would be at dinner. "The Vicar's lady's been taken ill," he said, "and they've gone to the vicarage to help."

"Not the scarlet fever, I hope?"

"No, no, merely a bad go of influenza. If you ask me it's the Vicar that needs them, not his wife. His is not the faith that moves mountains."

Mrs Gray now appeared, with Tamar Curle. Miss Curle was in looks tonight. She wore a gown of white tiffany over a satin slip, the front caught together by rosettes of seed pearls. A string of pearls adorned her throat, and her hair was arranged in soft ringlets that charmingly framed her countenance.

She came forward to make her curtsey to Lord Everley, who received her with gallantry, kissed her on both cheeks, escorted her to a place on the sofa, and showered her with so many roguish compliments that her face became quite pink.

Francis Warsop was the last of the guests to enter. He paused in the doorway just long enough to ensure that every eye was on him. He was not a big man, but his figure was as lithe and well-muscled as a cat's. He had a cat's indolent grace and a cat's bold green stare. It was easy to see why he was accounted a leader of the world of fashion. Nothing could exceed the perfection of his swallow-tail coat. His dove-grey pantaloons showed not a wrinkle. The glossiness of his boots spoke of champagne in the blacking. The cravat was tied in the *trône d'amour*, a nice touch, that. And it was all worn with exactly the right air of nonchalence. Not a doubt of it, Mr Warsop was the Prime Article.

He crossed the room to greet his host with formal courtesy; sketched a bow in the direction of his father and the Fromes; bestowed a nod on Mrs Gray and Mr Cleve; and came to stand before Tamar. Smiling down at her, he dropped a small package wrapped in silver tissue into her lap.

"A token of my esteem, puss," he said. "Think of me when you wear it."

Tamar quickly tore open the parcel. It contained a very pretty locket of gold and blue enamel edged with brilliants. As Tamar began to stammer her thanks, Francis sat down on the sofa, leaning his arm along its back.

"Look inside it," he suggested. "Shall I open it for you? The catch is a little stiff."

He took the trinket from her hand, and with a flick of his thumbnail, opened it. It contained two miniature portraits, and at sight of them Tamar gave a cry of delight.

"It's Mama and Papa! Francis, how clever of you! How did you come by these pictures?"

"Had 'em copied from the originals at Brampton House. According to Aunt C., they were done at the time of your Mama's betrothal. I thought this would make an appropriate gift."

Tamar gave him a glowing smile. "Indeed it does and I thank you. Nothing could have pleased me more."

"Try how it looks with this very fetching gown."

Tamar glanced at Mrs Gray. "Marion? May I?"

Mrs Gray, who had been watching Francis with an enigmatic expression, gave a tight smile. "Of course, my love. Come, and I'll fasten it for you."

The girl and her duenna moved towards the looking-glass that hung above the mantel. Mrs Gray unclasped the string of pearls from Tamar's neck, and replaced it with the locket, while Sir Sholto and Lord Everley looked on approvingly.

Francis Warsop rose from his place and sauntered over to where Alex stood.

"Well, Linslade," he said softly, "this time you may wish me happy."

Alex shrugged. "I wish Miss Curle happy."

"But not me? How very uncharitable of you! One might almost think you harboured a grudge against me!"

"I don't give a button for you, happy or unhappy; but I warn you that I have the happiness and health of Sholto Curle and his family very much at heart."

Francis widened his eyes. "Indeed? And why is that, I wonder? Do you plan to lay siege to the fair Lucilla? Not that I blame you. A dazzler, my cousin, and will inherit two fortunes, the St Clair and the Curle. You could do worse for yourself, much worse. But let me give you a hint, my lord. I doubt if you'll succeed in that quarter. The lady seems to have taken you in dislike."

Repressing a longing to plant Mr Warsop a facer, Alex said brusquely, "I don't propose to discuss Miss Pelham or anyone else with you. Remember what I've said. If any harm comes to Sholto Curle, I'll carry my suspicions to the Chief Magistrate at Bow Street. We're good friends. He'll listen to me."

Before Francis could reply, Alex turned his back. He almost cannoned into Jason Cleve, who was standing close behind him. Cleve must have moved up unnoticed. There could be no doubt that he'd heard the conversation. He made as if to speak but, catching sight of Alex's face, changed his mind and stepped back.

XI

ALEX DID NOT speak to Francis again that night. At dinner they were placed at opposite ends of the long table, and afterwards it was noticeable that Jason Cleve stuck close to Francis, as if to prevent further arguments.

Francis, for his part, ignored the Fromes and paid extravagant court to Tamar . . . an attention which she received with reserve rather than enthusiasm.

At nine o'clock the tea-tray was brought in. Nicholas slipped away to steal a last look at the treasures of the library while the Earl expressed his thanks to Sir Sholto for his hospitality.

"No need to hurry away, you know," the old man said.

Alex shook his head. "I fear there is, sir. I must see Nick safely to my grandmother's house. From there I go to London on urgent business."

"I understand. I shan't be astir when you leave, so I'll bid you farewell now. Mind you visit us again at Ringwood. And give my kind regards to Lady Linslade."

Alex completed his round of goodbyes, and left the drawing-room. The house was quiet, the passages deserted. He made his way to the Great Hall, where candles were set out on a table beneath the musicians' gallery. He picked one up and lit it from the candelabrum, but he did not at once go upstairs. The clash with Francis had left him feeling restless and irritable. One part of his mind warned him to forget the Curles and their problems. The other told him that this would not be possible.

He carried his candlestick over to the wall where the family portraits hung. It was easy to identify Sir Sholto's progeny. Charles Curle was Sir Sholto forty years ago, black-haired and blue-eyed, full of vigour, smiling. Next to him was his wife Caroline Curle, née Brampton, fine-featured and flaxen-haired like her cousin Francis, though without his look of arrogance. Hers was a melancholy visage, the delicate mouth drooping, the wide eyes shadowed with secret thoughts.

Alex scanned the upper row of portraits. Directly above the painting of Charles was an oval picture of a girl with red hair and blue eyes. He thought at first that it was Lucilla Pelham, but realized by the style of her dress that it must be her mother Elizabeth. Great determination looked out at him, charm, eagerness, the bright spirit of a girl who'd married an explorer and followed him to the ends of the earth.

He was searching for Sidney Pelham's portrait when he heard a sound behind him, and glanced over his shoulder to see Lucilla herself coming through the doorway under the minstrels' gallery. She wore a long cloak and carried a basket on her arm. He started towards her, and she held up an imperious hand.

"Stay where you are, Lord Linslade. I don't wish you to take the contagion."

Alex walked steadily on. "I don't fear it, ma'am. How is the patient?"

"More comfortable. If you will forgive me, Lord Linslade, I am very tired. I bid you goodnight."

"Wait, please." He stopped before her. "Nicholas and I leave early tomorrow. I want to thank you for your kindness to us during our stay at Ringwood."

Her eyes blazed suddenly. "A kindness you have grossly abused, my lord."

"Abused? In what way?"

"You know quite well in what way. You spoke to me of the tontine, and I told you, plainly, it had nothing to do with the attacks on my grandfather, yet you chose to poison poor Dr Chase against certain members of my family. You made vile accusations against them, accusations of murder . . . "

"Someone has attempted murder, Miss Pelham. My only concern is to protect Sir Sholto."

"I have no wish to discuss it with you, sir! I have heard the whole sorry tale from my cousin Francis."

"Perhaps Mr Warsop may be somewhat biassed."

Lucilla shook her head violently, as if to shut out his words. "I know who is biassed. It is you. You quarrelled with Francis years ago, over some woman, and you've chosen this despicable way to vent your spite . . . "

"Nonsense!"

"Is it? Do you deny there was a quarrel?"

"I do deny it," said Alex furiously. "My difference with your cousin went far beyond mere brangling, and I have no intention of speaking of it, to you or anyone else. If I have abused your hospitality, then I'm sorry for it. I wish you well, ma'am, and assure you that neither I, nor any other member of my family, will trouble this household again."

He bowed stiffly. Lucilla stared at him for a moment, then turned and rushed away, slamming the door after her with great force.

Alex swung on his heel, and was about to re-cross the hall when he heard his name called. Looking up, he saw a face peering down at him from the gallery. It was Mrs Gray. She raised a finger to her lips, and hurried down the spiral stairway that led to the floor of the hall. Reaching the Earl's side, she caught hold of his arm and said, urgently, "My lord, I heard what passed between you and Lucilla."

Alex regarded her coldly. "Eavesdropping, ma'am?"

"If you like." She sounded impatient. "Sometimes one

must do uncomfortable things, for the sake of those one loves."

"I'm afraid I don't know what you mean."

"The tontine." Her large eyes watched him feverishly. "I heard Lucilla speak of the tontine, and of accusations of murder. You think it was one of them that tried to kill Sir Sholto."

As he made no answer, she tightened her grip on his arm. "You think it, and so do I. They are desperate for money, you see? That's the only reason for this betrothal. They want the Curle share. Francis feels nothing for Tamar, nothing at all."

She looked, he thought, a little mad. He was tempted to make some snubbing remark, but he saw the agony of concern in her eyes, and relented. "I can't interfere, you know," he said. "It's for Miss Curle, and her family, to choose whom she'll marry."

"Choose? My poor darling has no choice, Lord Linslade, none at all. If she doesn't accept this marriage, then she will die an old maid, without position, without respect, without children of her own to cherish."

He frowned. "Surely you exaggerate? Miss Curle is pretty and accomplished, and of good family. She's bound to receive many respectable offers. Young Ayliffe, for instance, would marry her tomorrow, and there'll be others as willing, believe me."

"No, no, you don't understand. Giles Ayliffe is a case in point. His parents will never countenance the match. They have made that insultingly clear, and Sir Sholto will never allow Tamar to face such parental opposition." Seeing Alex shake his head, Mrs Gray said fiercely, "I know what is the truth, my lord. The Ayliffes forbid the match, because of the History."

"What history?"

Mrs Gray hesitated, then said in a low voice, "The history of insanity, sir. Caroline, Tamar's mother, suffered from a recurrent depression. She ended by taking her own life."

"That is very sad, but there are many causes of depression. The hardships of life . . . some shock . . . "

"Caroline Curle never knew a moment's hardship. She was a pampered darling, all her days."

"When did her illness begin?"

"After Tamar was born. I was called in to attend the birth, and I know that that was when it began . . . when my precious was born. Caroline refused to nurse her baby, would not touch her or even look at her. She fell into such a deep melancholy that the doctors feared she would die. She recovered but, from that time until her death, she was prone to the wildest swings of mood. Sometimes she was in alt, sometimes in the depths of despair. She feared to go about in society. She could not make the lightest decision. If I had not been at hand to care for the children, they would have lacked all that tender care that only a woman can bestow. Charles Curle was in the Army, fighting in one country after another, seldom here in England. I don't scruple to tell you that I've been mother and father to Tamar and Adrian, yet I have none of a parent's rights, I am powerless to protect them against life's vicissitudes. This marriage to Francis Warsop. I saw it first as the answer to my prayers. I thought Tamar would be safe with him, but when I came to know him . . . "

"'Came to know?' Surely, as Tamar's cousin, Mr Warsop must frequently have come to Ringwood?"

"No, not at all. He dislikes country life. Last year he spent a week or two with us. It was at that time that I began to . . . doubt him. There is something in his nature, some streak of malice, or cruelty, even, that frightens me. I'm not without friends, my lord, and I wrote to certain of them, those who live in London. The reports they sent me of Francis — his gambling, his wild behaviour — his libertine propensities — have given me sleepless nights, yet still I believed it would be best for Tamar to have the security of the Everley name and, some day, the title.

"I clung to that hope, sir. I blinded myself to reality. Even after the . . . the curious events of recent months, I tried to believe there was no malice abroad. I knew about the tontine. I knew Lord Everley and his sister Charlotte Brampton are surviving members. I began to think — fear — that perhaps the accidents to Sir Sholto were related to the tontine. When I heard Lucilla speak of it to you, tonight, I was shocked beyond measure. My worst nightmares are realized. Lord Linslade, I

86

am a woman without status, without influence. I can do nothing, but you can take action, you can . . . "

"No, madam," said Alex firmly. "You heard what was said here tonight, so you know that I have no influence in the matter. Nor do I wish to have. Chance brought me to this house and when I leave it tomorrow I shall do my best to forget all about it."

"You cannot be so craven! You cannot abandon us!" Mrs Gray clasped her hands in dramatic entreaty. "At least tell me that you will try to discover who was responsible for these dreadful events. You are a man of influence, you can raise questions in the right places . . . "

"You mistake, ma'am. It has been made very plain to me that I have no right to interfere."

"Ah, you have been offended by what Lucilla said; but I cannot, will not accept that you are indifferent to Sir Sholto's plight. For his sake alone, I beg you to do what you can. If you refuse, and the worst befalls, then that guilt must remain with you always. It was Fate that brought you to Ringwood, my lord, and you cannot avoid that Fate."

With these throbbing words, Mrs Gray swept away up the gallery stair. Lord Linslade was left standing in the hall, in the grip of a rising resentment. Hot wax from the candle spilled on to his hand and he swore aloud. A cheerful voice spoke behind him.

"Alex? I thought you were already abed."

"No," said his lordship bitterly. "I have been here, enacting a Cheltenham tragedy with a cast of bedlamites and a damned poor script! It's been a lesson to me, not to meddle in what doesn't concern me. Come, let's go up. We leave tomorrow, as early as possible, and I for one hope never to set foot in the place again!"

Mrs Gray went straight from the Great Hall to Lucilla's bedroom and found her seated in her night wear before her looking-glass, brushing her hair with short, angry strokes. Lucilla turned when she saw the duenna and said sharply, "What is it now, Marion?"

Mrs Gray sat down and folded her hands in her lap. "This betrothal," she said. "I have been wondering if it is right for Tamar? I have the feeling that Mr Warsop is . . . a thought

87

unsteady . . . not quite the sort of man to make our dear one a good husband."

Lucilla stared. "But, good God, you've said over and over that he's just the one for her! What's made you change your mind? Have you been speaking to Linslade? Has he been casting aspersions on Francis? Because if that's the case . . . "

"No, no. Lord Linslade never mentioned Francis."

"So, you have spoken to him?"

"I ventured to approach him, yes, to beg him to discover who has launched these dreadful attempts against Sir Sholto. My intentions were of the best, Lucilla, believe me, though I suppose you will think I took a liberty in speaking to him."

Lucilla did think so, but she saw the distress in the older woman's face, and sighed. "I think Linslade is the last man we should apply to. He detests Francis and could never be impartial in his views. And I should like to know why you've turned your coat so suddenly."

"I . . . I have heard rumours," faltered Mrs Gray, "that Francis's reputation is . . . somewhat tarnished."

"If you mean that he keeps a mistress," said Lucilla, "then let me tell you it's quite the fashion for a gentleman to have some lightskirt in tow. I'm sure Linslade is no better, in that regard, than the rest."

"My love," said Mrs Gray, much shocked, "pray guard your tongue a little. A lady of quality should never speak so."

"A lady of quality," replied Lucilla hotly, "would think shame to listen to slanders against her own kith and kin. Linslade has gone beyond what is permissible. I beg you won't mention his name to me again."

"But I thought . . . it seemed to me . . . that you were in a fair way to liking him."

"I was, until he chose to accuse the Everleys of murder. Now I devoutly hope that I've seen the last of him and all his clan. As for Tamar marrying Francis, surely the final decision rests with Tamar. Grandfather isn't Gothic, you know. He'll never force her to marry against her inclination, and Tamar herself has agreed to the match."

"I fear that is because I have over-persuaded her. I was so anxious to see her happily settled. Secure, as I have never been secure. I'm afraid she accepted Francis's offer to please me and Sir Sholto, rather than herself."

"That would be idiotic," said Lucilla roundly. "No one could be so poor-spirited."

"You might not. You have so much resolution, dear Lucilla; but Tamar is far more pliable, and, oh, I could not bear it if she entered into an unsuitable marriage because of my insistence."

"Nothing is final yet," Lucilla said. "A good deal can happen in the next few months. If Tamar changes her mind, she has only to say so, and that will be that." As Marion still looked unconvinced, Lucilla reached out and took her hand. "Don't fret," she said. "I'll speak to Tamar, if you wish, and tell her the choice is hers."

"Will you? Dearest Lucilla, that will lift such a weight from my mind."

Mrs Gray kissed Lucilla goodnight, and went away with a lightened step. Lucilla, sighing a little, climbed into bed and blew out her candle.

The Fromes left Ringwood directly after breakfast next morning. It was a quiet departure. The Steward Soan was on the driveway before them, to oversee the bestowing of their baggage and to insist that one of Sir Sholto's own grooms must accompany them to Evesham.

Adrian Curle came out of the house to shake hands, and promised to look them up as soon as he reached London. Dr Chase, too, emerged briefly, murmured his thanks to Alex, and said he would write to him in a day or so.

Of Miss Pelham there was no sign. Lord Linslade told himself that he was heartily glad of it; but he could not resist stealing a glance at her window. He thought he saw the curtain move slightly, but Lucilla did not appear, and he turned away to give instructions to Cheadle.

He climbed into the carriage, and Nicholas followed. The door was closed, the groom swung up to his perch, Cheadle gave a crack of his whip, and the vehicle moved forward away from the house, through the woods, to the highway. They passed at a brisk pace through Swallowford, and were soon travelling westwards towards Evesham .

XII

THE CURLES NOW went ahead with their own plans for removing to London. Jason Cleve having already departed on the Mail Coach, it was agreed that Lucilla, Tamar and Mrs Gray should travel with Lord Everley in his coach, while Adrian rode in the curricle with Francis.

The party would leave early in the following week, and travel by easy stages to Abingdon, where accommodation had already been reserved for them at an excellent inn.

It remained only for the ladies to fill the portmanteaux, valises and bandboxes brought down from the attic.

Tamar agonised a good deal over which garments she should take with her, but Lucilla advised her to pack as little as possible.

"What does quite well for Swallowford," she said, "will look very countrified in London."

"But that means we will have to have everything new," said Tamar. "It will be weeks before we can set foot outside the door."

Lucilla laughed. "Not weeks, days only. Aunt Charlotte wrote in her last letter that she has modistes and milliners standing at the ready, and I promise you I mean to indulge in a positive orgy of shopping."

"But won't that be vastly expensive?"

"Vastly," agreed Lucilla, with satisfaction. "Remember that this is probably the one time in our lives that we'll be encouraged to primp like peacocks. We may as well make the most of it."

She went off happily to the stables, to confer with the head groom about transporting her horses to Town. Left alone, Tamar returned to her study of the gowns in her wardrobe.

She was interrupted by a gentle tapping at her door, and opened it to discover the kitchenmaid Hannah, who timidly held out a folded paper.

"Miss, if you please, I was to give this to you."

Tamar took the paper. "Who brought it here, Hannah?"

"It were Jem, Miss, from Squire Ayliffe's."

"I see. Thank you."

Hannah bobbed a curtsey and retreated, and Tamar quickly unfolded the note. Its message was brief.

"Dear Tam" she read, "Mama has told me you are to leave for London on Monday. I must see you, to bid you Godspeed, and to tell you something of Great Importance. I shall wait for you in the arbour. Don't fail me.

Yr devoted servant,

Giles Ayliffe."

Tamar pressed the letter to her breast. She was torn between happiness and dismay. She had made a solemn compact with Giles that they would not meet in private again. It was too painful for both of them. She could not bear to see the sadness in his eyes, his noble fortitude was more wounding than any harsh reproof could be.

Grandfather had explained, oh so kindly and gently, that she must not hope to marry Giles. His parents were implacably opposed to that and, cruel though it might seem, it was not something that would change. If Giles went against his parents' wishes, it would make him deeply unhappy, and Tamar too.

She knew this to be true. She was not even sure that Giles would marry to spite his family. Once, in fun, she had suggested they make a runaway match to Gretna Green. Giles had been very much shocked. Nothing, he said, could persuade him to treat his dearest Tamar with such a lack of respect. If they could not marry with honour, they'd best not marry at all.

It was a decision that caused her to shed bitter tears, but she consented at last to marry Francis Warsop. If she felt no love for him, at least he was not a stranger, and he would not try to separate her from her family as some husbands were said to do.

She had made up her mind and she would not falter; but surely it couldn't be wrong to see Giles this once without others looking on, and to say farewell for ever. She needed some sacred memory to carry her through the months and years ahead.

Quickly she found her warmest cloak, put it on, and drew the hood close about her face. She kicked off her thin leather slippers and thrust her feet into stouter shoes. Then she went quietly to the back stairway, ran down it, and let herself out into the kitchen garden. From there, it was easy to slip through the orchard to the belvedere that overlooked the ornamental lake.

Giles was waiting, as he had promised. His face lit up at her approach and he put out both hands to clasp hers, and drew her into the shelter of the arbour. There was a bench there, and they sat down facing each other. Reluctantly, he released her hands.

"It was good of you to come," he said. "I'd never have asked it of you, except that this morning I received a letter that may change our lives." He was fumbling in the pocket of his greatcoat as he spoke, and he brought out a single sheet of paper and waved it at her.

"It's from Mr Amos Brocket," he said eagerly. "I never hoped for so quick an answer. I sent him my drawings and the specifications for my Steam Horse . . . and asked if I might have the honour of meeting him to discuss production. Brocket's an engineer, you know, with a manufactory in Southwark. Brocket and Sons is one of the foremost firms in England. If they buy my design, my fortune's made. Oh, Tam, don't you see that it will solve all our problems? With money in my pocket, I'll be my own man. No one will be able to prevent our marrying."

"No!" Tamar raised a hand in warning. "You promised you wouldn't speak of that."

"Then I must break my promise. When I gave it I thought I had nothing to offer you. Now I know different. I'll be rich one day. I'll be able to provide you with all the elegancies of life."

"I don't care a fig for money," cried Tamar. "I never have. But you know I'm not free. I'm promised to another. What you speak of can never be."

"I must speak, I will speak! You and I were meant for each other. If you truly wished to marry Warsop, if you truly loved him and desired to be his wife, then I'd swear to leave you in peace, but I know it's me you love. Look me in the eyes, Tam, and deny it if you can."

She glanced at him fleetingly, then sprang to her feet. "I can't stay, I should not have come."

He gave a triumphant laugh. "You see, you can't deny it. We both know what's in our hearts." As she tried to brush past him, he caught her by the shoulders and said in a quieter tone, "Hush, love, I didn't mean to scare you. But please believe that I'll never give up hope of marrying you. Trust me, Tam. That's all I ask. Keep faith with me just a little longer."

Tears glinted in her eyes. "How can I?" she said. "My engagement is to be announced in September. I can't alter that."

"Then give me till September. I'll have Brocket's answer long before then, and when I have it I shall go to my father, and to Sir Sholto, and make them see reason." He drew a clean handkerchief from his pocket and wiped the tears from her face. "There, my dearest, don't fret. All will come right. Now give me a smile."

Tamar managed a watery smile. Leaning down, Giles kissed her mouth. "I shall be in London next month," he said, "and the first house I call at will be Lady Charlotte Brampton's. Go inside now. I'll watch you all the way."

She turned and hurried away along the orchard path. Giles watched until she was lost to sight beyond the wall of the kitchen garden, then strode to the thicket where he'd tethered his horse, swung himself up into the saddle, and set off at a gallop for home.

That same evening, Sir Sholto summoned Lucilla to him for a private talk.

"About Linslade," he said, "I hear that you and he came to cuffs the night before he left?"

Lucilla coloured. "Who has been carrying tales?"

"No one. I'm not blind, my dear. I saw how you pokered up, every time his name was mentioned, and I asked Chase to put me in possession of the facts."

"Then you know the answer. Linslade accused the Everleys of planning the attacks on you."

"Not quite. He suggested, I think, that the surviving members of a tontine would have a motive for murder. He did not directly accuse the Everleys."

"It comes to the same thing. He has his knife into Francis, because of some sordid quarrel over a woman."

"My child, I've known a great many men in my long life, and I tell you, frankly, Linslade doesn't strike me as the sort of man to carry a grudge in that way."

"Then why did he say those abominable things?"

"I expect he felt it to be his duty." Sir Sholto gazed hard at his grand-daughter. "A lesser man might have held his tongue and left us to take our chances."

"You cannot believe that Uncle Henry . . . that Francis . . .?"

"No, of course not! I think the whole thing is a storm in a teacup, but I want you to remember that Linslade's father was my trusted friend. I like this young man, and his brother. I hope that when you reach London you will treat them with civility, for my sake if not for yours."

Lucilla stared straight ahead of her. "The Fromes are above our touch, Grandfather. I doubt if our paths will cross again."

Sir Sholto gave her a quizzical smile. "Stranger things have happened," he said.

XIII

OAKENGATES, THE HOME of the Dowager Countess of Linslade, was situated on a sunny hillside some five miles from Evesham. The house, of comfortable proportions and charming aspect, had been built by Lady Alice's own father, and she had retired to it soon after the death of her husband.

Her friends in the ton were inclined to commiserate with her on what they deemed to be an enforced exile, but she herself had never regretted leaving Foxfare. At Oakengates she was free to arrange things exactly as she chose, without having to confer all the time with her daughter-in-law and son. She could spend the winter months cosily entertaining her acquaintance, and in summer could remove to the exquisite house she owned in Grosvenor Street.

Her circle was that of the older Whig aristocracy, robust in its enjoyment of life, vigorous of mind, good-humoured and outspoken. She was as welcome at Devonshire House as she was at Brocket, the Lambs' delightful country home. She was a famous hostess, and one might find at her Town parties the foremost politicians and artists of the day. Many people came to her for counsel, for she was a shrewd observer of the world and its foibles. The success of her only son, Julian Frome the diplomat, had been due in part to her knowledge and advice.

Smallboned, elegant, with large hazel eyes and thick silver hair, she was still accounted a beautiful woman. She could have remarried had she wished, but she preferred her independence. Her feelings for her family had always been strong, and her grandchildren regarded her with warm affection and sought refuge with her whenever life at Foxfare became too uncomfortable to bear.

Alex and Nicholas, arriving at Oakengates around three in the afternoon, found her in her writing-room, dealing with a pile of accounts. She embraced her grandsons, rang for refreshments to be brought, and demanded an instant recital of what she termed The Curle Saga. "When Belper arrived here," she said, "covered in mud and babbling of having been waylaid by Mexican bandits, I confess I thought him to be in his cups."

"No, it was all quite true," Alex said. "There was a regular dust-up." He described the events on the highway, and later at Ringwood, without however mentioning the tontine, or the attacks on Sholto Curle.

Lady Linslade was enchanted. "Why is it," she demanded, "that I never experience such adventures? I have never clapped eyes on a footpad, nor heard a shot fired in anger. But how lucky that you should chance upon the Curles! I was acquainted with Sir Sholto, many years ago."

"So he told us. He said I must be sure to give you his kind remembrances."

"Delightful man! I recall he was something of a scholar. One was forever meeting him at Egremont's place at Petworth. They used to argue about Egremont's Claudes and Correggios, though I think Sir Sholto's interest lay more in books than in paintings."

"Lord, yes," said Nicholas eagerly, "his library is beyond anything I've ever seen, and he gave me free run of it. I was able to look up all manner of things about Delphi and the like, which will come in very handy when I write my own book."

Nick launched into an account of the expedition to Greece. Lady Linslade listened with keen attention, but at the end of an hour called a halt, saying that Nick was looking fagged to death and must rest for an hour before dinner. When he'd left the room she turned to Alex.

"He's been quite ill, hasn't he?"

"Yes, and I'm partly to blame. I took him from a sickbed, and plunged him into a blizzard, a shooting affray, and sundry domestic dramas. Luckily he had the services of a good doctor; and Miss Pelham produced some magic potion that brought his fever down quite amazingly."

"Miss Pelham is the older grand-daughter?"

"Yes, the child of Sir Sholto's daughter Elizabeth, and Sidney Pelham the explorer."

"I remember Elizabeth. Very lovely, and amusing, and high-spirited. Does this girl resemble her?"

"Miss Pelham," said Alex with asperity, "resembles no female I ever met. She wears breeches, rides like a Cossack, and has a temper as red as her hair."

"Breeches?" said the Dowager, fascinated.

"Not all the time." An unwilling smile touched his lordship's lips. "Only, she told me, when she is chasing bandits."

"Good heavens! Who else inhabits this remarkable household?"

"There are two other grandchildren, from Sir Sholto's son Charles: a boy aged eighteen who seems short of a few nuts and bolts, and a blonde chit of about sixteen. They're in the charge of Mrs Marion Gray, a distant cousin of Sholto Curle." The Earl paused, frowning, then said, "The girl, Tamar, is betrothed to marry Francis Warsop. Lord Everley, Warsop, and their tame lawyer arrived at Ringwood yesterday, to arrange the marriage settlements."

The look of laughter faded from Lady Linslade's eyes. "How very embarrassing for you," she said, "but I'm sure, my dear, that you handled it with your usual aplomb."

"Nothing of the kind." Alex sounded bitter. "I made a sad mull of things. I let it be known that I hold Warsop in contempt. That was not, as you may imagine, well received."

"You spoke to Sir Sholto?"

"No. To Dr Chase. He told the Everleys, and Warsop lost no time in tattling to Miss Pelham, with the result that I'm now cast in the rôle of the Demon King."

"I don't understand, my love. Why did this doctor carry tales to the Everleys?"

"Because I asked him to. I can't explain, Grandmama. There were . . . certain complications. I did my best, but I gave offence."

"To Sir Sholto?"

"No. He's a very tolerant man."

Lady Linslade perceived that she was not being told the whole story, but she did not press the point. Instead she said vehemently, "Sholto Curle must be out of his mind! Francis Warsop is a gazetted fortune-hunter, and his father's close to bankruptcy."

"Yes." The Earl picked up a paper-knife and turned it slowly in his fingers. "There's a Lady Charlotte Brampton, Everley's sister. Do you know her, ma'am?"

"I do, and avoid her when I can. She's an excessively cold, haughty woman, a high stickler of the worst sort. It's said she had numerous lovers in her youth — the on-dit was that Prinny was one of them — but if you ask me, she entirely lacks heart. When her daughter Caroline fell ill, Charlotte Brampton kept her cooped up in her room like a prisoner; she allowed her grandchildren to be raised by others. I find that unnatural."

"How close is she to Warsop?"

Lady Linslade shrugged. "They're both of the Carlton House set. That makes them birds of a feather."

"And the lawyer? A Mr Jason Cleve?"

"Clever Cleve," said her ladyship.

"A sharp, is he?"

"No, no. He's what you might call a society lawyer. Has a large practice, owns a house in Half Moon Street. He's the third son of old Sir Edward Cleve, who's a cousin of the Everleys."

"All in the family," said Alex, half to himself. He did not seem to have any further questions, and Lady Linslade decided to change the subject.

"How long do you mean to stay with us?" she enquired.

"No more than a day or two. I promised Castlereagh I'd be in London by the end of the week, and I can't fail him. He's being killed by overwork." The Earl suddenly laid aside the paper-knife, and said abruptly, "Grandmama, I've a favour to ask of you."

"What is it, my dear?"

"It concerns Miss Pelham. She's to make her come-out this year, with Miss Curle. They're to be launched by Lady Charlotte, who's Miss Pelham's godmama. While I was at Ringwood — before the brangling started — I promised Sir Sholto I'd do what I could for Miss Pelham. She's spent most of her life out of England and knows very few people. I don't imagine, in view of what's happened, that she'll wish for my support . . . but if you will agree to meet her . . . perhaps put in a good word for her . . .?"

"Of course I will. Does she have any particular interests? Apart, I mean, from chasing bandits?"

Alex thought a moment. "She desires to own a high-perch phaeton, in which she will very likely break her neck."

"On that score," said the Dowager firmly, "I shall offer her no advice whatsoever."

When Alex went upstairs to change for dinner, Lady Linslade remained at her desk, lost in thought. Though all her grand-children were dear to her, Alex remained her favourite. That did not blind her to his faults, the chief of which was his tendency to be easily bored.

He was not, she knew, the dedicated diplomat her son had been. He had told her more than once that he disliked the constant travel, and the endless conferences. She suspected that the unruffled calm and balanced judgement, that won him such high praise in official circles, sprang more from indiffer-ence than from self-control.

It was an attitude he carried over into his private life. He cared deeply for his family and for a few close friends, but was happy to let the rest of the world go hang. He enjoyed life, but in a casual, dispassionate way. For instance, although he was a notable athlete, he seemed to take no pride in his prowess. He never indulged in the neck-or-nothing exploits so dear to his fellow Corinthians. He did not race his curricle to Brighton or seek to go a few rounds with some champion of The Fancy. He gambled in schools where the stakes were high, but not to excess. He drank hard, at times, but he was never seen drunk.

It was the same in matters of love. His wealth, title and

splendid looks made him a highly desirable parti, and many were the lures cast for him by hopeful debutantes and their ambitious mamas. He eluded all these traps with ease.

Lady Linslade was aware that he enjoyed the favours of various birds of paradise. Only last year he'd installed a voluptuous opera-singer in a house in Montpelier Square. These affairs never lasted long. Alex quickly tired of his inamoratas, and discarded them, albeit on the most generous of terms.

His mama constantly bewailed what she called his rakehelly habits. It was his duty, Elvira said, to marry and set up his nursery. She was forever throwing eligible girls in his path, dreary dowds of impeccable rectitude, whom Alex treated with polite indifference. Though he flirted with a number of pretty and acceptable young females, he did not propose marriage to any of them. Society mamas were inclined to brand the Earl of Linslade a heartless philanderer.

Conscious of this, Lady Linslade found his reaction to Miss Pelham highly diverting. Alex had described the girl in less than glowing terms — a hoyden, he suggested, with a volatile temper, and little sense of propriety — but he had showed no sign of being bored by her.

Might one begin to hope that at last he had fallen in love?

The fact that peculiar difficulties lay in the way of such an attachment did not perturb Lady Linslade. If Alex wished to meet that challenge, well and good. If he did not, so be it.

She thought of writing to tell Elvira of the events at Ringwood, and decided against it. Elvira never failed to put the wrong interpretation on the written word. Better to speak to her when they met in London, after one had had time to consult with one's friends and discover more about Miss Pelham's antecedents and character.

In the mean time, the plans for removing to Town must be reviewed. Nicholas must be allowed to rest a little before embarking on another long journey but, all things considered, it should be possible to leave Oakengates on Wednesday of next week.

The Dowager sent for her butler and housekeeper, and warned them to be ready to set forth on that date.

XIV

THE RINGWOOD PARTY left for London on Monday morning at eleven o'clock, an hour that Lord Everley described as the crack of dawn.

The weather was sunny and the carriage well sprung, so that even Marion Gray, a poor traveller, experienced no discomfort. His lordship dozed in his corner for most of the way, and Lucilla and Tamar whiled away the hours chatting, observing the features of the countryside and playing solitaire on the portable board Mrs Gray had brought with her.

They reached the Lion at Abingdon by mid-afternoon to find Francis Warsop and Adrian already ensconced in the private parlour bespoken by Lord Everley. Adrian was in tearing spirits. He announced that they had "driven neck or nothing", had raced another curricle all the way from Charlbury to Woodstock, winning hands down, and had still found time to stop and sink a quart or two of the old home-brewed.

Supper was a convivial meal, and at its conclusion the ladies retired to bed, leaving the gentlemen to linger over a fine old French brandy the landlord produced for them.

The next day proved less enjoyable. Not only were they using hired horses, but a light drizzle made the surface of the roads dangerously slick and forced them to travel at a snail's pace. However, they were in High Wycombe by dusk, and on Wednesday had only to cover the relatively short distance from there to London.

Lucilla, who had visited so many strange parts of the world, had come to the Metropolis only once, as a schoolgirl. Everything was new to her, and exciting. As they bowled down the Bayswater Road she showered questions on Lord Everley. He replied cheerfully that he'd no room in his noddle for such flim-flam, and it was left to Mrs Gray to play the part of guide.

She entered into the rôle with enthusiasm, saying that she was a Londoner by birth and by affection, had a sister living in the neighbouring village of Islington, and retained warm links with her cousins in Wimpole Street. She suggested to his lordship that, as they had plenty of time in hand, it might amuse the girls to take the long way round, through Marylebone. Lord Everley good-naturedly agreed, and ordered the coachman to turn north to Regent's Park, laid out by Mr Nash after 1812, then south past the fine façades and noble Quadrant of Regent Street, then west again along Piccadilly.

Lucilla, bending eagerly to her window, thought she had never seen such a press of traffic. Vehicles crowded and jostled on every side: phaetons, curricles, and post-chaises, hackney-chariots and drays, the old-fashioned barouche, and the spanking-new cabriolet. They watched the Mail Coach come in from the north, marvellously trim and smart, its magnificent horses sweeping past with a thunderous trampling of hooves.

The noise of the town was deafening, for as well as the rattle of iron-bound wheels on cobbles, the crack of drivers' whips and the shouts of passengers thwarted in their wish to reach their destinations with all possible speed, there was an incessant hubbub from the crowded pavements. Hawkers cried their wares: hair-brooms and milk, small-coal and gingerbread, knives to grind, bellows to mend, chimneys to sweep! At one corner a ballad-singer lamented the recent execution of the Cato Street Gang. At another, a one-legged sailor in a cocked hat churned the handle of a barrel-organ.

The cacophony of sound appalled Tamar. "I shall never be brave enough to set foot in the street," she said. "It is like Bedlam!"

Mrs Gray smiled kindly. "You've no cause to be alarmed, my love. Lady Charlotte will never permit you to run the smallest risk. You will ride in a carriage, or if you have to go on foot you will be escorted by a footman with a stout cudgel in his hand. Not all families are as strict in their arrangements, more's the pity. There is a great deal of moral laxity in our modern society."

Lord Everley grunted heavily. "Too many people," he said. "When I was a lad, the streets were dirtier, and black as your boot after nightfall, but, damme, a man could walk without having hoi polloi treadin' on his heels! Nowadays, every ploughboy and yokel must needs leave the land and traipse up to Town, in the mistaken notion that he'll be able to pass his time in idleness in some rich man's household. Clerks ape their betters. Every manjack of 'em seeks to own his horse, and butchers ride in carriages dressed as fine as fivepence. The wealthy Cits flaunt their wives in satins and jewels, while we gentlefolk are hard put to it to keep the duns from the door!"

He seemed to realize that this last pronouncement came a little too close to the truth, for he cast a quick look at Tamar, and lapsed into gloomy silence. Mrs Gray said briskly, "At least we can be sure that no vulgar personages will come near our dear girls. Any such pretension would be instantly rebuffed."

Lucilla only half-listened to these remarks. She was gazing about her with sparkling eyes, and not even the admiring catcalls of two rudesbys on the flagway could persuade her to desert her window.

London, she decided, was a place of enchantment, and she determined to improve her knowledge of it at the earliest possible moment.

There was something a little forbidding about the façade of Lady Charlotte's home in Curzon Street. Brampton House had been built in 1768, and its structure lacked the grace of more recent edifices. Its front porch was heavily ornamented in the baroque style, its front door looked strong enough to withstand a siege, and its basement windows were barred as if the inhabitants lived in daily expectation of being burgled.

Inside the building the same heavy touch prevailed. The drawing-room, into which the travellers were first shown, was very splendid, but Lucilla could not imagine herself kicking off her slippers there, or curling up on a tapestried chaise-longue to read a romantic novel.

The walls were hung in rich cherry-red silk, and the entire ceiling was covered by a painting of the Judgement of Paris, framed by a triple corniche of gilded plaster. Gold paint masked the carved doors, above which were displayed the Brampton arms. The furniture was French, ormolu and marquetry work being much in evidence. A Savonnerie carpet entirely concealed the floor.

There were several portraits on the walls; the largest, by Gainsborough, depicting a young woman in a lilac satin gown whom Lucilla took to be Lady Charlotte in youth. More interesting were the two paintings, on the inner wall, of Caroline and Charles Curle, the originals of the miniatures in Tamar's locket. The two girls walked across to examine them, but were interrupted by the entry of Lady Charlotte herself.

She was an imposing figure, tall and erect, and without the embonpoint displayed by her brother. Her face was oval and her features well-cast, but she favoured the heavy maquillage of a past era, her lips being reddened and her cheeks heavily powdered to produce a somewhat mask-like effect. Her eyes were prominent, of a clear, pale blue; they stared with unblinking intentness at the two girls standing before her. Tamar seemed to pass the inspection without difficulty, but Lady Charlotte continued to stare at Lucilla for some moments. At last she spoke.

"You're very like your Mama, my dear."

"So they tell me, ma'am . . . as Tamar is like hers."

Lady Charlotte frowned. "A superficial likeness," she said, "nothing more. Caroline never enjoyed good health." She paused. "You look healthy enough. The Curles are a hardy lot. That's all to the good."

"Why," thought Lucilla, "she thinks of us as fillies up for sale. I wonder, will she desire to inspect our teeth?" The idea made her smile, and she saw her godmother narrow her eyes and compress her lips.

At that moment the butler appeared with wine and a dish of macaroons for the travellers. Lady Charlotte gestured to the two girls to sit down and at once turned her back on them and fell into conversation with Lord Everley. She cited the routs, assemblies and balls to which she proposed to take Lucilla and Tamar, and the people to whom they must be presented. (The name of his Majesty King George IV topped that list, though it seemed indeed to count for less than certain others.)

Lucilla quickly perceived that neither she nor Tamar, nor even Mrs Gray who sat ignored in a corner, was to be consulted about the programme for the Season. Everything was to be arranged for them, and their preferences were of no account whatsoever. Miss Pelham and Miss Curle were in London for the sole purpose of receiving Society's stamp of approval, and they must parade themselves in whichever ring they might best display their paces to the ton.

103

Tamar seemed to accept this high-handed treatment without demur. She sat quietly on the sofa, lost in a day-dream, her fingers idly twisting the fringe of her shawl. Perhaps, being better-acquainted with her grandmother than was Lucilla, she knew that argument would be swiftly quashed.

No one looking at Lady Charlotte's face could doubt her sharp intelligence or her formidable strength of will. This was a woman accustomed to getting her own way, even if that meant riding roughshod over the wishes of others.

Lucilla, who had been reared to fend for herself, was aware of a growing resentment. "For what is the use," she asked herself, "of escaping from Caribbean pirates and Mexican cut-throats, if one is then to be tyrannized by one's own relations?"

Such milk-and-water submission might do for a girl fresh from the schoolroom, but it was not to be tolerated by the daughter of Sidney and Elizabeth Pelham!

At five o'clock the discussion was brought to an end by the arrival of Francis Warsop and Adrian. Adrian entered first, and was received by his grandmother with a great deal more warmth than she had shown his sister or cousin. Lady Charlotte patted his cheek, remarked how he'd grown, and told him that she had had all his papa's books brought down from the attic and placed in his room. "You may browse to your heart's content," she said, "and what's more, I've had the piano tuned this very week. It awaits your touch, dear boy. We all look forward to hearing you perform, very soon."

Adrian murmured some vague reply. He was looking pale and strained, and Lucilla wondered if he'd been subject to another of Francis's neck-or-nothing dashes.

Francis himself now entered and made his bow to the company. He dropped a careless kiss on Lady Charlotte's brow and said, "Accept my apologies, Aunt, for being late. We stopped off at the Burning Babe in Highgate, to see a mill. The Highgate Battler against Flash Fred, but it all came to nought. Poor Fred was run down by a brewer's dray last night. Killed stone dead, poor fellow. So Adrian and I sank a flagon or two and came straight here."

The glitter in Francis's green eyes, and the flush on his face, suggested that he'd consumed more than one or two flagons, but Lady Charlotte accepted his excuses calmly, merely ordering him to forget his nonsensical prize-fighters, and go and talk to Tamar.

Francis meekly crossed the room to sit beside Tamar. He talked to her charmingly for some fifteen minutes, invited her to drive out with him the following afternoon, and then rose to take his leave.

"Can't keep my cattle standing in this east wind," he said. "Tamar, I shall see you tomorrow at three . . . and Lucilla too, of course, if she wishes to accompany us? Adrian, we'll make that visit to Cribb's Parlour within a day or so, eh? Aunt Charlotte, Mrs Gray, your most obedient. Papa, do you mean to dine at home tonight?"

"Yes, yes," said Lord Everley, waving an impatient hand, "I'll be along directly. Be off with you, now."

Francis departed. Lady Charlotte said briskly, "Mrs Gray, you and your young folk will want to refresh yourselves after your journey. Dinner will be at seven. Afterwards we will all enjoy a comfortable cose, and discuss the excitements in store. If you will ring the bell, there beside you, Mrs Talbot will show you to your bedchambers. Pray ask her for anything you may require."

As they followed the housekeeper up the stairway, Lucilla hung back to put an arm round Adrian's shoulders.

"Are you quite well?" she asked. "You look a bit peely-waley."

"I'm all right." He hesitated, then said in a low voice, "Francis lied. It wasn't a prize-fight he stopped for, it was dogs. Bull-terriers, matched two by two. I watched one poor brute torn to shreds, then I told Francis it was the most bestial and disgusting thing I ever saw, and I'd not watch any more."

"I thought dog-fighting was illegal?"

"It is, and so I told Francis. I said if he didn't leave immediately I'd report the matter to the authorities. Indeed, I think I shall do so anyway."

"Bravo!" said Lucilla. "Francis must have been bosky to attend such an exhibition."

Adrian made no reply. As they reached the top corridor he said, in an elaborately matter-of-fact tone, "Did you know that

Shelley and his wife Harriet were married in St George's Hanover Square, just around the corner from here? I mean to go and see his signature in the register. It must be truly uplifting to stand in the place where genius once trod."

"A great deal more uplifting," agreed Lucilla, "than paying good money to see a dog-fight."

XV

As soon as the visitors had left the drawing-room, Charlotte Brampton turned to her brother who was engaged in refilling his wine-glass.

"Well, Henry," she demanded, "how did things go at Ringwood?"

Lord Everley came back to his chair. "Oh, tol lol, you know," he said. "Sholto ain't up to the mark, these days. Dear fellow's aged a great deal since last we met."

His sister cast him an impatient glance. "We're none of us getting any younger. But the settlements? Was everything agreed?"

"Agreed, sealed and signed. Generous terms, too. Sholto was never one to bite on a shillin'."

"When is the betrothal to be announced?"

"On Tamar's seventeenth birthday." Lord Everley sounded defensive, and with reason, for Lady Charlotte wheeled on him with a look of extreme annoyance.

"Her birthday is not until September. That's five months away! How came you to forget that?"

"Didn't forget," said his lordship. "Sholto made it plain from the start there was to be no early announcement. Wants the child to try her wings a little before she marries."

"Her wings," said Lady Charlotte grimly, "may carry her straight to some other nest, the Fromes' for example. I gather that Linslade and his brother were at Ringwood when you arrived?"

"Who told you that?"

"Jason Cleve very properly wrote to warn me of the Frome presence."

"Warn? What d'ye mean, warn? No harm in Linslade. Very decent fellow, behaved just as he ought. Showed real concern about Sholto's accidents."

"What accidents?" said Lady Charlotte sharply.

"Didn't you know? Thought Cleve must have mentioned 'em, since he's been so busy!" Seeing a dangerous glint in his sister's eye, Lord Everley went on, "Someone's been persecutin' poor Sholto in the most wicked way. Sent him poisoned sweetmeats. Tried to shoot him. Sabotaged the bridge he crosses every day. Linslade thought the tontine might be the cause of it. Couldn't know he was aimin' his arrows at us, so to speak."

"Don't be so sure. Linslade holds no brief for our family."

"Rubbish, Charlotte. Linslade's a gentleman. Wouldn't dream of offerin' us a deliberate insult. No, no, he spoke from well-meanin' ignorance. Francis soon put the record straight for him."

"And, of course, Linslade made you an apology?"

"Well, no, why should he? I don't expect a man to apologize for his good intentions. I like Linslade. Fine sportsman. Air of distinction. At home to a peg in any company, and not a malicious bone in his body, which is more than can be said for Mister Cleve."

"There's no need to recite his virtues to me, Henry. I'm well aware that Linslade represents one of the greatest prizes in the marriage mart! He has a title, wealth, wit, and the family charm that seems to have befuddled your poor mind! In short, he's precisely the sort of man who might captivate an impressionable young girl like Tamar. Surely you can see that he could destroy all our plans?"

Lord Everley looked taken aback, but made a quick recover. "Balderdash," he said. "Linslade's no cradle-snatcher."

"And Francis is, I suppose? He's several years older than Linslade."

"No, dash it, the circumstances ain't the same."

"They seem so, to me."

"Well, take my word for it, Linslade made no move to fix his interest with Tamar. For my money, he preferred Lucilla. The two of 'em got on like a house afire, accordin' to Sholto. Fine girl, Lucilla, mettlesome piece, full of fun and gig."

"I shall take very good care," said Lady Charlotte through her teeth, "that Linslade doesn't come near either of our girls. I shall warn them both what sort of man he is, and instruct them to have nothing to do with him. And you, Henry, will kindly remember that Tamar is an heiress, a very pretty one, with an excellent lineage and a handsome dowry. She's bound to receive a number of flattering offers unless we announce without delay that she's engaged to marry Francis."

"I've told you, we can't announce it. Gave my word to Sholto that not a whisper would be breathed until her birthday, so don't imagine you can put it about, because I won't stand for it."

Lady Charlotte stifled the angry protest that sprang to her lips. Her brother was easy-going and indolent to a fault, but on one point he was resolute. He would not break his given word. No public announcement of the betrothal could be made. Of course, if Francis was seen to be Tamar's constant and chosen companion, then the ton might draw the obvious conclusions; but it wouldn't do to offend Sholto Curle. If his dictum were ignored, he was quite capable of forbidding the banns.

She thought she knew why he had imposed this waiting period. Sholto Curle might live far from the fashionable world, but he was no fool, and in matters touching the happiness of his grandchildren he could be maddeningly fussy. No doubt he wished to satisfy himself that Francis was ready to give up his gambling and womanizing, and to live a respectable married life.

"Does Francis understand," she said aloud, "that he's on five months' probation?"

Lord Everley chuckled. "Yes, and he don't like it above half."

"He will like a debtor's prison even less."

"Lord, it won't come to that."

"It will, Henry, I promise you. I instructed Jason to make enquiries into the extent of Francis's debts. I know precisely what the sum is."

"Damme, Cleve had no right to snoop into our affairs."

"He obeyed my instructions. It's I who pay his fees, Henry, not you. Good God, man, it's common gossip that you're at *point non plus.* Your creditors are snapping at your heels. You'll soon have to sell Everley itself."

"Oh come, it's not so bad as all that. I'll turn the corner never fear. All I need is a nudge from Lady Luck. The jade's deserted me these past few months, but that can't last forever, and if the worst comes to the worst, I know I can count on you to . . . "

" . . . do nothing!" Lady Charlotte spoke with icy clarity. "I told you, the last time I stood bail for you, you needn't look to me for help again."

"Blood's thicker than water, Charlotte!"

"It is indeed, and I don't propose to shed one more drop for you or your wastrelly son. You'd best din it into Francis's head that his only hope of keeping from bankruptcy and disgrace is to marry Tamar, and to achieve that, he'll have to mend his ways at once."

Lord Everley's face was a rich purple. He stared at his sister in silence for a moment, then heaved himself to his feet.

"I didn't come here to bandy insults with you," he said. "We'll talk again when you're in a more charitable frame of mind."

"I've forsworn charity," retorted Lady Charlotte.

"In that case," said her brother, mustering what dignity he could, "I will bid you a very good night."

He bowed stiffly and headed for the door. His sister's voice followed him into the hall.

"Don't forget to speak to Francis," she said.

Lord Everley reached his house in Grosvenor Square in a very ill temper. Charlotte had always had the knack of getting under his skin. The fact that she'd had the good fortune to marry money, and had invested it shrewdly, didn't give her the right to preach at those who'd been less lucky. It was unjust that she should live high on the hog, yet carp at him for wishing to do the same.

One had only to look at her house to know she was rolling in pelf, whereas Everley Park — the very home where she'd been bred and raised — was falling to rack and ruin. The Town house wasn't much better. Furniture shabby, cellar well-nigh empty, the duns yapping on the doorstep. It was too bad.

It didn't improve his mood when he found his son and heir lounging in a chair in the library, his legs outstretched to a comfortable fire, and a bottle of vintage claret at his side.

Lord Everley grasped the bottle by its neck and placed it out of Francis's reach.

"You've drunk enough," he said. "Half-seas-over when you came to y'r aunt's home tonight. Put me to the blush!"

Francis grinned lazily. "Aunt didn't mind."

"Ah, that's where you mistake, my lad. She don't think too much of you and your ways. She's had Cleve smousin' around and she knows how badly you're dipped. Says she won't shell out a brass farthing to keep you from the King's Bench. Says if you don't mend your ways, your pretty little bird will find someone better to marry, and land you in the suds."

"Don't fret, Papa. I don't propose to lose Tamar. I know how to handle her, and she's a biddable child, in any case. She'll do as Aunt C. bids her."

"That may be so, but it's not Tamar, or even m'sister, you have to worry about. It's my good friend Sholto Curle. He'll not put up with any nonsense from you."

"Sir Sholto's at Ringwood."

"Aye, but he has friends in London. If he hears that you're gamin', and drabbin', there'll be no betrothal party, I promise you."

"Have no fear. I shall be a model of propriety . . . for five months." Francis's green eyes sparkled. "Word of a gentleman," he said.

Lord Everley was not convinced, and when, after dinner, Francis collected hat and gloves from the hall table, his father watched him with a disapproving eye.

"Where are you goin'?" he demanded.

"White's. Why don't you come with me?"

"You keep away from the tables, Francis! Haven't I made it plain enough? There's to be no more gamblin'."

Francis shrugged. "Dear sir, I have nothing left to gamble with; but surely an evening of improving conversation with old friends can't come amiss?"

"Your friends," said his lordship bitterly, "are all hellbent for Tyburn! Stay away from them, Francis."

Francis smiled. "Goodnight, Papa. Pleasant dreams."

He clapped his curly-brimmed hat on to his head and sauntered down the steps to the square; there he hailed a passing hackney-chariot and directed the driver to convey him to an address in Edgware Road.

He planned to spend the next few hours with an Irish widow of his acquaintance. Mrs Brody was a woman of many talents, and, having been left in comfortable circumstances by the late Mr Phineas Brody, she did not demand immediate payment for favours granted.

XVI

HOWEVER MUCH LUCILLA and her godmama might differ in their attitudes towards the forthcoming Season, they were at one in their determination to appear suitably dressed.

The morning after the Ringwood ladies reached London, Lady Charlotte swept them off to keep an appointment she had made with Madame Bonamie of Albemarle Street.

Madame was not, as Lucilla at first feared, Lady Charlotte's own modiste, but one much in favour with the younger set of fashionables. Her establishment — one could not demean it with the title "Shop" — was a small but charming house with a capacious stable-yard where customers were permitted to leave their carriages.

Madame herself was Parisienne to the core: hard-headed and shrewd in matters of money, but with a flair for line, colour and cut that marked her a true couturière. In person she was small and thin, with black hair severely confined in a smooth chignon. Having no pretensions to beauty, she contented herself with being *jolie laide*. Her preference was for black gowns of discreet but elegant style and, though her manner was always deferential, she left her clients in no doubt that in matters of fashion they would be foolish to contradict her.

Having greeted Lady Charlotte and her party, she led them to a pleasant morning-room and offered them sherry, ratafia and sweet biscuits. She did not sit down but waited quietly, with clasped hands, while Lady Charlotte enumerated the items she proposed to purchase for her protégées.

It was a formidable list, beginning with Court Dresses for the Presentation, and continuing through gowns for morning-, afternoon- and evening-wear, to cloaks, shawls, pelisses, boas, gloves, parasols, reticules, and every sort of undergarment. On the subject of bonnets, slippers and boots, her ladyship expressed reservations. She rather thought that these must be acquired elsewhere, but possibly Madame Bonamie could advise them what to look for, and where?

Madame murmured that that would be a pleasure. Her sharp eyes were studying the two girls with dispassionate care, as if she already knew to a T what were their measurements, and was envisaging the styles and colours that would best become them. Lucilla, conscious that she was in the hands of an artist, began to enjoy herself.

A little time was spent on examining a folio of sketches of gigantic damsels in Court dress. That choice settled, Madame conducted them to a large salon, where the pale gold carpets and white-brocaded walls formed the perfect backdrop for a display of Madame's creations.

The ladies disposed themselves in comfortable chairs. Madame raised an imperious hand, and a troop of assistants fetched gown after gown from the cupboards at the far end of the room.

First to be shown were a number of morning-dresses; simple muslins and gauzes in delicate pastel shades, with high waists and small puffed sleeves. Lady Charlotte nodded approvingly, saying they were just what best suited a young girl. Tamar, encouraged by her grandmama, tried on first one and then another, professing herself quite unable to decide which she liked best.

Madame came to her aid. "If one may suggest," she murmured, "the pink, the lilac, and the green sprigged are perfect for Mademoiselle, and she may add to them later, when she knows more precisely what she needs. It is a mistake to buy too much, too soon."

This exemplary restraint impressed Lady Charlotte favourably, as it was meant to do, and she turned to Lucilla with an indulgent smile. "And now, my dear, what is your choice? The azure is charming. Do try it on."

Lucilla did as she was asked, but without enthusiasm. As she stood contemplating her reflection in the pier-glass, Madame came to stand behind her and, under cover of arranging a flounce, said in a low voice, "What is it that Mademoiselle Pelham has in mind?"

Lucilla glanced up to meet the sharp black gaze. "Something less commonplace," she said promptly.

Madame, far from being affronted by this description of her work, nodded briskly. "*Vous avez raison*," she said. "The mode is changing. Not dramatically, of course, but one sees where things will go. The sleeves larger, the waistline lower." She produced a sketching block and pencil from the table at her side and began to draw swiftly. "You see . . . the present silhouette is . . . so . . . straight and confined. The new silhouette is . . . so . . . as if one were to employ two triangles, the narrow ends at the waistline and the broad at shoulder and hem. It is a line that would suit Mademoiselle to perfection!"

Lady Charlotte, sensing a conspiracy in the making, leaned forward.

"What is that, Madame? What are you suggesting?"

Madame turned with a smile. "That the dresses I have this week from Paris will be *ravissantes* for Miss Pelham."

"Paris?" Lady Charlotte's tone implied that Paris was synonymous with Sodom and Gomorrah. "I think we need not look to foreign products, Madame! In my view, a young female appears her best in simple English styles. I desire nothing outré or immodest for my girls."

"It stands to reason one does not have such wares to offer," said Madame coldly. "However, one must accept the fact that Mademoiselle Pelham is no ingénue. What is right for Mademoiselle Curle is not right for a young lady of twenty. There is also the red hair, which requires careful thought. If your ladyship will but permit me to show you what I have in mind . . .?"

Rather grudgingly, Lady Charlotte nodded. Madame murmured instructions to an assistant, and within minutes the insipid blue muslin had been replaced by a gown of pale jonquil crêpe, cut with great simplicity, the full sleeves formed of overlapping petals lined with matching satin, and the skirt stiffened at the hemline with a narrow band of the same material.

Lady Charlotte, eyeing this confection, was forced to admit that it became Lucilla very well. She then demanded to know its price and, on being told, said at once that it was by far too expensive and could not be considered.

"Dear Aunt," said Lucilla, "Grandfather was most insistent that the charge for clothes for Tamar and me was not to fall on your shoulders."

"That is not to say," retorted Lady Charlotte, "that he would wish you to waste his money merely to gratify your vanity, Lucilla."

Lucilla nodded agreement. "That is perfectly true, Aunt, which is why it will be far better if I settle the accounts myself. I have a comfortable competence, you know, and would much prefer to bear some of the costs of my Come-out myself."

Lady Charlotte said repressively that people of quality would think it very odd for a young girl to be running up accounts all over Town; but Lucilla found an unexpected ally in Mrs Gray, who said quietly that dear Sir Sholto had enjoined her most strictly to see that Tamar and Lucilla were well turned-out in every respect. "He said that he wished *his* girls to be able to hold their own in the best company, and that expense was not to be a consideration. Moreover, I can't see what objection there can be to Lucilla's spending some of her own money. She's accustomed to do so, and can be relied upon not to overstep the mark. As to choosing what is appropriate and in good taste, I do think, dear ma'am, that we may depend upon Mme Bonamie to advise us in that regard."

This served as a gentle reminder to Lady Charlotte that Mrs Gray was no mere employee in the Curle household, but Sir Sholto's blood relation. Lady Charlotte, remarking that if Lucilla wished to flaunt herself as a female with more money than sense she could not prevent it, turned her full attention to Tamar.

Lucilla then selected, as well as the jonquil crêpe, a number of other morning-dresses; a walking ensemble in Lovat green grosgrain with a matching Paisley shawl; a pelisse in velvet that admirably set off the copper of her hair; two short spencer-jackets, one of taffeta and the other of embroidered muslin; an enchanting afternoon-gown of lilac cambric, the seams piped in darker satin; three silk dresses, a straw-coloured, a deep gold, and a soft apricot; and several exquisite and very costly evening-gowns. Lucilla could not decide which of these last delighted her most: the rose-doré with overdress of lace, fastened down the front with buttons of rose-quartz; the deep blue satin trimmed with appliqué; or the balldress of silk gauze, embroidered round the hem with motifs of pale green leaves, the sleeves puffed and finished with shallow falls of lace.

Mrs Gray became infected with the excitement and boldly ordered two evening toilettes, and Lucilla insisted on presenting her with a tippet of maribou feathers, snow white and long enough to reach the ground, with a matching muff lined with silk.

She left Mrs Gray turning this way and that before the looking-glass, and sought a quiet word with Madame Bonamie.

"Can you make me a riding-habit?" she enquired.

"But of course. I will show you some styles . . . "

"No," said Lucilla. "I know precisely what I want." She described this in some detail and, as she talked, Madame sketched rapidly on her drawing-block.

"Like this?" she said.

Lucilla studied the drawing.

"Dare I?" she said.

Madame spread her hands. "Why not? Of course, for *une bourgeoise*, such an ensemble would be impossible. One would be reminded of an equestrienne at Astley's Amphitheatre. But created by Bonamie, and worn by Mademoiselle Pelham, it will be, I promise you, a clap of thunder!"

"What material, and colour?" said Lucilla.

"Broadcloth, *teint de miel*," answered Madame.

"When will it be ready?"

Madame, ruthlessly dismissing the prior claims of a dozen clients, said that the first fitting could be in two days' time. After then, one would have to see, but not later than a week, all told.

It was now well past noon, and Lady Charlotte expressed

herself exhausted. She directed Madame to have all the purchases delivered to Curzon Street without delay; ascertained that she should take Lucilla and Tamar to Dubois et Cie for bonnets, and to Mr Garrett for footwear; and led her party off in triumph to the waiting carriage.

As the door closed after them, Madame summoned her assistants and said that in future she would herself deal with all requests from Lady Charlotte's household. For, as she later explained to her good friend Mme Dubois, Lady Charlotte's protegées represented a veritable goldmine which one must exploit to the full.

"Mademoiselle Curle," she said, "is nothing extraordinary. Pretty enough, but one may find a thousand pretty girls among the ton. But the other — the Mademoiselle Pelham — in her one recognizes *une originale*! She, I predict, will take the beau monde by storm. One week from now, her acquaintance will be entreating her to say who is her costumière, and who creates her bonnets. We must be sure, *ma chère Mathilde*, that it is the names of Bonamie and Dubois that rise to her lips."

When Mr Francis Warsop presented himself in Curzon Street that afternoon, to take his cousins driving, there was nothing in his appearance to suggest that the Everley purse was strained. His dark blue coat was made in the newest style, the sleeves full at the shoulder and the fronts lightly padded to suggest the "military chest". His pale buff pantaloons and gleaming Hessians did him and his valet credit.

He arrived in an open carriage drawn by his matched greys. Its side panel bore the Everley crest, and the coachman and groom were in the Everley livery. As Francis had that morning informed his papa, "Nothing will fetch the bailiffs in quicker than for us to appear short of the ready. Once they know the dibs ain't in tune, we're done for."

Miss Pelham and Miss Curle had decided against putting on new gowns, Lucilla holding that it would quite ruin the effect of a Bonamie creation to top it off with a bonnet bought at Mr Hopkins's Emporium in Oxford.

Adrian surprised them by electing to accompany them on the drive. He had that morning acquired a *Guide to London*, and as they travelled along Curzon Street, he regaled them with a great many unsolicited facts.

Hyde Park, he said, covered an area of three hundred and sixty-one acres, and had belonged to the monks of Westminster from the time of the Conquest until the Dissolution, when Henry VIII filched it from them and turned it into a royal hunting-ground. Deer, announced Adrian, had been hunted there until the middle of the last century, and might still be seen in secluded thickets. Charles I had caused a circular drive and race-course to be built, which had been popular with the smarts of his day. Under William and Mary, the roads across the park became infested by footpads, duellists, and other undesirables, and good order was only restored under the Georges.

This recital was accorded less than full attention by Adrian's companions, for Francis was advising his coachman how to bring the team through heavy traffic, and the girls were more interested in the present than in the past. They pricked up their ears, though, when Adrian told them that the red brick mansion at the end of Park Lane was Apsley House, built by the Adam brothers and at present the home of the Duke of Wellington. Here the Waterloo Banquet was held each year, in honour of the final defeat of the monster Bonaparte.

For Tamar, whose father had died a hero's death on the field of Waterloo, this was a poignant moment, and her cup overflowed when, just as the carriage turned westward past the gates of Apsley House, the Duke himself appeared, accompanied by another gentleman.

Tamar, forgetting all decorum in her excitement, turned round in her seat with a cry; and the Duke, who had always had an eye for a pretty face, gave her a smile and a cheerful nod of the head.

Francis was moved to say, in a rather snubbing tone, that Old Douro's reputation as a general was much over-rated.

"Most of his victories were won against vastly inferior adversaries," he said, "and though he won Waterloo, it was at the cost of thousands of lives."

Tamar grew quite pink with annoyance. "The people who belittle the Duke," she said, "do so out of envy. At Waterloo he trounced Napoleon, and no one can say that he is an inferior adversary. As to the cost in lives, my papa gave his, and I don't think he, or . . . or any of us . . . would say he died in vain!"

Francis, realizing that he had made a major faux pas, set himself to charm Tamar back to good humour. Adrian remained engrossed in his guidebook. Only Lucilla noticed that the gentleman strolling at the Iron Duke's side was none other than that arrogant and meddlesome creature, the Earl of Linslade.

While the young people were enjoying their drive, Lady Charlotte, at home, was in close conclave with Mr Jason Cleve.

They sat in the small boudoir her ladyship reserved to her own use, and a stranger observing them might have been amazed to see how indulgently her ladyship treated her guest. Her usual hectoring manner had vanished, and she addressed Mr Cleve as an intimate, even a confederate. Cleve, for his part, was very much at his ease, sitting with legs outstretched and weskit unbuttoned as he explained to her the terms of Tamar's marriage settlement.

"If Francis can pull it off," he said, "he'll be in clover. It's not just the girl's dowry one must consider. She'll come into her father's legacy when she's twenty-one, and a good deal more besides when Sholto Curle sticks his spoon in the wall."

Lady Charlotte frowned. "With regard to that," she said, "Henry told me some rigmarole about attacks against Sholto. Humdudgeon, I told him. Henry could never distinguish fact from fiction."

"The attacks, my dear, are fact, but it's all been placed in the hands of the Law. I doubt we'll hear of any further incidents."

"According to Henry, Linslade tried to suggest that the tontine was at the root of it."

"He did, yes. Your brother laughed it off."

"Did Francis?"

"No. Francis holds the Fromes in detestation. He bandied words with Linslade, but I was able to intervene in time to prevent a scene. No harm was done."

"Linslade should be called to account for uttering such a slander."

"He made no direct accusation that I'm aware. Lord Everley took no offence, so why should you?"

"I regard it as an intolerable impertinence!"

"And best forgotten. Come, Charlotte, you'll gain nothing by setting yourself up against the Fromes. For one thing, Sir Sholto took a great shine to 'em and won't hear a word against 'em. For another, they have a good deal of pull. Quarrel with Linslade, and you'll find yourself in Queer Street. My advice to you is, leave well enough alone."

He leaned forward to pick up his sherry-glass from the table at his side, and sipped delicately. After a moment, he said, "I must tell you, ma'am, that I've seen a sharp decline in your brother's health over the past few weeks."

Charlotte smiled. "Henry said the same of Sir Sholto."

"That's as may be, but during the journey to Swallowford, and our dealings there, I was able to observe Lord Everley at close quarters. His right hand is very tremulous. He often has difficulty in catching his breath, and he suffers from alarming lapses of memory. You should persuade him to visit his doctor."

"No doctor is ever going to persuade Henry to give up his gambling, his guzzling, or his brandy."

Mr Cleve gave an enigmatic shrug, and Lady Charlotte said sharply, "What is it Jason? What's on your mind?"

He gave her a bland smile. "Why, my dear, I was thinking that you're set fair to outlive both your brother and Sholto Curle."

"And inherit the tontine, is that your meaning?" She stared at him with narrowed eyes. "If I do, what's it to you?"

Mr Cleve tilted his head. "Naturally, as your man of business, I'd be glad to see your fortune augmented; but as your friend I consider the money of no importance. It's you I value." He raised his glass in a manner half-gallant, half-mocking. "I drink, my dearest Charlotte, to your continued good health."

The Duke of Wellington had invited Lord Linslade to Apsley House in order to discuss with him certain confidential matters:

questions to which answers might not be given by high officials of the Crown. As he was due to keep an appointment at White's Club in St James's Street, the two men strolled together along Piccadilly, talking as they went. Their topic was the presence in England of the disgraced Queen Caroline. The Duke was concerned that this might cause public rioting during the forthcoming coronation ceremonies of King George IV.

"The vulgar mob," said the Duke, "has an unaccountable fondness for Her Majesty . . . not as great as during her trial, perhaps, but strong enough to make them resent her exclusion from the Abbey. Captain Spencer has told me that Lady Sarah Lyttelton — you know what long ears she has — is convinced there'll be some uproar. There've already been stones thrown, and windows smashed, and the Queen takes care to keep emotions high . . . jaunts about Town in a shabby post-chaise drawn by hacks, as if she hasn't a penny to her name . . . and lives in the scruffiest house imaginable, to show how she's kept from her rightful place in the Palace. Temple says the hucksters are having difficulty selling seats in the stands along the processional route because people fear bloodshed. Poppycock, I told him, London's full of troops, we shall check any insurgency before it starts."

"Hardly what one would wish, sir, to use armed force against our own subjects?"

The Duke frowned. "I know Castlereagh's views on that well enough, my lord. The fact remains, we can't allow public violence. Once give the mob its head, and we shall end up forfeiting ours!"

The Earl was silent. It was scarcely more than a year since the Cato Street conspirators had plotted to murder the Cabinet and cause an insurrection. The plan had been scotched, and five of the guilty hanged, but there was still a simmering of unrest in London.

"I don't believe," he said at length, "that we have much to fear from Englishmen, provided we address the wrongs that afflict them."

The Duke grunted. "Bread and circuses," he said. "Well, we'll give 'em those." They crossed the street to the south side, and he said with an abrupt change of subject, "What of the

Bourbons? Will they speak on the Queen's behalf? One hears rumours."

The Earl shook his head. "I doubt if any of the foreign courts will take her part," he said. "Her stock's fallen very low because of her freakish antics."

"Damned pack of vulgarians," muttered the Duke; though whether he referred to the Bourbons, or to England's Royal House, was not entirely clear.

XVII

ONE EVENING A week later, Alex chanced to drop in at Tom Cribb's Parlour in Panton Street, where the bucks of the Town and the lads of The Fancy gathered to sink a quart and blow a cloud.

He had secured a tankard of ale and was carrying it to a corner when he heard his name called, and looked round to see a tall, fair-headed gentleman beckoning. Alex hurried across the taproom with hand outstretched.

"Den," he exclaimed, "by all that's wonderful. What are you doing here? I thought you were still in Vienna."

Captain Denby Shepstone pulled out the chair next to his and signed to Alex to sit down.

"Sold out," he said. "Devilish dull, y'know, the peacetime Army. Decided to become a farmer, instead."

Alex knew that this decision, though lightly voiced, must have cost the Captain much soul-searching. Everything about him — his military-style frock-coat and high leather stock, his fine curling moustachios, and the old sabre scar on his right cheekbone — proclaimed the professional soldier. Like his father and grandfather before him, Denby Shepstone had served his country with distinction. Only the most pressing of reasons could have made him choose to quit the Army.

"Den," Alex said, "you know if there's anything I can do . . . "

The Captain shook his head. "Nothing at all, Alex. Truth is, m'father's frail as a feather, these days, and Mama worries herself to shreds about him. Not that they've put any pressure on me to sell out, but . . . well . . . I know my place is at home, runnin' the estate. Made up my mind to it, so we'll say no more about it, if you please."

Alex nodded. His friendship with Den had begun at Harrow and endured ever since. Each knew he could place complete reliance on the other, something not common in a world where ambition and self-seeking were the order of the day.

Over the course of the next hour, Alex recounted the events surrounding his return to Foxfare: Nick's illness, the decision to move him to Evesham, and the extraordinary sojourn at Sholto Curle's home. When he spoke of the attacks on the old man, Captain Shepstone looked grave.

"Nasty business," he said. "If you ask me, Warsop's responsible. Twister, if ever I knew one. Beats me how any man could wish to see his grand-daughter leg-shackled to such a shabster. Surely the chit could do better for herself? Or is she an antidote? Buck teeth and a squint?"

"No, no, she's quite a beauty." Alex hesitated, then said, "Just for your ears, Den, I imagine Sir Sholto feels the odds are against her. Her mama was prone to melancholy and took her own life. Perhaps the old man feels Warsop will accept what others may jib at."

"Lord," said the Captain cheerfully, "most of the folk I know are dicked in the nob, and I still like 'em."

"If that's your preference, come home to dinner. My family arrived in Town this afternoon, and the place is a madhouse, but I can offer you some of my father's burgundy."

"Lead on," said the Captain, rising to his feet. "For that burgundy, I'd engage to go with you to Bedlam itself."

Although the Foxfare party had reached Frome House soon after three o'clock, it could not be said that they were settled in. The fourgon that had carried their baggage still stood in the yard, and a pile of valises, bandboxes and mantua-cases almost entirely blocked the front hall.

Lord Linslade and Captain Shepstone, entering the house from Berkeley Square, found themselves in the midst of a battle between the butler, Bungay, and Lady Linslade's dresser, Miss Perritt. The latter was demanding that the valise at the very bottom of the pile be instantly extricated as it contained her La'ship's stock of Godbold's Vegetable Balsam, the only thing that could be relied upon to soothe her palpitations.

Bungay, meanwhile, was insisting that all the medicines had been packed as they should be in the travelling medicine-chest, which had already been carried upstairs.

Both protagonists appealed to his lordship for support, but luckily, before he could speak, the Honourable Mrs George Frome appeared at the head of the stairway, and announced in her booming voice that everyone could stop buzzing around like flies in a tar-barrel as Lady Linslade had been prevailed upon to swallow a dose of Velmo's Syrup, and no longer required the Balsam.

The Earl took Captain Shepstone by the elbow and steered him towards the library, which lay at the back of the house; but before they could reach sanctuary, doors flew open to the left and right of them, revealing on the one side Miss Emily Frome, in a great panic because (so the Captain understood her to say) the pebble was under the settle; while on the other side stood George Frome, red-faced and furious, demanding that Alex join him at once in the drawing-room.

Assessing the field at a glance, the Captain offered his arm to Miss Emily and retired in good order to the morning-room. Alex followed his brother into the salon.

"Well, George," he said pleasantly, "what is the matter?"

George swept his arm in a wide gesture. "Look about you," he commanded. "Look about you and you will see. Where is the furniture, I'd like to know? Where's it gone, eh? What have you done with it?"

The Earl's bemused gaze slid from the Chippendale suite to the two rosewood settees with brocaded seats, took in the dropside table, the fine German pianoforte, and the matching cabinets full of Meissen china. He was about to say that everything seemed to be in place when light dawned.

"Ah, you mean the Egyptian stuff?" he said. "That was sold months ago . . . soon after I returned from Rome, in fact."

"Why?" shouted George, fairly dancing with rage. "I demand to know why?"

"Well," said Alex patiently, "for one thing it was purgatory to sit on, and for another, it was an eyesore. You may like sofas with crocodile feet, George, but I tell you frankly, every time I went near one of 'em, I'd the feeling my leg was about to be snapped off. I told Ross to sell the lot. They fetched a fair price."

"The price," said George untruthfully, "does not interest me. I ask myself how you could have brought yourself to sell objects which were our dear mother's pride and joy."

"Oh, come," Alex said, "Mama bought the suite in a fit of insanity because she wished to follow the Regent's lead. I don't know how many times she's said it was a wretched mistake and begged me to sell it."

"You may say so, but I promise you your actions have quite overset her. She's at this moment laid down on her bed and feeling very low, very low indeed."

"Then I'd best go and cheer her up." Alex gave George a friendly clap on the shoulder. "I've brought Denby Shepstone to dine with us. Be a good fellow and see he's given something to fortify his nerves. I'll be down again directly."

He went upstairs. George made a half-hearted attempt to find Captain Shepstone and failed, for the good reason that the Captain was now lying flat on his back on the morning-room floor, with his head thrust under an oak settle. Beside him knelt Miss Emily Frome, nervously wringing her hands.

"Can you see him?" she asked. "He's white, with brown ears."

"He ain't white now," returned the Captain. "I see him, though. Little beggar's right at the back upside down."

"He's stuck fast," Emily mourned. "I tried to pull him out, but I could only catch hold of his ears, and he shrieked so!"

"Got his paws jammed against the underside of the seat," said Denby, "and in a fine old panic, by the look of him. What's his name?"

"Pebble," Emily answered. At the sound of her voice, the trapped terrier uttered a heartrending whine and tried to struggle towards her, but only succeeded in wedging himself more tightly in his prison.

"Leave him to me," the Captain said. "You go and sit quietly in that chair, there's a good girl."

Miss Frome did as she was bid, and the Captain began to talk softly to the victim.

"Pebble," he said, "you are making a great cake of yourself. There's no need for this hysteria. I am going to get you out, do you see? Keep that thought in the forefront of your mind. Tell yourself that salvation is as sure as that night follows day."

Pebble, recognizing the firm authority of this new voice, lay still and began to breathe more quietly. In a short while the Captain was able to reach out and stroke the little dog's head, and then to turn him on his side and draw him to safety.

Pebble at once threw himself into a series of leaps, cavorts and caracoles expressive of his gratitude to his saviour.

"Thank you," Emily said, as the Captain got to his feet, "you are so very kind! He saw a rat . . . at least, he thought he did . . . he is always hoping to see one . . . "

" . . . and the wish was father to the thought." Captain Shepstone smiled, holding out his hand. "Perhaps, ma'am, I may introduce myself. I'm . . . "

"Denby Shepstone," Emily said. "The last time we met, you gave me a jarful of tadpoles. How could I ever forget the giver of such a handsome gift?"

The Captain dimly recalled a chubby six-year-old, missing her front teeth, who had trotted at her elder brothers' heels throughout a long summer holiday at Foxfare. She'd grown, he thought, into a handsome girl; a trifle on the tall side, but with an excellent figure, as well as the warm Frome smile and engaging manner.

"You must be Miss Emily," he said.

She nodded. "The same. Goodness, your coat is quite ruined, you're dust to the shoulder. I should have called a footman to help me, but the fact is, Pebble dislikes men in livery. He'd have set up a roar, and that would have brought George down on us."

"George, I collect, is anti-Pebble?"

"Well, he didn't wish me to bring him to Town with me, but I couldn't leave him at Foxfare. He was the runt of the litter you know, and I hand-fed him for weeks. Now he depends on me overmuch. If I leave him for more than a few days, he pines, and won't eat."

The runt, who was now rolling on his back on the hearth-rug, gave the Captain a knowing grin, as if to say that despite his tender years, he knew very well how to manage a woman.

"Give me your coat," said Emily, "and Bungay will see that it's brushed. I'm glad you're staying for dinner. The family behaves much better when there's company. And, if you please, don't speak of the rat to George because he'll be horridly righteous and say 'I told you so', and of all phrases, I think that one is the most detestable."

When the Earl entered his mama's bedchamber, he was not immediately able to see her, for the curtains were close-drawn, and the room in semi-darkness.

After a moment he discerned the frail figure reclining on the chaise longue near the windows, and moved cautiously towards it.

"Mama? Are you awake?"

The figure stirred slightly.

"Alex, my son, is that you?"

"It is indeed." He found her hand and raised it to his lips, then bent to kiss her forehead. "May I draw these curtains back? I should like to see your face!"

Lady Linslade lifted a languid hand in assent, and Alex pushed aside the heavy velvet drapes, allowing light to fall across the chaise longue.

He saw that his mama, prostrated though she might be, had found the strength to put off her travelling clothes and to don a very fetching dressing-gown of pale blue silk trimmed with swansdown.

"You look charmingly," Alex told her as he sat down on the nearest chair. "Did you find the journey very fatiguing?"

"It is not the journey that has brought me so low," said Lady Linslade in failing accents, "but your lack of filial consideration. How could you do such a thing, Alex?"

He shook his head, smiling. "My dear, I apologize for not having consulted you, but how was I to know you'd formed a passion for the Egyptian suite? I thought you detested it."

"I do not speak of that," declared her ladyship. "Material

possessions are nothing to me. No, it is what Nicholas had to tell me, this afternoon . . . "

"Nick was here? That's capital. How is he?"

"Like you, he is devoid of all proper feeling! Not only did he inform me that he prefers to reside with his grandmother in Grosvenor Street, he went on to report that you've been the guests of Sholto Curle! You have been living cheek by jowl with a passel of Everleys!"

"Well, not quite," murmured Alex. His mother ignored him.

"It is beyond my understanding, Alex, that you could consent to remain under the same roof as that set of reprobates. When I recall how Francis Warsop betrayed my beloved Arabella, and brought shame on us all . . . oh, it's too bad of you! Too bad!"

"My dear Mama, I had no choice in the matter. Nick was ill, and we were caught in a snowstorm. I promise you, the visit passed off without any unseemly incident." As he spoke, Alex was wondering if Nick had been fool enough to mention the assaults on their host, but he quickly realized that his mother's thoughts had taken quite another direction.

"According to Nicholas," she said, "there were Girls."

"Yes. Sholto Curle's two grand-daughters, Miss Pelham and Miss Curle."

"I don't wish to hear their names." Her ladyship shuddered delicately. "Nicholas described them as regular smashers. He said you had undertaken to help them make their way in Society. You must be out of your mind."

"Nick exaggerates," said Alex easily. "I told Sir Sholto I'd do what I can, but that's not much, you know. Lady Charlotte Brampton has far more influence among the high sticklers than I."

"You know that's not true." Lady Linslade raised herself a little on her pillows. "You are a Nonpareil. The hostesses will do as you ask them. But that is not the point. I regard it as a piece of gross impertinence for an Everley to seek the help of a Frome, and I won't countenance such a thing, not for a single instant."

"I do it for Sir Sholto, Mama, not for the Everleys."

"Don't bandy words with me, pray! Miss Curle has Everley blood, and Miss Pelham has been raised in the same evil nest, taught the same immoral, grasping ways. I've no doubt she will hold by the Everleys through thick and thin."

Alex, remembering Lucilla Pelham's quick defence of Francis Warsop, could not argue the point; but he said calmly, "On the other hand, Miss Pelham and Miss Curle both have Curle blood, and no one can cavil at that."

Lady Linslade pressed a handkerchief to her lips and closed her eyes. "Do not torture me," she implored, "by suggesting you mean to recognize these people. Have you no shame, Alex? No pride in the honour of our name?"

"As to that," said Alex, "Sholto Curle's name is as honourable as ours. I tell you plainly, Mama, I won't act shabby towards a man who gave Nick and me shelter when we needed it, and treated us with the utmost generosity."

"I see," said Lady Linslade, "that you are determined to thwart my wishes, but I trust you won't attempt to foist this pack of adventurers on me! I will never receive the Everleys. Never! The very name is anathema to me, and if any of them so much as sets foot in this house, I vow I shall leave it for ever!"

The Earl was tempted to make a sharp reply to this statement, but kept his temper in check, saying evenly, "Come, Mama, there's really no cause to distress yourself. I'll do what's civil towards Sir Sholto, and no more. Now let's come to pleasanter things. I've brought a friend to dine with us. You remember Denby Shepstone, I expect?"

"Of course I remember him. I'm not yet in my dotage. Though what can have possessed you to bring him to dinner, on our first night in Town, is beyond me. I'm sure there's nothing fit to set on the table."

"On the contrary, Gaston has planned a very handsome repast in honour of your arrival."

"Gaston's idea of what is acceptable, and mine, do not necessarily agree," said Lady Linslade coldly. "Be so good as to inform him, and Bungay, that I shall speak to them downstairs in half an hour from now. And ring for Perritt as you go out."

Lady Linslade turned her face away, and the Earl, seeing that it was useless to reason with her, left the room and went in search of Captain Shepstone.

The following morning Alex strolled round to Grosvenor Street to pay his respects to his grandmother. He found her at home; but Nicholas, she told him, had gone out an hour earlier to visit Montagu House.

"He desires to see the Elgin Marbles and to read some book that's lodged there in the King's Library. I must say, the voyage to Greece has quite settled him in his choice of a career."

Alex smiled. "Yes. I fancy that in a few years' time I'll be preening myself about my brother the famous archeologist."

The Dowager, sensing a certain constraint in her grandson's manner, enquired bluntly how his mama did.

"Well enough," he replied, "but somewhat miffed by our visit to Ringwood."

"That's hardly to be wondered at, you know."

"There's no need to make a Cheltenham tragedy of it. We're bound to come across the Everleys and Curles from time to time. I don't wish to live in their pocket, but I don't mean to snub 'em, either."

He switched the talk to other topics and left, after an hour, saying he was off to Jackson's Saloon for some sparring practice.

The Dowager, watching him stride away along the street, thought it a pity that he didn't box a few ears at home. Was there ever a more thoughtless, tiresome family than his? Take George, endlessly disrupting his brother's plans, carping at trifles, bridling at imagined insults; and Augusta, too greedy and too lazy to concentrate on anything but her next meal; and Elvira, so fretful and vapourish, so ready to drag the household from one melodrama to the next, regardless of the consequences.

While one could sympathize with Elvira's determination to keep the Everleys at a proper distance — particularly as Arabella and John Ruthven would be in London very soon — one saw that she was taking a disastrous line with Alex.

Tolerant he might be, and easy-going to a fault, but he would certainly not submit to being told how to run his life.

One would have to take Elvira aside, and somehow drum it into her head that Alex was near the end of his patience, and that any attempt to dragoon him might have highly undesirable results.

XVIII

THE DOWAGER'S FEARS were realized sooner than she had anticipated. Just three days after her grandson had visited her in Grosvenor Street, the Fromes and Everleys met in circumstances which made it impossible for them to ignore one another.

It was at breakfast that Lady Linslade informed the Earl that she required him to escort her to a party that evening. Alex, who was sorting through a pile of letters, shook his head abstractedly. "I'm sorry, Mama, I'm engaged to drive down to Newmarket with Den. Doubt if we'll be back before midnight. You'd better take George."

"Augusta and I," said George flatly, "are dining with the Onslows."

"Then Nick must stand in for me."

"Nicholas will not do," said Lady Linslade. "It's you I need, Alex, and I don't know why you should try to fob me off in this rude way. You've known for weeks that we're promised to the Cowpers tonight."

Alex looked up sharply. "The Cowpers? Oh, Lord yes. I'd forgot."

"A nice thing to forget your sister's first important party! Strictly speaking she should not go about in society until after the presentation at Court, but Emily Cowper assures me this will be a small, select gathering."

"I know Emily Cowper's small gatherings," Alex said. "Two hundred people crammed into a space designed to hold half the number. We wouldn't be missed."

"If," said his mother, "you wish your sister to dwindle into an old maid, by all means insult Lady Cowper. Go to Newmarket."

Alex sighed. He knew that there was no way he could escape going to the Cowpers' assembly.

It was not that he disliked Lady Cowper, indeed he enjoyed her company. She was an enchantingly pretty woman with soft dark hair and the complexion of a pale rose. Her mama, the late Lady Melbourne, had been regarded as something of a parvenu by the ton, but she'd become bosom bows with the Regent, and one of London's foremost hostesses. Emily Cowper had inherited her mother's talents. She was shrewd, accomplished, and possessed of the Lamb charm that attracted to her home the most brilliant and amusing members of the beau monde.

Many of these topnotchers would be present tonight, and while they might very well ignore young Emily Frome, they would certainly not ignore Linslade of Foxfare.

Alex smiled into his sister's anxious face. "Don't worry, puss," he said, "I'll see the lions don't eat you."

"I shan't know what to say to them," Emily replied. "I shall be numb with fright."

"No, you won't. All you need do is smile a great deal, and nod your head occasionally. People will declare you to be a very pretty-behaved young female, with an uncommon degree of understanding."

The evening began well. Lady Cowper, receiving her guests at the head of the stairway, greeted the Fromes with affection, complimented Lady Linslade on her gown, bestowed a kind word on Emily, and informed Alex that her brother William had sent particular messages from his country home that he hoped to see Linslade in Town very soon.

The civilities observed, the Frome party entered the first of three reception rooms that stretched from the front of the mansion to the back. A dense throng of people was gathered here, all of them talking and laughing in the hearty manner of those who have known one another for years and are perfectly convinced of their own importance.

All of them, Emily found, were acquainted with her mother and her brother. Their progress across the room was constantly interrupted by friends wishing to speak with them. Emily was presented to all of them, and they greeted her affably enough;

but she could see that this occasion was not intended for the pleasure of fledgelings but for birds of a far finer feather.

She followed Alex's advice, smiled, listened politely, and held her tongue; but her eyes feasted on the spectacle of the fashionable world, the fine gowns of the women, their sparkling jewels, the fantastical arrangements of their hair adorned with such high loops and puffs that one was at a loss to see how they could put on their bonnets.

The gentlemen, too, were very splendid. Their dress uniforms, their swallow-tail coats and form-fitting pantaloons, their curled and pomaded locks, were quite beyond anything she had been privileged to see among the country squires at home.

Even the oddities present — whom Alex referred to as the frumps and fribbles — were fascinating to her. The very stout lady in purple with the scarlet wig askew on her head was identified as Harriet, Lady Slade, whose racing-stables were renowned throughout the shires; while the two young men in earnest talk with the Prime Minister, Lord Liverpool, proved to be the Wynn brothers, known, because of their odd-sounding voices, as Bubble and Squeak.

Gaining confidence, Emily was actually able to pick out familiar faces: the Devonshires, who had stayed at Foxfare on several occasions, Frederick Lamb the distinguished diplomat, and red-faced, weatherbeaten Lord Althorp.

At the end of the first room they encountered Lady Jersey holding court to a group of her cronies. She chose to be gracious, and promised to send dear Lady Linslade vouchers to admit her and Miss Frome to the next assembly at Almack's. She then embarked on the latest on-dits of the Town. Sally Jersey was known as Silence by the irreverent, and, guessing that some of her anecdotes would be too salty for Emily's maiden ears, Lady Linslade signed to Alex to move on to the next room.

Here refreshments had been set out, and footmen were serving wine and other cordials. Alex secured champagne for his mother and himself, and a glass of lemonade for Emily. He was about to raise his glass to his lips when he heard his name spoken, and turned to find himself facing the satirical smile of the Princess Dorothea Lieven.

The Princess was a power to be reckoned with. She was the wife of the Russian ambassador (and, since the Congress of Aix in 1818, the mistress of the Austrian Chancellor, Prince Metternich). Alex had met her many times on diplomatic missions. He knew the acuteness of her mind and the sharpness of her tongue. She was, moreover, a member of the King's intimate circle — the Cottage Group, as it was called — and a patroness of Almack's Club.

It was not, however, the Princess's formidable reputation that caused Alex to stiffen, but her companions. At her right hand stood Lady Charlotte Brampton, and at her left Miss Lucilla Pelham and Miss Tamar Curle. There was no hope of escape. The Princess was beckoning. Even Lady Linslade recognized defeat, and the Fromes moved forward to greet the Everleys.

Alex, bowing over the Princess's languid fingertips, wondered if she sensed the tension in the air. He thought it probable. There was a streak of malice in the woman. She enjoyed setting a place by the ears. Yet her first words, spoken to his mother, were innocuous enough.

"Lady Linslade, I believe you're acquainted with Lady Charlotte Brampton? May I present to you Miss Lucilla Pelham and Miss Tamar Curle, who are to make their Come-out this year?"

Lucilla and Tamar made their curtsies, which Lady Linslade acknowledged with the faintest of nods. "I think, Princess," she said, "you've not met my younger daughter, Emily? She will also be presented this month."

The Princess smiled. "Then we shall see her at our little gatherings." The large blue eyes scanned Emily's face. "One sees the family likeness. She's very like Alex, is she not? It must rejoice your heart, ma'am, to have him in England again."

"It does." Lady Linslade's tone was terse. "Duty takes him from us far too often."

"Alas, yes," sighed the Princess. "That's the nature of a diplomat's work. I recall how little time your late husband was able to spend with you."

Lady Linslade reddened. Julian Frome's reputation as a statesman was equalled only by his reputation as a rake. She made a quick recover, however, and said with a smile, "You yourself, ma'am, suffer these same deprivations. It's to be hoped the dear Prince will soon return from Moscow?"

The Princess said Prince Lieven would certainly be in London for the Coronation, and the conversation turned to this comfortably safe topic.

Lord Linslade, finding himself ignored by Lady Charlotte, turned to Miss Pelham and Miss Curle and enquired how they were enjoying London. Miss Pelham replied, with cool politeness, that she had so far seen very little of it. Miss Curle was more enthusiastic. It was delightful, she said, to be continually coming across so many famous landmarks and notabilities.

"Like the Duke of Wellington," agreed the Earl. As Tamar glanced at him in confusion, he smiled. "I saw you drive past in Mr Warsop's carriage," he said. "Was your papa one of the Duke's officers?"

"Yes," said Tamar shyly. "He was with him at Brussels for several months. Then he was seconded to the 2nd Hussars. It was during their charge at Waterloo that Papa . . . that he was . . . "

Seeing that she was unable to finish the sentence, Alex said gently, "That was the charge that changed the course of the battle."

Tamar nodded. "The Duke wrote to my grandfather. Such a kind letter. It is one of our most treasured possessions."

The Earl glanced about him. "He's not here tonight, I think, but one day I must present you to him . . . if you'd like it, that is?"

"I'd like it above all things," said Tamar simply.

The Earl now turned his attention to Miss Pelham. She looked charmingly, he thought. Her fine skin glowed, and her burnished hair was simply dressed with a few soft curls falling over the ears. Her gown was of cream-coloured silk and, studying it with a connoisseur's eye, Alex decided that it was a departure from the current style. Certainly it was attracting the interest of every female in the vicinity. Remembering how he had first seen Miss Pelham wearing breeches and waving a pistol, he chuckled. She gazed at him enquiringly, brows raised, the picture of cool indifference.

Alex sighed. "I suppose it must be the butter," he said.

She blinked. "I beg your pardon?"

"The unmelted butter in your mouth, Miss Pelham."

She bit her lip and her eyes sparkled, though whether from amusement or annoyance he could not tell.

"If I'm silent," she said repressively, "it's because I have nothing of moment to say."

He shook his head. "That won't do, you know. In Society the more trivial your thoughts, the more vigorously you must give voice to them. You should begin with some perfectly insipid question such as, 'How do you like London?' From there you may progress to the weather, or ask after a relation's health. As, for example, 'How is my friend Sir Sholto?'"

Miss Pelham became less starchy. "He's well, thank you, and in less pain now that the weather's warmer."

"When does he come to Town?"

"Soon, I hope. Dr Chase has a scheme to bring him by canal, at least for part of the way . . . to avoid the jolting on the roads."

Alex said it sounded an excellent plan, and was about to enquire after Dr Chase when there was a flurry of movement near the doors of the drawing-room, and the Duke of York entered, accompanied by his hostess and his inamorata, the Duchess of Rutland.

The people in the salon drew back to give Royalty space. The group surrounding the Princess Lieven broke up, and Fromes and Everleys were quickly separated.

Lord Linslade was inclined to think that the night's encounter, having so to speak forced the issue, might spare him further argument with his mama. His hope proved vain: Lady Linslade complained all the way home that she had been exposed to intolerable embarrassment. She described Lady Charlotte as scheming, Miss Curle as harebrained, and Miss Pelham as unpleasantly bold. She warned Emily to have nothing whatever to do with any of them and, as soon as the carriage reached Berkeley Square, retired to her bed with a migraine headache.

Lady Charlotte was equally fierce in her criticism of the Fromes.

"Be on your guard against them," she told Lucilla and Tamar as they returned to Brampton House. "Lord Linslade is especially dangerous. He is a libertine like his father before him. For you to be seen in his company can do you no good with people of sound morals. I expect it amused him, Lucilla, to chaff you as he did, but I hope that if he tries to take such liberties again, you will give him a severe set-down. Not that I shall permit him to dangle after you. That is very far from being my intention."

"I don't think," said Lucilla pensively, "that Linslade is the sort of man to dangle after anyone. He has far too good an opinion of himself."

"Exactly so. Men of that kind, vain, overproud men, like to string scalps at their belts. Mark what I say, Miss. Linslade is not to be encouraged in any way."

Lucilla made no answer for, truth to tell, she was in some confusion of mind. Before she left Ringwood she had resolved to treat his lordship . . . should they by any chance meet . . . with no more than formal courtesy. She had been dismayed, and not a little annoyed, to feel her pulse quicken at the mere sight of him.

His cordiality, she reminded herself firmly, was only what was to be expected of a seasoned diplomat. She had been in London long enough to know that Linslade was famous for his address. In fact, one had to admit that he was everywhere admired. One had only to see how people had received him tonight — the gentlemen greeting him with easy camaraderie, the ladies hanging on his lightest word — to know that in the eyes of the ton he was indeed a Nonpareil.

By the same token, it had become plain to her that her cousin Francis was not well-liked. Naturally, people did not disparage him in her hearing, but Lucilla was an observant girl, and well able to interpret the sidelong glances and sudden silences that announced his arrival in a room.

She wondered if Tamar was aware of Francis's lack of popularity. If so, she gave no sign of it. She seemed to drift along in a dream, allowing others to make decisions for her, going wheresoever chance carried her.

One thing was certain: the animosity between the Fromes and the Everleys went very deep. Lady Linslade had been cool to the point of rudeness. It was not to be imagined that she, any more than Aunt Charlotte, would encourage friendship between the two houses.

Lucilla, a realist, decided that it would be best to put the Earl and his family out of her mind.

This good intention endured for almost the whole of May. It was easy enough, in those crowded days, to think only of the moment. First there was endless shopping to be done, and when all the necessary gowns, bonnets, and etceteras had been bought, there was the Presentation at Court to be accomplished.

This took place at the end of the second week in May. Lucilla wrote to describe it to Sir Sholto: "It was, to be honest, pure farce: a sprinkling of yawning Royals surrounding the throne, and a great many of us Nobodies, got up in hoops and feathers, and sailing past H. M. the King like a fleet under review. However, we now carry the official stamp of approval, and are ready to be let loose upon Society."

As the Season advanced, London became impossibly crowded. Lucilla and Tamar were invited to so many parties, routs and assemblies, that they often attended several in one evening. Lady Charlotte and Marion Gray shared the task of acting as chaperone, and Francis was usually in attendance.

Lady Charlotte was punctilious about providing Lucilla with suitable escorts to every event. The gentlemen she selected were invariably well-bred, comfortably-circumstanced, and au fait with the foibles of the polite world. They were also, in Lucilla's view, excessively dull.

If she preferred any of them, it was Lord Povall, whom she met at a performance of *The Merchant of Venice*, and who thereafter paid her flattering attention. He was what her godmama described as A Catch. His fortune was large. He owned a handsome house in Town and estates in Lincolnshire. Though he had, as he freely disclosed, more than forty years in his dish, and had been a widower for ten of them, he was excellent company. He possessed a dry sense of humour, did not pay Lucilla outlandish compliments, and talked amusingly on topics that interested her. He was generous and kind-hearted. For example, when he learned that Adrian loved music, he was at pains to secure him tickets for a performance of

Handel's *Messiah*, and later helped him to meet a number of talented musicians.

Lady Charlotte did all she could to foster Lord Povall's suit, praised him to the skies and looked with disapproval at the posies, trinkets, and romantic verses sent to Lucilla by various other gallants.

"Do not let idle flattery turn your head, my dear," she said. "You are a little too inclined to enjoy empty show. Sally Jersey told me the other day that you are becoming the toast of the younger set. It is not a soubriquet I welcome. Next, we shall hear it said that you are frivolous, or fast, or some such thing."

Lucilla met these strictures with a dutiful smile and a deaf ear. She made no attempt to change her ways; indeed, she could not. It was not in her nature to be demure and missish. She liked people and was happy if they liked her. London, she was beginning to love and, if she sometimes found the atmosphere at Brampton House oppressive, it was simple enough to escape. She could spend an hour or two with friends, stroll in the Green Park with Marion Gray, or go riding with her cousin Adrian.

It was on one such outing that she became involved in an incident that earned her a quite unwished-for notoriety.

XIX

LORD LINSLADE WAS accustomed to drive out most mornings of the week to exercise his bays. Often he was accompanied by Emily or Nicholas, but on the last Thursday in May, the weather being unseasonably chilly, he was unable to persuade either of them to quit the fireside and set out with only his groom, Belper, for company.

He had come through the gates of Hyde Park and was tooling his team along the southern carriage-way, when he saw that the vehicles ahead of him were drawing to a halt to allow passage to a detachment of foot-soldiers who were swinging along briskly to the tune of fife and drum.

He drew his curricle to the side of the road, halting behind a high-perch phaeton driven by a gentleman who, to judge by the multiplicity of capes to his greatcoat, and the profusion of spare

lashes threaded through his hatband, hoped to be classed as a
top sawyer. That he was no such thing was clear from the way
he yanked at his reins and cursed the nervous young chestnut
between the shafts. The animal had taken exception to the
martial music and was making strenuous efforts to bolt.

A considerable crowd, both horsemen and pedestrians, had
gathered behind the line of carriages. The Earl, idly scanning
this throng, found himself gazing directly at Miss Lucilla
Pelham and her cousin Adrian Curle.

They had not seen him. Mr Curle, mounted on a useful-
looking roan, was watching the parade. Miss Pelham, on the
palomino, Dandified, had ridden forward and was waiting to
cross the road to the equestrian track beyond. Looking at her,
the Earl mentally raised his hat in salute.

She was wearing a riding-habit of cream broadcloth whose
cut emphasized the lines of her admirable figure. Her jacket
was frogged at shoulders and cuffs with darker braid. Lace
showed at her wrists and above the high line of her white
cravat. On her auburn curls was set, instead of the formal
hunting-hat, a velvet shako trimmed with a pheasant's feather.
Tan leather gloves, tan half-boots and a riding-crop with an
amber handle completed this striking ensemble.

The marchers passed by and the crowd began to disperse.
The driver of the phaeton at once pulled out from the roadside,
disregarding the approach of a heavy cart laden with barrels
and drawn by a massive percheron.

The carter, being in possession of the road, yelled at the
gentleman in the phaeton to give over. The gentleman
responded by lashing out at the carter with his whip. The
chestnut reared and it seemed that the two vehicles must
collide. Even so, disaster might have been avoided, had not a
small child escaped from its mother's grasp and dashed out
into the roadway, straight in the path of the cart.

The carter hauled back, cursing richly. The percheron threw
its great weight backward, and stopped the dray almost dead,
but the jolt dislodged one of the barrels, which crashed
sideways and shattered the shaft of the phaeton. The chestnut
was brought down, to lie kicking and threshing, tangled in the
traces.

Handing his reins to Belper, the Earl jumped down and went to help the phaeton's groom who was trying ineffectually to free the chestnut. The animal was in danger of being impaled on the broken shaft, and its struggles made it difficult to unbuckle the harness that pinioned it. Alex directed the groom to hold the chestnut's head steady, and set to work to unbuckle the harness. A voice spoke behind him.

"Take this, sir. Cut the traces."

He looked up to see Miss Pelham, one hand outstretched to proffer a wicked-looking knife. Not stopping to enquire how she came by the weapon, he took it from her and slashed at the heavy straps. In a short while he was able, with the help of the groom and an onlooker, to lift the phaeton back, and get the chestnut on to its legs.

The animal was trembling and sweating, but it did not appear to be badly hurt. The groom, running a hand down its near foreleg, said he thought it was no more than a strain, and the Earl turned away to look for the owner of the phaeton.

He found him a few yards off, sitting in the roadway, his fine coat muddied and his hat crushed under him. His cheek bore a weal which had certainly been inflicted by a riding-crop. Standing over him, whip in hand, was Miss Pelham. Her right arm encircled the shoulders of a very grubby urchin who was bawling his lungs out. Her left fended off a stout woman in blue, who was endeavouring to belabour the fallen man with a battered parasol. She was being urged on by the driver of the cart, and a crowd of delighted bystanders.

The Earl thought it time to intervene. Stepping forward, he addressed the woman with the parasol.

"Madam," he said firmly, "is the boy your son?"

The stout woman wheeled about. "Aye, that he is."

"Then I suggest you take him home. He's had a nasty fright."

The stout woman swelled. "'Ome, is it?" she cried. "'Ome? And what about justice, I'd like to know? What about that? What about this great ruffian, 'ere, that attacked my poor boy and well-nigh murdered 'im? Knocked into coffin-nails, my Arthur'd be, if Miss 'ere 'adn't saved 'im! And look at 'is jacket! Ruined, that's what! I wants me rights, see? I'll 'ave the Law on this great bully, so I will."

140

Alex eyed the man in the roadway. "As to the ruined clothes," he said, "I fancy that you and this Jehu may cry quits. However, I agree that some compensation is due to you for the violence done to your son." He leaned down, grasped the gentleman's collar, and hauled him to his feet. "Give the woman a guinea," he directed.

"A guinea?" shrieked the gentleman. "I shan't pay her a penny, sir, not a halfpenny, not a brass farthing! That guttersnipe of a boy caused an accident that has wrecked my carriage and lamed a valuable horse . . . "

Miss Pelham took a step forward. "It was you that caused the accident," she said hotly, "by the worst piece of driving I've seen in years; and as if that weren't enough, you chose to assault a little boy who can't be more than five years old ·. . . "

"Four," declared the stout lady, making a threatening pass with her parasol. "Four year old, is Arthur, and suffers crool with 'is nerves. I doubt we'll raise 'im to man'ood, after what that ravenin' beast done to 'im."

The ravening beast wrenched free of the Earl's grip and pointed a shaking finger at Lucilla. "If the Law is to be called in," he said, "it is I who shall do the calling. This . . . this termagant struck me. She struck me in the face. I shall summon her before the courts. I shall demand full satisfaction for this dastardly attack."

Alex shrugged. "Of course," he said cheerfully, "if you wish to publicize your execrable driving, and make yourself a laughing stock, by all means do so. But really, I think you'll be well-advised to hand over that guinea. If you don't, I fear the crowd may turn ugly."

The crowd, neatly taking its cue, set up an ominous growl. The phaeton-driver turned pale.

"It's an outrage," he cried, "a rank injustice. I shan't pay the harpy a sou! I'd rather die."

"If dyin's yer aim," shouted the driver of the cart, "we'll 'elp yer to it, mister."

The phaeton-driver retreated to stand behind Alex. "Very well," he muttered, "very well, I'll pay." He reached into the pocket of his greatcoat, drew out a purse, extracted a gold coin and tossed it towards the stout woman. She caught it neatly and stowed it away in the bosom of her gown. The crowd raised a lusty huzzah, the urchin stopped howling, and the phaeton-driver limped away to inspect his damaged chariot.

Turning to Miss Pelham, Alex held out the knife. "Yours, I believe, ma'am. Do you always go armed to the teeth?"

She smiled. "No. It's only by luck that I'm using my hunting saddle today, and it has a knife-holster." She glanced towards the phaeton. "Is the horse all right?"

"Yes. A strained fetlock, nothing more."

"I suppose I ought not to have struck that creature, but I was so enraged by the way he shook the child, who was already quite hysterical with shock and terror . . . "

"He got his deserts," Alex said. "You'll hear no more from him."

This view was supported by Adrian Curle, who rode up just then, leading Lucilla's horse. "Good morning, my lord," he said breathlessly. "Thank you for coming to Lucilla's aid. I couldn't come near, for the crowd. But if you will be kind enough to stay with Lucilla for a few minutes, I've a few words to say to that lout."

"Mr Curle," said Alex. "I strongly advise you to let sleeping curs lie. We don't want another public shouting-match."

"I ought to call him out," protested Adrian.

"No, you oughtn't. It would be a shatterbrained thing to do."

"Why? I'm a good enough shot. It'd be a pleasure to wing the counter-jumper. The veriest whipster, too! I wouldn't give him charge of a governess-cart, let alone a high-perch phaeton." A throught struck Adrian. "It just shows, Lucilla, how unsuitable such a carriage would be for a female."

"I'm quite capable of handling a high-perch," retorted Miss Pelham, but her voice lacked conviction. A troubled expression had come to her face, and she gazed anxiously at Lord Linslade. "I'm afraid," she said, "that this story will be all round Town in no time."

Alex agreed with her, but he shook his head. "Our friend over there won't repeat it," he said. "His rôle was hardly heroic."

"I pray you're right," Lucilla said. "Truly, I have no wish to excite vulgar comment."

His eyes twinkled. He was thinking that Miss Pelham would be the subject of comment, vulgar or otherwise, until her dying day. No amount of effort was going to subdue her impetuous temper or her flair for unconventional action. Those who lived near her could not expect peace of mind. On the other hand, they would never be bored.

He came to a sudden and surprising decision. Providence had three times cast Miss Pelham in his way, and he must not let her escape him.

He lifted her into the saddle, and then, his hand on Dandified's bridle, said, "Do you still wish to buy a phaeton, Miss Pelham?"

"Yes," she said. "Why do you ask?"

"By chance, I am due to visit my coachmaker tomorrow," he answered. "It will give me great pleasure if you and Mr Curle will accompany me. Hooper and Sons is a reliable firm, and you may like to examine some of their work."

Lucilla hesitated. Though he spoke of coachmaking, he was offering friendship. Her godmother would not approve. Nor would Lady Linslade. The sensible thing would be to make a polite refusal.

"Thank you," she heard herself say, "that will be extremely pleasant."

"By Jove, yes," said Adrian.

Alex smiled. "Good. I shall do myself the honour to call for you tomorrow morning at eleven o'clock."

Having accepted Lord Linslade's offer, Lucilla felt duty bound to tell her godmother of it. Accordingly, as soon as she returned to Brampton House she told Lady Charlotte about the encounter in the Park and the proposed visit to Hooper and Sons.

"Linslade can give me the best possible advice, Aunt," she said. "He's a famous whip."

"He's a famous flirt," retorted Lady Charlotte. "I don't know how such a man dares to cast out lures to a respectable female. You will kindly sit down at the desk this instant, and write him a note to say you find yourself unable to accept his invitation."

Lucilla shook her head. "I'm extremely sorry to disoblige you, ma'am, but you know that before I left Ringwood I promised Grandfather I'd do nothing to offend the Fromes."

"You prefer to offend me, is that it?"

"Oh, no!" Lucilla came to sit beside Lady Charlotte on the sofa. "Indeed, indeed, I'm most grateful to you for all you're doing for us; but I can find no reason to insult a man who has shown me nothing but courtesy and consideration."

"There are reasons, girl, which you're too young to understand. There can never be friendship between Frome and Everley. The chasm that divides us is too broad for you to cross."

Lucilla met her godmother's angry stare. "Marion told me that Francis quarrelled with Linslade over a woman, but that was long ago. Surely we can put the past behind us?"

"No, we cannot," said Lady Charlotte grimly, "and, unless you wish to incur my very grave displeasure, you will give me your word that you will sever all links with Linslade and his crew."

"I can't make such a promise. Not on the grounds you offer."

Lady Charlotte nodded coldly. "So be it, then. I can't command one as headstrong and selfish as you, but be warned that when your grandfather comes to Town, I shall have a good deal to say to him."

"Aunt, I do sincerely wish to please you . . . "

"You wish to please yourself, Lucilla, and you will do so, no matter what pain it brings to those near and dear to you. Now be good enough to leave me. I have nothing more to say to you."

Lucilla hesitated for a moment, then rose and left the room. Lady Charlotte sat for a while with a hand shading her eyes. Then she rang for a footman and gave orders for her carriage to be brought round. A quarter of an hour later she was on her way to Mr Jason Cleve's place of business in Gray's Inn.

XX

As FRIDAY MORNING was sunny and windless, the Earl arrived in Curzon Street in an open carriage, with Cheadle driving and Belper perched up behind.

The splendour of this turn-out much impressed Adrian, who ran down the steps to meet it.

"Good morning, sir," he said, as Alex stepped on to the flagway. "Lucilla bade me say she'll be out directly. Jove, but this is bang up to the nines! Those greys! Some Arab in them, ain't there? Sixteen-mile-an-hour tits, I'll be bound."

Alex smiled. "Yes, they're sweet goers. A trifle light in the bone for long hauls, but ideal for Town work."

Adrian then begged to be allowed to travel beside Cheadle on the box, the better to observe the greys' paces, and to this Alex readily agreed, since it would leave him free to devote his full attention to Miss Pelham.

She emerged from the house a moment later, dressed in a gown of blue madras cotton, and a spencer-jacket of matching silk. Her bonnet of fine cream straw was trimmed with the same silk. She carried a small reticule, and a lace parasol.

She greeted the Earl with composure, but her expression was a little strained, and he guessed that she had come to cuffs with her formidable godmama. He handed her up into the carriage, took his place beside her, and kept up a flow of commonplace remarks until he sensed that she was at her ease again.

Hooper and Sons had their main workshop across the river, in Southwark, and Linslade instructed Cheadle to go there by way of The Strand and the newly-completed Waterloo Bridge.

Lucilla had never seen this part of London, and found it enthralling. There were so many people to be seen, of so many different callings — the dustman in his shovel-hat, the blue-aproned butcher, the seaman in coarse linen breeks and reefer jacket, the old-clothes dealer wearing three battered tall-hats, one above the other — all going about their business amidst a clamour and bustle such as she had never experienced.

On one corner they passed a little table mounted on wheels, with cupboards fitted to it, and an urn. That, Lord Linslade told her, was a saloop-stall.

"The urn is for brewing the saloop . . . it's an infusion of sassafras with sugar and milk. You may buy a bowl of it for three halfpence."

"Have you ever done so?" asked Lucilla.

"Yes, indeed, and found it mighty comforting at five o'clock of a winter's dawn. The common folk can't afford tea or coffee, but even a chimney-sweep may buy a dish of saloop to keep out the cold."

A little further along, the carriage was delayed because of an accident on the road ahead, and while they waited for the way to be cleared, they heard a voice crying very loudly, "Hot, hot, hot, pudding-hot!", and the next moment a man dashed past them, heading towards Charing Cross. He was dressed all in white, with a powdered wig, and carried a tray slung from his neck. He checked his headlong pace as a customer blocked his path, handed over a steaming pie, snatched a coin in payment, and was off again in the twinkling of an eye.

"That's the Flying Pieman," said Alex. "He owns a shop in Smithfield but sells his wares all over Town. They say he and his wife are up at daybreak to bake dozens of pies. The Pieman takes them on a cart to public houses in Clerkenwell, Blackfriars, Piccadilly . . . the taverners keep the pies hot, and the Pieman replenishes his tray from them as he makes his rounds."

They drew near to Aldwych and saw ahead of them the fringe of the City with its huddle of houses, shops and inns, and the spires of Wren's churches rising into a pale blue sky.

"How beautiful London is," Lucilla said. As the Earl made no reply, she turned to look at him. "Do you not think so?"

"What we see here is beautiful," he answered, "but there's an ugly side, too. Not half a mile from here is the Rookery. People there live in rotting hovels, ten or twelve to a room. They survive by crime. They speak a thieves' cant that honest folk don't understand. Children are twisted by starvation and disease and, if they reach manhood, are like to end their days in gaol or on the gallows. And in Seven Dials there are printers who exploit this misery. One shilling will buy you the Dying Speech of a Condemned Man. The ballad-singers declare that a really hideous murder will keep the presses busy for as much as a week."

There was a harshness in his tone that startled Lucilla. "How do you know these things?" she asked.

He frowned. "Oh, in my salad days it amused me to wander about the streets, observing how people lived."

"The streets of the Rookery and Seven Dials?"

"No. I went there of necessity, once or twice. I was . . . searching for someone."

She saw that he did not like to be questioned about that and, as they now turned south towards the river, she asked him to identify the buildings and quays along its banks. A short while later they crossed over the bridge, and soon reached the gates of Messrs Hooper and Sons.

"I don't know which to choose," Lucilla said, an hour later. "My head's in a whirl."

They had been conducted all round the work-yard by Mr Hooper himself, and had examined what seemed like dozens of coaches in the making, as well as numerous sketches of curricles, gigs, phaetons and dress-chariots.

Lucilla turned to the Earl. "Please tell me what to do."

He pointed to a vehicle a few yards from where they stood. "If you wish for a high-perch phaeton, that's an excellent design. Well sprung, well balanced, and good to look at."

"But you have doubts, don't you? You think I might end in the ditch, like that oaf in the Park?"

"It's not what I think, but what you think, that counts."

She sighed. "I think I'm competent, but perhaps I suffer from a swelled head."

He smiled. "All drivers do. The mildest citizen sprouts horns when he has the ribbons in hand. The point is that a high-perch takes a devil of a lot of driving. One can't take one's eyes off one's cattle for an instant. There's no time to gaze about and enjoy the passing scene."

"What do you advise me to choose?"

"A phaeton," he said, "but not a high-perch. That one over there, for instance. It's not so dashing as this one, but you'll find it much more enjoyable to drive."

Here Mr Hooper was moved to suggest that if Miss Pelham desired to try the phaeton for herself, he would have it sent to her address at any time she chose. Lucilla seized on this offer with gratitude, and went so far as to discuss with Mr Hooper the shade of paint- and leather-work she preferred. This important point settled, Mr Hooper enquired which day she was free to make the trial run.

Lucilla thought rapidly. "I have no engagements next Thursday morning," she said. A thought struck her, and she glanced uncertainly at Lord Linslade. "I don't know if . . . I mean, I have no right to ask you . . . "

Alex, who had already mentally cancelled an appointment with his man of business, smiled blandly.

"Thursday morning will suit me very well," he said.

That evening Cheadle and Belper, reviewing the events of the day over a stoup or so of home-brewed, came to the conclusion that this time his lordship was fair hooked.

"'Eard 'im tell Miss 'e were goin' to Almack's," Cheadle said. "Shows yer, don' it?"

Belper was shocked. "You musta' mistook," he said.

"Almack's," insisted Cheadle. "Asked 'er ter stand up with 'im in the second country dance. There now!"

Belper considered this melancholy piece of information, and sighed. "Ah, well," he said at last, "I s'pose it comes to us all, sooner or later."

Cheadle pursed his mouth. "There'll be ructions," he prophesied. "Frome an' Everley is chalk an' cheese. Wait till 'er La'yship 'ears of it. Then the fat'll be in the fire an' no mistake."

Francis Warsop, returning from a card-game late on Friday night, was annoyed to find Mr Jason Cleve ensconced in the library, drinking brandy and reading a novel by Miss Jane Austen.

The lawyer laid the book aside as Mr Warsop entered the room.

"Good evening, Francis," he said. "I trust you've enjoyed a profitable few hours?"

"Dashed if that's any of your business," said Francis disagreeably. "What do you want?"

"I'm here at the behest of your aunt," Cleve replied. "She wishes me to warn you that Alexander Frome is paying marked attention to your cousin Lucilla."

Francis scowled. "Aunt C. takes these freakish notions. All humbug, if you ask me. Linslade ain't likely to ally himself to one of our breed."

"The facts don't support your theory, my dear! Lady Charlotte told me she forbade Lucilla to have anything to do with the man. Lucilla refused point-blank to obey."

"Aunt shouldn't try to badger Lucilla. She's a strong-willed wench."

"She is indeed," said Cleve drily. "She was involved in a vulgar brawl in Hyde Park, yesterday, it seems. Struck a gentleman in the face with her riding-whip. Linslade intervened to protect her from an angry mob."

Francis slumped down in an armchair and regarded his guest with dislike. "You know, Jason, you're not only an eavesdropper, you're also misinformed. Lucilla struck the man because he attacked a child, and the crowd was entirely on her side."

Cleve's eyes narrowed. "How do you know this?"

"It's all around the Clubs," said Francis carelessly. "Wyvern told me he witnessed the whole episode. Said the man in question was Tugwell's whelp, who's still wet behind the ears. Said if Linslade hadn't stepped in, the fool might have been mauled by the crowd."

"I find it strange to see you take Linslade's part."

"Not Linslade's. Lucilla's. Take my advice, Jason, don't try to malign her. You'll come off worst if you do. Lucilla's all the crack, these days. The fashionables say she has style, and the dragons say she has excellent ton. She can marry Povall any time she likes . . . or look even higher."

"As high, perhaps, as Linslade."

"I've told you, Linslade's only amusing himself."

Mr Cleve got to his feet. "Have you thought," he said coldly, "that Linslade could be seeking to fix his interest with your cousin, in order to strike at you?"

Francis laughed. "Rubbish!"

"It is not rubbish! Let me remind you that your survival depends upon your marrying Tamar Curle. Linslade could pour enough poison in Lucilla's ear to destroy your chances."

"Poison? What poison?"

"The fact that you seduced his sister, and tried to blackmail his father."

"There was no blackmail," said Francis furiously.

"Linslade will say otherwise."

"Foh, Linslade is far too proud to wash his dirty linen in public!" Francis had been watching Cleve closely as he spoke, and now rose from his chair and approached the lawyer. "What's on your mind, Jason? You're sweating like a pig. Has Aunt C. been nipping at your heels? If so, be so good as to tell her I'll announce my betrothal to Tamar at the agreed time . . . and I'll thank her not to poke her nose into my affairs."

"You're making a fatal mistake. If Linslade . . . "

"Oh, the devil take Linslade, and you as well," shouted Francis. "You presume too much, Cleve. My aunt may permit you to take liberties, but I will not! Stick to your law-books and ledgers, and stay out of my way!" Francis reached towards the bellrope that hung beside the fireplace, but Cleve held up a hand.

"Don't trouble to ring. I'll show myself out." He picked up his hat, gloves and cane from a chair, and moved to the door. There he paused. "I'll convey your sentiments to Lady Charlotte, and to your father. No doubt they'll be reassured to learn that you feel your position to be secure."

"Do as you please," muttered Francis.

Cleve left the room, and soon there came the sound of the front door closing after him. Left alone, Francis returned to his chair and sat staring moodily at the cold hearth.

XXI

LORD LINSLADE'S DECISION to attend an Assembly at Almack's came as less of a shock to his friends than it had to his coachman and groom.

While no man in his right mind would term these parties enjoyable — the chief beverages served were tea and lemonade, and the entertainment on offer was equally insipid — Almack's was known to the worldly-wise as the Marriage Mart. The goodwill of its highnosed patronesses was indispensable to any young woman anxious to make a good match. Mothers of marriageable girls fought tooth and nail to procure vouchers for the assemblies, and as Miss Emily Frome was known to be making her début this year, it was generally accepted that Linslade's presence was a sacrifice on that altar.

The Earl encouraged the belief by conducting his sister round the reception rooms and introducing her to several eligible bachelors. As Emily was a pretty girl, with engaging manners, her dance-card was quickly filled, Captain Shepstone securing for himself the first and supper dances. Alex, freed of his responsibilities, was about to join a group of his friends when he was intercepted by his brother Nicholas, who wore an extremely lugubrious expression.

"I say, Alex! This is a devilish place, ain't it? Never seen so many drolls and trolls in my life!"

"What brought you here?" asked Alex, smiling.

"Grandmama. Had a three-line whip out. No escape."

"Is that so?" Alex looked thoughtful. "Where may I find her?"

"In the card room with old Aldborough. She wants to talk to you, at once if you please."

Alex made his way through the now-crowded drawing-rooms to the card room. He found the Dowager Lady Linslade enjoying a tête-à-tête with a venerable gentleman in a snuff-coloured wig. At Alex's approach this ancient rose and tottered away, leaving the chair next to the Dowager vacant.

Alex bent to kiss his grandmother's hand and cheek. "Good evening, ma'am. You're in great good looks tonight. I hope I didn't drive away your latest cicisbeo?"

"Aldborough? No. I sent him to fetch me a glass of wine. At his best pace it will take him twenty minutes to make the journey. Sit down, my dear. Tell me, what is this tale I hear, that you and Sholto Curle's grand-daughter provoked a riot in Hyde Park?"

"There are several versions doing the rounds," he said as he took his place next to her. "Which had you heard?"

"That Miss Pelham was attacked by a lecher named Tugwell, that you sprang to her rescue, and that the crowd tried to lynch Tugwell."

Alex sighed. "Colourful, but inexact," he said. "The truth is that a brat ran out into the road and caused two vehicles to collide. Tugwell's carriage was wrecked. He pounced on the brat, and Miss Pelham pounced on him. The crowd took her part and became rowdy. I thought it wise to intervene. I . . .

er . . . persuaded Tugwell to pay the brat's mama a guinea, and all was well."

The Dowager nodded brightly. "And then?"

"There was no 'then'. Everyone went home."

The Dowager shook her head. "I don't believe you," she said flatly. "I don't believe that any grandson of mine could be so poor-spirited as to share an adventure with a girl whom Dorothea Lieven describes as the Beauty of the Season, and fail to make an assignation with her."

Alex grinned. "Grandmama, you're incorrigible."

She leaned over and tapped him sharply on the wrist. "Did you, or did you not, make an assignation? And don't tell me to mind my own business, for you know quite well that that has never been my strong suit."

"I took her to visit Hooper and Sons," Alex said. "She wants to buy a phaeton."

The Dowager raised her brows. "A visit to a coachmaker! How romantical! I'm sure that can't have failed to excite Miss Pelham's passions. When do you expect to see her again?"

"Tonight, in all probability. All the world and his wife seems to be here."

"Don't trifle with me, sir. I take it you're engaged to stand up with her?"

"Yes, in the second country dance."

"Why not the waltz?"

"You know it would be quite improper for Miss Pelham to waltz before the gorgons have given her their blessing." A reminiscent gleam came into his eye. "She told me that she has no wish to invite vulgar comment."

"Beautiful young females," said the Dowager stringently, "will cease to excite vulgar comment when pigs have wings. Tell me, shall I like her, Alex?"

"I think so. She resembles you in many respects. She's brash, impulsive and has a highly original mind."

"Dear, dear," murmured the Dowager. "Well, see that you bring her to meet me some morning. Now I see Aldborough returning, *ventre à terre*. You'd best escape while you may."

As he rose to go, she fired a parting shot. "Miss Pelham arrived a quarter of an hour ago," she said, "under heavy

Everley guard. You'll have to arrange a diversionary tactic, if you hope to come near her."

He gave her his lazy smile. "Don't worry," he said, "I already have an ally within the camp."

It was almost time for the second country dance. Returning to the main assembly-room, Alex saw that Miss Pelham, Miss Curle and Mr Warsop were with a group of young people on the far side of the room. No other Everleys were in evidence. Mrs Gray was seated alone in a corner, and Alex strolled over to join her.

She greeted him with a comical mixture of pleasure and anxiety. It was most kind of him, she said, to show her such flattering consideration, but Adrian had already gone to procure her a glass of ratafia, and there was no need for Lord Linslade to trouble himself further. When Alex remained standing before her, she was obliged to invite him to sit down, but she remained very much on edge.

Lord Everley, she explained, had refused to attend the assembly, and as dear Lady Charlotte was confined to her bed by an attack of influenza, it had fallen to her to chaperone the girls tonight.

"It is a responsibility that weighs very heavily on me," she confessed. "Everything depends upon their making the Right Impression. If anything were to go wrong . . . "

"Nothing ever goes wrong at Almack's," said his lordship.

Mrs Gray cast him a glance under her lashes. He saw with some amusement that she regarded him as the greatest of her problems. He wondered what picture Charlotte Brampton had painted of him. Unbridled lust, probably, coupled with insufferable pride and insatiable avarice.

A little ruefully, he set himself to charm Mrs Gray out of her fears, reminded her of his indebtedness to Sir Sholto, and mentioned casually that his grandmother, his mama and his sister were all present at this assembly.

Soon the music struck up for the country dance, and he moved off to claim Lucilla. Watching him go, Marion found herself in great confusion of mind. Should she forbid Lucilla to take the floor with Linslade? Would Lucilla pay her any heed if she did? Who could deny that, in manners and accomplishments, his lordship was a Nonpareil? Nothing could have been kinder than his attitude to herself. As a widow, dependent for roof and board on the goodwill of her family, Marion had received her share of slights from the ton. To many of them, a poor relation was only a little better than a paid companion or a governess; someone to be treated with indifference, certainly not to be shown any special attention. Yet Linslade had always shown her courtesy. During his stay at Ringwood she had observed him carefully. He gave himself no special airs. He was thoughtful towards both his brother and Sir Sholto. He was, she felt, most truly the gentleman.

Her gaze shifted to where Tamar stood quietly at Francis Warsop's elbow. Francis had hardly addressed a word to Tamar all evening. He was talking to his cronies, ignoring her. It must be plain to everyone that he wanted her only for her money. Once he had married her, thought Marion bitterly, all pretence would be over. He would revert to his debauched way of life, leaving Tamar to loneliness, misery and humiliation.

There was no way of averting the tragedy. As long as Sir Sholto approved the match, so would the world. Tamar herself offered no opposition. She seemed resigned to marrying Francis. One might find that resignation heartbreaking, but one had to bear with it. There was no escape, none at all, either for Tamar, or for those who truly loved her.

As the Earl led Miss Pelham into the ballroom, he was conscious of the admiring glances she attracted. She was looking ravishingly pretty in pale, rose-coloured silk, with long gloves of matching French kid. A delicate diamond necklace glittered at her throat, and a single rose was tucked into the bosom of her gown.

What added to her charm was that she seemed unaware of the effect she was creating. She greeted Emily and Nick, who were part of his lordship's set, with friendly ease and, when the music started, went through the measures of the dance with obvious enjoyment, her head held high and her smile radiant.

Mrs Drummond-Burrell, standing with fellow-patroness Lady Sefton, said in her waspish way that Miss Pelham appeared to be Alex Frome's latest flirt. Lady Sefton answered that if that were so, then for once Linslade wouldn't have things all his own way.

Mrs Drummond-Burrell smiled thinly. "My dear," she said, "you know how it will be. The man has only to shake the tree, and the plum falls into his hand."

Lady Sefton shook her head. "This girl is different," she insisted. "She has character as well as looks. She's already received several flattering offers, so Charlotte Brampton tells me, but she's in no hurry to make up her mind."

"I dare say," said Mrs Drummond-Burrell with a sniff, "that she already has."

The Dowager Countess of Linslade would have agreed with that view. Seated beside Elvira Frome at the edge of the ballroom floor, she watched Alex and Lucilla Pelham approach in the final figure of the dance. They advanced hand in hand, the girl with that glow about her that speaks of brimming happiness, and Alex scarcely able to take his eyes off her.

Conscious of the stiff disapproval of her daughter-in-law, the Dowager essayed a placatory remark. "I must say," she said, "that I'm pleasantly surprised. I'd expected something . . . well . . . more farouche. I find Miss Pelham has style and a pleasing modesty."

"Modesty?! I beg, Ma'am, that you won't mistake that milky smoothness for modesty! It is a mask, I assure you. It conceals a shameless adventuress with ambitions to be a Countess. I, for one, do not intend to stay to see her flaunt herself in this encroaching way. I shall fetch my cloak. When the number ends, be so good as to tell Alex that I wish to be taken home immediately."

Lady Linslade gathered up her skirts and swept away. The Dowager made no effort to stop her. When Elvira was upon her high ropes, argument was useless.

The dance ended. Alex restored Lucilla to the charge of Mrs Gray, remained chatting to them for a few minutes, then answered his grandmother's beckoning finger.

As he reached her, she stole a quick look at his face. His eyes were bright with amusement. He looked so happy that she was tempted not to give him his mother's message; but she knew Elvira would not be content to let things rest.

"Your mama is tired," she told him. "She wishes to leave. Go with her, Alex. Nick and I will see Emily safe home."

He stood still for a moment, the laughter dying from his eyes. Then he nodded and went away without a word, to order his carriage to be brought to the door.

XXII

ONLY SIX WEEKS now remained before the crowning in Westminster Abbey of His Majesty King George IV. London was crowded to overflowing, not only with its own citizens but with an extraordinary influx of merchants and prelates, caterers and entertainers, soldiers and sailors, foreign dignitaries and petty officials, all of them converging on the capital in order to play a part on the glittering coronation stage.

Lucilla immensely enjoyed this pageant. Although she had no wish to lead a hectic life year in, year out, it was amusing to experience it at least once. What woman would not take pleasure in wearing elegant clothes, meeting famous and fascinating people, and being courted and admired to the extent of being dubbed "The Inimitable", "The Incomparable", or even "The Divine" Miss Pelham?

Yet, as the month of June passed, she realized that her enjoyment depended less and less on these frivolities, and more and more on the presence of Alexander Frome. She found herself hoping, each time she approached a roomful of people, that he would be there. To catch a glimpse of him across the street was to feel a lift of the heart, while to see his face light up at sight of her was unimagined bliss.

Although London was a vast city, the world of the ton was comparatively small. Its members lived very much in one another's pockets. Even so, Lucilla was amazed how often she encountered Lord Linslade.

On the very first occasion that she drove her new phaeton in the Park, his lordship happened to be walking there with friends, and readily agreed to be taken up by her and to give her one or two pointers on how to negotiate the heavy traffic at the exit gates. She met him strolling in Bond Street when she was visiting the Lending Library, at the Opera and at the Play. At formal balls she could rely upon him to solicit her for two dances, the most that propriety permitted, and he always made a point of asking her which parties, routs and assemblies she was engaged to attend. In short, Lord Linslade was paying her very flattering attention.

Delightful as this was, it created grave difficulties. Lady Charlotte's dislike of the Earl had in no way abated, and she made this abundantly plain to him every time they met. Her manner to Lucilla was one of icy correctness. Although she never expressed a direct criticism, she used silence with devastating effect. Any attempt to talk about Linslade was simply ignored. It made Lucilla feel both guilty and ungrateful, and bruised her ardent spirit.

To make matters worse, Lucilla was not absolutely sure of Linslade's affection. When she was with him, she felt that he was genuinely attracted to her, even that he was falling in love with her. At times he seemed to be on the brink of making her a declaration. Yet, somehow, he always allowed these moments to pass. He would turn the subject, or make some funning remark, as if he were deliberately shying away from a commitment.

Sometimes she woke in the small hours to remember her godmother's warning . . . that Linslade was wooing her only to strike at her cousin Francis. Try as she might, she could not rid her mind of that poison. Nor could she bring herself to break with Linslade. She lived in hopes that today, tomorrow, some time soon, he would speak the words she so much longed to hear.

Alex, too, was suffering. His mother kept up a barrage of attacks on the Everleys in general, and Miss Pelham in particular. She resented every moment that Alex spent with Lucilla, and vented her misery on those about her, indulging in so many tears, megrims and fits of the vapours that the whole house was in an uproar. She insisted that Alex's lack of consideration was sending her into a decline, and dressed so regularly in black or lilac that her friends were prompted to enquire whether there had been a death in her family.

Alex's lot was not made easier by his brothers and sisters.

Emily, whose friendship with Captain Shepstone was beginning to look most promising, and who now counted herself an authority on matters of the heart, took a high romantic line.

"I know you're in love with Lucilla," she said one morning when she was out riding with Alex, "and I know Mama is dead set against the match, but you mustn't let her stand in your way. If you can't be married here, or at Foxfare, you must fly to the Border. It's the only way."

"Gretna?" Alex smiled at Emily's solemn face. "I don't think that will serve."

"Why not?"

"Well, for one thing, an elopement would be so deuced uncomfortable. All those dubious taverns on the road north, not to mention the hue and cry, and the risk of a duel at the end of it."

"You needn't fear a duel. No one will dare to challenge such a famous shot as you."

"I fear that Warsop might feel obliged to do so. Then I should have to put a bullet in him, and how would that advance my suit, pray?"

"So you admit there is a suit?"

"No, I do not!"

"But if you love Lucilla . . . " cried Emily passionately, "you cannot deny her. There can be nothing worse, in the whole world, than to deny the true dictates of one's heart."

"I don't propose to discuss it, puss."

"But Alex, surely you see . . . "

"No, Emily! You mustn't interfere. We'll say no more about it, if you please."

His tone was so firm that she dared not protest further, except to inform the sky that if he let Lucilla slip through his fingers, it would be the most tragical thing imaginable.

George's reaction was even less acceptable. He cornered Alex when he was going over his accounts in the business-room and advised him bluntly to remove to Foxfare for a spell.

"Staying in Town won't fadge, Alex. Bound to keep bumpin' into the Pelham filly. You can't hope to marry her. Her family would never countenance it. The deeper in you get, the unhappier it makes you, Mama and the rest of us. Go back to

Foxfare. Put the gal out of your mind. Plenty of other good fish in the sea."

To this Alex replied that when he wanted George's advice, he'd ask for it. This caused George to swell up like a tickle-toby.

"A loyal son," he expostulated, "does not marry to disoblige his family. You may say it's not come to marrying, yet, but the buzz is all round Town that you're nutty on the girl. Lord knows what you see in her. I must tell you, she doesn't please me at all. Too flighty by far. Flaunts herself in a very immodest way. Appears to enjoy bein' the target of vulgar gossip."

The Earl's eyes glinted dangerously.

"Only a vulgarian pays heed to vulgar gossip," he said. "Miss Pelham certainly won't stoop to do so. As to you, George, I must ask you to keep a civil tongue in your head when you refer to that lady. If you don't, you'll have me to reckon with."

"Oh?" replied George in a sneering voice. "and what will that betoken? Will you throw me out of the house?"

"Out of this house," said Alex grimly, "and out of Foxfare too."

"A fine thing! A fine thing for you to be threatening your own flesh and blood, for the sake of a damned Everley!"

"Think it over," advised the Earl. "Think it over very carefully, George, for I mean what I say."

George carried the report of the quarrel straight to his mama, and the atmosphere in the house grew considerably worse. Alex himself was now so angry that he would tolerate no reference at all to Miss Pelham. He went about his affairs as usual, but he was clearly worried and unhappy. Only Nicholas understood the real reason for his distress.

"It's Bella you're thinking of, ain't it?" he asked, and Alex nodded.

"Of course. How could I insult Bella by marrying into the family of the man who all but ruined her life? How can I ask the Ruthvens to accept Francis Warsop? How could I ever invite him to my home? On the other hand, how can I bar him from it without giving Lucilla good reason?"

"Tell her the truth."

"I'm not free to do that. I can't tell her what puts Warsop beyond the pale without betraying Bella's secret. I wish we had never come near Ringwood . . . that I'd never met Lucilla. George is right, damn his eyes! I ought to leave London and not see her again. Leave her to marry Povall or some other deserving man. But God knows where I'll find the courage."

"Grandmama will back you," Nicholas said. "Take Lucilla to see her . . . "

"I can't do that, either. To take Lucilla to meet my grandmother would be as good as making a proposal of marriage. I can't mislead Lucilla in that way. The truth is, Nick, that it doesn't matter a tinker's cuss who is for or against me. I have to make the break myself, and I have to make it soon." He paused, then said heavily, "I must stay in London for the Coronation. After that, I shall go abroad for a while."

Nicholas carried the problem to the Dowager, but to his chagrin she said that Alex was right. "The decision is his," she said. "We must leave it to him."

"Bella wouldn't bind him to silence if she knew. She's devilish fond of Alex. Wouldn't want to queer his pitch in any way."

"Bella has a husband and four children to consider. John Ruthven has been an angel to her, but I doubt if he's angelic enough to welcome Francis Warsop to the bosom of the family."

Nicholas frowned. "Francis is a loose fish, I agree, but why must we condemn the whole Everley clan because of him? Adrian Curle's sound as a bell, provided you keep him off music. Good company, good horseman, never oversteps the mark. Tamar Curle's a bit of a widgeon, but dashed pretty, and nothin' to mislike in her. As to Lucilla Pelham, I think she's top o' the trees, and even if I didn't, I'd never say so, because I know Alex is daffy upon her."

"Has he said so?"

"Doesn't need to," said Nick gloomily. "Any fool can see how it is with him."

The Dowager sighed. "I wish I knew what to do," she said. "We're all of us in a sad old muddle!"

XXIII

THE MUDDLE WAS compounded by the arrival in London, on the last Wednesday of June, of Sir Sholto Curle.

Lucilla was in the sewing-room at the top of the house, setting a stitch in the torn flounce of a gown, when she heard a commotion in the street below. Going to the window, she was amazed to see her grandfather's huge old-fashioned travelling-coach, with John Coachman and a groom on the box, three postillions riding alongside, and Ramon, mounted on a mettle-some black horse, bringing up the rear.

As she watched, the cavalcade clattered to a halt, the steps of the carriage were let down, and out sprang Mr Giles Ayliffe, resplendent in jacket of dark blue superfine, fawn pantaloons, and gleaming Hessians. He was followed in a more leisurely manner by Dr Chase, and finally by Sir Sholto himself. Lucilla hurried down to meet the newcomers.

All three of them were in high spirits, and quite unrepentant for having arrived unheralded. When Lucilla apologized for being the only one of the family at home to greet him, Sir Sholto said cheerfully, "Tush child, I never expected to find the red carpet rolled out. Where is everyone? Out on the strut?"

"Aunt Charlotte and Tamar are making morning calls, and Adrian has gone to Epsom for the races. Lord Linslade was kind enough to invite him to join his party. I thought there could be no objection to it."

"None in the world," agreed Sir Sholto. "Good for the cub to learn to tell a stepper from a slug, and Linslade will see he don't get in over his head." He turned to the butler, who was hovering discreetly a yard or so away. "You're Neame, are you not? Well, Neame, I'm glad to see you after all these years, and I wish you would find my friends and me something to eat, for we're empty as a row of kettles. Tell the cook not to make a to do of it . . . some beef, bread, cheese, ale and wine will fill the bill nicely."

Neame, much gratified to be remembered by name, bustled away to order the refreshments, and Lucilla led the travellers to the drawing-room.

"I must say," she said, as she helped Sir Sholto to settle himself in a wingchair, "that you look in fine fettle. How far have you come this morning? Did you sleep at Windsor, or closer to Town?"

"Spent the night at the Chiswick Arms," said Sir Sholto, looking very pleased with himself. "Came there by water. Young Giles, here, planned it all. Hired a river-boat, a very splendid affair, made me feel like Pharaoh on the Nile. Bespoke rooms for us at various points along the river, and sent my carriage ahead, to convey us from Chiswick to London. The whole thing went as smooth as silk. Never more comfortable in my life."

Dr Chase was equally enthusiastic. "Just the thing for your grandfather," he said. "A leisurely journey, through pleasant country, and first rate hostelries at night." He added, in a lower tone, "He's taken no harm from it, my dear. Done him the power of good to get away from Ringwood for a spell."

"Was all quiet there?" she asked. "No more incidents?"

"None. Your grandfather was right. The events must have been the work of some deranged individual. There'll be nothing to fear in London."

"I hope you're right."

"I'm sure I am. And now, if you'll permit, I'll go and have a word with Rogers. He came with the baggage fourgon, and has my medicine-case in charge."

Dr Chase left the room, and Lucilla moved to speak to Giles, who was standing by the window, staring moodily out at the street.

"I'm so grateful to you, Giles," she said, "nobody could have managed things better."

As the young man shook his head deprecatingly, she went on, "Have you fixed on a place to stay? I'm sure that if Aunt Charlotte were here she'd invite you to make this your home for as long as you're in London."

"No," said Giles quickly, "that wouldn't be suitable. I've reserved a room at Long's Hotel in Bond Street."

"Just around the corner," approved Lucilla. "We shall look forward to seeing you often."

He gave her a strained smile. "I shall certainly call on you, and . . . and Tamar . . . but I expect to be pretty busy, you know, with my Steam Horse. I've an appointment to see Mr Amos Brocket in the last week of July. I've already sent him my drawings and the working model. If he likes the concept, my fortune's made."

"I'm sure he'll like it," Lucilla said.

Giles nodded, then said abruptly, "Is Tamar well?"

Lucilla hesitated. A few weeks ago, she would have made some casual rejoinder, but now she knew all too well how painful it was to be in love, yet unable to speak of it to anyone.

"I think," she said at last, "that she'd be all the better for seeing you. Come and visit us soon, Giles."

"Thank you," he said, "I will."

He stayed long enough to eat some of the food that Neame brought in, but soon after said his goodbyes and went off to find a hackney-cab to convey him and his bags to Bond Street.

Sir Sholto, left alone with his grand-daughter, beckoned her to him.

"Well, my dear," he said, "from what my old friend Holland wrote me, you've become the Toast of the Town. Tell me about your triumphs."

She laughed and, taking her place beside him, entered into a lively account of the grand parties she'd attended, and the droll characters she'd encountered.

When at last she paused for breath, he regarded her with his head on one side. "All very fine," he said, "but what of your heart, Miss? Are your affections yet engaged, or is all this expense to no purpose?"

His tone was teasing, but she caught an undertone of concern and replied evenly, "I've received three respectable offers, sir, from Lord Povall, Mr Edmundson and Sir John Braby."

"But . . .?"

"I don't feel able to accept any of them."

"I see." He watched her for a moment, then said quietly, "What of Linslade, puss? My information is that he has been most particular in his attentions."

She glanced up quickly. "Information? Did Aunt Charlotte . . .?"

"Your Aunt Charlotte and Henry Everley have both written to tell me of Linslade's interest. Perhaps they are mistaken in their view?"

She sat with downcast gaze. "He . . . he seems to feel . . . kindly towards me."

"Come, now, it goes further than kindness, surely? For a man like Linslade to be dancing attendance on a female can only mean he's developed a *tendre* for her."

She looked up unhappily. "Aunt Charlotte doesn't think he wishes to marry me. She thinks he has . . . some other motive."

The old man shifted in his chair. "If she imagines Linslade will try to give you a slip on the shoulder, she's all about in her head. Linslade's not the sort to deceive an innocent girl."

Lucilla nodded. "So I believe. There are times when I'm sure he loves me, but . . . he doesn't speak. There must be a reason for his silence. I've racked my brains to think what it could be, but I can find no answer . . . except, perhaps, that it has to do with Francis."

"Why do you say that?"

"I've heard that there was a quarrel between them, years ago. A quarrel over a woman."

She looked searchingly at her grandfather as she spoke, but he chose not to answer her implied question. Instead, he said, "Was it Francis who told you of it?"

"No. Grandfather, if there was such a quarrel, then I must tell you I don't believe Linslade was at fault."

He smiled at her quizzically. "You could be prejudiced."

"Perhaps. Since I came to London, I've learned certain things about Francis."

"Yes?"

"That he drinks too much and gambles heavily. His friends are a ramshackle lot."

"My child, you've just described half the fashionables in Town."

"I know, but Francis isn't honest. He's lied to Tamar more than once. I don't believe he cares for her as he should."

Sir Sholto frowned. "Is he unkind to her?"

"Not unkind, no. Indifferent, rather."

"You think he's marrying her just to line his pockets?"

"Oh, no." Lucilla smiled. "Perhaps I'm too romantical in my notions. I've learned, since I came to London, that people in our walk of life don't marry for love. I can't hold it against Francis if he wishes to marry for practical reasons."

"A marriage without mutual affection and respect is not practical at all," said Sir Sholto bluntly. "How does Tamar feel, do you know?"

"She floats along from day to day."

"She's only sixteen," said Sir Sholto uneasily.

"I know, but there's something unnatural in such detachment. It's as if she's waiting for something to happen . . . as if her thoughts were fixed on some distant, secret place." Lucilla made a helpless gesture. "I can't explain, Grandfather. You'll see for yourself."

At that moment there was the sound of flying footsteps in the hallway, and the door burst open to reveal Tamar, still wearing her pelisse and bonnet, with Lady Charlotte a few paces behind her.

"Where's Giles?" said Tamar breathlessly. "Neame says he was here."

Lucilla moved swiftly towards her cousin. "He was indeed, but he left a while ago to go to his hotel." Catching hold of Tamar's hand, she gave it a warning squeeze. "Come and welcome Grandpapa."

Tamar turned for the first time towards Sir Sholto. He held out his hand to her and she ran over to embrace him. Her smile was open and sweet as ever; but none of the three people watching her could miss the expression of bitter disappointment in her eyes.

XXIV

OVER THE NEXT three days Sir Sholto settled into the pattern of life in Curzon Street. Lady Charlotte, an excellent hostess, made every possible provision for his comfort. He was given a set of rooms on the same level as the dining-room, and if he desired to move to another floor, a footman was always at hand to assist him.

He was tired after his long journey from Swallowford, and as the weather was inclement he was well content to remain within doors. It gave him time to rest, to read the journals, to receive visits from old cronies, and above all to acquaint himself with the moods and behaviour of the members of his family.

It did not take him long to find that the relationship between Lucilla and her godmother left much to be desired. Lady Charlotte, when taxed, insisted that the cause of the trouble was Lord Linslade.

"Lucilla is being talked about," she said. "Not that that seems to bother her. She's a foolish, headstrong girl, and won't listen to a word I say."

"My dear, if your method has been to slate Linslade, then it's hardly surprising Lucilla won't listen to you. Can't you see she's head over heels in love with the man?"

Lady Charlotte made a moue of distaste. "'Being in love', Sholto, may be all very well for members of the lower orders, but for people of our rank and standing, it is nothing but self-indulgence! Lucilla has received several advantageous offers, and refused them all . . . and though I'm happy to say that none of the gentlemen in question has as yet cried off, one can't expect their patience to last for ever."

"Why do you blame Linslade for that?"

"Because he's merely toying with Lucilla," said Lady Charlotte. "He has no intention of marrying her."

"Perhaps he has honourable reasons for not asking for Lucilla's hand. We both know, Charlotte, how deep the rift runs between our family and his. I've long wished to mend it. For Lucilla to marry Linslade might be the answer."

Lady Charlotte reddened. "Ask him what his intentions are, if you're looking for answers."

"I shall, at the right time. These two young people have known each other only a few weeks. Perhaps they wish to be sure of their feelings before rushing into matrimony. Our best course is to deal kindly with them, for any unkindness may force them into action we would deplore."

"Lucilla is enjoying my hospitality, my patronage. I'm doing my best to see her properly established in life. Do you call that unkindness?"

"No, my dear. Heaven knows we're all deep in your debt. Don't think us ungrateful." Sir Sholto paused and smiled. "We old fogies can't play the rôle of Cupid. In matters of the heart, no one ever heeds advice. All we can do for these young people is offer our support and show we have confidence in their good sense." As Lady Charlotte made no answer, he continued. "Now I wish to speak to you about Tamar. She's far from happy. That upsets me very much."

"Young girls take these freakish starts," said Lady Charlotte impatiently. "She's homesick for Ringwood, and the people she knows. Once she's betrothed, she'll soon perk up."

"It's the betrothal that troubles me. Yesterday I asked her point blank if she wished to marry Francis. She replied that that would only be decided on her next birthday. She doesn't seem to grasp that Henry Everley and I have already agreed on the terms of the marriage settlement . . . that Francis expects an announcement to be made in a matter of weeks."

"Tamar's only a child. She'll do as we bid her."

Sir Sholto stared fixedly into Lady Charlotte's angry eyes. "Would you bid her marry against her true feelings?"

"She has none. She lives in a dream world."

"Yes, and that's precisely what disturbs me. Dream worlds are dangerous. Your daughter Caroline lived in a dream world, and the dreams became nightmares and drove her to suicide. For God's sake, Charlotte, consider . . . "

"I have considered," cried Lady Charlotte in a desperate voice. "Do you think that I can ever put Caroline from my mind? Every time I look at Tamar's face, I'm reminded of my lost child. And Tamar is like Caroline, in character as well as looks. The same indecision, the same self-deception. The history of morbid depression is in the Brampton blood, Sholto, and we cannot wish it away. The people in our circle don't forget that Caroline lost her sanity and took her own life. What mother of an eligible son is going to encourage him to take on that legacy? Francis is willing to do so. He'll give Tamar an honourable name, a safe home. He'll save her from dwindling into spinsterhood. If you think she'll contract any other marriage as advantageous, it's you who are living in a dream world!"

"Young Ayliffe would marry her today."

"Giles Ayliffe has no prospects. His head's full of nonsense. Added to which, his parents are bitterly opposed to the match. You've presented these very arguments yourself, I don't know how many times."

"Perhaps I was wrong to do so. If I was, then I won't force Tamar to pay for my error."

"May I ask what you propose to do, Sholto?"

He leaned his chin on his clasped hands, thinking. At last he said, "For the moment, I shall do nothing but wait and watch." He gave her his gentle smile. "I'm glad to be here, Charlotte, and I'm sure that between us we'll find a way to resolve all our difficulties."

Lady Charlotte carried the news of Sir Sholto's change of attitude straight to her brother, and that afternoon a council of war took place at Everley House. Present were Lord Everley, Lady Charlotte, Francis Warsop and Mr Jason Cleve.

Lord Everley was in a towering rage. He railed against his old friend Sir Sholto accusing him of reneging on their agreement. He berated his sister for failing to make Tamar toe the line. When Mr Cleve attempted to defend Lady Charlotte, Lord Everley rounded on him, called him an incompetent shyster and threatened to turn over the family affairs to another lawyer, a threat which caused Mr Cleve to turn very white about the gills.

But the loudest peal his lordship rang over his son's head. "I've warned you before, Francis," he thundered, "that this marriage is your last hope. If you can't pull it off, then I've done with you, once for all. I'm sick to death of your loosefish, good-for-nothing ways, and if you can't mend 'em, you'll find yourself out on the street, and not a feather to fly with."

Francis raised a sulky face. "Don't blame me," he said, "if the chit's lovesick for Giles Ayliffe."

His father's scowl grew fiercer. "Ayliffe? Ayliffe's a mere boy, a mooncalf without title or fortune. You call yourself a man of the world, yet you can't compete with him? You can't win over a green girl of sixteen? If you've failed, my lad, you've no one to blame but yourself. Spent your time in the gaming-hells, instead of with her. Played the ninny, wasted your efforts and my money! I'll have no more of it, d'ye hear? I don't wish to see your face again until you can bring me better tidings. And now, get out! Get out, the pack of you! I declare, the very sight of you makes my stomach queasy!"

But as the guests filed towards the door, Lord Everley spoke again.

"Cleve. Wait."

Mr Cleve returned to stand before the old man's chair.

"I mean what I say," Lord Everley said, "so don't think to play fast and loose with me. I've been watching you, these past few months . . . watching my revenues decline, while you and that sister of mine grow plump as partridges."

Cleve assumed an air of injured dignity. "My lord, I have always served you, and Lady Charlotte, to the best of my ability."

Lord Everley gave a sneering laugh. "Oh, you've served Charlotte well, in every sense of the word. Don't think I don't know what's gone on between the pair of you, all these years. I've turned a blind eye to your bedroom antics. Didn't want any scandal. Didn't want the Clubs sayin' m'sister has a jumped-up pettifogger for a lover. But don't think you can try any tricks on me. Do I make myself plain?"

Cleve's face worked. "Does your lordship presume to accuse me . . . to threaten me. . . ?"

"Take it how you like," said Lord Everley rudely. "Take it that I mean to keep a careful eye on you, and if I see aught that I don't like, you'll answer for it."

Mr Cleve opened his mouth, closed it again, bowed stiffly and withdrew. Out on the flagway he stood for some minutes frowning and tugging at his lip before striding away towards Half Moon Street.

Next morning, fired by his parent's harsh strictures, Francis called at Brampton House. He dressed with care in a Wellington frock-coat of sober cut, dark grey trousers and a plum-coloured waistcoat. His linen was snowy, his boots gleamed, his cravat was tied *à l'Irlandais*. He had discarded his diamond tie-pin, and only the Everley seal hung on his fob-chain. Surveying himself in the glass, he felt that he presented a suitably staid appearance . . . the picture of a man determined to abandon his old ways, and embark upon matrimony.

He was disconcerted, and not a little annoyed, to find on his arrival in Curzon Street that he had been forestalled by Giles Ayliffe, who was cosily ensconced in the morning-room, regaling Miss Pelham and Miss Curle with the latest Swallow-ford gossip.

Francis's first thought was to go to his aunt and demand the immediate ejection of Mr Ayliffe, but he realized that that would damn him forever in Tamar's eyes. She was in a glow of happiness at seeing Giles, drank in every word he spoke, and laughed delightedly at his smallest witticism.

Francis had to content himself with greeting her in a proprietary manner, taking the chair next to her, and pretending to share in the general bonhomie.

Lucilla, in his opinion, was being unnecessarily kind to Ayliffe. She positively encouraged him to prose on about his Steam Horse, a topic that Mr Warsop found very tedious. Francis was contemptuous of this new fad of steam-propulsion and felt sure that it must quickly pass. Never having done a day's work in his life, he despised a man who was ready to soil his hands like a common labourer.

Yet for all his superior airs, he knew that in Giles he faced a dangerous rival. That inventive mind, that driving energy, could carry Ayliffe far . . . and if he could, he'd take Tamar with him. Francis saw his own prospects of wealth and security dwindle before his eyes.

His fears increased as the days passed. Giles was always underfoot. He visited the house daily. He hired a carriage and took the girls to see a fireworks display on Battersea Fields. He secured, under the aegis of Sir Sholto, an invitation to the Seftons' dress ball and danced twice with Tamar and once with Lucilla. Though he never presumed or overstepped the mark, he was constantly, maddeningly, there, and Francis could think of no way to be rid of him.

Giles, after all was said and done, remained a close friend of the Curles; and while Lady Charlotte might look at him sideways, and speak witheringly of his "lunatic machines", she could hardly forbid him the house.

Adrian Curle was Giles's firm ally. The two of them rode out together most mornings of the week, and they were often accompanied by Nicholas Frome. It seemed to Francis that the Fromes' influence now outweighed the Everleys' in Curzon Street. This view was confirmed when he saw Giles and Lord Linslade sauntering together along Piccadilly, apparently on the best of terms.

When next he saw Giles, Francis took it on himself to issue a warning. "I shouldn't become too friendly with Linslade if I was you," he said. "Lady C. doesn't like him above half."

Giles looked astonished. "Lord," he said, "I can't claim friendship with Linslade! Never met him but once, at Swallow-ford. Didn't expect him to recall my name when I chanced to run into him at Jackson's Parlour. But he did remember, and was kind enough to go a few rounds with me, too. Very handy with his fives, I can tell you. Rattled my bonebox more than once, and never let me plant a hit on him. Jackson told me that if Linslade hadn't been born to the purple, he'd have made a career for himself in the Ring."

"One must suppose that that explains his penchant for prize-fighters and other low sorts," said Francis spitefully.

Giles's mouth tightened. "Linslade," he said, "has the common touch. There isn't a snobbish bone in his body, else why would he waste time talking to me? He was kindness itself. Enquired about my Steam Horse and told me that if I needed any help in promoting it, I might apply to him."

"Very generous! I expect he hopes that you'll put in a good word for him with Lucilla."

That made Giles burst out laughing. "I, put in a good word for the Nonpareil? Come now, Francis, that's doing it too brown. Linslade doesn't need me to speak for him. Any fool can see that Lucilla's nutty upon him."

With this cheerful remark, Giles went off to keep an appointment at Tattersall's where he hoped to purchase a hunter for his father.

Francis was left to brood on the evils of his situation, and to wonder how in the world he could end them.

Lady Charlotte resented Mr Ayliffe's presence quite as much as did Francis, but she was clever enough not to say so. She made no further approach to Sir Sholto, but concentrated on wearing down Tamar's resistance to the betrothal. She harped endlessly on the need for a young female to make a respectable marriage. She spoke of the felicity of owning both a house in London and a country seat. She mentioned, not more than two or three times a day, the benefits of being Lady Everley. She reminded Tamar frequently of the debt she owed her grandfather. "How sharper than a serpent's tooth," she observed, "is an ungrateful grandchild. I trust that you are not so lost to all sense of duty that you will bruise the heart of that beloved and saintly gentleman."

These tactics would have had little effect on Lucilla, but they were acutely distressing to Tamar. She began to look quite haunted whenever Lady Charlotte approached her. She lost her appetite and slept badly, so that dark shadows appeared under her eyes. She was torn between her longing to be with Giles and her dread of her grandmother's tongue.

Marion Gray, watching the girl's health deteriorate, became more and more anxious. Normally she would have turned to Dr Chase for advice, but the Doctor had returned to Swallowford for a spell, to attend to his patients' needs. Taking her courage in both hands, she spoke to Sir Sholto.

"Lady Charlotte means well," she said, "but she is putting too much pressure on Tamar. The child's constitution won't stand such persecution."

Sir Sholto smiled. "Pray, Marion, don't exaggerate. It's hardly persecution to wish to see Tamar well established. This passion the child has for young Ayliffe is no more than a passing fancy, I'm sure."

"I don't agree," said Mrs Gray. "Tamar may be young, but she's very staunch in her affections, and they are fixed on Giles Ayliffe."

Sir Sholto regarded her thoughtfully. "Do you believe she should marry him?"

"I didn't say that. I know only too well the obstacles along that path. But why must she be forced to marry Francis Warsop? In a year or two perhaps, when she's more mature, she may meet someone she can truly love and respect, and contract a union in which she will be sincerely happy."

"Marion," said Sir Sholto with deliberation, "do you think I'm such an ogre that I'll compel Tamar to marry against her will?"

"No, of course not. Dear Sholto, I know you to be the best of men, the kindest, the most generous . . . but that doesn't alter the fact that Tamar is under great strain. Her nature is not sanguine, you know. I fear that if she's tried too far, she may do . . . something desperate."

Sir Sholto leaned over and grasped Mrs Gray's thin hand.

"My dear, you mustn't fret so. I won't let Tamar come to harm, but nor will I rule out all chance of her marrying Francis. I won't throw away substance for shadow. Let us all be patient, and see how things turn out. You must try to be calm and suppress these morbid imaginings. They do nothing to help the case." As Marion opened her mouth to protest, the old man held up an admonitory hand. "No, that's enough. I wish to hear no more about it, from you or from Lady Charlotte. You must both of you trust me to do as I think best."

Mrs Gray went away in a despairing frame of mind, convinced that her last court of appeal was closed. She believed that Tamar was playing a dangerous game with Francis Warsop. One did not jilt such a man. His nature was vindictive. To be publicly slighted, and at the same time to lose his hope of a comfortable income for life, would very likely prompt him to some petty act of revenge. His glib tongue could damage Tamar's reputation beyond repair.

As the weeks passed, Marion grew more and more perturbed. Giles Ayliffe was forever in Curzon Street. He accompanied Tamar on many of her walks and rides, and as they were friends of long standing it was impossible to forbid these outings. Giles's manner towards Tamar remained perfectly correct, yet it was easy to see that he worshipped the ground she trod on.

Worse, Mrs Gray was beginning to see that Tamar was building all her hopes on the success of Giles's cockamany invention. If that failed, the disappointment could have disastrous effects on the child's always volatile spirits.

Mrs Gray had neither money nor a home of her own. She had to endure the pain of being unable to offer any haven to the person she loved most in the world. All she could do was watch events, and pray that a merciful Providence would show her some way out of the dilemma.

XXV

LUCILLA'S TWENTIETH BIRTHDAY fell in the second week of July, and Sir Sholto had earmarked the date for a small family celebration. It was Giles who hit upon the idea that this should be held not at Brampton House, but on the riverboat Sir Sholto had hired, which was still moored at Chiswick.

The notion found instant favour with the younger members of the household, who at once set about planning the excursion. A team of workmen was despatched to clean and polish the barge from stem to stern, and to furbish it up with awnings, carpets, cushions and the like, until it looked, in Giles's phrase, "fit for the Grand Panjandrum and his court."

Everyone took some share in the arrangements. Sir Sholto caused lanterns to be hung in the trees surrounding the mooring-place. Mrs Gray purchased sticks of incense, which she proposed to burn on deck to keep away midges and other insects. Adrian was inspired to hire a quartet of indigent musicians to entertain the guests, and Lady Charlotte undertook to provide all the necessary refreshments.

"An elegant cold collation," she said. "Nothing elaborate, just some cold ducks, ham, chicken, a pie or so, bread and butter and cake. Fruits and cheeses, wine, of course, and lemonade. And champagne. Yes, definitely champagne. It lends a festive note. You may say it's unnecessary, when we shall be simply *en famille*, but in my opinion what's worth doing, is worth doing well."

"Won't be just the family," Sir Sholto said. "Linslade and Nick Frome are coming, too."

Lady Charlotte stared as if she could not believe her ears. "You must be mad," she said. "Francis and the Fromes? It's unthinkable."

"Francis ain't invited."

174

"Not invited?! The man who is to marry your grand-daughter, not invited?! I declare, I was never more shocked in my life!"

"Well, it's no good putting on that Friday face," said Sir Sholto calmly, "for my mind's made up. This is Lucilla's birthday, and she's to have what guests she likes, which is to say, Linslade and Mr Frome."

"I won't countenance it," she said.

"You'll have to, I'm afraid. The invitations have already been sent."

"In that case," said her ladyship, "I can only pray that the Fromes have enough delicacy of mind to refuse you. Not that I have much hope of it for, by all I know of them, they have about as much refinement as a cockerel on a dungheap."

Lord Linslade found the invitation awaiting him at the breakfast table, next morning.

The only other person who had so far come downstairs was Nick, who was working his way through a plateful of bacon and buttered eggs, while at the same time trying to decide on the likely winner of the afternoon's race at Newmarket.

"Whirligig," he suggested, in a somewhat muffled voice, "has the pace, but can he stay the distance? Can't count on it. Then there's the bay, Johnny-Come-Lately, and I s'pose one shouldn't overlook Mischief Maker. Came fourth last time out, you recall, and finished strongly. What d'you think?"

Receiving no answer to his question, Nicholas glanced up. Alex was standing behind his chair, staring abstractedly at the white card in his hand.

"Alex?" said Nick. "Is something amiss?"

Alex shook his head. "No. We're invited to Lucilla Pelham's birthday celebration on Sunday evening."

"What? In the lions' den?"

"No, it's to be held aboard Sir Sholto's houseboat at Chiswick. An alfresco meal."

"Sounds diverting. Shall you go? I shan't, otherwise."

The Earl took some time to answer, and at last said, almost to himself, "I must go, I think. I must speak soon."

Nicholas opened his mouth to enquire whether Alex meant

175

to pop the question at last; but a glance at his brother's tense and frowning countenance made him change his mind.

The problem of what to give Lucilla for her birthday taxed the minds of all in her immediate circle. Lady Charlotte wrote a short list for their guidance, but as it included such items as a collection of sermons by the Dean of Canterbury and a book on *Cooking for the Chronic Invalid*, her suggestions were ignored.

Tamar, who was an excellent needlewoman, had already embroidered a silk reticule for Lucilla. Sir Sholto paid a visit to Asprey's in Bond Street and chose a very pretty diamond and pearl bracelet. Lady Charlotte decided that a tartan shawl she had had for some months, but had never liked, would suit Lucilla's tawny colouring very well. Adrian purchased a small bottle of attar of roses. Nicholas sent a posy and a box of glazed chestnuts.

For Lord Linslade the choice of a gift was difficult. He thought too highly of Lucilla to offer her anything trumpery, yet what he bought must be impersonal. It must not arouse any false expectations.

He spent three unhappy days inspecting the wares in every shop he could think of, and it was quite by chance that he hit upon the perfect answer. In one of the lanes off Regent Street he found a small painting of Swallowford village, showing the weir, and the Merry Man beside the green, and even giving a glimpse, above the hanging forests, of the roof of Ringwood. Alex ordered it to be despatched, with his note of good wishes, to Brampton House.

Also exercised in her mind was Marion Gray. Her pocket was not deep enough for the smart shops of Bond Street, but she was persuaded that she would find some charming trinket or geegaw at the Pantheon in Oxford Street.

This one-time assembly-room had been transformed into a bazaar, and boasted a great number of stalls where milliners, perfumers, florists and drapers sold goods at a fraction of the prices charged in the larger emporia of the Town. Moreover, it was an amusing place, with a gallery for strollers and a conservatory with a Zoo containing monkeys, parrots and tortoises.

Mrs Gray spent an hour or so wandering about the precincts, and decided at last that she could not do better than purchase a few yards of blonde lace, very reasonably priced, which would serve to trim one of Lucilla's evening petticoats.

She paid for the lace, and was watching the stall-woman wrap it in a sheet of tissue paper, when she was disturbed by shrill female laughter that seemed to come from the aisle behind the stall. Peering past the array of cloaks, caps and bolts of material piled on the shelves, Mrs Gray discerned a woman standing talking to someone who was hidden from view.

The woman was tall, and of ample proportions. Her hair, under an exaggeratedly high poke-bonnet, was of that hard red that speaks of the henna bottle, and her complexion owed much to rouge and powder. She was expensively dressed in Chartreuse silk. The Spanish shawl draped about her shoulders was secured by a large brooch studded with brilliants, and she carried a parasol with a handle of carved ivory. Mrs Gray identified her unhesitatingly as one of the demi-mondaines who lived in the Edgware Road. By the way she was fluttering her lashes, and pouting up her lips, Mrs Gray judged her to be talking to her protector.

At that moment the woman stepped backward, and her companion followed, putting out a hand to tuck a wad of folded banknotes into her corsage. Mrs Gray saw that the man was Francis Warsop.

Her first thought was that he must not see her. Picking up her parcel, she moved swiftly to the cover of a florist's stall where she remained motionless, staring at Francis.

There could be no doubt that it was he, and no doubt about his relationship to this doxy. They were laughing and bantering with the familiarity that spoke of long-established intimacy. After a while, he bent to plant a kiss on the woman's thick white wrist, and the two moved away together, towards the exit to the street.

Mrs Gray moved to a bench and sank down upon it. Her heart was pounding and her hands trembling with mingled disgust and rage. All her suspicions, all her fears, were justified. Francis Warsop was still conducting his life as if Tamar had never entered it, and if he could behave so during the time of courtship, what hope was there that he would become a faithful husband?

He was a libertine, a cheat, and a liar, and under no circumstances must he be allowed to marry Tamar.

But how to prevent it?

Useless to confront him with his duplicity. He would merely laugh, and deny all. A jealous old woman, he'd call her, whose eyesight couldn't be relied on.

Dr Chase, always such a good friend, was still away in Swallowford. Lucilla? Lucilla was no more than a girl, herself. One couldn't burden her with such an indelicate story. And Sir Sholto had shown himself to be unreceptive to criticism of the marriage, and in fact instructed Mrs Gray to say no more on that subject.

There was nothing to do but wait, wait for further evidence of Francis's perfidy, wait for an opportunity to expose him for the villain he undoubtedly was.

Clutching her package, Mrs Gray made her way slowly back to Curzon Street. There she retired to her room, to stretch out on her bed and sip a draught of sal volatile, in a vain attempt to calm her jangled nerves.

Lucilla's birthday began promisingly. The weather was fair and warm, and the preparations were concluded without a hitch. After breakfast she examined and exclaimed over the presents she'd been given, after which the family attended morning prayers at St James's Church in Piccadilly.

At two o'clock the cook, Mrs Grampound, and various of her minions left for Chiswick in Lady Charlotte's chaise, followed by Sir Sholto's fourgon laden with a mountain of food, wine, buckets of ice, baskets of china and cutlery, and all the paraphernalia Mrs Grampound held to be indispensable to the serving of a picnic supper.

The carriages of the guests gathered at Curzon Street, and after some initial chopping and changing, left there at three o'clock. Sir Sholto, Lady Charlotte and Tamar travelled in her ladyship's barouche. Mrs Gray rode with Giles in the gig, and Nicholas Frome accompanied Adrian Curle, who drove Lucilla's phaeton.

Lucilla herself was taken up by Lord Linslade in his curricle. He was dressed for the occasion in riding-clothes; a dark green coat, the collar rolled high and falling to broad lapels; fawn breeches, and boots with white tops; a plain weskit, and a tall hat with a curling brim.

Miss Pelham was attired in a gown of pale mauve muslin, embroidered with sprays of flowers around the hem. On her head was a hat of chip straw, trimmed with long velvet ribbons. She carried a parasol of lilac lace, which cast delicate shadows on her face and deepened the colour of her eyes to violet.

For the first mile or so, she left the Earl to steady his greys, which were skittish after a day or two in the stables; but once the traffic thinned, and they were bowling along the Fulham Road, she thanked him for his birthday gift.

"It's so exactly what I like most," she said. "A present that reminds me of some happy place or circumstance."

He glanced at her, smiling. "I know. I was tempted to keep it for myself, for that very reason." He hesitated, then said quietly, "I shall always think of Swallowford . . . of you, and your family . . . with such deep pleasure."

Something in his tone made her heart miss a beat. She said, half-teasing and half-apprehensive, "You speak as if Ringwood might disappear, like a castle in a fairytale. It won't, you know."

"Not Ringwood, no. Myself, perhaps."

"You're leaving London?"

"I'm afraid so. Tomorrow I go down to Foxfare to see to certain matters there. I'll be back in Town for the Coronation, but after that I expect to be sent to Vienna."

"Sent? By whom?"

"The King plans to make a ceremonial tour of Europe. Lord Castlereagh has asked me to accompany the royal party. It's not what I desire, believe me. I'd far rather stay here and continue to . . . to see you. But there are problems I can neither explain nor resolve. I beg you to understand."

He spoke with intensity. She realized that he had rehearsed these words many times in his mind, and that it gave him pain to speak them. She longed to question him, but guessed that if she did, she would get no satisfactory answers. The fear she had been fighting for weeks, surged to engulf her. Alex was going away. She could not hold him. The knowledge gave her such anguish that for a second she could not utter a word. Then she clasped her hands tightly in her lap, and nodded.

"I do understand. I know that whatever you do is for the best. I hope that . . . that one day you'll return, and . . . and tell me whatever it is that can't be told now."

He made no reply, and she sighed. "How long will it be before you leave?"

"I'm not sure. After the Coronation. A week, perhaps. Ten days."

"I see." She sat for a time in frowning thought, then said briskly, "I hope at least you'll be able to attend Aunt Charlotte's ball. It's set down for the Friday after the Coronation."

He met her gaze. "Lucilla, my dear, I don't know."

"Don't refuse out of hand. Leave the decision open, and come if you are able."

He nodded, and turned the conversation to some indifferent topic. By the time they reached Chiswick they were able to present calm countenances to the world.

Lucilla had never before visited Chiswick, and thought it a charming village. They reached the Mall soon after leaving Hammersmith, and Alex was able to point out Walpole House, which dated from the seventeenth century, and the graveyard of St Nicholas' Church, where the painter William Hogarth lay buried.

Hogarth Lane led them to Duke's Avenue, opposite the main entrance to Chiswick House, with its fine gates and magnificently wooded Park. In the distance rose the mansion built by the Third Earl of Burlington, on the lines of Palladio's Villa near Vicenza.

Reaching the riverside at last, they found the houseboat safely moored at a wooden landing-stage, and already teeming with activity, the servants busy setting out the repast, and the guests enjoying a glass of wine under the shade of the awnings. Much interest was displayed in the prospect across the Thames to the fields and forests of Mortlake and Kew, and Giles

Ayliffe's cup ran over when one of the new steamboats came into view, forging along in midstream, and churning up all manner of mud and weed with each sweep of its giant wheel.

Setting out the picnic, and consuming it, took the better part of three hours. Lucilla was grateful for the time it gave her to collect her thoughts. She joined automatically in the laughter and repartee of her companions, but part of her mind was busy with Alex's announcement.

She was in a puzzle what to make of it. On the face of things, he was saying goodbye, yet she could not believe that he wished to leave her. He had spoken of a problem he "could neither explain, nor resolve". Was it something to do with his work for the Government, or a personal matter? She wanted desperately to talk to him, to break down the barrier of reserve he had raised between them. Once or twice, she caught him watching her with painful intensity, as if he were trying to stamp her image in his memory.

The afternoon wore on. The light failed from the water-meadows, and Sir Sholto ordered the lanterns lit on the barge, and in the trees round about. Lucilla's thoughts grew quieter. Her earlier panic evaporated, to be replaced by a resolve to find out exactly what had prompted Alex's decision.

Once she felt he was about to revoke it. As the sky grew dark, and the stars blossomed over the roofs of Chiswick, he came to stand beside her. She sensed that he was fighting an urge to take her in his arms. She put out a hand to him, but he at once stepped back, and moved away to talk to Giles and Adrian at the far end of the boat.

She did not follow him, nor did she try again to have private speech with him. When the time came to return to Town, she suggested that it would be easier if she drove with Adrian in the phaeton, and he took Nicholas in his curricle.

He nodded tersely. "As you wish."

She gave him her hand. "Don't leave the country without saying goodbye to me."

He bent his head and kissed her palm. "I shan't, I promise."

Adrian brought the phaeton to where they stood. Alex helped Lucilla to climb up into it. She thought she heard him murmur the words, "Goodbye, my love", and she swung round quickly in her seat, but he was already striding away towards his waiting carriage.

Lucilla told her grandfather, next day, that she might not see Lord Linslade for some time as he was going first to Foxfare and later to Vienna.

The old man looked at her without speaking for a moment, and then said bluntly, "You'll miss him, puss, won't you?"

"Yes, I shall, but I don't wish to speak of that to anyone but you, Grandpapa."

"Very well, it shall be our secret. Did Linslade give his reasons for this sudden departure?"

"Not the true ones, I think. No doubt I'll learn them, in time."

That was all she would say, and thereafter she went about her daily round with a cheerful face. Sir Sholto knew that Lucilla was not the girl to show her disappointments, but he guessed that she was suffering, and he devoted much thought to what he might do to help her.

XXVI

LONDON WAS NOW in the final frenzy of preparation for the Coronation of the King on July 19th.

Westminster Abbey and Westminster Hall had been transformed by armies of carpenters, joiners, painters and upholsterers. The Abbey was fitted with tiers of benches covered in crimson cloth, boxes and galleries had been installed under the western windows overlooking the nave, and extra seats placed in the choir, and in the north and south transepts.

In Westminster Hall, where the Royal Banquet was to take place, a whole new floor of wood covered in blue cloth had been laid, and banks of seats stood against the cloth-draped walls. The King's musicians were to be accommodated in a gallery above a Gothic arch at one end of the Hall, while at the other was a dais for the King and the Royal Dukes. Long dining-tables stretched down either side and, here, three hundred and twelve peers of the realm would in due course sit down to the feast. The peeresses, to Lady Charlotte's intense disgust, were to be confined to the galleries, unhonoured and unfed.

Parliament had voted no less than £243,000 for this feudal splendour, and it was rumoured that the King's own robes had cost the colossal sum of £24,000. They were the cause of much hilarity among the ton; "For how," asked Emily Cowper, "will poor Prinny move at all, in a train twenty-seven feet long, and in a hat trimmed with ostrich-feathers and a heron's plume?"

Despite what the cynics said, there was now only one thought in every mind. Not a man, woman, or child but was determined to be part of Coronation Day, and argument raged about what should be worn, what food prepared, and from which vantage point the spectacle might best be viewed.

Lady Charlotte had long ago procured places in the public stands for the younger members of her family and Mrs Gray, but the unexpected arrival of Sir Sholto, Dr Chase and Giles Ayliffe severely taxed her mind.

"Seats are not to be had for love or money," she said. "Every balcony along the route is already bespoke. Chase and Giles may take their chances with the common crowd, but that's not to be thought of for Sholto."

The day after the picnic at Chiswick, however, Sir Sholto received a very welcome letter.

"From Linslade," he announced. "He writes that he has reserved the house opposite the Speaker's residence in Westminster. His family prefers not to use it, and he offers it to me and such friends as I choose to invite. Uncommon civil of him, I think. Marion, you may give your seat on the stand to Giles, and you and Dr Chase will bear me company. How's that?"

Mrs Gray, who had been secretly wondering how she would endure a whole day of noise and crush, accepted this offer thankfully. And though Francis muttered that he didn't care to take charity from a Frome, no one paid any attention to his ill-humour, since all were busy discussing the fine detail of their plans of campaign.

Lord Linslade was by this time at Foxfare, and in a thoroughly depressed frame of mind. While he knew he had done the correct thing in breaking off his association with Lucilla, he missed her abominably and found himself unable to think of anything else.

There was work to be done on the estate, but it did not fill his time. Most of his neighbours were away, gone to London for the festivities, and he found himself dining alone every night, which did nothing to lift his spirits.

Far from curing him .of his longing for Miss Pelham, the isolation intensified it. He grew daily more sure that she was the only woman in the world for him; and since Fate had put her forever out of reach, he foresaw for himself a life of crabbed bachelorhood.

On the eve of the Coronation he returned to London to find his household in a state of wild confusion. Within an hour of his arrival, he had found it necessary to summon all the servants, and review the orders his mama had given them; devise a scheme whereby Nicholas, Emily, George and Augusta could be conveyed to their seats before the main roads were closed to carriages; raise and distribute various sums of money to people who had not dreamed how much the excursions were going to cost them; restrain the terrier Pebble from biting a man who delivered his mama's diamonds from the Bank; and rebuke Emily for announcing in an airy manner that she had made up her mind to marry Denby Shepstone and would like Alex to give his consent forthwith.

"No doubt one day you will marry Den," Alex told her, "but we'll do things the proper way. No, don't bridle at me, if you please. At least have the decorum to wait until Denby requests your hand, before you puff off your plans."

"I don't need to wait," protested Emily, turning very red in the face. "I know that Den wishes to marry me."

"Has he said so?"

"No . . . but he doesn't need to. He loves me. I know it. A woman knows these things without being told."

In ordinary circumstances, Alex would have treated this worldly wisdom with amusement, but tonight it touched on raw nerves.

"When Den wishes to be betrothed to you," he said sharply, "he will speak to me and to Mama, to seek our permission.

Until that time comes, be good enough to remember what I've told you."

At this Emily stamped her foot, called Alex a brute and a heartless tyrant, and rushed headlong up the stairs. Alex would have followed and tried to mollify her, but at that moment a courier arrived with an urgent message from Castlereagh. Certain minor royalties had taken exception to the places allotted them in the Abbey. Linslade was, please, to call upon them at once and smooth their ruffled feathers.

This errand took two hours to complete, and the Earl returned to Berkeley Square to find the family about to sit down to dinner. A glance around the table told him that Emily had already poured out her heart to her mother, who bestowed on Alex a look of deep reproach. Alex ignored it. He wished only to get through the meal with the appearance of calm. Later he would make his peace with his sister.

All went well through the first course. George and Nicholas plied Alex with questions about Foxfare and its doings, and Lady Linslade insisted on being told, for not more than the fourth time, precisely how she was to be conveyed to Westminster on the following day.

But when the meat-dishes had been removed from the board, and the dessert brought in, Augusta precipitated a crisis.

"Such a pity, Linslade," she remarked, as she helped herself to Floating Island Pudding with whipped cream, "that you weren't in Town for the Hortons' dress party. There was never anything more enjoyable. All the guests were in historical costume. Lady H. herself wore a Venetian domino, with a steeple wig and a mask, and stood in a gondola, handin' out gifts. Gave me a set of Pandean pipes. Lord knows what I shall do with 'em! Your Miss Fulham was there. Quite took the shine out of the rest of us. She was *en Grecque* . . . Atlanta or some such thing, and carried a golden apple. There was Povall, and John Braby, callin' to her to toss the apple, but she would not. If you'd been there, she must have thrown it to you. Pity you had to choose this week to rusticate."

Alex returned some curt response to this, and the subject might have been allowed to lapse had not the Devil entered Emily. Still smarting from her brother's snub, and unaware of the unhappy state of affairs between him and Lucilla, she decided to roast him a little.

"I think, Augusta, you have that name wrong. Surely you mean Miss Balham, not Miss Fulham?"

Augusta shook her head. "Don't know any Miss Balham," she said. "I refer to Miss Fulham. Pretty copper-nob, Sholto Curle's grand-daughter, has a *tendre* for Alex, here."

Emily achieved a fluting laugh. "Oh, but that isn't Miss Fulham," she cried, "that is Miss Peckham. If you don't learn to get names aright, Augusta, they'll be carting you off to Bedlam!"

Nicholas, catching sight of his brother's darkening face, tried to intervene, but it was too late. Augusta was protesting loudly that she knew Fulham from Peckham, thank you very much; Emily was giggling and egging her on; while George hammered on the table with his fist and commanded them both to hold their tongues and pass the creamboat.

At the height of the uproar Lord Linslade's temper snapped. He rose to his feet and in a thundering voice shouted, "Silence! Silence, all of you!"

The din ceased as if by magic. Five shocked faces turned towards him.

"It is distasteful," said his lordship in a voice shaking with fury, "to see how this family comports itself at the dinner-table! Yelling and sniggering like a bunch of Yahoos! You, Emily, have behaved in such a pert and forward way that I've a good mind to send you back to Foxfare to learn some conduct. And you, Augusta, will oblige me by referring to my friends by their correct titles, and not by whichever misnomer first enters your head. The lady you speak of is Miss Pelham, Miss Lucilla Pelham. P-E-L-H-A-M."

"That's what I said. Pelham," answered Augusta, "and I see no reason for you to dislike it. Perfectly good name, Pelham. Nothin' to be ashamed of. Not like Ramsbotham, or Mudd, or Pigg. What's more, I like the gal. Pretty to look at, and pretty-behaved, too. Don't know for the life of me why you don't marry her."

"Be quiet, Augusta," said George desperately. She fixed him with an enquiring gaze.

186

"Why? I never had any objections to the match."

George made feeble hushing signs to his wife, but his Mama now took up the cudgels. "You may not object to it, Augusta," she said, "but I assure you, I do. I will never permit such a *mésalliance* to take place."

"Don't see how you can prevent it," said Augusta reasonably. "Alex can wed whom he likes. No need to ask your permission, ma'am."

"If Alex marries Lucilla Pelham," said Lady Linslade awfully, "all will be over between us. He will never set foot in my house again."

She shifted round to face Alex as she spoke, her chin raised defiantly; but seeing his expression, she faltered and leaned back in her chair. Nicholas got quickly to his feet and came to place a hand on Alex's arm. "Don't say any more," he pleaded. "We're all above ourselves. Wait till tomorrow."

Alex jerked free of Nick's grasp. "No," he said. "What has to be said, will be said now, and it is this. I have always tried to act in the best interests of this family, and I hope to do so in the future; but this is my house, and while you live in it you will observe the rules I set down. I shall invite what friends I wish to it and, if you dislike them, you may stay away. I will marry how, when and whom I please, and nobody — not even you, Mama — need presume to offer me advice on the subject. Now I consider that I have earned a little peace. I am going out. I bid you all a very good night."

With that, he turned and strode from the house. Out in the hall a footman sprang to open the front door for him, and Bungay hurried to offer him his hat and gloves; but the Earl marched past them without a halt, and with such a look of white rage on his face that both men stepped back without daring to address a word to him.

His lordship's anger carried him as far as his grandmother's house in Grosvenor Street, but by the time a flunkey had admitted him, and was conducting him to the small parlour on the first floor, his sense of proportion had begun to reassert itself.

He found the Dowager alone. She had exchanged her formal

dress for a loose garment of pale grey damask, the sleeves ruched in the Marmaluke style. A lace cap was set on her silver hair. It made her look kittenish rather than dignified. She was engaged in a game of patience and, at the moment of Alex's entry, was searching covertly through the pack of discards in her hand. Finding the trey of diamonds, she extracted it, placed it in position on the table and turned to smile at her grandson.

"I'm allowed three cheats in an evening," she said. "This is only the first." Her gaze sharpened as she took in Alex's wild-eyed look, and she stretched out a hand.

"Come and give me a kiss," she demanded, "and tell me what has happened to make you look like Jove-athunder."

Alex dropped a kiss on her cheek and sat down on the far side of the table.

"I went mad," he said. "I insulted Mama . . . Emily . . . Augusta. God knows what got into me." He shook his head dazedly. "For a moment, Grandmama, I was ready to murder the lot of them! Can you credit it?"

"Oh, easily," said the Dowager. "I don't know how you've kept your hands off them for so long."

"It's not a laughing matter. I shouted. I told Mama to mind her own business. I ranted about it being my house, not hers . . . "

"A fact which Elvira has managed to ignore for years . . . "

"I behaved like . . . like a barbarian."

"A Berserker," agreed the Dowager cheerfully. "It happens, on occasion, to people like you . . . over-conscientious, self-contained people who've been too much put upon. It happened to me, once."

"You?" Alex stared in disbelief, and the Dowager tranquilly placed a black two on a red trey.

"Yes. I went wild. I cut the tails off every coat in your father's wardrobe, and then, for good measure, I took ten bottles of his best brandy — it had to be smuggled in, you know, on pack ponies, at great risk to life and limb — and I broke the lot. I will never forget the satisfaction it gave me, to see the stuff running all over the floor."

"What made you do it?" said Alex, fascinated.

"Linslade did something to provoke me. I forget, now, precisely what it was, but in any event he never did it again. The cause of going berserk can be quite trivial, you see. The last straw, in fact. What set you off?"

Alex rubbed a hand over his forehead. "Augusta called Lucilla Pelham Miss Fulham. Emily set up a tease. Mama said she wouldn't permit me to marry Lucilla, and I . . . exploded like a petard."

"Very natural," said the Dowager. She lifted a line of cards and moved it to the right. "Are you in love with Miss Pelham?"

"Yes," he said at once, "beyond recall. But you needn't be anxious about it. I've already told her I'll be going abroad very soon, with H.M.'s party."

"And how did she receive the news?"

"I think it made her . . . unhappy . . . but she's not the sort of girl to . . . to . . . "

" . . . wear her heart on her sleeve?"

He nodded. "I think Lucilla's been expecting something of the sort. I've tried not to . . . not to . . . oh, be damned, whatever I say makes me sound a coxcomb!"

The Dowager laid aside her cards. "Did you consider telling her about Francis Warsop's seduction of Arabella?"

"No, how could I? It's Bella's secret, not mine."

Lady Linslade considered him quietly. At last she said, "Stay here, Alex. I'm going to order some tea. I shan't be long." She rose, patted him gently on the shoulder, and left the room.

Alex leaned back in his chair and closed his eyes. Now that his anger had faded, he felt an extraordinary lassitude of mind and body. Perhaps that was always the effect of berserker rage. Tomorrow he would have to apologize to his family, but for the moment he was content to remain where he was, empty of all thought.

Presently the door behind him opened, and he heard the chink of the teacups. He started to get to his feet.

The person bearing the tea-tray was neither his grandmother nor the butler, but a young woman not yet turned thirty, with fair hair curling about her face, and the delicate features of a Botticelli Venus.

She was dressed in the height of modality, in a gown of

wheaten silk trimmed with blonde lace. She came forward to kiss Alex, her smile registering both pleasure and a certain mischievous amusement. He took the tray from her and set it on the table.

"Bella," he exclaimed, "I'd forgot you were due to arrive today! Is John with you?"

"Not he. He says that if the rest of the nation wishes to waste its blunt putting a crown on a porker, he does not. I brought the children, though."

"All five of 'em?"

"All five." Arabella gave him a quizzical look. "If you can persuade any right-minded child that to stay home is preferable to coming to London for a Coronation Parade, then you're cleverer than I am." She settled herself behind the tea-tray. "Sit down, my dear, and tell me all there is to tell about the beautiful and modish Miss Pelham."

"Who," demanded his lordship, sitting down as he was bid and accepting a cup from his sister, "told you about her?" As Bella only smiled, he said, "I suppose it must have been Grandmama, since you only reached Town today?"

"Heavens, no," said Arabella lightly. "The rumours began to reach Lincolnshire as much as a month ago. By the end of June we had it on good authority that you were fairly hooked. In the first week of July we heard that White's was giving ten to one on your announcing your engagement. When you mysteriously fled to Foxfare, last week, your price went out a bit. I'm told Lord Povall is now the favourite in the betting."

"Destestable!" muttered Alex.

"Odious," agreed Arabella, "but I'm sure you can regain the lead if you set your mind to it."

"You know quite well, I was thinking of the gossip. To subject Lucilla to that . . . "

"Well, my love, there's one sure way to keep tongues from wagging, and that's to put a notice of your betrothal in *The Times*."

"There will be no betrothal. I've told Lucilla that I'm going abroad when the King makes his tour of Europe."

"Poor Miss Pelham. Pursued, only to be slighted. I must say, I thought better of you, Alex."

"I was wrong, I know. All I can do now is remove myself from her life, and hope she finds someone more deserving."

"Poppycock," said Arabella roundly. "No one could be more deserving than you, and though I hesitate to inflame your vanity, you know quite well that you're considered the most desirable parti in England." Arabella took a few sips of her tea and then set down her cup with a firm gesture. "I think," she said, "that you should go to her at once, and tell her you have changed your mind, and propose to stay in England and marry her."

"Bella, please . . . "

"No, don't interrupt. It's quite obvious that you have, as always, been moved by the noblest of motives to forswear your own interests. It's crystal clear you're doing so to protect me. What great nonsense, Alex! Do you really imagine I'll allow my youthful peccadilloes to blight your life? When I was sixteen I committed a great folly in running off with Francis Warsop. I don't forget the hurt it caused my family, and John; I don't seek to gloss over the gravity of my action; but I do say this. What happened is old history. Francis and I belong to the real world, not to some fusty old melodrama. I've met him any number of times, over the years, and I assure you we feel nothing but indifference towards each other. I've told Mama, time and again, that I wish to end the silly feud between the Everleys and us. There's no reason for it to continue . . . and no reason in the world why you shouldn't marry Lucilla Pelham."

"You're generous to say so, Bella, but *I* don't forget that you have a husband and children to think of."

"John and I are completely at one on this, and the children are in no way concerned with the decisions of their olders and betters."

Alex got up from the table and took a few restless paces about the room. Returning to gaze down at Arabella, he said, "If it was only between ourselves . . . but there's Mama, too. She won't relent."

Arabella laughed. "Mama will enact a Cheltenham tragedy or two, of course; but I'll warrant you that a week or so after you announce your engagement, she'll be helping Lucilla to choose her bride-clothes and debating whether your first-born . . .

who will naturally be a boy . . . must be named William after Sir Guillaume de Frome, or Simon after Simon Curle the Crusader."

As Alex still looked uncertain, Arabella rose and gave him a quick hug. "There's no time to be lost," she said. "It's too late for you to call at Brampton House, but you may write a note to Miss Pelham, and hand it in at her door on your way home. Do make haste to put the poor girl out of her misery."

Alex's face was suddenly transfigured by the broadest of smiles.

"Bless you," he said. "I believe I'll do just that."

"You'll find pen and paper in the library," Arabella told him.

He hurried away, and ten minutes later left the house, bound for Curzon Street. From behind the morning-room curtains his grandmother and sister watched his departure with every mark of satisfaction.

XXVII

LONDONERS WERE THAT night divided into two camps: those who were resolved to stay up till dawn, to secure their places along the Coronation route or to join the many celebrations in course throughout the city: and those who were resolved to retire early to bed, to fortify themselves against the exertions of the great day.

Adrian Curle, Giles Ayliffe and Nicholas Frome were of the former persuasion. As soon as they had eaten their dinners they met at an agreed point in Piccadilly and set out on a round of sight-seeing, beer-swilling and general jollification.

The other inhabitants of Brampton House stayed home. Dr Chase, who had returned to Town from Ringwood two days earlier, insisted on giving Sir Sholto a tisane to ensure him a good night's rest. The old man for once didn't argue, but retired to bed at eight o'clock, on the strict understanding that he was to be roused at four the next morning. "We shall be the first to leave the house," he told Dr Chase. "We must be at Westminster not later than six, or we shan't be allowed through."

Lady Charlotte and Tamar went upstairs not long after,

leaving only Lucilla, Dr Chase and Mrs Gray to gather round the evening tea-tray.

The excitements of the week had worked on Marion's nerves, and she said fretfully that she was sure none of them would succeed in reaching their seats in time.

"Don't worry," Lucilla told her. "Everything will go swimmingly, you'll see. John Coachman will take you to the house Lord Linslade has lent us, you'll have Mrs Grampound and Neame to look after you there . . . "

"What if they can't come through the crowds?"

"They're already at the house," said Lucilla patiently. "They'll spend the night there, and very pleased they are about it, too, for they'll have the best view of His Majesty in London."

"If I'm not here," mourned Mrs Gray, "who will see that the rest of you rise in time? Who will . . .?"

"That is all taken care of. Aunt Charlotte will be fetched by Lord Everley at six. Francis will drive Tamar and me to our places, and Giles will go with Adrian."

"Food," said Mrs Gray, "and drink! All those hours you will be forced to spend in the hot sun . . . "

"The stand is covered, and we have enough in the picnic hampers to sustain us for a week. Do, pray, set your mind at rest, Marion."

Mrs Gray was prevented from raising any further difficulties by the entry of a footman bearing a letter for Lucilla. Recognizing the handwriting, she took it quickly and broke the wafer that sealed it.

"It's from Linslade," she said. "I hope there's no upset in the plans!"

She read the missive through, then nodded to the footman. "Thank you, Timothy. There's no answer."

As the man retreated, Lucilla read the letter through a second time. Mrs Gray, watching her sharply, saw that she had turned very pale.

"Lucilla? Not bad news, is it?"

Lucilla shook her head a little confusedly. "No, no . . . not at all. He writes to tell me that he does not, after all, have to leave England . . . and that he hopes to have the f-felicity of calling upon Grandpapa, and me, as soon as may be convenient to us."

Mrs Gray struck her hands together delightedly. "Oh, Lucilla, what joy!"

Lucilla shook her head quickly. "I don't think you should read too much into it, Marion."

"Nonsense," said Mrs Gray. "There's only one construction to be put on it. He means to offer for you, but wishes to speak to your grandfather first. Very proper of him."

"It may just be some matter of business."

"That would not give him felicity! It's quite plain what he intends." Mrs Gray leaned forward. "How does he address you, may I ask?"

Lucilla blushed. "As 'my dear, dearest Miss Pelham'."

"There you are, then," said Marion. "Not a doubt of it! You may expect a flattering offer in the very near future. Oh Lucilla, my love, I do wish you very happy!" She sprang from her chair and planted a warm kiss on Lucilla's cheek. "I must tell Tamar," she said, already hurrying towards the door. "If only she's not already asleep. Indeed, I shall waken her."

"Marion," said Lucilla, "pray wait . . . " But Marion was out of the room and running up the stairs. Lucilla turned to Dr Chase. "He makes no mention of marriage," she began, but Dr Chase shook his head.

"My dear, there's no need. It's been obvious to us all, since I don't know when, how matters stood between you two. Smelling of April and May! Allow me to offer you my sincere felicitations. He's an admirable man and will make you very happy, I'm sure. If I was you, I'd write to him and suggest a time when he may call on you."

"It can't be tomorrow," Lucilla said.

"The day after, then," said Dr Chase comfortably. "I doubt if he'll change his intentions in the space of two days."

His Majesty King George IV passed that night in the home of the Speaker of the House of Commons, not far from St Margaret's Church in Westminster.

The robes he was to wear for his coronation had already been conveyed there, removed from their packing and spread out so that the crimson velvet train, spangled with golden stars, might not be crushed. On a special pedestal rested his huge black Spanish-style hat trimmed with feathers.

It is doubtful if His Majesty slept well that night, for the churchbells were pealed every half hour from midnight until dawn, and from time to time cannons boomed across the river, and rockets hissed upward into the dark sky.

Added to these sounds was the hubbub of the streets: the constant clop of horses' hooves as carriages, hackneys, gigs and cavalrymen passed to and fro; the rumble of wagons and drays conveying mountains of food, wine, ale and water to various points along the main roads; and, over all, the voices of the people who were already thick along the route. Every window overlooking it had its complement of watchers. Every seat on every stand was sold. Many citizens had climbed to rooftops or the upper branches of trees. On every corner, honest folk rubbed shoulders with pimps and pickpockets, the drunk mingled with the sober, the London-bred with the country-dwellers who had never before set foot in the city. Yet all this polyglot crowd was united by a common purpose, a will to be part of that greatest of all national events, the crowning of a monarch.

Lucilla sat late at the window of her bedroom, which afforded her a glimpse down Clarges Street to Piccadilly. Her eyes were on the living pageant that streamed along the highway; but her thoughts often strayed to Linslade's letter, which she held tightly clasped in her hand.

Coronation Day dawned sunny, a good omen which put the waiting population in a cheerful mood and did much to prevent the unrest feared by the authorities.

Sir Sholto and his companions were among the first to catch sight of their sovereign, for the house secured by Lord Linslade was directly opposite that of the Speaker, and its windows overlooked the carriage gate through which the royal coach must reach the street.

This was due to happen at ten minutes to ten; but there was a delay of almost half an hour, a circumstance which caused Sir Sholto to say acidly that Prinny must be having trouble with his corsets. (An unjust criticism, as it happened, the problem being that Lord Gwydyr, the acting Lord Great Chamberlain, had torn his clothes while dressing.)

At last the great gilded carriage rolled through the archway, and the watchers at the windows were afforded a brief glimpse of the King's face as it passed. The huzzas of the crowd burst forth rolling down towards the river; bells began to peal, their joyous sound spreading west to Knightsbridge and east to the City and, just before half-past ten, King George IV of England arrived at the doors of Westminster Hall.

He made a dramatic entrance. As Mr Benjamin Robert Haydon was later to record, "Something rustles, and a being, buried in satin, feathers and diamonds, rolls gracefully into his seat. The room rises with a sort of feathered, silken thunder. Plumes wave, eyes sparkle, glasses are out, mouths smile, and one man becomes the object of attraction to thousands. The way in which the King bowed was really royal. As he looked towards the peeresses and foreign ambassadors, he showed like some gorgeous bird of the east."

Some, like the Duke of Wellington's inamorata, Mrs Arbuthnot, might mock the King's appearance and think that his brown wig, with thick curls falling over forehead and neck made him look perfectly ridiculous; but most conceded that somehow Prinny had acquired an impressive dignity, and that the whole scene had a splendour that quite outweighed its comical aspects.

Even the Elizabethan costumes that His Majesty had designed for those Privy Councillors who were not in the House of Lords, looked quite in keeping with the occasion; and Sir Walter Scott, who had travelled to London from Leith in one of the new steamships, was seen to be nodding his approval of the assembly, as if he saw there material for one of his romantic histories.

Lucilla, Tamar, Francis, Adrian and Giles had taken up their places early that morning, and were by now on amicable terms with their neighbours on the stand. These were, on their right, a country squire and his lady, who had come up from Dorset; and on their left, Mr and Mrs Hosea Hogpenny, with their family of three daughters and four sons. Mr Hogpenny was the owner of a shipyard. Lady Charlotte would have condemned him unhesitatingly as a wealthy Cit, but Lucilla found him amusing company. He had a fund of information on all manner of subjects, and was able to tell her which dignitaries were to take part in the procession, which regiments were stationed along their particular stretch of the road, and what music was to be performed during the solemnities in the Abbey.

When Lucilla complimented him on his knowledge, he rubbed a hand down his large red face and said affably, "Well, ma'am, to the likes of us, information is money, and we put it to good use. Prinny may be glad of it, too, for he comes to the City when he's short o' cash. Reckon we've built more palaces and bought more works of art for the nation, than many that hold up their noses at City brass."

Mrs Hogpenny's picnic baskets cast the Curles' hampers in the shade, and she lost no time in pressing a variety of delicacies upon those about her, adjuring them to eat hearty and keep up their strengths, as it was going to be a long day. Tamar repaid this kindness by offering her handerchief, soaked in lavender-water, to the youngest Miss Hogpenny, who showed signs of succumbing to the heat. Adrian found in Mr Augustus Hogpenny an amateur musician of some experience, and the two requested Francis to move to the end of the row, so that they might better pursue their discussion on mediaeval plain-song. Giles struck up a conversation with Herbert Hogpenny, who worked in his papa's shipyard, and was eager to learn Mr Ayliffe's views on steam propulsion.

In short, there very soon developed between the two groups the camaraderie that is quite alien to the British character except on such rare occasions as coronations, State funerals or royal weddings.

Halfway through the morning they were warned by a burst of cheering in the vicinity of Westminster Hall that the King had begun his progress to the Abbey. A hush fell on the watchers. The soldiers were called to attention. Every head strained for a better view of the raised walkway along which the procession would approach.

First to appear was the King's Herb Woman and her six young attendants, clad all in white, and scattering herbs and heavy-scented flowers as they went — a custom, Mr Hogpenny said, originally thought to ward off the plague.

Next came the Officers of State, bearing the crown, the orb and the sword. (Mr Hogpenny informed Lucilla in a piercing whisper that Messrs Rundell, Bridge and Company were owed nigh on £33,000 for those baubles, and he doubted they'd see their money within a twelvemonth.)

After the Regalia, followed three bishops, carrying a paten, a chalice and a bible. Then to a great burst of huzzaing and saluting of troops, and shouting and jostling of people on the street, appeared King George himself. Everyone on the stand surged to their feet, and Lucilla had to rise on tiptoe to see the figure pacing slowing past.

The King walked in front of a canopy of cloth of gold. The Barons of the Cinque Ports, who bore the canopy, had been ordered not to carry it over the royal head, as the King wished to be seen by the people in the garret windows and on the rooftops. As he drew level with Lucilla, he checked, and she heard him say to the pages carrying his train, "Hold it wider. Hold it wider."

Then he moved on. The cheering and applause moved with him, the people on the stand slowly resumed their seats, and Lucilla was able to study the rest of the procession. The peers would pass, she knew, in order of seniority, so she had some idea of when she might see Linslade; but she had not bargained for the disguising effect of the ceremonial robes, and could not immediately discern him. As she scanned the rows of faces, she unconsciously gripped Mr Hogpenny's arm for support. He glanced down at her and said kindly, "Looking for a friend, are you, ma'am?"

Lucilla nodded. "Yes, but I don't see him, yet." Her eye picked up Linslade's tall figure and she said quickly, "Yes, I do, though!"

Mr Hogpenny's shrewd blue eyes surveyed her eager face, the shining eyes and parted lips, and smiled.

"Give 'im a shout for you, will I?"

"No," cried Lucilla, appalled, but it was too late. Mr Hogpenny rose to his feet, took off his hat, and waved it over his head, at the same time roaring in stentorian tones, "God Save His Gracious Majesty! Long Live the King!"

Every head, including Lord Linslade's, turned towards the voice. Lucilla, seizing her chance, stood up and waved her kerchief wildly. Alex saw her, and a beaming smile spread over his face. His hand rose in a half-salute. Next moment the procession had passed them by.

Lucilla faced Mr Hogpenny. "Thank you," she said. Mr Hogpenny gave her a grin and a wink. "A loyal subject knows when to speak up," he said, and at once changed the subject, thus establishing him in Lucilla's book as a man who combined delicacy of mind with kindness of heart.

Sir Sholto and his party saw the procession arrive at the great West Door of the Abbey at about eleven o'clock, and, as the King entered the building, heard the choir within burst into the Hallelujah Chorus, while the assembled congregation cheered lustily.

It was a moment that moved Marion Gray to tears, and even the prosaic Dr Chase was heard to blow his nose and clear his throat once or twice.

Inside the Abbey, the ceremony began. It was to last for five hours, and those watching reported later that at times the King, weighed down by his robes, the regalia and the heat, seemed likely to collapse. However, he restored his strength by taking sips of sal volatile, and recovered sufficiently to behave in what the Duke of Wellington felt to be a most improper fashion, glancing about him and bestowing soft looks on certain ladies of his acquaintance.

These improprieties were cut short by the sermon of the Archbishop of York, who said sternly that a monarch must encourage morality and religion, and preserve the morals of the people from the contagion of vice and general depravity.

During the actual crowning, the King's demeanour was exemplary and, at its end, those present showed their delight by waving their caps and coronets, and shouting at the tops of their voices, "God Bless the King!" Braced by this enthusiasm and further sips of sal volatile, the King at four o'clock returned to Westminster Hall for a splendid coronation banquet. Three hundred guests awaited him at the tables, and many more watched from the galleries above.

Lord Denbigh afterwards described the scene to his mama in glowing terms. "The spectacle," he declared, "exceeded all imagination. Picture to yourself Westminster Hall lined beneath with the peers in their robes and coronets, the Privy Councillors, Knights of the Bath, and a multitude of different attendants and Chief Officers of State in most magnificent dress, and with a double row of galleries on each side above, filled with all the beauty of London, the ladies vying with each other in the magnificence of their apparel and the splendour of their head-dresses, some of them being literally a blaze of diamonds. Prince Esterhazy is said to have had jewels on his person estimated at £80,000, and the rest of the foreign ministers and their ladies were as splendid as jewels and fine clothes could make them."

When the King, heralded by the shouts of the populace without and by the blare of trumpets, at last entered the Hall, crowned and walking under his golden canopy, the people there were so deeply affected that they one and all broke into vociferous huzzas.

For a description of the banquet, and the events surrounding it, the Curle family had to rely upon the report of Lady Charlotte, who reached Brampton House shortly before midnight. Lucilla heard the carriage draw up at the front door and hurried to meet her godmother who, despite the exhaustions of the day, was in high good humour.

"A triumph," she announced, as she entered the house. "I confess I was most pleasantly surprised to see how well it all went off. How has your grandfather withstood the exertions? I trust he is safe in bed, by now?"

"Not at all," returned Lucilla with a smile, "he's not to be moved until he's heard everything you have to tell. Have you had anything to eat, Aunt? Mrs Grampound has prepared a small collation to tempt your appetite."

"It needs no tempting," said her ladyship roundly. "We peeresses of the Realm don't count for much in the minds of His Majesty's caterers, let me tell you. Not a morsel of food were we offered. All we could do was look down on such a spread as boggled the mind! Soups, salmon, turbot and trout, venison and all the common meats, ham and savoury pies, daubed geese, lobster . . . with dishes of mounted pasty, and hundreds of side dishes, hundreds of sauce-boats, vegetables, jellies, creams . . . enough to feed all the armies of Europe! His Majesty left about half-past seven to return to Carlton House. After he was gone the peers and bishops set about the feast with a will, while we were forced to watch and starve! One gentleman wrapped a capon in his handkerchief and tossed it up to his family, but that did not feed the five thousand!"

Lady Charlotte allowed Neame to relieve her of the scarlet robe and coronet she still wore, and instructed him to bring the food prepared to the drawing-room, with a bottle of good claret.

"We can talk as I eat," she said, linking her arm through Tamar's. "Where are Adrian and Giles?"

"Gone to Hyde Park," said Tamar, "to see the fireworks."

"With a bunch of rowdies, I've no doubt. There was a good deal of unruliness in the streets as we drove home, but the people seemed good-humoured enough. What about Francis?"

"He went home," Lucilla said. She did not know if she spoke truth, suspecting that Francis had gone off on some private celebration.

The answer seemed to satisfy Lady Charlotte, however. "I'm glad to hear it," she said, "for I must tell you that I'm most troubled about my brother's health. He was seated at a table just below me, and I could see that his face was purple. The heat and the stress of emotion must have been harmful to a man in his sanguine condition. I feared at one point to see him fall down in a fit. Francis should call the physician to him tomorrow."

In the drawing-room they found Sir Sholto, Dr Chase and Marion Gray awaiting them. For the space of an hour the family exchanged impressions of the day's events, and Sir Sholto then sent for more wine, so that they might all join in drinking the health of their new monarch.

At last, worn out, they prepared to go to bed; but as Lady Charlotte collected her candlestick from the table in the hall, Sir Sholto drew her aside.

"A word with you, my dear."

"Is it important, Sholto? I'm worn to rags."

"I think you should hear this tonight. Before you returned,

Lucilla showed me a letter she received last evening from Linslade. He wishes to call on me. Evidently he intends to offer for her."

For a moment Lady Charlotte was silent, and her face, which usually reflected her lightest emotion, remained blank.

"Will you approve the suit?" she said at last.

"I shall welcome it," replied Sir Sholto. "He'll make Lucilla happy. As to the difficulties involved, we'll overcome those if we set our minds to it."

"I hope you're right," said Lady Charlotte. Again she gave him that curiously blank stare: then, turning, slowly mounted the stairs to bed.

XXVIII

LUCILLA WAS IN fact mistaken in thinking that Francis had gone off on a drinking-spree. After taking leave of his cousins at Brampton House he had strolled round the corner to Half Moon Street, where Jason Cleve lived. His intention was to borrow money, but he met with short shrift.

"Impossible," said Mr Cleve shortly. "Your father's given explicit orders, you're not to have any more."

"He's a skin-flint, a cheeseparing miser!"

"He's tired of footing the bill for your follies." Cleve's voice was a little slurred. He had, Francis observed, consumed the better part of a bottle of brandy, and the glitter in his eyes said he was not quite sober. Francis adopted a wheedling tone.

"Come, Jason, have a word with Aunt C. She'll hand over the dibs if you ask her."

"The last time we talked," Cleve reminded him, "you made insulting remarks about your aunt. I don't forget insults, to myself, or to her."

"Dash it, I meant no harm. Spoke out of turn. Beg your pardon for it. But have a heart, man. Don't let the bailiffs take me!"

Cleve regarded his guest with cold eyes. "You think the streets are paved with gold, don't you? Well, they ain't. If you've landed youself in dun street, you'll have to get out of it as best you may."

"I'm desperate, Cleve! If I can't pay off the worst of my debts, it's the King's Bench for me. You won't allow that, surely?"

Cleve shrugged, and his eyes scanned Francis with contempt. "It's no use snivelling to me, I can't help you. Why don't you ask Sholto Curle for a loan, since you're to marry his grand-daughter?"

Francis stared. "Don't be a fool. You know that's not possible."

Cleve's only answer was to yawn and pick up the book he had been reading. After a moment Francis, seeing there was nothing to be gained by further appeals, took his leave.

He considered walking over to Brooks's Club, but decided that he might meet too many of his creditors there, and headed instead for the Royal Dragoon, a tavern in Shepherd Market which did not enjoy the patronage of the ton.

It was, in fact, what his Aunt would unhesitatingly have described as a Low Haunt. It was favoured by labourers, the servants of the great houses round about, and such young bucks as liked to keep low company and drink more than was good for them. Tonight, it was packed to capacity, and very few of its customers were sober.

Francis managed to elbow his way through to the tapman and procured a glass of Last Shift, a concoction guaranteed to put a grin on the gloomiest face. Since there was no chance of finding a seat in the taproom, he remained where he was, sipping his drink and wondering how the devil he could raise enough money to bring him to the rightabout.

After a few minutes he felt a nudge at his elbow, and looked round to see a thickset man, dressed in nankeen trousers, a velveteen jacket and a moleskin cap with ear-flaps. The man's visage was heavy and brutish, disfigured by a broken nose and a burn-scar that ran down his cheekbone to the corner of his mouth. He leered at Francis, displaying a mouthful of black and broken teeth.

"Evenin', yer honour, Mr Warsop! I 'opes I sees yer well?"

Francis scowled at the man with distaste. "What are you doing here?" he demanded.

The man's grin grew broader. "Why, I aim ter drink the 'ealth of 'Is Majesty," he said, "an' wot else would I be wishful ter do, loyal subjick as I am? Mebbe you'll see yer way clear ter buy me a nip o' Nelson's Blood, sir?"

"I've no blunt to waste," said Francis roughly. The man chuckled.

"Mr Cleve turned yer down flat, 'as 'e?"

"What do you know of Mr Cleve?"

"I know 'e 'olds the purse-strings! Seen the pair o' you together, more'n oncet. Got eyes in me 'ead, see?" He leaned towards Francis and said in a whining tone, "'Ow's about it, yer honour? A glass o' rum, eh? Let's say, fer past services? Cheap at the price, though I says it meself."

Francis ignored the plea. Reaching out, he caught the man by the lapel of his jacket. "What are you to Jason Cleve?" he said fiercely.

"Why," returned the scarred man, "I'm 'is good friend. Same as I'm a friend ter you, sir. Done 'im a few favours, I 'ave. Give 'im a mort o' good advice. Told 'im which prads are like to win, an' which will still be runnin' come Lammas-tide."

Francis glanced about the room. The way to the door was blocked by a group of apprentices who had linked arms and were bawling out the verses of a bawdy song. He reached into his pocket, drew out a coin and tossed it to the tapman.

"Give him rum," he said, pointing at his companion.

The scarred man lifted a finger to his temple in mock salute. "Yer honour's 'umble sarvint," he said. "Lay a guinea or so on Neck Or Nothin' next time out."

"I've had enough of your tips," said Francis, "and enough of your begging, too. I warn you, don't trouble me again."

"There's gratitood fer yer," mourned the scarred man. He turned to collect his shot of rum from the tapman, and Francis seized the chance to escape, pushing through the crowd to the inner door, and so through the private bar to the street.

The scarred man noted his departure with a sardonic grin. "Scared," he remarked to the world. "Scared, the 'ole pack o' them, as well they might be." He raised his glass in silent salute, not to His Britannic Majesty King George IV, but to the profits to be gained by a fly bird as knew how to suck a living out of a rich man's fears.

Francis would have been greatly disturbed to know that his encounter with the man in the moleskin cap had been witnessed by certain of his acquaintance.

Adrian Curle, Giles Ayliffe and Nicholas Frome had chosen to drop in at the Royal Dragoon at the end of a tour of the neighbouring taverns. While it must be said at once that none of them was sober, none of them was so far gone as not to recognize Mr Warsop. Indeed, Adrian had attempted to attract his cousin's attention, hailing him repeatedly from the far side of the room; but his shouts were drowned by the singing of the apprentices, and he gave up the attempt. ·

"Don't much want to talk to him, anyway," he told his companions. "Be honest with you, don't much care for Francis. Loose fish. Ramshackle."

Giles, who became a trifle ponderous when in his cups, said that that was not a kind thing to say. "Francis," he said, "ain't all bad. More flash th'n foolish. Keeps bad company, thash all."

Mr Curle did not argue the point. His gaze was on the shifty character standing next to Mr Warsop and addressing him in what seemed to be a very encroaching way.

"Villain," opined Mr Curle solemnly. "Cut your throat, soon as look at you."

Mr Ayliffe looked pained. "No, dash it, can't say that! Man's your cousin, after all."

Adrian giggled. "Not Francis. Ruffian with him."

Giles and Nicholas both turned to stare at the man in the moleskin cap.

"Ugly," conceded Giles, "but can't condemn a man for his looks. Honourable scars, p'raps. Hero of ... of ... somewhere 'r other." He frowned. "Don't care for his hat. Moleskin. Not at all the thing."

Nick was rubbing a hand across his eyes. "Seen him before," he muttered.

"Can't have," said Adrian firmly. "Not the sort of fellow one sees."

At this point Francis broke off his dialogue with the burly man and made his headlong exit from the tavern.

"Seen him," insisted Nick. "Seen him at . . . dash it, I wish my head didn't spin so."

"Newmarket?" suggested Adrian helpfully.

"Newgate," supplied Giles.

Nick closed his eyes. "Can't recall. Gone, gone, gone." He leaned forward suddenly and rested his head on his arms.

"Don't you go," said Giles. He seized Nick's shoulder and shook him. "Wake up, man!" Nick did not move. A faint snoring sound began. Giles got to his feet.

"Have to get him home," he said. "Lend a hand, Curle."

Between them they succeeded in rousing Nicholas enough to get him on his feet. The three young men edged and elbowed their way out of the tavern and made their uncertain course through crowds of roisterers to Berkeley Square. There they handed Nick into the charge of a poker-faced Bungay, who promised to get him to bed without disturbing the rest of the household. Giles and Adrian retraced their tracks to Brampton House, it being agreed that Giles should spend the night there rather than attempt to return to his hotel.

"You think Nick really knew that rogue?" said Giles. Adrian shook his head.

"No," he said. "Bosky, tha's all."

Giles was not so sure, but he sensed that Adrian found the association of the scarred man with his cousin Francis distasteful, and did not pursue the matter.

XXIX

LORD LINSLADE PRESENTED himself at Lady Charlotte's home the next morning at eleven o'clock. Marion Gray, who chanced to see his curricle draw up at the door, hastened to tell Lucilla of his arrival. She found her standing before the pier-glass in her bedroom, regarding her reflection with disfavour. A pile of discarded gowns lay on the bed.

"It's not suitable," Lucilla mourned. "Nothing I own is suitable."

Mrs Gray laughed. "My love," she said, "there are no rules about what should be worn to receive a proposal of marriage. Why, when Mr Gray came to pay me his addresses, I was working in the garden, wearing an old stained gown and boots! It did not seem to deter him in the least."

"My hair," said Lucilla distractedly. "I look quite frumpish!"

"Give me the comb," Marion said, "and sit down! Let me see what I can achieve."

Lucilla sank down on the chair before the looking-glass and allowed Marion to coax her curls into order. As the job was completed, there came a tap on the door, and a maidservant brought in a bouquet of yellow roses. Lucilla felt for the note among the blooms. It was short.

"My dear Miss Pelham," it read, "I hope to have the privilege and pleasure of speaking with you a little while from now. Until then, believe me to be your most ardent and devoted admirer. Linslade."

Lucilla pressed bouquet and note to her bosom. "This dress," she said. "It won't do! This colour, with yellow roses!"

Marion leaned over and removed the posy from Lucilla's grasp. "The colour is neither here nor there," she said, "since you won't be carrying these when you meet his lordship. Sit quiet, Lucilla, and compose your mind a little."

"He may not wish to marry me. It may only be a matter of business!"

"Pigs may fly," said Mrs Gray.

Lord Linslade, meanwhile, was himself suffering considerable apprehension. Though he was sure of Lucilla's affections, he was very much aware of the animosity of the Everley clan. Lady Charlotte made no secret of the fact that she disapproved of him. Might she not have influenced Sir Sholto? The old man was kind and courteous, but would he allow Lucilla to marry a Frome?

During a restless night Alex had rehearsed various ways of putting his case to Sir Sholto. He had decided at last that his best approach was to be entirely frank, and to trust in the old man's sound good sense.

To the critical eye of Neame, who admitted him to the house, he appeared perfectly at his ease, a gentleman paying a routine morning call. Under this calm demeanour, however, Alex felt as nervous as a callow youth on his first assignation.

Sir Sholto was discovered reading in his book-room. He greeted the Earl with great affability, invited him to sit down and gave him a glass of sherry wine. He then enquired politely about the health of the members of Alex's family, conversed a little on the triumphs of yesterday's ceremonies, and said, finally, "But you've better things to do, Linslade, than listen to the ramblings of an old codger like me. I expect you wish to see Lucilla?"

Alex set down his empty glass. "Not immediately, sir. It's you I wish to speak to. You're no doubt aware that I hold your grand-daughter in the highest possible regard. She is to me everything that is most admirable in a woman . . . not only beautiful, but spirited, generous of mind, kind . . . "

"Yes, yes," agreed Sir Sholto, "she's a charmin' filly. A trifle hot at hand, sometimes, but not an ounce of vice in her."

Alex smiled. "Exactly, and the fact is, sir, that I wish for nothing more than to marry her. I'm here to ask your permission to pay her my addresses."

"Very proper," said Sir Sholto briskly. "Not that we old fogeys have the final say in the arrangement of the modern marriage." He frowned, as if at some inward thought. "Young women, these days, prefer to make up their own minds. But for what it's worth, you have my permission."

Alex was a little thrown by this unexpected compliancy. "I'm conscious," he said, "of the . . . the difficulties that have existed between our two families. I don't want Lucilla to be made miserable by . . . well . . . continued feuding."

"Won't happen," said Sir Sholto. "I shan't permit it on my side, and you won't on yours. I'm tired of playing at Capulet and Montagu. Time we all behaved like civilized folk. I like you, Linslade, I believe Lucilla loves you, and I fully expect you to deal extremely together."

"Thank you," Alex said. "That brings me to my second point, the matter of my financial circumstances. My affairs are in good order, and I'm well able to supply Lucilla with the elegancies of life . . . "

"'Course you are," Sir Sholto agreed. "We're neither of us men of straw, eh? We can settle those mercenary details at our leisure."

"I'd prefer to do so at once," Alex answered, "always provided Lucilla will have me. My lawyer is Thomas Shooberry. If you'll give me the name and direction of yours, I'll arrange for them to meet and draw up a preliminary document for you to look at."

Sir Sholto chuckled. "Hard man to shift, aren't you? Very well, your Mr Shooberry and my Mr Baldrick may consult whenever you wish. Now go and talk to Lucilla. I won't accompany you. Yesterday's junketings have tired me somewhat, and Chase has ordered me to stay put until further orders. Go along to the drawing-room, if you will, and I'll see she comes to you there."

Alex hesitated. "Should I not speak to Lady Charlotte, first?"

"No," said Sir Sholto. "Leave her to me." He waved a dismissive hand. Alex rose, repeated his thanks, and made his way to the drawing-room.

Lucilla did not keep him waiting long. She came quickly into the room, checked, made her curtsey, and stood smiling at him a little uncertainly. He moved towards her and took both her hands in his.

"That letter I sent you . . . it was very bad . . . it didn't say the half of what I meant . . . "

Lucilla met his eyes. "I'm glad you don't plan to leave England," she said.

"I plan to stay here, with you. Miss Pelham . . . Lucilla . . . I'd composed such a fine speech for you, and now it's flown out of my head. I can only say that I love you with all my heart, and ask you very humbly if you will be my wife. Will you, my dearest one?"

"Yes," said Lucilla. "Oh, yes!"

His lordship did not appear to find this forthrightness at all unmaidenly. Taking Miss Pelham into his arms, he kissed her with a thoroughness that left her in no doubt of his sentiments. Releasing her at last, he said, "Lucilla, there's something I must explain to you. I couldn't speak of it, before, but now that you're to be my wife, I can tell you the whole. I hope it won't make you change your mind about me."

She shook her head, smiling. "Nothing could do that."

He sat down with her on the sofa, and told her the full history of the liaison between Francis Warsop and his sister; their elopement, and the events that followed. Lucilla listened with a strange sense of relief. She had thought his restraint sprang from a dislike of something in herself. By comparison, a skeleton in the closet seemed very unimportant, something that could be exorcized by a little goodwill and good sense.

When he had made an end, she said, "Thank you for telling me these things. They don't alter my feelings, but are you sure that your sister won't dislike the idea of our marrying?"

"Arabella told me that if I didn't make you an offer, she'd wash her hands of me."

"And your Mama? The rest of your family?"

"We may expect a few squalls at first, but we'll come safe to port, never fear. When shall we announce our engagement?"

Lucilla thought. "Friday night, at Aunt Charlotte's dress ball? Is that too soon?"

"Not an instant. Er . . . are you sure I'm invited to it?"

"You, and all your family."

"Lady Charlotte mayn't see it quite your way."

"Yes, she will. For one thing, she's too practical to fight the inevitable. For another, she'll do what Grandfather wants, because he's footing the bill for the party, and who pays the piper, calls the tune."

As Lucilla predicted, Lady Charlotte took the news of the betrothal without protest, if without enthusiasm, and agreed it be announced at Brampton House on Friday night.

As she later explained to her brother, "When Sholto's mind is made up, there's no use arguing. It offends every sentiment to think of Lucilla married to Linslade, but I don't see how one can prevent it."

Lord Everley shrugged. "I've no objection to it, myself. I call it generous of Linslade to offer to bury the hatchet. I tell you, Charlotte, I'm weary of squabbles. I'd like to spend what time's left to me, in peace."

Lady Charlotte looked at him in some concern. His health had deteriorated markedly over the past few days. His body had become bloated and his colour was far too florid.

"You should let Princeton bleed you," she said severely, "and you should drink less. He's warned you often enough."

For answer, Lord Everley drained his glass and refilled it. "Princeton's an old woman. I've lived as I chose, and damme I'll die as I choose."

Lady Charlotte did not press the matter, knowing that argument was bad for him; but Francis, who arrived soon after with Jason Cleve, was less considerate. He launched at once into a stinging attack on the Fromes in general, and Linslade in particular. His father cut him short.

"You seem to have forgotten," he said, "that it was you that wronged the Fromes, and not the other way about. If Linslade is good enough to forget the past, then you should be grateful, instead of ranting on like a schoolboy."

"Linslade good? You're all about in your head if you think that, Papa. Why, his intention is to destroy us. He's wormed his way into that old dotard's good books and, once he's married to Lucilla, he'll rule the roost, you may count upon it."

"If you're calling Sholto Curle a dotard, my boy, then it's you who are gone in the attic! He knows just what he's about. Linslade's a splendid catch. Your Aunt Charlotte recognizes that, if you don't."

"Aunt C. is blinded by his money. She never could resist the jingle of gold. And if she expects me to attend the ball, she's making a very great error. You don't get me under the same roof as a passel of Fromes."

"Then you're a bigger fool than I took you for," retorted his father. "Do you think Society will take your part against Linslade? This will be the match of the Season, and you'd best accept it with good grace or you'll make yourself a laughing stock. And don't upset Lucilla, or you'll be sorry. The Curles are a clannish lot. Cross them, and you can forget about marrying Tamar. If you've the sense you were born with . . . and that's nothin' to boast of . . . you'll attend the ball, do the pretty by Lucilla, and speak to Linslade with circumspection. Now get out of my sight. You give me the megrims."

The old man closed his eyes, breathing heavily. Francis slouched away, but Jason Cleve remained, staring down at Lord Everley.

"My lord," he said softly, "are you wise to force a confrontation between Francis and Linslade?"

"There'll be no confrontation," said Lord Everley. "Sholto won't allow it. Nor will I." He opened his eyes and said in a slurred voice, "Go away, Cleve, for God's sake."

The lawyer left the room. Lord Everley's gaze shifted to the worn fabric of the curtains, the paint flaking in one corner of the ceiling, the film of dust on the hearth.

"Past carin'," he muttered. "Long past carin'."

Lord Linslade had stretched the truth when he spoke of "squalls" in his family. "Tempests" would have been a better word. His mama, when informed that he proposed to marry Miss Pelham, was seized by such severe spasms that a doctor had to be sent for. In the days that followed she adopted the mien of high tragedy, broke into tears at the mere sight of her firstborn and vowed that nothing remained but for her to retire from the world and spend the rest of her days in religious seclusion.

She refused point blank to meet or to write to Lucilla, and declared that nothing would persuade her to attend Charlotte Brampton's ball. Her doctor agreed, saying that her ladyship must take things quietly for a week or so.

George, predictably, slated Alex for causing their mother so much pain. He declared flatly that he would not go to the ball, but found to his chagrin that Augusta had already accepted for both of them. Taken to task, Augusta for once defied her husband. "'Course we're goin'," she said. "Alex deserves our support, I like Miss Fulham, and the Bramptons set the best table in Town."

Arabella and John Ruthven declined on the grounds that they would be in Lincolnshire with their children. Emily and Nick, wholeheartedly on Alex's side, squabbled violently with George and adopted a less-than-respectful attitude to their mama.

The tensions at Berkeley Square increased by the hour, and it was only the intervention of the Dowager that prevented open conflict. She arrived one morning in militant mood, and went straight upstairs to her daughter-in-law's bedroom. Surveying the patient with a steely eye, she told her briskly to pull herself together.

"It's not the least bit of use for you to lie here like a corpse at a wake," she said. "The world goes on, Elvira, whether you like it or not. Alex is going to marry Miss Pelham, and unless you wish to lose him entirely, you will put a good face on it and make her welcome."

"I hope," said Elvira in a failing voice, "that I know my duty, Mama. When I am strong enough, I shall leave this place. Then Alex may do as he chooses. But nothing . . . nothing . . . will prevail upon me to attend that odious woman's party!"

The Dowager sniffed. "Just as well, perhaps. The affair will be testing enough, without our having to look at your Friday face. But you might give some thought to what people will make of your absence. They'll search for reasons, and most probably they'll light on the very thing you're trying to hide . . . that sorry old tale about Bella and Francis Warsop."

This produced a faint moan from Elvira.

"Exactly," said the Dowager. "That is a situation we all hope to avoid. Since you have thrown in your hand, I must do what I may. A fortnight from now, I shall hold a soirée. I shall invite the starchiest of my friends. You and the children will attend, and you will all of you display your delight and gratification at Alex's choice of a wife. Is that clear?"

Lady Linslade, knowing that in this mood her mama-in-law was not to be gainsaid, nodded dumbly, and the Dowager swept away to give the other members of the family a dose of the same medicine.

Finally, she requested Alex to bring Miss Pelham to tea in Grosvenor Street that afternoon. The two ladies enjoyed a comfortable cose, the Dowager regaling Lucilla with anecdotes of Alex's childhood escapades that caused him no little embarrassment.

At parting, she embraced Lucilla warmly, and said she looked forward to drinking her health at dear Lady Charlotte's ball. Not to anyone would she have admitted that the thought of Fromes and Everleys being thrown together in such a hugger-mugger way filled her with apprehension.

XXX

IN ACCORDANCE WITH his undertaking to Sir Sholto, the Earl made an early call on his man of business to discuss the matter of marriage settlements.

Mr Thomas Shooberry had been legal and financial adviser to Alex's father, and still handled the management of the Frome fortune. A lawyer by training, he had built on a natural flair for turning pence into pounds, and was now able to choose his clients from a very select list. Numbered among them were men highly placed in Government, the City and the world of banking. Mr Shooberry was in consequence one of the best-informed people in London.

He held Lord Linslade in great esteem, and was delighted to learn of his betrothal to Miss Pelham.

"One heard rumours, of course, but one was inclined to discount them in view of your past differences with the Everleys. May I offer you my sincere felicitations, my lord? Perhaps you'll take a glass of the Amontillado, to mark the occasion?"

The sherry was poured and enjoyed, and discussion ensued about the terms of the settlement. At the end of half an hour Mr Shooberry leaned back in his chair and coughed delicately. "There is one point I should raise," he said. "It's no secret that Miss Pelham is a very wealthy young lady. The bequest from her father, Mr Sidney Pelham, and the inheritance from the St Clair estate, together amount to well over two hundred thousand pounds. How does your lordship propose to . . . er . . . make the money secure."

"It's Lucilla's," said Alex. "I wish her to have control of it."

Mr Shooberry pursed his lips. "Sir, for a young female, however competent, to be in charge of such a large sum, could have disastrous consequences."

Alex smiled. "I hope and expect that Lucilla will come to me . . . and to you . . . for advice, but she must come from choice, not compulsion. She's managed her own affairs since she was sixteen years old. She's of independent mind. I don't want to change that."

"Perhaps," suggested Shooberry, clutching at straws, "she may like to place her fortune in trust for your children?"

"She may. By all means suggest it to Mr Baldrick and Sir Sholto. If Lucilla likes the notion, well and good. And now there's another matter I wish to raise with you. It concerns the financial situation of Lord Everley, his son, Francis Warsop and his sister, Lady Charlotte Brampton."

Mr Shooberry nodded sagely. "I'm glad you've seen fit to mention it, my lord. Since you will in some sense be marrying into that family, I feel I must warn you that their circumstances are, to say the least, precarious."

"Don't beat about the bush, Shooberry. I feel sure you know to a penny what they're worth."

"One has made . . . ah . . . discreet enquiries," admitted the lawyer.

"What have you learned?"

"That Lady Charlotte Brampton is a wealthy woman. Her late husband left her well-provided-for, and by shrewd investment she has built up a sizeable fortune."

"Do you act for her in any way?"

"No, certainly not, else it would be quite inadmissible for me to speak as I do. No. Her ladyship's affairs are in the hands of Messrs Thring and Godbold, a very reputable firm."

"What about Henry Everley?"

"There, I'm afraid, the picture is less rosy . . . in fact, not rosy at all. Not to put too fine a point on it, Lord Everley is a ruined man. His house in Town is mortgaged to the hilt, and most of his property in Leicestershire was sold years ago. A pity to see such valuable assets frittered away. If the management of them had been in my hands . . . "

" . . . instead of in the hands of Jason Cleve?"

"Precisely."

"You have a low opinion of him?"

"Let us say he is not well-regarded in the profession. He's too anxious to puff himself off as a man of the world. Ostentation does not become a man of the Law, in my opinion."

"Lady Charlotte seems to think highly of him."

"Not as a man of business," said Mr Shooberry tartly. "They are said to be lovers, but it's not for me to judge on that score."

"Do you think Lady Charlotte is the source of Cleve's income?"

"I doubt it. Perhaps she tosses him a bone, now and again, but she's far too canny to let him control her pursestrings."

The Earl nodded. "Are you aware," he asked, "that Lord Everley and Lady Charlotte are members of a tontine?"

"Yes. And a very foolish form of investment I think it."

"Would the capital of the tontine be enough to save the Everley bacon?"

"Lord, no! Nothing short of a miracle can do that. The tontine money is invested in property, and will bring in little more than twenty thousand . . . a drop in the bucket compared with what the Everleys owe."

The Earl sat thinking for a while, then said, "Would it be lawful for me to offer to buy the tontine properties?"

"Why, yes," said Mr Shooberry with a puzzled look, "but there are a thousand better ways to invest your blunt."

"They wouldn't achieve my ends," said Alex. "Find out which properties the tontine covers, will you, and make an offer for them? A generous offer."

"At least," said Mr Shooberry, "permit me to make some enquiries, first. One must be sure that the properties are worth buying, that the title deeds, and the books, are in order . . . "

"Certainly, do whatever's necessary," agreed the Earl. "In fact, I want you to do more." He drew a sheet of paper towards him, took a quill from the inkstand on the desk, and wrote rapidly. "I wish these people to be kept under constant surveillance," he said. "You are to arrange it and see that reports of their activities are made to me on a regular basis."

Mr Shooberry picked up the paper, scrutinized it, and nodded. He itched to know the reason for this request, but he saw, by the closed expression on Lord Linslade's face, that it would be useless to question him.

*

By a stroke of misfortune Giles Ayliffe's appointment with Messrs Brocket and Sons of Bermondsey had been set down for the morning of the Brampton House ball, a fact which Lady Charlotte deplored.

"Why you had to choose this day of all days, to go gallivanting off on some wild-goose chase, I cannot think. Mind you're here in good time tonight, Giles. Nothing is worse than to be short of gentlemen at a ball, and there are some very plain girls who must be supplied with partners."

Cheered by the prospect of spending his evening dancing with antidotes, Giles set off for Bermondsey. Mr Amos Brocket met him at the yard gate and led him to a poky office in the corner of the main shed. He was a short, chunky man who looked as if he'd been smelted from iron ore, and he lost no time in destroying Giles's hopes.

"This model o' yourn," he said. "It won't do, lad. I'm sorry, but there it is. No point in leadin' you on."

Giles swallowed. "Do you mind telling me why you reject it?"

Mr Brocket sighed. "Out o' date," he answered.

"But . . . but I've studied every past design," protested Giles. "I've made improvements on them. I've incorporated features in my Steam Horse that no other designer has used. Surely . . ."

Mr Brocket held up a grey-veined palm. "No doubt that's true, lad, and I take off my hat to you, workin' all alone, out there in the wilds. Thing is, we build engines to do the work we need, which is carry coal from Stockton to Darlington. That's the line we're in, see, and your design ain't what we need. Too light, and would cost too much to make. We've thought it over, very careful, and the answer is 'no'. I'm sorry."

Giles nodded. "I see. I understand. Thank you for having given me the benefit of your time, and experience." He paused, then said, "Perhaps if I were to make modifications?"

Mr Brocket shook his head. "Wouldn't serve. There's others who are one jump ahead, see?" He studied Giles's mortified face and said, "What you need to do is come to London, work wi' folk that's already in the business, learn the ropes, so to speak."

"I'll do anything," said Giles quickly. "Would you have a

217

place for me, Mr Brocket? I don't mind hard work, and I want to learn."

"Lad," said Brocket, "I've seven sons of me own, all aimin' to join me here. But there's other companies as good as this'n. Mebbe you'd like to try 'em. Wait." He went to the high desk in the corner, found paper, and scrawled several names on it. "Ask 'em," he advised. "Never know your luck, though in these hard times, vacancies don't happen all that often."

Giles thanked Mr Brocket, put the list in his pocket, and returned to his hotel. His disappointment was so acute that he felt numbed. It seemed impossible that the work of years had come to nothing, that all his dreams were destroyed. He had no chance, now, of marrying Tamar. It would be dishonourable even to think of such a thing. He had no fortune and, with the best will in the world, he couldn't expect to establish himself in the business of steam-haulage for many years to come.

He knew he could expect no support from his parents. Their reaction would be, forget Tamar Curle, come home to Swallowford and settle down to the life you were born to.

It was a prospect that cast Giles into despair. He left the hotel and walked the streets for hours, trying to find some way past this crushing defeat. He could think of none.

By late afternoon he had come to a decision. He must tell Tamar the truth at once, tell her that to marry him was out of the question, and urge her to marry Francis or some other worthy gentleman.

It would be agony to say goodbye, but he had no other choice. Much as he loved Tamar, he knew her frailties. She could not leave a life of wealth and luxury to become the wife of a penniless inventor. She would never survive the hardships of such an existence. It would be better to cut the ties quickly and cleanly, and retain at least the unspoiled memory of the love they had shared.

In this mood of heroic self-sacrifice, Giles returned to his room, to make ready for Lady Charlotte's dress ball.

Charlotte Brampton was not noted for her sensibility, but even she had grasped the hazards of bringing Fromes and Everleys together in too precipitate a fashion. For that reason, she did not invite the Fromes to dine in Curzon Street before the ball, giving as her reason that so large a gathering would overtire Sir Sholto.

Lucilla was worried that Alex might feel slighted, but he reassured her by saying easily, "No, love, it's a wise move. Don't put yourself in a pucker about it. Tell your aunt, please, that I look forward to leading in our contingent at nine-thirty precisely."

The dinner in Curzon Street was not a happy one. Lady Charlotte's mind was naturally on the arrangements for the ball, and she several times interrupted the meal to give last-minute instructions to her wine-steward and butler. Sir Sholto and Adrian, in the manner of mere males, chatted casually about a shooting-party they planned to hold at Ringwood in the autumn. Lord verley, after addressing a few heavy compliments to the ladies on each side of him, sank into a lethargy. Lucilla, Marion Gray and Dr Chase kept up a semblance of polite conversation at their end of the table, and Francis confined himself to flirting desperately with Tamar.

Watching him, Mrs Gray decided that he was acting very strangely. He'd had a good deal to drink, and his green eyes held a hard glitter. He leaned close to Tamar, murmuring things that seemed to embarrass her, and when she blushed and turned her face away, he laughed. Marion longed to intervene, but she was seated too far from the young couple. Dr Chase saw her concern and said in a low voice, "Where's young Giles? Wasn't he asked to dine?"

Marion gave a faint shake of the head. "I've not set eyes on him all day. He was to visit that firm, you know . . . the one considering his invention? If it's been rejected, I fear it will be a great disappointment to . . . to all of us."

Dr Chase studied Tamar's white face. The child looked ill, he thought. Poor girl, with her unhappy history, she should not be subjected to so much stress. Warsop wasn't the man for her. He should be shielding her at this time, gentling her into a more confident mood. Instead, he was treating her like some demi-mondaine, putting her to the blush. It was shameful.

Mrs Gray answered his unspoken thoughts. "Giles will be at the ball," she said. "Whatever his feelings, he won't shirk. We must be ready to comfort Tamar if it's bad news."

*
219

At nine o'clock Lady Charlotte took her place at the head of the wide stairway, ready to receive her guests. Lord Everley was at her side, and Sir Sholto sat in his wheeled chair, further along the gallery.

The front door had been thrown open, and flunkeys and footmen were in position in the hallway. Outside, linkboys lit their torches, and stable-lads prepared to stand to the heads of carriage-horses.

Lady Charlotte's chief fear . . . that the ton would prefer other parties above hers . . . soon proved to be groundless. The line of smart vehicles banked up along the street and deposited such a bevy of the titled, the famous, the rich and the beautiful as exceeded her ladyship's wildest dreams. Lady Charlotte perceived that tomorrow her party would be accorded the ultimate accolade, that of being described as a sad squeeze.

She attributed her success to her own brilliant reputation as a hostess, but Jason Cleve, who was standing with Francis on the west side of the gallery, knew better.

"Word's got out that Linslade's spoken for Lucilla," he said, "and they've come to see if it's true." He turned a lazy smile on Francis. "I trust we shall soon hear your own betrothal announced? Tamar's too pretty a pigeon to fly about alone. If you don't snare her, someone else will."

"Don't trouble your head on that score," said Francis. "She's mine, signed and sealed, as you very well know."

"I know it," sighed Mr Cleve, "but does she? Does the bucolic Mr Ayliffe know it? Watch that they don't take a leaf from your book and make a runaway match of it!"

"Damn you, mind your own business," said Francis fiercely.

"I speak as a friend, my dear fellow."

"Then you may save your breath! Ayliffe's no danger. He hasn't a penny to his name."

"And nor have you." Mr Cleve moved back, laughing, as Francis took a threatening step towards him. "Spare me the dramatics, Francis. I know your financial position to a T, and I advise you to clinch your engagement to your cousin with all possible speed. Sweep her off her feet, if need be . . . though I do urge you to stop short of another unsuccessful elopement."

Francis lifted a fist, as if to smash it into Cleve's smiling face;

220

but he changed his mind, and strode away towards the main reception room. Mr Cleve returned to his contemplation of the guests in the hall below.

XXXI

LORD LINSLADE, AS he had promised, arrived at Brampton House at half-past nine, an hour which many of his contemporaries would have termed unfashionably early.

Nothing in his manner suggested that this was to be one of the most important nights of his life. He was dressed, as always, with quiet perfection, the only touch of flamboyance being the ruby pin set in the folds of his cravat.

He brought with him the Dowager Countess of Linslade, his sister Emily and Denby Shepstone. An acute observer might have seen in his companions certain signs that this was no ordinary occasion. The Dowager was magnificent in a gown of gold tissue. She wore the Linslade diamond tiara, and diamonds sparkled at her throat and wrists. Emily too had made special efforts with her toilette; while Denby Shepstone, in unaccustomed civilian dress, managed to retain a military air, as if he might at any moment dash up the stairway and take the Everley camp by storm.

The Fromes did not at once join the people moving slowly up to the reception point, but lingered in the hall to await the arrival of George, Augusta and Nicholas, who had travelled in the second carriage.

The Dowager sized up the guests with a practised eye. "Devonshires, Granvilles, Melbournes. Very tonnish."

"No Royals," said Emily, disappointed.

"That is what makes it tonnish," said the Dowager drily. Her gaze shifted to Lady Charlotte at the head of the stair. "Dear me," she said, "puce satin. To accord with her brother's complexion, I suppose."

"Grandmama," said Alex severely, "you're to behave yourself tonight. Remember we're sitting on a powder-keg."

"I'll strike no sparks," she promised.

The meeting went off very well. Lady Charlotte, seeing the

Fromes approach, put on the gracious smile that Sir Sholto called her camel-look. The Dowager, going one better, kissed her hostess warmly on both cheeks. Augusta reminded Lord Everley, with a hearty laugh, that the last time they'd met had been out with the Quorn, when they both took a toss at a regular stitcher. Adrian arrived and bore the younger members off to the ballroom, and Alex stood for some minutes chatting easily to Sir Sholto. The line of guests was held up for all that time, and when at last the Fromes moved on, no one was in any doubt that they were to be counted the guests of honour.

Alex, going in search of Lucilla, found her in an ante-room with Lord and Lady Sefton. She was wearing a gown of ice-blue silk, with an overskirt of lace. Her hair was dressed high, the better to display the sapphire earrings Alex had given her as an engagement present, and in her hand was the posy of small white rosebuds he'd sent her that morning.

They moved together from group to group, chatting to various of their friends, and there was about them that almost visible glow that illuminates those newly in love.

Lady Sefton, coming to sit beside Lady Linslade, said, "So the on-dits are true. When is it to be announced, Alice?"

"Tonight," said the Dowager, smiling. "Sholto will do the honours."

"Are you pleased?"

"Delighted. She's just the girl for Alex, suitable in every possible way."

"A love match," nodded Lady Sefton, "that meets all the requirements of birth and background; what could be happier than that?" She hesitated, then with the licence of long friendship, spoke her mind. "I think Miss Curle is less fortunate in her choice."

"I'm not well acquainted with Miss Curle. She looks to me to be a pretty pea-goose, but I may be wrong."

"She doesn't deserve Francis Warsop," Lady Sefton said. "It can only end in disaster. She hasn't the force of character to cope with that gentleman's tricks."

"Perhaps they won't marry," said the Dowager. "Sholto Curle isn't the man to force the girl into a distasteful marriage."

Lucilla, too, was worried about Tamar. She saw how her

cousin's eyes kept straying towards the door, and how her face grew whiter and her hands more tremulous as the night progressed.

"She's fretting her heart out over Giles and his wretched invention," Lucilla told Alex, "and, to make matters worse, Francis is behaving like a satyr and frightening the wits out of her. Oh, I wish I knew a way out of this tangle!"

"Don't worry about it tonight," he said. "Tomorrow, if you wish, I'll have a word with young Ayliffe, and see if I can help him."

"Tamar's not your responsibility," demurred Lucilla, but he shook his head.

"You mistake. Now that I'm to marry into your family, I intend to meddle in everyone's affairs. It will be quite useless to try to dissuade me. Come and dance with me."

Giles arrived at the ball just as Lady Charlotte was about to quit her post and move to the ballroom. She scolded him sharply for his tardiness.

"I told you this morning that I counted on you to see there are no young ladies left without partners. It's time you thought of others, Giles, instead of always putting your own pleasures first."

Giles swallowed this rebuke without protest, but it angered him so much that he made no effort to rescue any wallflowers. Instead, he hung about the edge of the gathering, talking to no one, drinking glass after glass of wine, and watching for Tamar.

After an hour of waiting, he began to think she was deliberately avoiding him. He decided to speak to Mrs Gray but, before he could go in search of her, he found himself face to face with an affably-smiling Lord Linslade.

"Evening, Ayliffe," said his lordship. "How did the interview go?"

"Badly," Giles said. "Brocket turned me down. He thinks the Steam Horse is too light for his sort of work, and will cost too much to build."

"Perhaps some other manufacturer . . . " began the Earl, but Giles cut him short.

"No. I spoke to two others, and they confirm Brocket's view." He dredged up a smile. "The effort wasn't wasted, though. It seems I've the ability to be a designer, but I need training, and to work in London with men who know the trade."

"I see. Have you any particular firm in view?"

"Yes, sir, I have. Brocket gave me a list of names, and one of them is a Mr Hosea Hogpenny. It happens I've met him . . . on the stand, at the Coronation. I was in discussion with his son, and he told me their company is one of the leaders in the building of steam-ships. I intend to seek employment with them."

"In what capacity?" asked Alex. Giles met his eyes squarely.

"As an apprentice," he answered. "This time, I'll start at the bottom and work my way to the top. I can do it."

"I'm sure you can," said Alex, smiling, "but it occurs to me that if you were to bring some capital into the firm, you might start a little higher up the ladder? It would give me pleasure to lend you whatever you need."

Giles reddened. "Thank you," he said quickly. "I appreciate the offer, but I can't borrow from you. I don't know when I'd be able to repay you."

"Don't turn me down out of hand," Alex advised. "I have confidence in you, Giles, and a great deal depends on your making a success of things." He clapped the younger man on the shoulder, and went away to speak to Lord Althorp, who had just arrived.

Giles emptied his glass and set it down. Talking to Linslade had in some way strengthened his resolve to do what must be done. He pushed through the crowd in the anteroom and took up a position in a corner of the ballroom, from where he could watch the dancers.

Tamar was dancing with a man in Hussar uniform, but of Francis Warsop there was no sign. The music ended, Tamar returned to her seat, and her escort moved away. Giles crossed the room to her side.

"I must talk to you alone," he said.

Tamar looked at him with anxious eyes. "I can't. Not now. Grandpapa is to announce Lucilla's betrothal. If I'm not here, my Grandmother will miss me, she'll be so angry, and Francis will . . . "

"Forget them," said Giles brusquely. "This is more important. I'll wait for you in the library. Don't fail me, Tam." Turning on his heel, he walked rapidly towards the door.

Tamar rose uncertainly to her feet. She saw that Sir Sholto had had his chair wheeled to the foot of the musicians' rostrum, and that Lucilla and Lord Linslade were standing next to him. Guests, smiling and chattering, were beginning to stream in from other rooms, and footmen moved among them carrying trays laden with glasses of champagne.

Tamar's gaze shifted to Giles. He had reached the door of the ballroom, and directed one speaking glance at her before disappearing from view. She knew that if she did not go to him now, he would leave the house, and her life, for good. She snatched up her reticule from the chair and began to make her way through the advancing guests. She caught a glimpse of Marion Gray, watching her anxiously from the far side of the room, and raised a hand in a placatory gesture. Crossing the antechamber, she reached the deserted gallery and hurried along it to the library.

Giles was standing in the centre of the room. He came to meet her, hands outstretched.

"I knew you'd come! I had to see you, Tam. My love, it's to say goodbye."

"No!" She placed her hands in his. "No, Giles, I will never say goodbye to you, never as long as I live."

"We've no choice," he said desperately. "Brocket turned me down."

"It makes no difference."

"But it does. You must see, now my invention's failed, I've nothing, no hope, no fortune . . . "

"I don't care for fortunes," burst out Tamar, "I care for you. I mean to be with you always. I mean to be your wife."

"Darling, that's not possible. If I were such a cur as to offer for you, your grandfather would send me packing, and quite right, too. You must put me from your mind."

"Never, never, never." Tamar began to sob. "I beg of you, Giles, don't leave me. Take me away with you. I can't live without you, I shall die if you leave me!" She threw herself forward, clinging to him, wrapping her arms about him. For a moment he returned her embrace, holding her close and burying his face in her hair. Then he thrust her away.

"Don't," he said huskily. "It only makes it worse for us both. Goodbye, my dearest Tam. Remember, I shall always love you."

Still Tamar tried to cling to him, but he pulled free and almost ran from the room. She called his name, but he took no notice. She heard his footsteps hurry along the gallery and down the stairs.

She sank down on a sofa. Her head was spinning, her hands were ice-cold, the tall tiers of books seemed to be about to topple down on her. She leaned her head on her hands.

"Very touching," said a voice. "The Lovers' Farewell! Worthy of Covent Garden, 'pon rep!"

Tamar looked up to see Francis smiling at her from the doorway.

In the ballroom Sir Sholto had made his announcement, and the guests were clustered round Lucilla and Alex, offering congratulations and laughing compliments.

Lady Charlotte, standing near the engaged couple, was taking the credit for what Society clearly saw as an admirable match. Turning to her brother, she said, "Well, Henry, that has gone off very well, I think. Now we have only to settle Francis and Tamar." She glanced about her, frowning. "Where is Tamar? She should be here, with us."

Lord Everley shrugged. "How should I know?"

Jason Cleve spoke in his soft voice. "I saw her leave the ballroom, before Sir Sholto began to speak. Francis followed her. Planning a tête-à-tête, in some quiet corner, no doubt."

"Rubbish," snapped Lady Charlotte. "Tamar knows better than that."

Cleve studied his fingernails. "But does Francis?" he murmured.

A look of alarm crossed Lady Charlotte's face. "Go and find them, Jason! Tell them to come here at once!"

"I fancy," said Cleve, with his malicious smile, "that our Mrs Gray is already conveying that message to them. I saw her go out a moment ago, with Dr Chase."

226

"Oh, this is too tiresome! What use is Marion? They won't listen to her, or to Dr Chase, for that matter. I shall have to go myself. Henry, your arm, if you please!"

"We don't know where they are," protested his lordship. "Demmed if I'll play at hide-and-seek with 'em!"

But his sister had hooked her hand through his arm, and was fixing him with a quelling stare. Shrugging his shoulders, he allowed himself to be led away.

In the library Francis advanced to stand over Tamar. "A touching scene," he repeated, "if perhaps a trifle overplayed. I gather Ayliffe's invention is not about to take the world by storm?"

Tamar got unsteadily to her feet. "That is none of your business," she said hotly, "and I think it ungentlemanly in you to be eavesdropping on a p-private conversation."

Francis raised his brows. "Indeed. I would have called it ungentlemanly in your bucolic Adonis to seek to engage your affections when he cannot offer you marriage!"

Tamar clenched her fists. "Go away, Francis," she said in a low voice. "Leave me alone."

For answer, Francis took a step closer to her. "But that's the last thing I'll do, my dear. Unlike Mr Ayliffe, I intend to remain constantly at your side. Have you forgotten that we are soon to be married?" He reached out a careless finger and touched a tress of her hair. "Come," he said, "make the best of things. Since true love has flown out of the window, take the bird in hand! We shan't fare so badly together."

Tamar struck his hand aside. "Go away," she said, her voice rising. "I shall never marry you. I detest you. I detest the very sight of you."

Francis laughed. "Devil take it, but you have some spirit, after all. I like you the better for showing a little fight!"

Tamar tried to brush past him, but he caught hold of her, pinioned her arms in a rough grip, and began to kiss her face and throat. She struggled, and his grasp tightened, his free hand groping at her breast. Turning her face aside she screamed, but Francis, half-drunk and in the grip of a blind rage, forced her backwards against the sofa, his weight bearing

227

her down. She screamed again. Footsteps pounded along the gallery, the door burst open, and Marion Gray ran headlong into the room, rushed over to Francis, and began to belabour him with her fists. Behind her, in a frozen tableau, stood Lady Charlotte, Lord Everley and Dr Chase.

Lord Everley recovered his wits first. He strode forward, leaned past Marion Gray, seized his son by the collar and hauled him to his feet.

"Have you run mad?" he thundered. "You're damned drunk, sir. You're a damned disgrace to your name! Leave the house at once. I'll deal with you tomorrow."

Francis broke into sneering laugher. "I may be drunk, but I'm not blind, my dear Papa! I can see what's before my eyes, that this little baggage has been playing fast and loose with Ayliffe . . . "

His father struck him backhanded across the face. "Get out of this house!" he shouted. "Get out, before I have the lackeys throw you out!" He thrust Francis aside and bent over Tamar.

"Hush, child, hush," he said. "There's nothing to fear. My son is drunk. He forgot himself. Accept my apologies tonight. You shall have his tomorrow."

Tamar shook her head violently from side to side, tears pouring down her face. "Marion," she sobbed. "Marion."

"I'm here, darling." Marion sat beside Tamar, cradled her in her arms and rocked her like a baby. Lady Charlotte waved a bottle of smelling-salts under Tamar's nose. Francis stood for a moment staring at the three women. Then he rounded on his father.

"I'll go," he said, "but I tell you to your face, you're an old fool and I've done with you. D'you hear me? I've done with you, and your skinflint, sermonizing ways."

Lord Everley appeared not to hear him. His hands lifted to clutch his head, he gave a great cry, and his face slid into a grotesque grimace, the right side drooping, the left twisted in agony. He swayed, and crashed headlong to the floor.

Dr Chase ran to kneel beside the fallen man. "Francis! Lend a hand, help me lift him."

Francis ignored the plea. He plunged from the room, pushed

past Jason Cleve, who was standing in the doorway, and ran from the house.

XXXII

THE SEIZURE SUFFERED by Lord Everley was severe enough to preclude his being moved to his own home. On Dr Chase's instructions he was carried to a bedroom on the lower floor of the house, and his own surgeon was called to his bedside.

Sir Henry Halford concurred with Dr Chase, that Lord Everley had suffered a stroke which had left the right side of his body paralysed. The stricken man could neither move nor speak, and lay as heavy as clay, breathing with difficulty.

Lady Charlotte at first felt that the ball must be allowed to continue; but when the two doctors made it plain to her that her brother was gravely ill and might at any time suffer a further attack, she went to Sir Sholto and asked him to bring the festivities to an end. By one o'clock in the morning, the last of the guests had driven away, and the linkboys, who had earlier lighted their way, were now employed in scattering straw along the street to deaden the sound of the carriage-wheels.

Sir Sholto's chief concern was to find Francis. "A dreadful thing it will be," he said, "if Henry dies without his son at his side."

"It was Francis who brought it on," said Lady Charlotte grimly, "first by his dissolute ways, and then by creating an uproar tonight. If Henry dies, I will hold Francis responsible."

Sir Sholto shook his head. "Henry's been on borrowed time these many years," he said. "Harsh thoughts won't help him. Go to bed, Charlotte, you're worn to a shade."

"I must stay with Henry."

"It serves no purpose. We'll call you if there's a turn for the worse. Marion and Lucilla will sit with him, and Chase will be in constant attendance. But we must find Francis. Adrian must find him and bring him here."

At this point Lord Linslade and Denby Shepstone, who had remained behind after the other guests left, offered to go with Adrian to search for Francis. Sir Sholto accepted the suggestion gratefully. "To speak truth," he said, "Adrian's too green to go into Francis's favoured haunts. I'll wager he's holed up in some gambling hell or whore's bedroom."

"We'll find him," Alex promised.

The three young men set off on their mission; but though they combed the gambling-dens of Jermyn Street, and the taverns of Covent Garden, they found no trace of Francis.

Lord Everley lay unconscious for three days. At the end of that time, his condition seemed to improve very slightly. He recognized Lady Charlotte when she approached him, but he could still neither move nor speak.

"It's a matter of time," Lady Charlotte said. "Lord Inver suffered just this kind of attack last year, and he's out and about again. We must be patient."

Dr Chase, when Lucilla asked him point blank what were her uncle's chances of recovery, shook his head. "Very small," he said. "He has undermined his constitution, for years, by his drinking. His heart is weak, and his pulse erratic. I doubt he'll last the week. All we can do is keep him comfortable."

"If only we could find Francis!"

"Why bother?" said Dr Chase bluntly. "The fact is that they detest each other. It's a melancholy truth that father and son aren't always close. If you want my opinion, keep Francis at a distance."

He repeated this view to Mrs Gray while they were watching, one night, at the sick man's bedside. She nodded vehemently.

"We're better off without him," she said. "Let him stay with his mistress, and not come here to trouble us."

"Mistress?" said Dr Chase, startled.

"Why, yes. I saw him with her at the Pantheon Bazaar. A horrid, vulgar creature. He paid her money. They were clearly on intimate terms."

"Then let him remain with her," Dr Chase said. "He can't help his father."

Marion did not say that her concern was not for Lord Everley, but for Tamar. Since the night of the ball, Tamar had not left her room. She lay on the great fourposter-bed, cocooned in misery. She made no response when spoken to, and the food sent up to tempt her appetite was left untouched. Marion feared that she was sliding into the morbid depression that had afflicted her mama, and was determined that if Francis did return to Brampton House, he must not be allowed near Tamar.

Thinking that Giles Ayliffe might be able to comfort the child, she went in person to his hotel. The porter, a fatherly man, was unable to say where Giles had gone. "Lit out fer 'ome, most like," he said, "or found hisself a cheaper lodgin'. These young bucks come ter Lunnon, spend like nabobs, and soon find their pockets to let."

Mrs Gray wrote to Giles in care of his parents' address at Swallowford, but she had little hope of bringing him back to Town. Nor would Sir Sholto consider allowing Tamar to return to Ringwood. Lady Charlotte, he said, needed the support of her family at this time.

All Marion could do was watch over Tamar with anxious care, and hope that in time she would recover her spirits.

Lord Linslade called regularly to enquire after Lord Everley and to offer such help as he was able. Jason Cleve was also a frequent visitor. He claimed that he came to console Lady Charlotte, but Dr Chase thought he was more interested in Lord Everley's chance of survival.

"When the old man goes," the Doctor said to Mrs Gray, "Cleve loses his meal-ticket." He disliked Cleve, and steadfastly refused to let him into the sickroom.

"His lordship can't speak, you know. I doubt if he knows night from day. Let him go in peace."

"As his man of business," insisted the lawyer, "I have a duty to try to communicate with him."

"Communicate with Lady Charlotte. She has his power of attorney."

Cleve sought out Lady Charlotte. "It's a matter that can't be dodged," he told her, brushing aside her protests. "In a sentence, there's been an offer to buy the tontine properties."

"Oh, that!" Lady Charlotte made an impatient movement. "I was told of it yesterday by Mr Thring. It seems to be an advantageous offer. I told him to make the necessary enquiries."

"Who made the offer, pray?"

"I don't know, yet. Thring will tell me in due course."

"Your brother's in no state to consider such a sale."

"My brother is dying." Lady Charlotte looked at Cleve out of weary eyes. "I have to accept it. I must do what's best for him, and for Francis."

"Does Francis wish to sell?"

"He has no say in the matter. It's between me and Sholto Curle. Sholto has an open mind." As Cleve seemed inclined to argue, she waved a dismissive hand. "I'm very tired, Jason. We'll talk of it some other time. I must rest, now."

With that Cleve had to be content, and he took his leave of her ladyship, albeit with an ill grace.

Lucilla took her turn at nursing Lord Everley. It was arduous work, and Alex took her driving in the Park, whenever possible, to give her a change of air. She was deeply depressed about her uncle's situation.

"It's heartbreaking to see him so helpless," she said. "I could wish him a speedier end, except for the hope that he may be reconciled with my cousin. If only we could find Francis."

"We will," Alex said. He was silent for a space, and then said quietly, "Lucilla, I want you to promise me something."

"What is it?"

"To take special care of Sir Sholto. See that he doesn't go about London unguarded. Send that Mexican of yours with him."

She stared at him in alarm. "Why do you say this?"

"I'm afraid there may be a revival of the attacks on your grandfather."

"But why? Has something happened? Alex?"

"No, no, only a pricking of the thumbs." He tried to sound casual. "However, it can't hurt to take precautions. Do it, my dear, just to please me?"

She nodded unhappily. "Very well." She said very little for the rest of the journey. The thought of the tontine lay unspoken between them.

On the Frida after the ball Alex received news of Francis. The bearer was Giles Ayliffe, who seemed to have difficulty in saying what was on his mind. "I shouldn't have come," he said, as Alex led him to the morning-room. "You'll think me grossly impertinent."

"I'll think you a loose-screw if you don't sit down and tell me what this is all about."

"It's Warsop," said Giles, plumping down in a chair. "I've heard rumours. I don't like to listen to gossip, but in this case . . . I have a personal reason . . . a duty . . . oh, damn it all, Linslade, they're saying that Warsop tried to kill Sir Sholto."

"Certainly an ugly tale," said Alex calmly. "Where had you it?"

"From Petersham. He's my second cousin, you know, and spoke to me out of friendship. Says the story's in all the Clubs. Of course I told him it was humbug, but . . . well . . . I confess I've been vexed in my mind. Didn't sleep a wink last night. Kept remembering those mishaps at Ringwood." He paused, gazing unhappily at the Earl. "I mean, if Warsop planned those, then he's no better than a cold-blooded murderer, and should be under lock and key. You may say it's none of my business," Giles went on, turning red as fire, "but it is, because of Tamar. I must do what I may to protect her."

"Why do you come to me?"

"Because you're to marry into the family, and because I know you won't try to gammon me. I need a plain answer. Have you heard the rumours, and do you believe them to be true?"

"I've heard suspicions voiced," Alex said carefully, "and I'm trying to discover if there's any truth in them. Certain enquiries are afoot."

"I beg pardon, sir," said Giles, "but there's no time for long-drawn enquiries. In a matter of days Tamar could be engaged to marry Warsop."

"I think not," Alex said. "Francis queered his pitch on the night of the ball." He told Giles of the scene with Tamar and the quarrel with Lord Everley. "I doubt if Tamar will let him near her," he said, "and you can be sure Sir Sholto won't countenance the match after what happened."

"That may be so," said Giles, "but Sir Sholto's an old man. He could stick his spoon in the wall, any day. When he goes, Tamar will come under Lady Charlotte's control, and she'll press for the marriage. Linslade, I love Tamar with all my heart, but I'm not blind. She's the sweetest, gentlest soul in the world, but she hasn't the strength to stand up to Lady Charlotte. She'll be hounded into marrying Warsop . . . and that will be as good as signing her own death-warrant, because it's her fortune he wants, not her."

"I think you exaggerate."

"No, sir, I do not. That's why I've come to you, to beg you to see that Tamar's kept safe until I have Sir Sholto's permission to marry her."

The Earl looked up in surprise. "You think you'll get it?"

"Yes, I do. Sir Sholto has no objection to me as a man. It's simply that I have no security to offer a wife. Well, I intend to rectify that. I can't promise Tamar immediate wealth, but I'll be a rich man one day . . . perhaps sooner than anyone thinks."

"How?" said the Earl, fascinated.

"Hogpenny," returned Giles. "I spoke to him yesterday. He's agreed to employ me."

"I see. You don't think that perhaps Sir Sholto will baulk at the idea of Tamar marrying into the . . . er . . . shipping trade?"

"He may, of course, but I shall convince him," said Giles stoutly. "Hogpenny and Sons is already in a fair way of business. They expect in a year or two to be building vessels to trade with the Americas. Steam vessels. Steam is going to revolutionize the world, my lord, and those of us who are sharp enough to invest in it now, will make fortunes. Take my word for it." He coughed. "Which brings me to my second reason for coming to see you."

"Ah! What is that?"

Giles swallowed. "Last time we met, sir, you were kind enough to say that if ever I needed to borrow money, you would be prepared to lend it."

"Just so."

"Well, at the time, I rejected the offer. Didn't like the notion of being beholden to anyone. I see now that that was mere vanity. To be brief, Mr Hogpenny has told me that if I can put up some capital, he'll be ready to make me a junior partner in the firm, like his own sons. I know it's a great deal to ask of you . . . to put money into what you must think is a wildcat scheme . . . "

"I don't think it," replied Alex. "I've asked a few questions of my own, and I've been told, by men whose opinions I respect, that steam is indeed the coming thing. I may add that steamships appeal to me a great deal more than steam-trains, because they'll be so much further from Foxfare."

234

Giles's face shone with pleasure. "Then may I inform Mr Hogpenny . . . "

"Tell him that I shall do myself the favour, some time in the very near future, of calling on him to discuss the nature, extent and terms of my investment in his company."

"Thank you, sir! Thank you, indeed. I swear you won't lose by it." Giles sprang to shake the Earl's hand. "We shall be richer than Golden Ball in no time."

"Very gratifying," Alex said. "May I make one other suggestion? Go to Tamar, and tell her what you've told me."

"There's nothing I'd like more," Giles said, "but I'll hardly be welcome at Brampton House."

"True," said Alex. He thought a moment. "Are you invited to the Melbournes' musicale, on Tuesday night?"

"Yes, but I mean to cry off. I'm not much for music."

"But the Curles are. Brace yourself, Giles, and attend it. You may find a chance to speak to Tamar on neutral ground."

XXXIII

At the same time as Giles was conferring with Lord Linslade, Marion Gray ended a spell of duty in Lord Everley's sickroom. The anxieties of the past few days had exhausted her, and longing for her bed she made her way along the gallery towards her bedroom. She was about to enter it when she heard the front door of the house open and close softly. Thinking it must be Lady Charlotte, she moved to the balustrade and peered over; but the person moving on tiptoe across the lower hallway was Francis Warsop. He looked grubby and dishevelled, and walked with the over-careful gait of a man who had had too much to drink.

Marion shrank back into the shadows. She had no wish to talk to Francis but, before she could reach the shelter of her room, she heard a second person hurrying across the marble flags of the hall, and Lady Charlotte's voice raised in sharp enquiry.

"Francis? What are you doing? Come here at once!"

Francis remained where he was, one foot on the lowest step of the stair. Lady Charlotte came into sight and stopped close to him.

"Where do you imagine you're going, pray?"

"Dear Aunt," came Francis's reply, "I'm going to visit my papa, as a good son ought."

"You'll do no such thing! How dare you come here in this condition? You're not wanted in this house. You're the cause of all our troubles, the cause of your father's illness. If he dies, I shall count you his murderer!"

"Hold your tongue, you old witch!"

"Murderer," repeated Lady Charlotte fiercely. "I know what you've been about, all these months. Scheming to rob your papa, and to injure our dear Sholto Curle! My eyes were blind for a time, but they're open now!"

"Open, are they?" Francis caught hold of Lady Charlotte's arm and jerked her towards him. "And who has opened them, madam? Which of your poisonous friends taught you that slander? No, you needn't say. It was Cleve, wasn't it? What a fool you are, my dear Aunt, to believe that lying toad!"

He started up the stairs once more, but Lady Charlotte hurried round to head him off.

"Get out of my house," she said between her teeth. "Get out before I call the servants to throw you out!"

Francis checked. For a moment it seemed that he would push Lady Charlotte aside. Then he said in a quieter tone of voice, "I'll see my father, ma'am, if I have to obtain a court order to do so. I will see Sholto Curle, as well, and tell him where to look for thieves and murderers. Inform your paramour of it, next time he seeks to bring you tales against me."

He made his way back across the hall and out of the house. Lady Charlotte sank down on the stairs and leaned against the balustrade, eyes closed. Above her on the gallery, Marion Gray, her face blank with shock, retreated to her room and closed the door.

That evening, Alex called at Brampton House to deliver a book he had promised to lend Sir Sholto. Lucilla came downstairs to tell him her grandfather was not at home.

"He drove out soon after three," she said, "to play a rubber of

236

whist with Colonel Makepeace. He promised to be home by six."

"Don't fret. I expect they're swapping tales of the good old days. Is Ramon with him?"

"Yes." She smiled faintly. "Tricked out in groom's livery, and in a very bad temper. It's not that that troubles me." She reached into the pocket of her gown and produced a folded paper. "A boy delivered this, not half an hour ago. It's from Francis."

Alex took the letter. It was inscribed to Lucilla, and its heading was The Prince's Saloon, Jermyn Street. The writing was blotched and shaky, the text almost incoherent.

"Lucilla," it read, "the bailiffs are at my heels, I shall be in the King's Bench if they catch me. You must know that Aunt C. and that dog Cleve plot against me they wish me dead they will keep me from my father. I beg you to speak to Sir Sholto. He must be told the truth, he must consent to see me. He is the only one who can save me, now. Believe me to be y^r affectionate cousin, Francis Warsop."

"He sounds in despair," Lucilla said.

"Foxed, more like," Alex answered. He was thankful that Lucilla, being housebound, could not have heard the rumours Giles had spoken of.

"What's to be done?" Lucilla said. "I thought of going to this Saloon, but perhaps it's not the sort of place for a female?"

"It certainly isn't." Alex folded the letter and handed it back to her. "I'll go myself. When Sir Sholto returns, show him this, but warn him not to follow me. It may be a trap."

"Trap?" Lucilla looked at him with eyes full of anxiety. "Why would Francis wish to set a trap?"

"I can't explain now." He was already halfway to the door. "Tell your grandfather, if you will, that I shall hope to bring Francis back here within the hour."

The distance from Curzon to Jermyn Street was not great, and Alex reached The Prince's Saloon soon after seven o'clock. The light was fading fast, but the street lamps were not yet lit. Few people were about, for the gambling hells that crowded the area were busiest between midnight and dawn.

He climbed the steps to the heavy front door, and knocked. A burly janitor admitted him and indicated by a jerk of the thumb that he was free to enter the main entertainment hall. This had been decorated some years past, in the flamboyant style made popular by the Regent at Brighton; but time had tarnished the gilt pillars and stained the brocaded walls.

There was a billiard-room at the back of the building, and along the side walls curtains concealed recesses where private parties might be held. A balcony circled the central well, with further rooms off it.

It was not the sort of place to be patronized by respectable folk. The company was invariably of a low sort, though not necessarily of low rank. It was said that one of the habitués was a bishop who augmented his income by crooked horse-deals; and glancing about him, Alex recognized several members of the peerage engaged in drinking, smoking and making ribald by-play with the demireps and Cyprians who had free run of the premises.

Button-holing a pot-boy, the Earl demanded to know where he might find Mr Warsop. The boy indicated one of the upper rooms, and Alex climbed the stairs, knocked on its door and walked in.

The room was evidently reserved for gambling, most of its space being taken up by a large table and several chairs. Seated at the table was Francis. He had thrown off his coat; and his shirt, which was none too clean, hung open to the waist. An empty brandy bottle stood at his elbow. He was more than two parts drunk, but his gaze, as it swept over his visitor, had lost none of its insolence.

"Linslade. Unexpected pleasure. Who set you on?"

"Lucilla showed me your letter." Alex drew out a chair and sat down. "Where have you been these past few days? We've searched high and low for you."

"And found me low." Francis picked up the empty bottle, reversed it, shook his head, and tossed the bottle to the corner of the room.

"Warsop," said Alex quietly, "there's no love lost between us, but take my advice. Come back with me to Curzon Street."

"F'r what? Converse wi' my sainted papa? Chat wi' my dear Aunt Brampton?"

"She might appreciate a visit."

Francis laughed. "You mistake. Sh' wants none'v me. Said she'd have me thrown out. Please her migh'ily t'see me rot in gaol."

"I'll help you to meet your debts."

"What?"

"I will lend you what you need."

Francis lifted his head to stare. "Why?"

"It would please me to end the antagonism between us."

"Would it, though? Ver' generous, I'm sure. Linslade'll play the goo' Samaritan. Bask in th'glow of Social 'proval, while Warsop is the pa-pariah. Tha's my rôle, ain't it. Rôle the Fromes devised f'r me."

"For God's sake," Alex said impatiently, "it was you that chose to abduct my sister."

"An' you that chose t'say I was after her money. Umh? Never thought, did ye, that I loved her? Bella, charmin' Bella. All I wished of life. But you . . . you treated me li' dirt, you an' y'r pratin' papa." Francis straightened in his chair. "I thank you, Linslade, but I'll not touch your money. 'D'rather rot in the King's Bench."

Alex leaned forward. "The past is past, man. Let me lend you what you need."

Francis gave a faint chuckle. "Don't know what I owe, do you, my bucko?"

"I've a fair idea. Will fifteen thousand cover it?"

Francis blinked. "Nosed into my affairs, did you? Well, it won't fadge."

"But you'd accept a loan from Sholto Curle?"

"Who said so?"

"Why else do you want to see him?"

Francis was silent. His lips worked. "Doesn't c'ncern you."

"Let me take you to Sir Sholto."

"Not there. Nest'v vipers. Tell him t'come here. Moun . . . mountain t'Mommet . . . Mahom . . . Ommet." Francis drooped, slumped forward and sprawled across the table, arms a-dangle.

"Devil take him," Alex muttered. He got up and moved round the table, lifted the lolling head, tapped the flaccid cheek. There was no response, not a chance in the world of getting the numskull back on his feet.

Sighing, he left Francis where he was, and went downstairs and out into the street to find a hackney carriage.

He was out of luck. Every hackney he saw was already engaged. He walked to the end of Jermyn Street and was about to turn down St James's when a closed carriage approached at a brisk pace. It slowed to take the corner, just long enough for him to identify the Curle crest on the panel, and to see Ramon sitting, arms folded, on the groom's perch seat.

Alex shouted and waved to the coachman to draw rein, but his voice was drowned by the rumble of the wheels on the cobbles. The carriage dashed on. Swearing, Alex sprinted after it, though it was obvious that his best pace couldn't match that of Sir Sholto's bays.

He was still a hundred yards behind when the vehicle halted outside The Prince's Saloon. He saw Ramon leap down and help Sir Sholto to alight. The two moved slowly towards the steps of the Saloon. In the same instant, five men ran out of the mouth of the alley beside the building. They were dressed all in black, with mufflers wound about their jaws, and cudgels in their hands. Quick and quiet as a pack of wolves, they raced towards their victims. John Coachman, busy with his horses, did not hear their approach.

Alex shouted again, and put on a burst of speed. The men in black heard him, and checked just long enough to allow Ramon to thrust Sir Sholto up the steps. Then they came on in a rush, cudgels flailing.

Ramon kicked the leader in the groin and sent him writhing to the gutter. Alex, catching up with a second, spun him round and delivered a haymaker blow to his jaw. A cudgel whistled past his ear and caught him a numbing blow on the shoulder. He staggered, but recovered in time to lash out at a masked face, and aim a kick at a passing belly. From the corner of his eye he saw John Coachman stand up on his box and lay about him with his heavy whip. On the steps, a cudgel felled Sir

Sholto. Then Ramon was back, dancing like a cat and brandishing a wicked-looking knife. In the building, an upper window was thrown up, and a woman began to shriek hysterically for the Watch.

As suddenly as they had come, the attackers fled, vanishing along the shadowy alley. Alex bent over Sir Sholto who was sitting hunched against the railing of the steps, breathing stertorously.

"Are you all right, sir?" he asked.

Blue eyes regarded him balefully.

"As right as any man can be that's been trampled by a herd of elephants. Help me up."

Alex put an arm round the old man and lifted him to his feet. Sir Sholto nodded briskly. "Thank 'ee, Linslade, thank 'ee kindly. If you'd not happened along when you did, those Mohocks would have had my purse and watch."

"Sir Sholto," Alex began, "I believe you should consider . . . "

"Mohocks," interrupted Sir Sholto, firmly. "That is what we will say when we return to Brampton House. Understand?" As Alex hesitated, the old man took his arm in a tight grip. "I have to protect my family," he said, "and especially the females of my family. I rely on your support, Linslade. Now tell me, where is Francis?"

"In the Saloon, sir."

"Be so good as to fetch him out."

"I'm afraid he's drunk as a wheelbarrow."

"Is he? Then wheel him out," said Sir Sholto cheerfully, "wheel him out, and let's take the silly fellow home."

XXXIV

ON REACHING CURZON Street they were relieved to find that Lady Charlotte had retired early. They were able to have Francis carried into the house and put to bed unchallenged.

Sir Sholto was in a fractious mood. He refused to allow Dr Chase to examine him, declaring that a few bruises wouldn't kill him, and he'd thank everyone to stop treating him as if he were made of china. When the doctor offered him a paregoric draught, he was advised to pour it down the nearest drain.

"I've no wish to sleep," Sir Sholto said. "Got too much thinking to do. Have to plan what to say to Francis tomorrow. I mean to ring such a peal over his head as he won't soon forget!" He cocked an eye at the Earl. "How badly is he dipped, d'ye know?"

"As I judge, to the tune of fourteen or fifteen thousand."

"Well, I must bail him out, for Henry's sake if not for his own. Tomorrow he can go back to his own home, but not before I've made it plain to him that he won't play fast and loose with *my* blunt." He held out his hand to Alex. "Francis mayn't thank you, Linslade. He's an ungrateful sort of fellow, but I thank you for all you've done tonight."

"There's no need," Alex said. "I consider myself part of the family."

The old man smiled. "So do I. So do I. Now you'd better go and talk to Lucilla. I expect she's worked herself into a proper flurry, over all this."

To describe Lucilla's state of mind as a flurry, fell far short of the truth. She had spent an anguished hour wondering how Alex was faring at The Prince's Saloon. She had attempted, without success, to prevent Sir Sholto from following Alex to that den of vice. She had had to contend with Marion Gray, who, having chanced to overhear Lucilla's conversation with Lord Linslade, had worked herself into a state of hysteria and made a string of wild accusations against Francis. He would, Marion insisted, abduct Tamar by force, and very likely murder them all in their beds.

Lucilla slapped Marion, to bring her to her senses, and told her tartly it was time she cured herself of her habit of eavesdropping, as it caused a great deal of unnecessary trouble. Marion dissolved into damp contrition, protesting that she acted only out of love for her dear ones, and Lucilla had to put her to bed with a hot brick at her feet and a cold compress on her forehead.

No sooner was that done, than Sir Sholto and Lord Linslade arrived with Francis. The sight of the three gentlemen, one of them totally inebriated and the other two bearing the marks of a dangerous brawl, did nothing to calm Lucilla's temper. Her strained nerves snapped, and Linslade, because she loved him best in the world, was the obvious target for her rage.

Meeting him as he left Sir Sholto's room, she demanded to be given a full account of the evening's events.

Alex described them as best he could. He was himself tired, and his shoulder was aching abominably, facts which made him miss the high colour in Lucilla's cheeks and the sparkle in her eyes.

She heard him out in silence but then said, in a brittle tone, "Are you trying to tell me that Grandfather was set upon by a gang of Mohocks?"

"That's his opinion," said Alex carefully.

"But is it yours?" As Alex made no reply, Lucilla moved a step closer to him. "Before you left here," she said, "you spoke of a trap. Did you mean that Francis had set a trap for Grandfather?"

"I thought it possible," admitted Alex.

"And I suppose you also think that what happened tonight is linked to the accidents at Ringwood?"

"Lucilla," Alex began, but she cut him short.

"I know you have good reason to dislike Francis," she said. "I know him to be weak and feckless, but nothing will persuade me to believe that he's capable of murder."

"I sincerely hope you're right."

"You hope!" Lucilla regarded him with withering scorn. "I take leave to doubt your sincerity, sir. You've thought from the start that Francis was guilty of these horrible crimes. You've not only suspected him, you've succeeded in turning his own flesh and blood against him!"

"That is completely untrue!"

"Is it? Then I take it you will now try to clear him of suspicion and reinstate him in the eyes of the world?"

"I will try to discover the truth. Good God, Lucilla, surely you can see that our chief concern must be for your grandfather? He must be protected at all costs. Why else do you think I instructed you to keep him here tonight?"

"Instructed? Since when am I your servant, pray, to perform your orders?"

Alex, now as angry as she was, strove to hold on to the shreds of his temper.

"We'll talk of this tomorrow," he said, "when we are all in a calmer mood."

"There's nothing to discuss," cried Lucilla. "Nothing I wish to discuss with you, ever! I never wish to see you again."

Alex made a move towards her, but she stepped back from him.

"Please leave at once," she said.

He stared at her for a moment, then gave her a stiff bow and strode out of the house. As the door closed after him, Lucilla fled upstairs to her bedroom, where she burst into a flood of tears.

Back in his dressing-room at Berkeley Square, Alex was rubbing liniment into his aching shoulder when there came a tap on his door, and Nicholas walked in. Nick grinned at him.

"What have you been up to? Boxing the Watch?"

"You're not far out," Alex said, and related what had occurred at The Prince's Saloon.

"Is Sir Sholto all right?" asked Nick anxiously.

"Right as a trivet," Alex replied. "I left him rehearsing the trimming he plans to give Francis tomorrow."

"Trimming? He should rather have the brute thrown into prison! It was Warsop lured him to that den of thieves. If you hadn't chanced along, the old Trojan would be crows' meat by now." Nick checked, frowning into space. "There's something I should recall about Warsop. Trouble is, I was badly foxed that night."

Alex looked up with an arrested expression. "What night?"

"Night of the Coronation. We was at the Royal Dragoon . . . Ayliffe, Curle and I. Warsop was there, too, hob-nobbin' with a rogue in a moleskin cap. Ugly-looking customer with a scarred face. Rang bells with me, I can't think why."

"Try Ringwood," said Alex quietly.

"Ringwood?" Nick looked blank for a moment, then struck his fist into his palm. "By thunder, you're right! It was the man on the grey . . . the one that loosed off a shot and near took off your head. He was facing the other way that night, so I never saw the scar, but it's the same ruffian, I'll take my Bible oath on it!"

"Your oath won't cut much ice in a court of law, Nick. The first time you saw the man, you were half off your head with fever, and the second, by your own admission, you were drunk."

"Nonetheless," insisted Nick, "the man on the grey was the man I saw talking to Warsop in the Royal Dragoon. I'll wager anything you like it was Warsop paid him to fake those accidents at Ringwood, and tonight's little affair as well. Surely Sholto Curle can see what's going on?"

"He sees, all right," Alex said.

"Then he'll hand Warsop over to the constables?"

"I think he's more likely to settle his debts, and send him home."

"Settle his debts?! Great God, Alex, you won't sit by and let that murderer run loose?"

Alex set down the liniment bottle and buttoned his shirt. "I agree that something must be done," he said. "The Chief Magistrate at Bow Street is an old friend of mine. I think I shall have to pay him a visit."

Next morning the Earl breakfasted at half-past eight, a departure from custom that caused his valet to say to his butler that he feared love had addled his lordship's brain.

At nine he strolled into the library, to greet Mr Thomas Shooberry, to whom he had the night before sent an urgent message.

Mr Shooberry had already spread a great many papers on the large map-table, and he began at once to expound on them. He led the Earl through a veritable maze of facts and figures, citing accounts and payments, amounts deposited in or withdrawn from sundry banks and counting-houses, balances here and deficits there, properties sold, bought, or leased, the whole dialogue so larded with legal phrases that after ten minutes Alex threw up a protesting hand.

"Shooberry, you're making my head spin. Pray tell me in simple terms what all this means."

Mr Shooberry leaned back in his chair and steepled his

fingers. "It means extravagance," he said. "It means living above one's touch, and running into debt. It means falling into the old trap of robbing Peter to pay Paul. In a nutshell, my lord, it means peculation on the grand scale."

"Can you prove that?"

"Not yet. To secure a conviction in court, I need to study official documents, and certain ledgers and records in the possession of . . . ah . . . private persons. I can arrange that, of course, but it will take time, and time," he cocked a shrewd eye at the Earl, "is not, I think, on our side."

"Very true. Tell me, how did the tontine members react to our offer?"

"Much as one would expect. They instructed their lawyers to investigate the merits of the offer. The lawyers will make the same enquiries I have made, and arrive at the same conclusions. They will discover that the tontine cupboard is bare . . . which brings me, sir, to the second of your commissions."

He produced a sheaf of papers which he placed before the Earl. "These are the reports of the agents I set to watch the persons you listed. You will see that these persons' actions are, for the most part, quite innocuous. Visits to friends, parties, shopping excursions and the like. But this one . . . " Mr Shooberry tapped the topmost report, . . . "makes interesting reading."

Alex studied the closely-written pages for some minutes. When he looked up, his expression was grim. "It suggests an accomplice," he said.

"Yes," agreed Shooberry. "The suspect meets the other man three times, each time in the unsavoury kind of place where no questions are asked and no faces remembered. You will see that the agent describes the second man's manner as aggressive, even threatening. He adds that on two of the three occasions, he was given money. If we could put a name to him . . . "

"I think we may do so. The description is exact."

"Do you wish me to set up a search for him?"

Alex did not at once reply. He had not told Mr Shooberry of the attempts on Sir Sholto's life, nor did he wish to do so. To

246

uncover embezzlement in the family circle was bad, but it could be lived down. Murder was quite another matter. Somehow he must find a way to bury that skeleton, once for all.

"How long do you need," he said at last, "to bring us to the point where we can press charges."

Shooberry pursed his lips. "Two days, perhaps three."

"Then make that your aim, please."

Shooberry frowned. There was a hesitancy in his noble client that he couldn't quite like.

"I trust, my lord," he said, "that you won't delay too long. The suspect may become suspicious, he may do a bolt and escape justice. That we can't allow."

The Earl gave the lawyer a half-smile. "You're right in theory, of course, but I confess I'm more anxious to protect the innocent than to punish the guilty. Do but consider the scandal, Shooberry, the disgrace to family and friends. I'm not sure I care to have that on my conscience."

Shooberry hesitated, torn between disapproval and curiosity. Curiosity won. "May I ask," he said, "what your lordship has in mind."

The Earl's smile broadened. "As a start," he said, "I shall pay a call on the Chief Magistrate of Bow Street."

When Mr Shooberry had taken his leave, Alex selected certain of the papers on the library table and packed them into his despatch-case. He then ordered his town carriage to be brought round to the door, and had himself conveyed to Bow Street Magistrates' Court.

The Chief Magistrate, Sir Nathaniel Conant, welcomed him warmly, and desired to know in what way he might serve his lordship.

Alex gave him a full description of the theft of the tontine money, though without mentioning the accidents that had befallen Sholto Curle. He then handed over his portfolio of papers, which Sir Nathaniel read with care, saying at the end that he concurred with Mr Shooberry's views.

"You've a prima facie case of fraud," he said, "but you'll need more evidence to secure a conviction."

"Shooberry is confident he can supply what we need within a day or so."

"Excellent. Let him come to me when he's ready to lay charges." Sir Nathaniel paused delicately. "Forgive my asking, but what precisely is your interest in this case?"

Alex gave a careless shrug. "I'm engaged to marry Sir Sholto Curle's grand-daughter. I feel I have a certain . . . family responsibility."

"Ah, yes." Sir Nathaniel's expression was bland, and Alex wondered if he might have heard the rumours circulating in the Clubs. If he had, he didn't say so, merely asking if there was any other matter Lord Linslade wished to raise.

"Yes," Alex said, "one. You'll have noticed that the agent describes an accomplice . . . a low sort of fellow, the merest jackal, I suppose . . . but it might be helpful to question him. It occurred to me that one of your Runners might be able to tell us who the man is, and where he may be found."

"We'll ask Sperritt," said Sir Nathaniel. "One of my best men, Sperritt. Knows every rogue in London. If he can't help us, no one can."

Mr Sperritt proved to be a small man, with short bowed legs and a barrel chest under his bright red Runner's weskit. He looked, Alex thought, like a duck dressed as a man. Impossible to imagine him raiding gambling-hells, putting down riots, arresting cut-throats or performing any other of the dangerous deeds for which his Force was famous. But a glance at Sperritt's visage made him change his mind.

The eyes staring fixedly at him were the cold, pale blue of a winter sky. The mouth was set in a flat, uncompromising line. The jut of his jaw suggested that rank and wealth impressed him not at all. Mr Sperritt, his lordship thought, was as rigid in his view of the Law as Mr Shooberry, and probably a good deal more ruthless in his determination to uphold it.

He listened without comment to what Alex had to say, asked one or two questions, and then said, "It's my guess, y'r lordship, that you've ter deal wi' Sam Rudge. No mistakin' that scar o' his. Got it from a doxy as planted 'im a facer wi' a hot weasel-iron. Broke 'is neb, it did, an' burned 'im t'the bone, but di'n't teach 'im no sense, simly."

248

"What's his lay?" asked Alex.

Sperritt sniffed. "Man o' parts, is Samivel. Used ter ride at Newmarket, oncet . . . won a mort o' races, too . . . but 'e took ter nobblin' the prads, an' that was the end o' that! Now 'e touts, an' pimps, and does whatever else yer might think ter name."

"How about blackmail?"

Mr Sperritt tilted his head. "Mebbe. Bin arter y'r lordship, 'as 'e?"

The Earl ignored this piece of impertinence. "I've had no dealings with Rudge," he said.

"Ah. Come on be'alf of a friend, p'raps?"

"Perhaps."

"An' what might yer be wantin' of 'im, sir, should yer find 'im?"

"I'd like to ask him a few questions. Do you know where he lives?"

"Seven Dials," said Sperritt promptly, "but don't you go trying to roust 'im out, sir. His morts'll set on yer an' slit yer throat."

"I'll be happy to leave the work to you," Alex promised. "I will, of course, pay any reasonable expenses."

Mr Sperritt glanced at Sir Nathaniel, who nodded. He turned back to Lord Linslade.

"Right y'are then," he said. "I'll keep me glims on Sam Rudge, an' when you've a mind to talk to 'im, you tip me the wink. This address'll allus find me."

With that he withdrew; and the Earl, after exchanging the commonplace courtesies with Sir Nathaniel, made his way home to Berkeley Square.

During the days that followed, Lord Linslade had ample time to reflect upon his situation. It did not please him. Lucilla still refused to see him. He had called twice at Brampton House, only to be told that Miss Pelham was resting and not to be disturbed. He was forced to resort to the artifice of sending Nick to Curzon Street to glean what information he could, and it was sparse.

Sir Sholto was in good health, but Lord Everley's strength was ebbing slowly away.

Francis Warsop had returned to his father's house and, as

Nick indignantly announced, was behaving in a very brazen fashion, attending various ton parties, and showing no proper remorse for his actions.

In Berkeley Square, things ran more or less smoothly. Lady Linslade had chosen this inopportune moment to become reconciled to her oldest son's betrothal, and spoke, albeit in a die-away manner, of holding a reception at Foxfare to present Lucilla to the local gentry.

Captain Shepstone danced attendance on Emily. George and Augusta, complaining that the heat of London was past bearing, departed to Brighton to enjoy the sea-breezes.

The terrier, Pebble, overcome by delusions of grandeur, attacked a carriage-dog in Hyde Park, and had to be taken to the farrier to have a torn ear stitched.

This ho-hum existence was disrupted on Tuesday evening when the Earl, returning from dining at White's, was informed by Bungay that a Mr Sperritt wished to speak to him.

Fetched from the kitchen to the morning-room, Mr Sperritt declined to sit down, saying that he couldn't bide more than a minute or so.

"On'y come ter tell yer, m'lord, that yer bird's about ter flit. Booked a passage t'Ostend, on the barque *Esmeralda*. Sails on the tide at six termorrer mornin'. But p'raps yer lordship knows o' that, a'ready?"

Alex met the Runner's insolent stare. He knew that Sperritt was accusing him of conniving at an escape in order to avoid the scandal of a trial. It was an idea that had occurred to him more than once over the past few days, but he had resolutely suppressed it. One couldn't protect Sir Sholto and his family by allowing a criminal to bolt.

What was far more disturbing was the realization that Sperritt knew a good deal more than he should, and meant to use his knowledge.

Disposing himself comfortably in a wing-chair, Alex said calmly, "No, this is the first I've heard of such a move. May I ask how you learned of it?"

"Why, sir, it's me business to know such things," Sperritt answered, "seein' as Sir Nat's been good enough ter gimme the case."

"Has he, indeed? I expect, as my friend, he wished me to have the best. Tell me, do you have a warrant of arrest?"

"No, I don't." Sperritt scowled heavily. "I took the liberty o' goin' ter see your Mr Shooberry, soon as I larned of the *Esmeralda*. He says 'e's got enough to make out a warrant, but Sir Nat's gone out o' Town, ternight, so we're 'amstrung."

"Where is Sir Nathaniel?"

"Dinin' at 'Olland 'Ouse. Mr Shooberry's druv down ter see 'im, an' get 'im ter sign the dociments, but I doubt we'll lay 'ands on those afore midnight."

"Can't you make an arrest, Sperritt?"

"No, m' lord, I can't. 'Thout I 'ave doo authority, me 'ands is tied. Can't enter a private 'ome, noways. A man's 'ome is 'is castle, even if 'e do be a thief an' a murderer."

"There's no talk of murder here, Sperritt."

"Ah, but there is, sir." Sperritt's teeth showed in a wolfish grin. "Talk in 'igh circles, an' in low. But talk's cheap, m'lord, an' won't put no chicken in our pot. There's on'y one man can 'elp us now, an' that's yerself. Delayin' tactics is what's needful. A gennelman o' rank an' fashion, like yerself, can go where a plain man like me can't."

Alex thought. "I expect I can gain access to the house," he said at last. "Will you bring the warrant there?"

"I will, sir, as close ter midnight as I can manage . . . if that's agreeable ter y'r lordship?"

"Agreeable is hardly the word. Acceptable, is better."

Mr Sperritt spread his hands. "'At's it, sir! A gennelman ain't never at a loss fer the right word! Don't trouble ter ring fer that Bungay. I can find me own way out."

The Earl chose to perform this office himself. As he opened the front door, he said casually, "Have you spoken to Rudge himself, Mr Sperritt?"

The Runner shot him an appreciative glance. "Not yet I 'aven't, sir, but I likely will. I'll bid yer goodnight, now, an' good 'untin'." He made an odd, bobbing movement of the head, which the Earl judged to be the nearest to a bow Jack Sperritt would ever make. Then, slapping his tall hat on to his head, and tucking his stave under the crook of his arm, he ran down the steps and trotted briskly away towards Piccadilly.

251

XXXV

Giles Ayliffe took Lord Linslade's advice about attending the Melbournes' musicale. He arrived at their mansion in Whitehall soon after eight o'clock, to find the reception rooms already crowded with elegantly-attired members of the ton.

He was informed by a stout lady in lavender satin that the reason for the excellent attendance was that the artist was to be none other than Madame Gemelli, who would perform on the pianoforte several of J. S. Bach's lesser-known works.

Reflecting that love demanded these sacrifices, Giles went off to secure a glass of wine, which he carried to a vantage-point near the main entrance to the music-room. He had been standing there for some minutes when he caught sight of Francis Warsop on the far side of the salon. Mr Warsop was exquisite in a dark coat, dove-grey pantaloons and gleaming Hessians. His expression of smug complacency slipped noticeably when he saw Giles.

Giles bowed stiffly. Francis gave him a curt nod and turned his back. Insolent devil, thought Giles furiously, to peacock about when he was under suspicion of murder!

People were streaming into the salon, laughing and chattering. Giles kept his gaze on the doors that gave admission from the stairway. He hoped to spot Tamar and detach her from whoever was her chaperone tonight; but the minutes dragged on, and she did not appear.

At twenty minutes past the hour Lady Cowper, who was acting as hostess for her brother, his own wife's reputation being sunk past recall, began to shepherd the guests towards the concert-chamber. Giles consulted his watch and decided that Tamar was not, after all, coming to the musicale. He had half made up his mind to leave when he saw Lady Charlotte Brampton advancing through the main doorway, with Adrian Curle and Nicholas Frome at her heels. Giles hurried forward to make his bow.

"Good evening, ma'am," he said with a smile. "Adrian, Nick. Your servant."

Lady Charlotte ignored this civil approach. She reached out and caught Giles's arm in a fierce grip.

"Where is Tamar?" she demanded. "What have you done with her?"

Giles stared blankly. "Ma'am, I've not laid eyes on her. She's not yet arrived."

"She must have done!" Lady Charlotte's tone was feverish. "She left home over an hour ago. We have been waiting downstairs for the past twenty minutes."

"Perhaps," said Giles confusedly, "she mistook the address?"

Adrian Curle shook his head. "Couldn't have done. Marion's with her, and Marion knows this house. Been here a score of times."

"That's true," agreed Giles. "Besides, John Coachman wouldn't miss his direction."

"Tamar didn't take any of our carriages," said Lady Charlotte distractedly. "Neame says Marion made him summon a hackney-cab. God knows what possessed the woman . . . "

This news was sufficiently odd to give Giles pause. He said slowly, "At least, ma'am, Tamar will be perfectly safe with Mrs Gray. Depend upon it, they've changed their minds and gone off to some other party. Can't really blame 'em! I mean, an evening of Bach ain't everyone's cup of tea."

Lady Charlotte brushed this aside with contempt. "How can I be sure she's still with Marion?" she demanded. "She may have given her the slip. She may be wandering about, quite alone and unprotected."

Lady Charlotte had begun to shiver uncontrollably, and Giles put out an arm to steady her. "My dear ma'am," he said, "pray don't be in such a pelter. There's not the slightest cause for alarm. Nick, be a good fellow and fetch Lady Charlotte a glass of brandy."

Lady Charlotte thrust his arm away. "I don't wish for brandy," she cried, "and you may spare me the fatuous clichés. You know nothing of what I'm suffering. It's the same horror, all over again. The depression, the flight, the . . . "

"You're right," said Giles, rubbing a hand over his face, "I don't know what this is all about. If you will explain your meaning, perhaps I . . . "

253

"The meaning," said Lady Charlotte with a rising voice, "is that Tamar has lost her mind! It was the same with my darling Caroline. She played this very same trick on me, ran off without warning and threw herself into the river! If Tamar kills herself it will be my fault! I've been too hard on her, too hard, but I wanted nothing but her happiness. To see her safe married. I should have paid her more heed, but this past week there's been so much on my mind... Henry's illness... Francis... still, I should have found time to speak to her. I should have told her I'd not force her into a distasteful marriage. She's not bound to marry Francis."

"Indeed she is not," said a new voice, "since Francis has not the smallest desire to marry her."

Giles swung round to find Francis standing close by, smiling, his eyes bright with malice. In the momentary silence they heard a burst of music from the next room.

Francis pulled a handkerchief from his pocket and dabbed it delicately to his lips. "Truly," he said, "this is a storm in a teacup! Aunt, I'll lay odds that your precious pair is already on the way to Swallowford. Not that I blame 'em. It must be excessively tiresome, always to dance to your tune!"

Lady Charlotte regarded him with loathing. "This is your doing," she said loudly. "You've sent Tamar away, to spite me."

Francis sighed. "I am growing very tired," he said, "of being held responsible for all your petty misfortunes. So far you've accused me of debauchery, attempted rape, and murder. Now you seek to blame me for the aberrations of your woolly-witted grand-daughter. I assure you I've no idea where she is. Why don't you ask young Ayliffe, here? It wouldn't surprise me to find he's smuggled her off to some bucolic love-nest."

He started to move away, but Giles caught his shoulder and spun him round.

"You'll apologize for that, Warsop, or answer to me!"

"I make no apology to you, bumpkin!"

"Then I take leave to say, sir, that you're a thief and a murderer!"

Francis drew back his fist and aimed a blow at Giles's head that made him stagger. Nick tried to step between the two men, but was thrust aside by a sweep of Giles's arm.

"Warsop, I demand satisfaction!"

"Don't be a fool." Francis turned away, but once again Giles seized hold of him, and this time dealt him a backhanded blow across the mouth.

"Will you name the time and place?"

Francis hesitated. The fury in his face died, to be replaced by an expression of sardonic amusement.

"Very well. Let it be Copenhagen Fields, at five tomorrow morning."

Giles gave a stiff nod. "The weapons?"

"Oh . . . pistols, I suppose." Francis glanced at Mr Curle, who was staring at him in horror. "Adrian, you'll act for me?"

"No, it's farcical," Adrian began, then spread his hands in resignation. "Yes . . . if you must . . . "

"I must," Francis said. He directed a half-bow at Lady Charlotte, and sauntered away.

Giles faced Nicholas. "Frome?"

"Of course, if you wish . . . though I'm not sure . . . I mean, I never before . . . "

Giles cut him short. "Collect me at three-thirty. Twenty-five, Albemarle Street. Don't be late."

He strode towards the door.

"I think," Adrian said, "we're supposed to dissuade them." He and Nicholas hurried after Giles.

Left alone, Lady Charlotte collapsed on to the nearest chaise-longue. She opened her mouth and gave vent to a series of shrieks that challenged the brisk arpeggios in the music-room.

As Lady Cowper later remarked to one of her cronies, it was a counterpoint that Mr Bach had never envisaged.

XXXVI

A LITTLE AFTER eleven o'clock on that same night, Lord Linslade set out on foot from Berkeley Square. The spell of hot weather had ended in steady drizzle, and he wore a light drab overcoat with the collar turned high, and a curly-brimmed hat tipped over his eyes. In each of the two deep pockets of the coat nestled a loaded pistol, for he suspected that his prospective host might prove recalcitrant.

He strolled down Curzon Street, turned into Half Moon. Street, and stopped at a handsome bow-fronted building with a neat Greek portico. The ground floor of the house was in darkness, but lights shone in the windows of the first floor.

Lord Linslade reached up and tugged on the chain hanging beside the entrance. A bell jangled faintly, within. Presently footsteps sounded, a key turned and bolts were drawn back. Jason Cleve's face, sharp with suspicion, appeared in the crack of the door.

The Earl nodded affably. "Evening, Cleve. May I come in?"

Cleve made a petulant movement. "My lord, it's past eleven! I was about to retire. Unless your business is urgent . . . "

"It concerns Lord Everley," Alex said.

"Are you saying he's died, sir?"

"No, no. If anything, he seems a thought better." The Earl removed his hat and shook raindrops from it. "It's devilish damp out here, y'know. Really, you should invite me in."

Cleve hesitated, then with a faint shrug, opened the door. The Earl followed him across the hallway and up a shadowy staircase to a study off the first landing.

The room was in considerable disarray. Cabinets stood with doors ajar, drawers hung open, files and dossiers were carelessly stacked on every table and chair. Although no fire was laid in the grate, Cleve must have been burning papers there, for the air smelled of smoke, and fragments of scorched parchment had drifted on to the hearth.

"Preparing for your jaunt to Ostend?" enquired his lordship.

Cleve wheeled about with an angry scowl, then checked as he saw the pistol in his guest's hand.

"Sit down, Cleve," Alex said.

Cleve attempted bluster. "This is outrageous. How dare you threaten me in my own house?"

"Sit down!" Alex waited until Cleve had complied, then drew forward a chair and took his place on the other side of the desk. "Keep your hands in full sight," he warned. "If you make any sudden move or sound, I'll shoot you. It would give me pleasure to do so."

Cleve leaned back slowly, spreading his hands palm-down on the desk.

"I demand an explanation of this . . . this atrocious insult . . . "

"You shall have it. As I mentioned, I'm here to discuss your dealings with Lord Everley."

"Dealings? I'm his lordship's legal adviser . . . "

" . . . under cover of which title, you've cheated him out of something in the region of thirty thousand pounds in seven years."

Cleve forced a laugh. "I can only suppose you to be drunk, sir, or mad. What gibberish is this?"

"No gibberish. We've enough evidence to send you to gaol, for a very long time, on charges of embezzlement; but that's not why I'm here. I've come to talk about the tontine . . . that very large sum of money that led you to attempt murder."

Cleve opened his mouth to speak, but the Earl held up a warning hand.

"You've always lived beyond your means, Cleve," he said. "This house, for instance . . . your gambling . . . your pretensions to be a Pink of the Ton . . . it must all have cost you a pretty sum. To pay your bills, you stole from Lord Everley. No doubt he was easy game, he's never been the man to count his pennies. Two years ago, you suffered a disastrous loss on 'Change and, to get yourself in the clear, you sold the tontine properties, forging the signatures of the rightful owners. You kept the capital, paying them no more than the interest they expected.

"The surviving members are three in number . . . Sir Sholto Curle, Lord Everley and Lady Charlotte Brampton. The Everleys are related to you by blood, and Lady Charlotte has besides been your mistress for many years. Don't protest! I've been on the Town long enough to know its on-dits.

"These three people trusted you, and never troubled to examine your handling of the tontine funds. You knew that while they lived you could avoid discovery. But in December of last year, Lord Everley suffered his first apoplectic stroke. For a while he was at death's door. You realized time was running out for you.

"If Lord Everley died, his estate, including his investment in the tontine, would come under scrutiny. Your thefts must be uncovered. Lady Charlotte might be prepared to hold her tongue. Sir Sholto would not. Faced with the certainty of disgrace and prison, you looked for a way out.

"You persuaded yourself that if Sir Sholto died first of the three, there was hope for you. The Everleys wouldn't wish to see the family name dragged in the mud. They would take their loss in silence.

"You set about planning Sir Sholto's death. You paid a criminal named Samuel Rudge to stage a series of accidents. In February, my brother and I became embroiled in one of these. We actually saw Rudge riding away from Ringwood. His is a face one can't mistake, you'll agree."

Again Cleve made as if to speak; but the pistol in the Earl's hand moved delicately, and he relapsed into silence.

"At first," Alex continued, "I suspected Francis Warsop of the crimes. I knew him to be loose-moralled, and ruinously in debt. Thinking to frighten him off, I persuaded Dr Chase to tell Lord Everley that the Law was to be called in. That, of course, amounted to telling you, since Everley kept no secrets from his sister, and she kept none from you. The attacks stopped as if by magic.

"The Curles came to London and, for a time, things went on quietly. Then, two weeks ago, Everley suffered his second, massive stroke. The doctors confirmed that he had not long to live. Your situation was once again perilous. You decided to stage another attempt on Sir Sholto's life, and to arrange it in such a way that the blame would fall on Warsop.

"You set it about in the Clubs that Francis was responsible for the earlier 'accidents'. You poisoned Lady Charlotte's mind against him, so that she forbade him the house. When he took refuge in The Prince's Saloon, you followed him there and urged him to borrow money from Sholto Curle."

"Lies," muttered Cleve.

"No, Cleve. The truth. I've had you under observation for some days. You were seen yesterday afternoon at the Saloon. You were in urgent conversation with Warsop."

Cleve licked his lips. "I went there as a friend, to beg him to return home!"

"Strange, but he doesn't appear to have had any faith in your friendship. In the letter he sent to Lucilla Pelham, he stated that you were plotting against him. That you wished him dead."

"He was in his cups. Can I help it if a drunken sot misinterprets a friendly gesture?"

"Was it kindness that made you meet with Samuel Rudge three times in the past few days? Was it kindness that prompted you to pay him money on two of these occasions? Or did you pay him to hire the thugs who attacked Curle? Or was it merely hush-money? I'm told that blackmail's his lay. No doubt he's extorted plenty from you, these past months."

"Rudge is a racecourse tout, a tipster. I allow him to place bets for me from time to time. You can't make anything of that, Linslade!"

"It might amuse me to try. It might tickle my fancy to tell my friend Sir Nathaniel Conant about the events at Ringwood, about Rudge's part in them, and about your cosy chats with Rudge."

As he was speaking, Alex caught the sound of carriage wheels approaching along the street. They slowed, and halted outside the house, but Cleve did not seem to notice. His whole attention was fixed on Alex.

"If you accuse me," he said venomously, "I don't suffer alone. I'll drag 'em all down with me, the whole passel of Everleys. Do you care to marry into the family of a gaolbird, my lord? I think not. You're too proud, too careful of your damned consequence."

"My consequence," said Alex coolly, "means nothing to me. What does matter is the safety of those I love. They are not safe while you're at liberty, therefore I intend to see you gaoled for embezzlement. I'm prepared to remain silent on the charge of attempted murder . . . provided you comply exactly with the terms I shall lay down."

"Terms!" Cleve laughed, a glimmer of hope in his eyes. "You're in no position to dictate terms! You've no case to bring, and you know it."

The Earl stood up. "I advise you to think very carefully," he said. "There's a man downstairs, a Bow Street Runner by the name of Sperritt. He has a warrant for your arrest on charges of embezzlement. He's a very singular character. He has a consuming hatred for criminals of your sort. He's already traced Samuel Rudge. He's picked up the rumours of murder that you so rashly started. He's caught your scent, Cleve, and he'll follow it to the kill. If I tell him what I know, he'll persist until he sees you hanged. I'd not shed a tear over that, were it not that your demise would cause shame and distress to your family. For that reason, and that alone, I'm prepared to strike a deal with you."

Cleve was silent, his eyes desperately scanning the Earl's face. At last he whispered, "What do you want of me?"

"You will confess to the theft of the tontine monies," Alex said, "and to spreading false rumours against Francis Warsop. You will make it crystal clear to Sperritt, to Sir Nathaniel Conant, and to whatever court may try you, that you have acted alone at all times. You will remain silent, for the rest of your life, about your plots against Sir Sholto and your dealings with Rudge."

A heavy pounding sounded on the front door of the house. The Earl kept his eyes on Cleve.

"Well," he said, "do you accept?"

Cleve stood up slowly. His gaze flickered round the room, came back to the pistol in the Earl's hand.

"I accept."

The rain had stopped, and out in the street the lamplight shone on the wet cobblestones, and on the black paintwork of the shabby carriage drawn up next to the flagway.

Two men stood beside the coach: Sperritt, and a man who held a long-barrelled horse-pistol.

Sperritt's left hand wagged a warrant at Cleve, while his right twitched open the carriage door.

"Get in," he said.

Cleve stumbled forward and climbed into the coach, followed by the man with the horse-pistol. Sperritt took a step towards the Earl.

"Why did he pay Rudge?" he asked.

"To back horses," Alex answered.

Sperritt's mouth flattened in contempt. "That for a tale!"

"You won't shake him."

"Don't reckon I will." Sperritt's cold eyes glinted suddenly. "They'll 'old to that lie, to save their skins. Mootual benefit, like. Kind of a tontine."

XXXVII

ALEX ACCOMPANIED SPERRITT and his prisoner to Bow Street, and remained there to hear Cleve make his formal confession. Only when this had been transcribed and signed did he feel free to return home.

He reached Berkeley Square at half-past three. Not being the sort of employer who expects his servants to wait up all night for him, he was puzzled to see lights blazing in several parts of the house, and to have the front door opened to him by his sister Emily, fully clad and in a state of great agitation.

"Alex," she cried, "thank God you've come! We've been scouring the town for you!"

"Why, what's wrong?" he asked, stripping off his hat and coat. "Not Mama, I trust?"

"No, no, she's all right . . . at least, as right as one can expect. Bella says we shouldn't send for Dr Princeton . . . not yet, at any rate."

Alex caught hold of Emily's shoulders and gave her a slight shake. "Will you please stop talking in riddles! What's amiss?"

Emily closed her eyes, opened them, and drew a deep breath. "Tamar Curle has run away," she said, "and Francis Warsop accused Giles Ayliffe of abducting her. Giles called Francis a thief and a murderer. They're to fight a duel tomorrow . . . no, this morning at five o'clock."

"A duel?" said Alex, seizing on what he saw as the salient fact in this farrago of nonsense. "Rubbish, Em! No one fights duels in this day and age."

"Yes, they do . . . or they will if you don't prevent them." Large tears began to course down Emily's cheeks. "They'll b-both be k-killed, or f-forced to f-fly the country! We shall never see our dear ones more."

261

Alex found a handkerchief and thrust it into Emily's hand. "Dry your eyes, puss. This ain't the time for watering-pots."

Emily gulped, and dabbed at her face with the kerchief. "I know, but I've b-been so frightened, with you from home, and G-George away, and Nick gone . . . "

"Gone where?"

"To be Giles's second," said Emily in a hollow voice. "I begged him not to, but he searched through those old manuals in the bookroom, and found the one entitled *The Proper Conduct of Affairs of Honour*, and it said that the first rule was for a second to persuade the challenger to withdraw, which Giles won't, Nick says, because he has the bit between his teeth, and the second rule is for the second to stand by his Principal to the last."

"Very noble. It might have been better for Nick to have stood by you."

"He would never have told me anything," said Emily, swift to Nick's defence, "except that Lucilla came here in a great pelter and blurted it all out. She hoped to take you with her, but I made her take Denby instead."

"Where?" said Alex patiently.

"To find Tamar. You see, Lucilla is convinced that Mrs Gray has taken Tamar to see her own sister in Islington, and she thinks that if she can persuade Tamar to come back with her, she may be able to stop the duel. She said that if Tamar hasn't been abducted, then there's no reason for Giles and Francis to fight about it."

"Very sensible."

"Yes, but it wasn't so sensible for her to tell Mama that Dr Chase has gone with Adrian Curle to the duelling-ground, because as soon as Mama heard the word 'doctor' it brought on one of her worst spasms. Alex, don't you think you should go and comfort Mama?"

"No," he said flatly. "There's no time. We must leave her to Heaven and Arabella. Did anyone think to tell you where this absurd affair is to take place?"

"At Copenhagen Fields. Do you know it?"

"I do. Run and fetch a warm cloak, Em, while I have the horses put to. You can tell me the rest of the tale as we go."

He strode out to the mews to wake Cheadle and Belper. His first thought had been to drive himself in his curricle, for that would certainly be the quickest mode of travel; but he remembered with a cold feeling at the heart that he might find injured or dead men at Copenhagen Fields, in which case a large carriage would be a good deal more practical.

Ten minutes later, the carriage swept round to the front door. Emily was waiting on the doorstep, enveloped in a dark cloak, and with the dog Pebble tucked under one arm.

"You can't take that animal," Alex said.

"I must," answered Emily, springing up to take her place beside him. "If I don't, he'll shriek the house down, and Mama will find out I'm missing, and very likely go into convulsions."

Accepting the force of this argument, Alex signed to Belper to shut the carriage door. Within minutes, they had swept round the Square, and were headed at.a spanking pace towards the New Euston Road.

Denby Shepstone's journey to Islington was one which he devoutly hoped kindly Time would erase from his memory. Lucilla forced her horses along at breakneck pace. It was a miracle they didn't all end in the ditch, and, when he ventured to suggest that it was foolish to risk their necks on what might be a wild-goose chase, Lucilla merely tossed her head.

"They're with Mrs Howard," she said. "I know it in my bones."

They reached the outskirts of the village before dawn. A sleepy ostler at the King's Head Inn directed them to the home of Mrs Howard, and a few minutes later the phaeton checked outside a neat house, half-timbered, with mullioned windows that glittered in the moonlight.

Denby flinched from the thought of waking the occupants at this hour of the night, but Lucilla felt no such qualms. Throwing the reins to him, she leaped down to the ground, advanced up the front pathway, and beat a heavy tattoo on the door. This had no immediate effect, but when she redoubled her efforts, an upper window was thrown open, and a head crowned with a nightcap demanded irascibly to know who was there?

Lucilla stepped back from the shadow of the porch. "I'm Lucilla Pelham," she said. "I desire, if you please, to speak to Mrs Howard."

"Mistress Howard is abed and asleep," Nightcap replied, "like all good Christians. Be off with you, now."

Lucilla stood her ground. "Then be so good as to waken her," she commanded. "I have a message for her sister Marion Gray. It's a matter of life and death."

"B'ain't no Mrs Gray lives here," retorted Nightcap. "Be off with you, afore I sends for the Beadle!"

Lucilla went back to pummelling the door. Nightcap set up a shrill invective. Lights appeared in the neighbouring houses, and dogs set up a cacophony of barking up and down the road. The Captain, suppressing a craven longing to drive away, begged Lucilla to be quiet. At the height of the uproar, the front door was suddenly thrown wide. Tamar stood there, candle in hand, with Mrs Gray behind her.

Nicholas had selected the Fromes' gig as the best vehicle for his particular purpose. For one thing it would attract no attention in rural surroundings, and for another old Dapple, the gig-horse, could be relied upon to stand still if it became necessary to stop and seek directions.

He reached Giles's lodgings in Albemarle Street at the appointed time, and found Giles waiting for him on the doorstep, a trifle pale of face, but perfectly calm.

They set out at once, their first target being Battle Bridge. From there, they had only to follow the old lane to Highgate, and quite soon arrived at Copenhagen House, an inn standing alone on a small hill.

The building looked to be of some antiquity, part of it being in the style of the seventeenth century. Around it stretched pleasant country: pastures, hayfields and woodland, with here and there an isolated cottage. Nick began to wonder how they might locate the duelling-ground, but a stable boy appeared who informed them that it was over to duck-pond, and if they was to follow the cart-track over the hill, they'd find it for sure.

The sky was by now paling from red to dusty pink, and it was quite light enough for them to follow the winding track. Nick felt bound to make another attempt to dissuade Giles from the contest but, before he could begin, Giles produced two letters, sealed and addressed, which he asked Nick to take.

"One's for my parents," he said, "and the other's for Tamar. Of course, you'll only deliver them if . . . if things don't go well for me."

Nick pushed Giles's hand aside. "I shan't need those," he said. "You won't . . . you can't . . . persist in this farce."

"It's no farce," said Giles. "I mean to kill Warsop if I can."

"Then you're a greater fool than I took you for. Good God, man, you know duelling's illegal. If you kill Warsop, or even wing him, you'll make a criminal of yourself."

"The fellow deserves to die. He's a murdering blackguard."

"That I don't believe! Alex wouldn't have fetched him back to Brampton House unless he knew that tale to be false. No, and Sir Sholto wouldn't have paid off his debts, either. You don't bail out the man that's trying to kill you. I'll be frank with you, Ayliffe. I think you hate Warsop because he came near to marrying Tamar. And that ain't a capital offence, whatever you may feel about it."

"He insulted me. He accused me of abducting Tamar. As if I'd ever harm a hair of that angel's head!"

"If you ask me," said Nick shrewdly, "Warsop said that out of mere spite. He knows Tamar's daffy on you. He knows you've the stuff in you to succeed, which he hasn't. He's not worth shooting, Giles. Withdraw the challenge. Forget the whole silly episode."

"Don't argue with me," Giles said. "I'll not change. Did you bring the pistols?"

"I brought my father's case. He always used to say they fired truer than any other he'd handled. Not that he used them for anything more than target practice. He said it was barbarism to offer to shoot a fellow human being. The manual says that it's perfectly honourable for a gentleman to . . . "

"Damn your manual," exploded Giles. "D'ye think Warsop will trouble his head with such flim-flam? D'ye think he'll delope? He wants me dead. My only hope is to kill him before he kills me."

They had reached the crest of the hill, and found themselves overlooking a charming prospect. Below them stretched a broad and grassy basin surrounded by sheltering woods still blue with the dawn mist.

At one end of the depression was a duck-pond on which a few plump birds paddled. Directly below them, on the gentle-sloping ground, a flock of sheep grazed.

"Well," said Giles, swinging himself down from the gig, and gazing about him with a countryman's critical eye, "at least we've chosen a good place for it."

Alex and Emily did not have a comfortable journey, for on the Earl's instructions, Cheadle was springing his horses whenever he could, and at times the carriage rocked alarmingly.

Although Emily had recovered a little of her composure, and did her best to tell her brother what she knew of the events at Melbourne House, her knowledge was sketchy. This troubled Alex. He knew that even if he arrived at the duelling-place in time, he still had to find a way to stop the fight. That could only be done by an appeal to reason, a commodity that seemed at the moment to be in short supply.

Giles, besides being naturally stubborn, was in love, and not to be placated on anything affecting Tamar's welfare. Francis, in Alex's view, was in a very dangerous state of mind: weighed down by debts and by his father's illness, unjustly accused of the vilest of crimes, he might well be bent on taking revenge, not only on Giles, but on the family and the society that had wronged him.

It wanted only ten minutes to five when they reached Copenhagen House. The stable lad waved them to the cart-track, and Cheadle took it at a speed that threatened to wreck the springs. The carriage swept up the hill and halted at the lip of the valley beyond. Alex and Emily jumped down to the ground.

A surprising sight met their eyes. Five people stood in the centre of the glade below. Dr Chase was arguing hotly with Giles Ayliffe, who held an ornate silver-mounted pistol in his right hand. A few paces off, Nick was addressing Francis Warsop, who was also holding a pistol. Nick was brandishing a small book, and appeared to be calling on Francis to read a section of it. Adrian Curle, a handkerchief dangling from his upraised fingers, stood between the two couples, looking bewilderedly from one to the other.

Suddenly Francis seemed to lose patience. He thrust Nick aside and said something to Giles, who nodded, stepped forward, and turned to stand back-to-back with Francis. Adrian, whether by intent or accident, dropped the handkerchief, and the two duellists began to pace slowly away from each other. At ten paces they would turn and fire.

Alex shouted and started to race down the slope, but the sheep, in the idiotic way of their kind, took fright and clumped together, barring his way. He shouted again. Neither of the combatants took any notice. Alex, knee-deep in sheep, ploughed forward, yelling like a banshee, and certain that he could not prevent catastrophe.

It was Pebble who saved the day. Seeing, as he thought, the master of his house being savaged by strange beasts, he sprang to the rescue. His sharp teeth nipped a tail here, a leg there, his shrill barks rent the morning air.

The sheep responded by moving downhill, first at a smart trot, and then in full stampede. Pebble veered to the right, shrieking defiance, and the sheep obediently swung left. They bore down on Francis just as he turned to face Giles. Engulfed, he staggered, retreated, was caught up on the woolly tide, and carried inexorably towards the duck-pond. At the edge of the pond the flock divided, flowing smoothly to safety, but for Francis there was no escape. He tottered on the mossy turf, threw up his arms, and with a heavy splash fell backwards into the water. Cloaked in green slime he rose, sank, rose and sank again. The doctor and seconds rushed to his aid.

Lucilla, Tamar and Denby Shepstone, dashing up in the phaeton at that moment, believed they had come upon a scene of tragedy. Dr Chase, Nick and Adrian were engaged in dragging Francis's weed-draped body from the pool. Giles was standing bemused in the centre of the glade, his pistol still in his hand. Emily ran distractedly to and fro on the opposite hillside, tearing her hair and calling for her dog. While Alex, apparently in the grip of overpowering grief, sat on the turf, his head bowed in his hands and his shoulders shaking uncontrollably.

Each of the three new arrivals naturally ran to the aid of the beloved. Tamar rushed with arms spread wide to embrace Giles. Denby proceeded rather more decorously to calm Emily. Lucilla flung herself on her knees at the Earl's side and gasped, "Alex, for God's sake, are we too late, is he dead?"

Alex threw back his head and gave a crack of laughter. "No, no, he's very much alive, though I doubt the shepherd of that flock will be, if he dares to show his face."

"We must go down to them," said Lucilla agitatedly, "we must talk to them before they begin all over again."

"They won't." Alex wiped tears of laughter from his eyes. "No one could contemplate staging a duel after such a fiasco. Oh, Lord, what a sight! I wish you'd been here to see it." He put up a hand to brush back a strand of Lucilla's tumbled hair. "Well, Miss Pelham? Am I forgiven?"

She caught his hand and held it to her cheek. "Oh, my love, there's nothing to forgive, the fault was all mine. I don't know why I ripped up at you as I did. I'm so very, very sorry."

Alex stood up and drew her to her feet. "Come," he said. "Let's go and suggest to our hot-headed friends that as Francis isn't a murderer, and Giles is not a seducer, we'd best resolve our differences over breakfast at Copenhagen House."

XXXVIII

SOME SIX WEEKS after what Nicholas liked to call The Battle of Copenhagen Fields, the Frome family, with the exception of George and Augusta who had already left Town, gathered for an informal dinner at the home of the Dowager Countess of Linslade.

London was by now very thin of company, most members of the ton having departed to see to their country estates, join shooting parties or recover from the exhaustion of a particularly strenuous Season.

Lord Everley had died in the last week of August at the same time as the scandal of Jason Cleve's arrest broke. Lady Charlotte, crushed by this double tragedy, travelled north to attend her brother's funeral, vowing she would never return to

London. Soon after, she wrote Linslade a typically arrogant letter, desiring him to place Brampton House on the market. As he felt in some part responsible for her current woes, he complied.

Sir Sholto, Tamar, Marion Gray and Dr Chase left at once for Swallowford, and the Dowager invited Lucilla to stay with her for a few weeks.

"You'll wish to be near Alex," she said, "and besides, it will allow us to become better acquainted."

The arrangement proved to be a happy one. Lucilla and the Dowager became fast friends, and Alex's mama was able to enjoy the pleasure of helping Lucilla choose her bridal-clothes, without having to put herself out in any way.

On this evening, dinner being over, the company had assembled in the drawing-room to hear the contents of the letter Lucilla had received from Mrs Gray. Marion, like many people with an over-developed sense of drama, wrote excellent letters, and her efforts were much valued by everyone present.

"As you may imagine," she wrote, "Swallowford is abuzz with the news of the Romantic Attachment between our dearest Tamar and Giles Ayliffe. The Squire and Lady Ayliffe were at first adamant that no engagement could be contemplated, saying that Giles could not be burdened with a wife, etcetera. Sholto dismisses this argument out of hand. He has made enquiries about Mr Hogpenny and found him to be well-thought-of in the City, and as shrewd a man of business as one could wish. Sholto says that with Hogpenny as his mentor, and Lord Linslade as his patron, Giles is like to become a pioneer of the Science of Steam Propulsion, and a man of great affluence.

"Giles and Tamar, meanwhile, exchange so many letters that I believe the revenues of His Majesty's Mails must have increased markedly. We are all to come to London in the Spring, and I believe we may expect to hear wedding-bells in the Autumn of next year.

"You will remember Mrs Faversham, of Nutley House? She has this week returned from taking the waters at Bath, and brought us riveting news! It seems Lady Charlotte has bought a house near the Pump Room, and is setting up to become the doyenne of Bath Society. She has already attached the interest of a Mr Darcy Boone who, though he has eighty years in his dish, and swears and takes snuff to excess, is as rich as Golden Ball. Mrs F. says they appear to deal extremely together. For my part, I say they deserve each other!

"Mrs F. told me that Francis Warsop is in Paris, where he's taken up with a very fast female, a French Countess, which I understand is vastly superior to an English one." Here Lucilla cast an apologetic glance at Lady Linslade, who sniffed and said French nobles might give themselves airs, but the fact was that they were all impoverished, and Francis could not hope to feather his nest that way.

Lucilla shook her head. "It seems the lady has been married twice before, and her second husband was a diamond merchant from Amsterdam, who left her with a handsome fortune, a house in Paris and a château in the Loire valley. Perhaps Francis has landed on his feet at last."

"I dashed well hope so," Nick said, "else we shall have him back here, spongin' on all and sundry, and involvin' us in every sort of trouble."

"Never mind Francis," Emily said. "Go on with the letter. How's my darling Sir Sholto?"

Lucilla smiled. "In excellent form. Marion writes that Dr Chase believes the excitements of the year have actually done him good . . . shaken him out of invalidism, and given him a new lease on life."

"Good," said Emily. "And what does she say about you, pray? When does she predict your wedding-bells will ring?"

"Emily," said Lady Linslade sharply, "that is a very pert question. It's no business of yours when Linslade and Lucilla choose to marry."

"Well, but it is," said Emily reasonably. "Denby and I can't tie the knot till they have, and we don't wish to wait for ever."

"Lucilla," said her mama repressively, "is in mourning for her uncle. A large wedding would not be proper at this time."

The Dowager, who had been watching Lucilla's face, said gently, "A small wedding, however, would be quite in order. Just the family and our closest friends, at Foxfare."

Lucilla opened her mouth to speak, but her future mother-in-law was before her. "I won't consider anything so shabby," she said. "We must remember what's due to Linslade. He may not be a French Count, but he's the Head of the House of Frome. I venture to think people will expect to be invited to his nuptials. When I married his Papa, two hundred guests sat down to the wedding-breakfast, and there was a party for all the tenants that night, with fireworks."

Wrangling broke out. Lucilla rose from her place and went quietly to join Alex, who was standing in the window bay, an expression half-amused, half-impatient on his face.

He took her hand. "Well, my love," he said, "when do you think we should be married? Yours is the only opinion that counts with me."

Lucilla put on a mournful expression. "It's hard to decide," she said. "Whatever I say, I will give offence to someone."

"There's one powerful reason why you should marry me without delay."

"What is that?"

"Augusta has taken to calling you Miss Botham. The sooner you change your name to Frome, the better."

"True," said Lucilla, "but on the other hand, perhaps I shouldn't rush into this marriage? I might do so much better for myself. You are, after all, only an English Earl."

Alex drew her into his arms and kissed her. "Miss Pelham," he said, "I adore you, and I wish you will tell Mama that we propose to be married at Foxfare before Christmas of this year."

Miss Pelham considered the request for all of five seconds and, as she could find no fault with it, decided to do as he asked.